whisper beach

SHELLEY NOBLE

wm
WILLIAM MORROW
An Imprint of HarperCollins*Publishers*

This is a work of fiction. Names, characters, places, and incidents are products of the author's imagination or are used fictitiously and are not to be construed as real. Any resemblance to actual events, locales, organizations, or persons, living or dead, is entirely coincidental.

HarperCollins books may be purchased for educational, business, or sales promotional use. For information please e-mail the Special Markets Department at SPsales@harpercollins.com.

FIRST EDITION

Designed by Diahann Sturge

Chapter opener image © iofoto via iStock.

Library of Congress Cataloging-in-Publication Data has been applied for.

ISBN 978-0-06-231916-6

15 16 17 18 19 OV/RRD 10 9 8 7 6 5 4 3 2

whisper beach

Also by Shelley Noble

A Newport Christmas Wedding (Novella)

Breakwater Bay

Stargazey Night (Novella)

Stargazey Point

Holidays at Crescent Cove

Beach Colors

To
Nancy Brown, Yvonne Marceau, and Irene Webb
I couldn't ask for better friends

Acknowledgments

From start to finish the creation of a book takes a village. Thanks to my village:

As always my agent, Kevan Lyon, and my editor Tessa Woodward, and to Elle Keck who picked up in the middle of the game and guided me through.

The William Morrow Art Department for another beautiful cover.

Gail Freeman and Charity Scordato who introduced me to the special world of living at the shore, answered my crazy questions, drove me on lengthy recces, argued plot points, and showed me all the best places to eat.

You guys are the best.

Chapter 1

VANESSA MORAN WAS WEARING BLACK. OF COURSE SHE always wore black; she was a New Yorker . . . and it was a funeral. She'd dressed meticulously (she always did), fashionable but respectful, chic but not different enough to call attention to herself.

Still, for a betraying instant, standing beneath the sweltering August sun, the gulls wheeling overhead and promising cool salt water nearly within reach, she longed for a pair of faded cutoffs and a T-shirt with some tacky slogan printed across the front.

She shifted her weight, and her heels sank a little lower into the soil. The sweat began to trickle down her back. She could feel her hair beginning to curl. She should have left after Mass, sneaked out of the church before anyone recognized her.

But what would be the point of that?

When she saw Gigi sitting bolt upright in that front pew, Van suddenly felt the weight of the years, the guilt, the sadness, the—

and by the time she'd roused herself, the pallbearers were already moving the casket down the aisle.

She bowed her head while her cousin and, at one time, best friend passed by, but she couldn't resist glancing up for just a second. Gigi looked older than she should; she'd gained weight. And now she was a widow.

Her cousin Gigi. Practically the same age, and best friends from the first time Gigi poured the contents of her sippy cup over Vanessa's curly hair. Vanessa didn't remember the incident, but that's what they told her. Of course you could hardly trust anything the Moran side of her family said.

And Van knew she couldn't leave without at least paying her condolences. Wasn't that really why she'd come? To make her peace with the past. Then let it go.

So she followed the others across the street to the cemetery, stood on the fringes of the group, looking across the flower-covered casket to where her cousin stood between her parents. Gigi leaned against her father, Van's uncle Nate, the best of the Moran clan. On her other side, Aunt Amelia stood stiffly upright. Strong enough for two—or three.

Behind them the Morans, the Gilpatricks, the Dalys, and the Kirks stood clumped together, the women looking properly sad in summer dresses, the men in various versions of upright—nursing hangovers from the two-day wake—wilting inside their suit jackets.

The one person Van didn't see was her father. And that was fine by her.

Gigi, whose real name was Jennifer, was the good girl of the family. Except for the sippy cup incident, she'd always done the right thing. Boring but loyal, which Vanessa had reason to know and appreciate, Gigi was now a widow at thirty-one. It hardly seemed fair.

Then again, what in life was fair?

Van passed a hand over her throat. It came away wet with sweat. This was miserable for everyone, including the priest who was fully robed and standing in the sun in the middle of a New Jersey heat wave.

He opened his hands. It was a gesture all priests used, one that Vanessa had never understood. Benediction or surrender? In this case it could go either way.

". . . et Spiritus Sancti . . ."

Vanessa lowered her head but watched the mourners through her lashes. In the glare of the sun it was hard to distinguish faces. But she knew them. Most of them.

"I wondered if you'd show."

Vanessa's head snapped around.

"Shh. No squealing or kissing and hugging."

"Suze? What are you doing here?"

Suzanne Turner was the only person Van had kept in touch with since leaving Whisper Beach. And that had been sporadic at best. She hadn't actually seen Suze in years. But she was the same Suze, tall and big-boned, expensively but haphazardly dressed in a sleeveless gray sheath and a voile kimono. A college professor, she looked fit enough to wrestle any recalcitrant student into appreciating Chaucer.

Suze leaned closer and whispered, "Same reason you're here. Dorie called me."

"And where is she?"

"Probably over at the pub setting up the reception. She demands your presence."

Vanessa closed her eyes. "I suppose I have to go."

"Damn straight. Dorie said if you sneaked out again without saying good-bye, she'd—and I quote—follow your skinny ass to wherever and give you what for."

Vanessa snorted. Covered it over with a cough when several disgruntled mourners turned to give her the evil eye.

"Let us pray."

Suze pulled her back a little ways from the group. She was trying not to laugh. Which would be a disaster. Suze had a deep belly laugh that could attract crowds.

Vanessa lowered her voice. "How does she know I have a skinny ass? For all she knows I could have gained fifty pounds in the last twelve years."

Suze glanced down at Vanessa's butt. "But you didn't. Did you ever think that maybe Dorie is clairvoyant?"

Vanessa rolled her eyes. She certainly hoped not. She moved closer to Suze, gingerly lifting her heels out of the soil.

"A bitch on shoes, these outdoor funerals," Suze said. "You look great by the way. You're bound to wow whoever might be here and interested."

Van narrowed her eyes at Suze. "How long have you been here? Who else is here?"

"I don't know. I just got a cab from the station. The train was late and I was afraid I'd miss the whole thing. Changed clothes in the parish office. Nice guy, this Father Murphy."

Another snort from Vanessa. She couldn't help it. "You're kidding. His name is Murphy? Really?" Every Sunday her father would drop her mother and her off at the church with a "Going over to Father Murphy's for services. I'll pick you up afterwards." Mike Murphy owned the pub two blocks from the church. Mike was short on sermons, but his bar was well stocked and all his parishioners left happy.

Seemed nothing much had changed in Whisper Beach. They'd be going to the other Father Murphy's as soon as Clay Daly was laid to rest.

"In the name of . . ."

It was inevitable that someone would recognize her. As the amen died away and eyes opened, one pair rested on her. Van stood a little straighter, lifted her chin. Pretended that her confidence wasn't slipping.

There was a moment of question, then startled recognition, a turn to his neighbor and the news rippled through the circle of mourners like a breeze off the river.

Van helplessly watched it make its way all the way to the family until it hit Gigi full force. Van could see her startle from where she was standing. The jerk of her head, the searching eyes. Van stepped farther back from the crowd and wedged herself between Suze and the Farley Mausoleum.

It was a desperate but futile attempt. Gigi found her, and almost as one, the entire family, the Morans, the Gilpatricks, the Dalys, and the Kirks, turned in her direction.

"Busted," Suze whispered.

"This is exactly what I didn't want to happen," Van whispered back.

"Then you should have come earlier and made your condolences . . . before the public arrived. You can't expect them not to be curious. It's been twelve years, and half of the people here thought you were dead."

Suze was right. She could have called. Warned them she was coming. Asked if she would even be welcome. She hadn't.

She wasn't even sure why she had come, except that everything had coalesced at once. Her staff had been urging her to take a vacation. Dorie's letter had arrived at the same time. And Van thought what the hell; she blocked out two weeks of her schedule, made reservations at a four-star hotel in Rehoboth Beach, and got out her funeral dress.

Even once she'd packed, dressed, and picked up the rental car, she was still deliberating. She almost drove straight past the parkway exit to Whisper Beach. But in the end she'd come.

She'd known Gigi had gotten married. She'd even sent a gift. But without a return address. Maybe Gigi was relieved not to have to write a thank-you note.

Van had called her once after she left, just to let Gigi know she was all right. Gigi begged her to come home, but Van couldn't, even if she'd wanted to. And couldn't explain why.

How could she tell Gigi that she was living in an apartment with way too many people, most of them strangers. That she was afraid. Hurt. Angry. Sick. For a long time. That she'd nearly died before she caved and called Suze—not Gigi—for help.

Gigi had already done enough. Cleaned out her bank account to help Van get away. Almost two thousand dollars, her college savings—all stolen while Van slept on the train ride to Manhattan.

"I'm beginning to think I shouldn't have come at all."

"Don't worry. The worst is over."

Oh no it wasn't. Van only hoped that she would be gone before the worst reared his ugly head.

"Well, you can't leave now. Everyone has seen you. Besides, I didn't have time for breakfast and I'm starving."

Gigi passed by, still supported by her father on one side and her mother on the other. Amelia was the only one who looked toward Van and Suze. And Van knew in that instant that regardless of the twelve years that had passed, she hadn't been forgiven.

"I'm not sure I can do this."

"You can and you will." Suze took her by the elbow and force-marched her toward the street. "We're both going. We're going to say our condolences to Gigi. Say hello to Dorie, eat, and then we can leave."

"I thought it would feel great to come back successful, independent, and well dressed. But now I'm thinking they'll hate me for it. I'm out of place here. What was I thinking? I won't be welcome. I know Aunt Amelia wishes I hadn't come."

"She's one person. And quite frankly, do you really care? You've come to pay your respects, and if they get the added benefit of seeing the success you've made of your life, well, good for you." Suze grinned.

Van couldn't help giving her an answering smile. It would be nice for everyone to know she'd survived. That she'd made something of herself. And maybe she did have a few things to answer for. To some people. Not all. There were some people she would never forgive.

She'd left a lot of unfinished business here. She'd begun to think it could stay unfinished, but standing here, being back even for an hour, drove home how impossible that was. Maybe it was time she just got it done.

She turned abruptly and started around the back of the church.

"Hold up, where are you going?"

"I'm staying out of sight until the last possible moment."

"And making a grand entrance?"

"God, no. We're going in the back way."

Joe Enthorpe sat at the bar in Mike's Pub, nursing a beer he didn't want and would be too early to drink if he was just getting out of bed instead of finishing up a long ten hours of night fishing.

He knew he was stupid to come to Mike's knowing that Clay Daly's funeral repast would be in the party room down the hall. He hadn't gone to the funeral. Wouldn't have gone even if he hadn't been out all night. Still, he couldn't stay away.

The door opened, and the first of the mourners came in. He probably should say his condolences, but he smelled like sweat, beer, and fish. Better he just went home.

He ordered another beer.

Mike just slowly shook his head and slid a mug of Guinness in his direction. Seems like today everybody remembered the summer he crashed and burned. Most of it took place right here at Mike's, before Mike kicked Van out for being underage.

The trouble with living in a place all your life—people didn't forget shit.

He plunked down a twenty and headed for the door.

"I'm guessing this ain't a big tip," Mike called after him. "I'll keep your change till you come back for it." Mike's laugh was the last thing Joe heard before he stepped out into the blinding sun.

Dorie Lister was in the caterer's kitchen at the pub when she heard the first mourners arrive. They'd left their sadness at the door and were ready to eat, drink, and if not be totally merry, at least have a good time. Best way to mourn your dead was to send them off with a party.

Rumor was, Gigi didn't have a penny to her name. Nate and Amelia had to pay the funeral expenses, including the wake before the funeral and the repast after it. So Dorie had offered the catering services of the Blue Crab, free of charge. It was the least she could do. So what if she had to scrimp.

She dismissed the two girls who'd helped with the setup and sent them back to the restaurant to set up for dinner. It was the last Saturday of the season, and there would be a handful of tourists to be fed.

She pulled her cell phone out of her apron pocket. Something she had been doing all day. She'd gotten the message from Suze that she was on her way. Nothing from Van. She wasn't surprised, but she was disappointed. Fool that she was, even after all these years, she'd expected Van to come.

Things had begun to unravel for Whisper Beach all those years ago. And it hadn't stopped. Maybe it wouldn't. Maybe she'd just have to sit back and watch all those young lives swirl right down the drain.

It was already too late for the likes of her, but she'd made her bed a long time ago. And all in all, it wasn't such a bad place to sleep.

Dorie dropped the phone back in her pocket, grabbed a hot pad, and pulled a tray of freshly browned Italian bread slices out of the oven. She placed the pan on a trivet and was just reaching for the bowl of tomato bruschetta when the door to the hall opened and Kippie Fuller slipped in and closed the door behind her.

"What? Out of shrimp bites already?"

Kippie shook her head. "You'll never guess who I think I saw at the funeral."

Kippie was big and moved slow, but she had a quick eye for gossip.

"Who?"

"I'm pretty sure it was her."

Dorie began to feel a glimmer of—not hope—exactly, but interest. Yes, interest, nothing more. She waited for Kippie to expound on the subject. She would; she always did.

"I didn't get a good look, but Pete Moran said it was her."

"Huh." Dorie untied her apron and threw it on the counter. Patted her hair, freshly blond from Lucille over at Sea Breeze Beauty.

"Well, don't you want to know?"

"Sure." Dorie checked her lipstick in the coffee urn. Smacked her lips a couple of time.

"Robbie Moran's daughter. What's her name."

"You mean Vanessa?"

"Yes, that's the one. The one who ran off and left her daddy alone, poor man."

Short memories, Dorie thought.

"Poor soul, I hear he's pretty bad off."

"Kippie, Robbie Moran was born bad off and went downhill from there. And he brought it all on himself."

"The idea of her coming back after letting everybody think she was dead all these years."

Nobody who bothered to look for her, thought Dorie.

"Whole family's a little wacko if you ask me. Including that daughter of his. She's got her nerve showing up like this. There'll be trouble. You mark my words."

Chapter 2

I THOUGHT THE GRASS WAS HARD ON MY HEELS." SUZE SHIFTED her suitcase to her other hand as they tiptoed their way through the graveled lot at the back of Mike's. They had stopped by the parish office on their way over; met the new priest, Father Murphy; retrieved Suze's bag and laptop, which Van was carrying; and were headed to the other Murphy's.

Suze shifted the suitcase again.

"What do you have in there?" Van asked.

"Hard copies of a couple of books I couldn't find online."

"In case Mass got boring? Or maybe you were planning to send a few e-mails?" Van lifted the laptop.

Suze looked offended. "I'm going to stay at Dorie's for a while. I need to visit with my parents, but I can't get any work done at their house. And I'm under the gun."

"I want to hear all about what you're working on. In fact, we could ditch the reception. I'd be just as happy to drive to the nearest upscale bar for a gin and tonic. And look," Van said with forced enthusiasm. "Here's my rental car."

"You parked in the pub parking lot to go to a funeral?"

"It was the only place I could find. Besides, funerals always end up at the pub." Van shot a longing look at her car. "Last chance."

"The heat's making you cranky." Suze grinned at her. "But I will put my suitcase in the trunk."

Van popped the trunk. "I'm not cranky."

"Well, well. What do we have here?" Suze raised both eyebrows at Van's overlarge suitcase. "What's under this blanket?" She lifted it up to reveal Van's laptop and printer.

"I'm on my way to Rehoboth. Two weeks of vacation. Fun in the sun, who knows what in the moonlight."

"Oh, meeting someone there?"

Van shook her head and pushed her suitcase over to make room for Suze's.

"Going by yourself?"

"Yeah, what's wrong with that?"

"Nothing." Suze hoisted her suitcase into the trunk. "Except it's bound to be boring. Why Rehoboth?"

Van shrugged. "It seemed as good a place as any. And close enough to the city in case I need to get back to the business."

"Doesn't look like you left the business behind."

"They might need me. And plus I'll have time to work on some plans for expansion. I'm thinking about opening a branch in Boston or Philly."

"Why don't you stay here instead? I'm sure Dorie has the room."

"But not the amenities of the four-star hotel I have booked in Rehoboth."

"Probably not. But I bet her crab cakes are better than the ones in the restaurant there."

"Probably." The Blue Crab was famous for its crab cakes. For Dorie's crab cakes. When they were the special of the day, she had to call in extra waitstaff. People lined up to get into the restaurant. Though Dorie always managed to put some aside for the staff to enjoy at the end of their shift.

Dorie was good like that. But it was dangerous to remember the good times. Because you couldn't remember them without remembering the other times. And Van had no intention of revisiting them.

They were nearing the back door to the pub, when a dark gray truck careened around the building and onto the street.

Suze yanked Van out of the way. "Ass—oops. Guess I shouldn't swear at a funeral."

"Just a local baboon, drunk at high noon. Some things never change." Van smoothed her dress and marched across the parking lot. Realized Suze wasn't coming and turned around.

"You're a poet."

"What?"

"A baboon at high noon? It might not make any of the literary journals, but it made me laugh."

"Come on. The sooner we get this over with, the better."

Van stopped at the back door of the pub's kitchen, exchanged a look with Suze, and opened the door.

Two women were standing across the room. Van didn't recognize the one facing them, but she knew the other one without having to see her face. Scrawny in a black-and-white print pantsuit minus the jacket. Hair suspiciously the same color as it had been twelve years ago. The "Sunday" pearls she wore on special occasions, clasped at the back of her neck.

"Dorie?"

Dorie pushed the other woman into the other room and closed

the door. When the pounding started, she turned and leaned back against it until the woman gave up and went away.

She'd been staring at Van with a blank expression. Now she crunched up her face, accentuating the wrinkles that had always been there, testament to the three-pack-a-day habit she'd acquired with the opening of the Blue Crab forty years before. "Do I know you?"

Van frowned. "Dorie? It's me. Vanessa Moran. You sent for me."

Dorie snorted herself into a laugh that Van remembered well.

"Had you going, didn't I?"

"Not funny."

"Hell, I thought it was funny. Did you think it was funny, Suze?"

Suze threw up her hands. "Neutral territory here."

Dorie started across the room. Van braced herself, not sure if Dorie was planning a hug or a slap or if she'd just keep walking right out the door and into the parking lot. Van had gotten all those reactions from Dorie at one time or another.

"Whatever I think you need at the time," she'd explained once after a particularly harrowing standoff. "Treat my friends and relations just like I play the piano . . . by ear."

Dorie had been their surrogate mother. Kids who'd come for summer jobs and were staying in the hotel dormitory, or locals working at the restaurant and going home at night.

She had always been the one you went to when you were hurt. When you'd missed curfew and were locked out of the dorm. When your parents threw you out or you were too drunk to go home. When you were broke, or your boyfriend dumped you, or when you were sure everybody hated you.

Dorie was an equal opportunity comforter. Her house was a haven for those who had no place else to go.

It was Dorie whom Van had come to that night. Dorie whom she'd stayed with, wanting to tell her what happened and not being able to. Dorie who waited patiently for her to get around to talking, while she gave her a bed where she found no sleep and food that she couldn't eat.

She'd left three days later, without having talked to Dorie, without a thank-you, without ever looking back.

Van smiled tentatively. Dorie shook her head and gathered both of them into a hug.

Dorie was tall, about five seven, a bit taller than Van, but much shorter than Suze, and much thinner. So they were clasped in a leaning tower kind of a hug. Awkward and off balance, soft and bony, familiar and safe.

"I wondered if you'd show up."

The same thing Suze had said.

"I was just following orders." Van gave Dorie a salute, but the gesture fell flat. "So why did you summon me? I already know they're not that glad to see me. At least Aunt Amelia isn't."

Dorie looked at the ceiling, her idea of calling the saints to witness. "All in good time. Now you two get out there, say your sorrys and mingle, while I get these platters out to the party." She raised her hand and shook a jangle of bracelets at Van. "And don't even think about sneaking off again."

"I can't stay."

"Of course you can. I have it on good authority that you're on vacation."

"How did you—"

"I called your office. I've kept up with the tech revolution. I've googled you. Anyone who looked for you over the last few years could find you."

But Dorie was the only one who'd contacted her, and only because of the funeral. For some reason that made Van feel sad, which was ridiculous because she didn't want to be found or contacted.

"Did you think I had to weasel your whereabouts out of Suzy here?"

That's just what Van had thought. "Dorie, I really can't—"

"So it's settled. Now get on out there before people begin to wonder if you bolted again."

"Not fair."

"No? Prove it."

Van shot her a look but started toward the door. "Suze, are you coming?"

"Not if you're going out there angry."

"I'm not angry."

"Ha."

Van started to open the door, but Suze grabbed it and kept it shut.

"Van. I know angry. I've studied the classics."

Van forced a smile. "How's this?"

"Maniacal and inappropriate, try again."

"Oh God, I give up. Let's just get this over with."

Van pushed the door open. The party was in full swing. The noise level was typical for a postfuneral bash. Mike Murphy was dispensing beer from an aluminum keg. A bartender was mixing the heavier stuff. Gigi must have married rich, because this would be costing her a fortune.

She caught sight of her cousin across the way, standing in a loose reception line of family members. The crowd didn't suddenly stop talking, or all turn to stare, though a few people did step out of their way as Van cut diagonally across the room.

"Like Moses and the Red Sea," Suze whispered.

Van frowned at her.

Suze shrugged. "Funerals always put me in a biblical frame of mind."

They were still several feet away when Gigi turned and saw them. After a moment's hesitation, she shoved her glass into the nearest relative's hand and ran.

She hit Van full force, both arms clasping around her as if she were afraid Van might slip away. Something Van wished she had the power to do.

"I knew you'd come. I'm so glad to see you."

Van patted Gigi on the back. "I'm glad to see you, too. I wish it were under happier circumstances."

"It's just been awful." Gigi burst into tears. Van could only stand there, while Gigi sobbed and gulped. Suze was being no help, and after a few uncomfortable seconds, she saw someone she knew—or pretended to know—and stepped away to talk to them.

"Gigi. Take it easy. I know you're hurting, but you've got to be strong." Empty words. And hard to say with Gigi choking her and half the attendees looking on. Van tried to ease out of Gigi's ironlike grip but couldn't manage it without causing a bigger commotion.

Van saw Amelia walking toward them, and she felt relief and a bit of trepidation. Amelia had always thought Van was a bad influence on Gigi. Somehow it didn't occur to her aunt that everything Van did was just trying to stay alive.

Amelia took Gigi by the arm. "Gigi, pull yourself together. You're making a spectacle of yourself."

She switched her attention to Van. There wasn't an ounce of any feeling showing on her face except consternation. This is why Van hadn't wanted to come. She'd moved on, but it seemed as if others hadn't.

"I suppose I'm glad you came but you could have given us a little advance warning and maybe we could have avoided this total breakdown." Amelia gave her daughter a tiny shake. "Gigi. Mr. and Mrs. Salcani are here to pay their respects." She peeled Gigi away from Van and herded her back toward the wall where the Dalys and Morans were lined up like a . . . firing squad, Van thought.

Van was left alone and embarrassed in the middle of the floor. The crowd that had been watching the reunion finally lost interest and turned back to their conversations. There would be plenty of fodder for talk at the bar tonight.

No one came up to say hello, and Van's confident façade began to slip. She looked around for Suze. Saw her talking with a good-looking man, around thirty or thirty-five, and hoped to hell it wasn't someone they knew. She'd never get Suze out of here.

She caught Suze's eye, motioned to her to meet her in the kitchen. Then, nodding and smiling but not stopping to talk, Van retraced her steps through the crowd.

The kitchen was empty. And Van slumped against the table. She'd give Suze two minutes, then she was out of here. This had been a mistake.

But when the door opened, it was Suze and Dorie. She wouldn't get away that easily.

"Dorie, don't start. It was a mistake for me to come."

Dorie pursed her lips, accentuating the wrinkles around her mouth. "It was a mistake for you to leave in the first place—at least not the way you did it."

Van started to protest, but what was the point? "Suze, you want to have dinner before I leave for Rehoboth?"

Suze cast a look at Dorie, who looked innocent. "Dorie said Gigi and her children have been living with her mother."

Dorie nodded. "The bank foreclosed on her house."

"That's too bad." Van turned toward the door.

"Van, you wouldn't leave her like this," Dorie said.

Suze grimaced. "She does need a friend."

"Then stay and be a friend." Van didn't owe any of them anything. Where were they when—when she needed them? Did she really have to ask herself that question? Suze had gotten her medical attention, let her stay while she recovered. Dorie had always been there for her, every time she didn't have a place to stay because her father was too drunk for her to go home, and Gigi had handed over her college fund so Van could get away.

"We'll never get a hotel room," Van said halfheartedly. "It's the end of the season and every hotel will be packed." She'd had to sell her soul to get two weeks at Rehoboth.

"You can stay with me; I could use the company," Dorie said, looking sad and forlorn.

Van didn't buy it for a second.

"You can't take a few days off for a grieving friend and a lonely old woman?" Dorie grinned. "I exaggerate somewhat on the second half of that."

"What about Harold?" Van asked in a last-ditch effort to get away.

Another jangle of Dorie's bracelets. "Don't worry about Harold. He won't be any trouble."

Van rolled her eyes. She was trying to remain calm, strong, determined, but inside she was beginning to panic.

And then Gigi walked through the door, looking totally defeated and needy and hopeful, and Van felt herself giving in. She looked over at Suze.

"A few days," Suze said.

Van blew out air.

Gigi sniffed and gave her a hug. "I'm just so glad you came. You don't have to stay . . . for me."

Van looked over her head to Dorie and Suze and caved. "Of course I'll stay. I want to." She nearly choked on the words. Because the truth was she'd rather be anywhere but here.

Van didn't return to the reception. She figured she and Gigi had made enough of a scene to keep everyone talking for the next few days. After Van promised Gigi to come visit her the following morning, Dorie took Gigi back into the party room.

"Whew," Suze said. "Such a scene. Really, Van."

"I didn't do it."

"I know. And even though it was a bit embarrassing, I'm glad you promised to stay. Gigi is a mess. Do you know anything about her husband? What was he was like?"

"Nope. One of the Daly clan. I don't remember him. It's not like Whisper Beach is actually a small town."

"Just gossips like one," Suze said. "Guess that's why they call it Whisper Beach." Suze grinned at her.

"Until the whispers turn into the roar of the latest scandal; kind of a microcosm of every town on the Jersey shore."

"Not like my town," Suze said, leaning against the counter, and resting her hand in a spill of marinara sauce.

"That's because only rich people live in your hometown."

"Mostly," Suze said, licking the sauce from her fingers. "Where the scandals are worse, and hidden more deeply," she intoned.

Van tossed her a dish towel and watched while Suze wiped her hands.

"What?"

"Just thinking . . ."

"About what?"

"About how you always fit in even though you hired on at the Blue Crab on a lark, not because you needed the money."

Suze laughed. "So that I could spend my summer at the beach, not commute to New York to intern in an office."

"Yeah, but you didn't have to work at all."

"Are we really having this conversation? Everybody has to work. Else you end up a brain in a bowl."

Van laughed. It was one of Suze's favorite expressions, taken from some *Star Trek* episode they'd watched one late night of reruns. The landing party had discovered a planet where the people were so advanced they no longer needed their bodies so their brains were contained in bowls. Only it turned out they needed bodies to survive. And the brains were dying. There were only three left.

"That brain-in-a-bowl thing really appealed to your imaginative sense, didn't it?"

"Yeah, and think of all the fun we would have missed if we hadn't worked at the Blue Crab together."

It had been fun. And look where it had gotten Van; after the disastrous beginning, her life had turned out pretty well.

She looked around the kitchen, warming ovens, an old Frigidaire—did they even make those anymore? Linoleum that had seen the feet from who knew how many birthday parties, anniversary celebrations, funeral receptions. Van had been to a few, worked a lot more.

And here she was right back where she started. A shiver racked her body.

"Oh hell, it isn't that bad."

Yeah, it was. Van already felt the ache deep in the pit of her stomach. The same feeling she'd had when she jumped on the train with Gigi's money and cut her ties to the past.

Only they weren't cut. If she'd had any doubt, Gigi flinging her arms around her in front of the entire room had put an end to that idea. Suze was right. Van had some unfinished business in Whisper Beach. Maybe this was as good a time as any to finish it.

The image of the Rehoboth hotel and spa rose momentarily in her mind. Maybe she could make the second week. "Do you think it's rude if we just cut out without saying good-bye?"

"So what? You didn't even say hello. But first a little sustenance." Suze found a foil container and began filling it with food. She pinched the top onto the container and put it in a bag. Held up a package of unopened crab puffs. Looked a question at Van.

"Why not. We'll pay her back. Are you done? Can we get out of here before someone else wanders into the kitchen?"

Suze dumped the crab puffs into a shopping bag. "Okay, let's go. Just stop by the Save a Lot. I don't mind staying for a day or two, but I refuse, absolutely refuse to drink white zin."

Van stopped. Narrowed her eyes at Suze. "How do you know Dorie drinks white zin?"

Suze shrugged. "I don't. But I bet she does, and I'm not going to. Now come on." She bustled past Van. Van followed more slowly. "Have you stayed in touch with Dorie?"

"Off and on. But I didn't spill any secrets if that's what you're worried about."

"I'm not." But she was.

They hurried back to the car. Van unlocked the door and was hit by a blast of hot air. "Just stand outside while I turn on the air conditioner."

"You are such a sissy. Lower the windows. It'll be just like the old days."

They got in. Van lowered all the windows. She didn't want to remember the old days.

"Yeow!" Suze jumped out again. "The seat's hot. Okay, forget the old days, turn on the air."

While they waited for the car to cool off, Suze said, "Remember that old Pontiac, it belonged to . . . what was his name, the guy with the stringy hair and big nose?"

"Johnny."

"Yeah, Johnny. We drove it down to the marina, only we took a wrong turn and ended up in the marshes."

Van smiled in spite of herself. "Had to get it towed out and then pay for getting it cleaned."

"I forgot that part. But I do remember the guy who drove the tow truck."

"As well you should, since you went out with him the next weekend."

"Now what was his name?"

"Can't help you there." They got in, and Van put the car in gear and pulled into the street and a stream of cars. "Ugh, I forgot about traffic."

"It's the last throes of summer," Suze said.

"It's worse than I remember it."

"It can't be as bad as Manhattan."

"I don't drive in Manhattan."

"Don't you ever get to the shore? Ever? I mean maybe not here, but somewhere?"

"Jones Beach. Once a year maybe. I've been busy. This was going to be my first vacation since starting the business." She sighed. "My extremely efficient staff threatened to quit if I didn't go away. I guess I run a pretty tight ship."

"Strangling, I bet."

"So I'm thorough and expect the same of my employees. I pay them very well."

"I'm sure you do."

"Do you ever get back to the beach?"

"Van. My parents live at the beach. Yeah, I get back. A lot. That's why I'm staying at Dorie's this time."

They drove in silence for a few minutes. If you could call it driving. More stop, start, stop, start as traffic inched toward the beaches.

When they finally got to the discount liquor store, there was not a parking space to be had. "Okay, just let me out, drive around the block, and pick me up back here. I'll hurry."

"Not a problem; you'll probably be out before I get back." Van tossed her purse over to Suze. "Take some money."

The driver behind them honked, then sat on the horn.

"Jackass. We'll settle up later." Suze jumped out of the car, gave the driver an emphatic hand gesture, and went inside the store.

Van inched her way to the corner and made the turn. When she stopped in front of the store ten minutes later, Suze was standing at the curb next to a gawky stock boy and a hand cart loaded with two boxes. Suze opened the back door and he slid both onto the backseat.

Suze handed him a tip and jumped into the car. "Romeo."

"What?"

"The tow truck driver. His name was Romeo."

"You would remember." She quirked her head toward the backseat. "Plan on moving in? I'm only here for a few days max."

"And you're probably still a stingy drinker."

Van sighed. "Considering my family history, I try to stay on top of things."

"On everything," Suze mumbled.

"I heard that."

"Of course you did or I wouldn't have bothered saying it."

Van laughed. She couldn't help it. Suze was eccentric and brilliant, clumsy and absentminded, told it like she saw it, but never let you down.

"So what did you buy?"

"Three reds, two whites, a magnum of white zin for Dorie, a bottle each of gin, vodka, and rum, a couple of bottles of girly mixes in case we're inclined to have something pink and sweet with a little umbrella in the glass. And two bottles of Moët & Chandon. It was so cheap I couldn't resist."

"And we would be celebrating what?"

"I don't know. We'll think of something."

Chapter 3

NORMALLY AFTER TAKING OUT A GROUP FOR NIGHT FISHING, Joe would drive straight back to the marina and fall into bed. Sleep most of the day then find someplace to have dinner. But he lay in bed, sweating and frustrated, in the house that as caretaker and marine boss he got rent free. His eyes felt like they were filled with glass, and yet when he closed them, he didn't like the pictures he saw. And he couldn't seem to get past those pictures into a blissful unconsciousness.

The tide was in on the river, but there wasn't enough breeze to blow the lingering stench of the mudflats away. He was tired of being in town, of eating at Mike's three or four times a week.

He could be living with his family on the farm—what was left of the farm—wake up still to the sweet-smelling grass until rush hour when the commuters would leave their condos and drive past on their way to the office, leaving their exhaust fumes over the fields.

These days when you walked out to the front porch, you could see their windows light up as they moved from bathroom to kitchen, the rooms growing dark as they went to bed. No evidence there had ever been acres of green grass there. The ink hadn't even dried on the bill of sale before the bulldozers arrived. At least they'd been able to keep the barn, and the building that housed milking stations for two hundred cows. They would adapt well for what he had planned.

He'd been at college when most of the land had been sold. Joe laughed bitterly and turned over, trying to find a cool place among the sheets. He'd been taking a full course load as well as working part-time to finish his farm management degree and go home to turn the dairy around.

He'd had some great ideas. But like most great ideas, they came too late.

Over a hundred years of Enthorpe blood, sweat, and, yeah, there were tears, and yeah, some of them had been his own. While he was away, the herd was auctioned off, the land parceled, and much of it sold.

They managed to keep twenty acres, but his brother Drew had gone off to the air force, and Brett opened a hardware store in the next township. His sister Maddy married and moved to Ohio of all places; Elizabeth was at college. Which left his mother, father, granddad, and two younger brothers, Matt and David, to manage.

They'd made money on the deal, but when they gave up the farm, they lost the Enthorpe spirit.

So Joe had decided to do something about that, too. It had been hard fought and barely won; his granddad resisted, his dad was cautious. It had taken Joe, Drew, and Brett to convince the older two Joes into going for it. Joe's plan would hopefully give them something to look forward to, be easier on them physically, make them more competitive in the market, and give them a real reason to get up each morning.

They couldn't get their land back, but maybe they could start over. The last three years had seen more blood, sweat, and tears, more than a few anxious moments. Finally, this would be the first year they would have a large enough crop to actually harvest.

They'd started over, and it looked like they might actually succeed.

His eyes closed. *Start over.* Maybe now that the farm was operating again, *he* could start over. Maybe that's what he'd been waiting for all along.

Van slowed the car down, looking for a parking place near Dorie's house, not that she expected to find one. In a few days there would be a mass exodus away from the beach and to the malls for school clothes and supplies. Back to work. Back to normal life. A few stragglers would hang around until they too would wander away. Then the streets would be empty and you'd have your choice of parking spaces.

But these last few days would be hell on parking, on waiters and waitresses, who would have to work overtime to fill in for the departing college and high school students who had been the bulk of the summer staff.

Van slowed as she reached Dorie and Harold's driveway.

Suze, who practically had her nose pressed to the window, exclaimed, "Wow, they still have that old Cadillac."

Van stopped the car. "Holy crap. Think it still runs?"

"Tires still look good from here."

"Want to drive around the block and hope someone has decided to go home or should we—?"

"Pull onto the grass. Do you think Dorie has put in central air?"

"What are the chances?"

"One can always hope."

Van turned into the drive, bumped over the cracked cement, and pulled onto the grass at an angle to the Caddy.

As soon as they were stopped, Suze jumped out, grabbed her suitcase and computer case from the trunk, and lugged them to the porch of the old Victorian beach house.

Van moved more slowly, a thousand emotions and forgotten memories vying for attention.

At the first sight of the weathered old house, Van's insides did a little leap of recognition. Now standing here looking at the porch with the old aluminum furniture, the seashell wreath on the door, familiarity warred with pleasure and a little knot of pain.

So many times she'd taken refuge here, so many times they'd talked into the wee hours. Sitting on the lemonade porch in the dark, laughing or crying and fanning themselves with pieces of cardboard while citronella candles cast their light and scent into the darkness.

Do not think of the good times. They were seductive, but they didn't last. Only pain and hurt lasted. And she didn't need any reminders of that.

"Van, you're going to melt if you stand there much longer. And since all the windows are closed, I'm guessing there might actually be air-conditioning inside."

Van slung her computer case over her shoulder and bumped her suitcase up the steps. She'd have to come back for the printer later.

Even if she didn't need it while she was here, she didn't want to leave it in the trunk, prey to heat and passing felons.

The suitcase rattled across the old floorboards as she made her way to the front door. She reached for the doorknob, but stopped. "We didn't think to get the key."

"When did Dorie ever lock her door?"

"She should." Van turned the doorknob. The door opened and they walked in. Right into—

"Harold!"

Harold Lister was in his seventies, but he hadn't changed at all, except maybe having less hair. Medium height, scrawny with a little belly that hadn't grown any that Van could tell, a prominent nose embellished with a mole that still held its usual place of prominencc.

Harold was never handsome, not even on a spruced-up day. But for some inexplicable reason, the ladies loved him and he loved them right back. The female staff did not. Most were college students or younger and they put up with his daily pinches, pats, and occasional groping with gritted teeth and determined silence. Working at the Blue Crab was a good job, and they didn't want to lose it.

He was wearing linen trousers and a short sleeve sports shirt and reeked of aftershave. Never a good sign with Harold.

The two large suitcases that sat by the door weren't either.

"Van, Suzy. Aren't you gonna say hello to old Harold?" He came forward and Van braced herself. He wasn't much taller than she, but he managed to get her in a tight hug and patted her butt when he let go.

She gritted her teeth but let it slide. He was Harold after all, the old dog of old dogs. And Dorie's husband.

"Harold," Suze said as he changed course for the larger woman. "Good to see you." She blew him a double air kiss and breezed right by him. "Going on a trip?" she asked from behind him.

Harold, turned, smiled, winked. "Thought I'd give you all a little girl time." He made a show of looking at his watch, which Van swore was a Rolex. "Gotta run. Have a good time. Mi casa su casa." He wiggled his fingers at them, grabbed the bags, which nearly knocked him off balance, and banged them through the open door.

Van turned to Suze. "What do you make of that?"

"Those bags were packed for serious traveling if you ask me."

"Off on one of his escapades?" Van ventured.

"Off on the arm of some clueless arm candy."

"Do you think Dorie knows?"

"About this time? She will soon enough."

Van pushed the handle of her suitcase down. "Like I believe I've said, some things never change."

"And some things do. There's air-conditioning. Let's get these things upstairs and go back for the booze."

Van picked up her suitcase just as she heard the Caddy fire up and back out the driveway. "Good riddance," she said. "I just don't understand why Dorie has put up with him all these years."

Suze turned to look down at her. "You would have dumped his ass after the first indiscretion."

It stung, but it was true. "That's what modern women do." That's what she had done.

"Uh-huh," Suze said and preceded her up the stairs. "But what are we going to tell Dorie?"

Dorie massaged her lower back while she oversaw her busboys returning the funeral things to the Blue Crab's kitchen. Damn, it had been a long morning and afternoon. Dramatic, too.

Well, heck. It was good to shake things up every now and then. And by the time she took Gigi back into the party room, the story of Van's return had made the rounds and interest had waned as people crowded around the food and the open bar. Of course, Dorie heard plenty about the reaction, mainly from Kippie Fuller and Sue Ann Blaine while they helped her clean up.

It was after two when the party broke up, and most people who hadn't gone home had moved into Mike's regular bar. A bunch of them would be there for the rest of the day.

Now it was going on four. Downtime for the restaurant, though several tables were occupied with late lunchers or early diners. Fine by her. For the next few weeks she'd have to close except on the weekends. After that she'd close up for the winter.

Hopefully Harold would be back by then to help out. Of course he might not be. You never knew with Harold. He might not have even left yet. He hadn't said anything. He never did, but over fifty years of marriage, she'd learned to recognize the signs.

Starting with the trips to the attic for the suitcases. The surreptitious packing and shoving them under the bed in the guest room. The haircut, the new shirts and ties.

She wondered what or who it was this time. But she really didn't care. Maybe she'd go to Florida for a few months. Her half sister lived down there. They used to have good times together.

But why the hell go to Florida when you had the beach here right outside the door? The weather down there was boring, and she'd just done summer up here.

Dorie tossed the keys to Cubby, her assistant manager, waiter, head busboy, and occasional dishwasher when the kitchen got backed up. "Move the van to the parking lot, hon. I'll walk home."

"You comin' in tonight?"

"I don't know. I've got company." At least she'd better have company after all the trouble she'd gone to to get it.

"You mean like a date? What'll Harold say to that?"

"Harold's out of town," *Or should be soon.* "Doesn't mean that gives me license to cavort."

"Huh? What's cavort mean?"

Damn, what was wrong with the teachers these days? "It's what lambs do in the spring."

"Uh, right." Cubby shook his head and climbed into the white-paneled *The Blue Crab Chases the Blues Away* van and drove away.

A young couple jogged past her. In this heat? It couldn't be healthy. All the old people came early or late in the day, away from the worst of the heat, attempting to walk off bad cholesterol, high blood pressure, and old age. And they usually ended up at the Crab to undo all their good work with some artery-clogging fried seafood.

You wouldn't find Dorie exercising in front of the whole world. Anyway, she ran around enough working at the restaurant. Forty years of it. Sore feet and cheap tippers, hurricanes and blizzards, broken air conditioners and broken furnace. Broken hearts . . .

Sometimes she wondered why she kept at it. But not often. Dorie wasn't given to introspection all that much. She was of the school that too much thinking led to impotence. And life had proved her right.

She wasn't what you'd call impetuous, either. Though she'd kind of jumped to a decision about this funeral thing. Now she was afraid she might have a situation on her hands.

Dorie walked over to the railing, looked at the steps to the beach, just a sliver of sand between the pier and the river. It was open to the public nowadays. So much fighting and carrying-on to take that beach away from the hotel. But they did, and Whisper Beach became just some more sand in the town's public beach. And the dumbest part was nobody even used it. It was a pretty stretch of sand, protected by dunes and a seawall holding the river out. But no matter how crowded the big beach got, it hardly ever spilled over to Whisper Beach. And that's how the locals liked it.

It might be public, but something unspoken said, private keep out.

Now the hotel had been sold, which Dorie guessed was a good thing, since it hadn't been rebuilt after Sandy. Which was stupid if you asked her. It was beachfront property if you didn't count Ocean Avenue that ran between it and the boardwalk.

Maybe they'd build another more modern hotel and her business would boom again. Or they might put up fancy condos with a four-star restaurant that charged four times as much as she did and didn't cook half as well.

Well, it was what it was, and out of her hands. She would adapt. She always did.

VAN AND SUZE sat in Dorie's parlor, the funeral food spread out on the coffee table and a bottle of cabernet in the center. They'd changed into more comfortable clothes as soon as they'd arrived.

Suze was wearing gauze harem pants and a tank top. Her naturally blond hair was pulled back into a ponytail leaving a fringe of fuzz around her face. It made her look young and carefree, not like a professor hoping for tenure and waiting for a grant that would support her research in order to get it.

Van always kept her hair short. It was more efficient and made her look more professional. And the cut, one that cost a fortune, was precise and sleek. Like her. Though Van had to admit that as she sat on the chintz-covered couch, watching Suze slumped comfortably in the old chair and drinking wine out of a jelly jar, she felt a little overdressed in her pressed capris and silk tee.

Well, they would have looked great at the bar in the hotel. Which reminded her. She reached for her phone, keyed in the numbers to the hotel, and postponed her reservation.

She hung up to see a grinning Suze, who handed her a glass, spilling a few drops on the coffee table as she did.

Van took the glass and wiped up the drops with the efficiency that had made her successful.

"It's like nothing changed," Suze said, oblivious to the spill and cleanup. "The same pastel walls. Same white gauze curtains. This same saggy chair."

"Don't forget the new air-conditioning," Van said. It was the first thing she'd noticed when they'd entered. Well, the first thing after Harold.

"Thank heavens for that. I wasn't relishing the idea of sleeping au naturel and sweating under an open window. And she still has those god-awful shades on the windows."

"What shades? I don't recall seeing any in my room."

"Because yours isn't on the side of the house with the fire escape. Don't you remember? She put them up after the boys climbed the fire escape and saw Dana naked. She screamed so loud the neighbors called the police."

"I think it was Gigi who screamed. They were sharing a room that night."

"Well, that would make more sense." Suze looked over the plate of hors d'oeuvres. "Dana probably basked in the attention."

"Probably. They were a little put out."

"The cops or the neighbors?"

"The cops."

"You have to admit it was pretty funny."

"I remember," Van said. But she didn't want to. She didn't want to be beguiled into reminiscences. Not about Gigi, Suze, or Dana, especially not Dana.

"The next day Dorie went out and got those ugly beige shades. After she let us have it for causing a scene."

"We didn't cause a scene. It was Gigi."

"Some things never change. Poor thing—she was always such a wuss."

Van rolled her eyes. "I know. She was sweet. I always thought she was too wishy-washy, but she came through when I needed her."

"Or maybe she just didn't have the guts to say no to you."

Van thought about it. "I didn't ask for the money. Gigi offered it. I didn't want to take it at first, but she insisted. So I did." Van had gratefully accepted it. For all the good it did either of them.

"Push that plate of crab puffs over here, will you?" Suze said. "With all the drama at the pub, I hardly got a chance to eat anything but a couple of miniquiches. Both at the same time. So gauche. Not that that crowd would notice. They were lined up three deep at the bar."

"Hmm." Van reached for her glass of wine. What she really wanted was a big glass of water. She drank, but not often and not much. Tonight, though, she was tempted to break her own rules and enjoy a glass or two.

She could feel the past tugging at her memory. She fought it. There had been fun times. But most of her teenage years, especially after her mother was killed, was one long desperate attempt to stay housed and clothed and fed. What she remembered most was hard work, grief, and anger.

Best not to go back even in conversation. She put down the wineglass.

"What, don't you like cabernet?"

"Sure, I just— Like you said, I'm a stingy drinker."

Suze looked concerned and a little uncomfortable.

Van didn't want to go there, but she knew she had better set things straight. "Don't worry, I'm not my father. I can drink without falling down and yelling profanities and letting people— I'm just so busy I rarely have time to enjoy good wine."

"Van, it's okay. You don't need to talk about that stuff. I told Dorie it might be rough on you to come back. She didn't understand. It hurt her that you left without a word.

"At first we all thought you ran away, which it turns out you did, but no one knew why. Gigi never told. Then when you didn't come back or let anyone know where you were, Dorie was afraid something had happened to you."

It had. "You set her straight though, right?"

Suze closed her eyes, opened them. "Eventually, but at first I didn't know any more than she did. But after you called me . . . well, I did call her once I knew you'd be all right. I didn't tell her anything, just that you were okay and that you didn't want anyone to know where you were. That's all, I swear. But I think she deserves to know why you left. She took good care of you, of all of us. And it really hurt her that you didn't come to her with whatever was hurting you."

Van leaned back on the couch and closed her eyes, opened them. "I've made a good life for myself. I own a successful business, and I'm thinking about opening another branch. I don't want to go back. I don't want to be reminded of where I came from."

She put out her hand to stop Suze from saying anything. "And yes, I remember. We had some good times. Some really good times. But I had some that were just awful. And it's impossible to remember one without the other."

"I'm sorry. I didn't mean to dredge it all up."

"Don't be. You know more about me than most people." Strange, since they'd never been that good friends. Which maybe had made it easier for Van to seek Suze out when she'd been completely down and out and close to death.

"And I . . ." Van shrugged. She didn't know how to say what she felt. To thank Suze for not judging her. Or if she had judged her, for keeping it to herself and helping her anyway.

"Don't say it. Have a crab puff." Suze shoved the rose-edged plate toward her.

"Thanks, but I'm not really hungry."

Suze wiggled the plate at her. "You need sustenance. I have a feeling you are going to get a barrage of questions from Dorie."

Van took a crab puff. "She still has the same plates."

"Amazing. I break a plate or cup at least once a week. I must have gone through five sets of dishes since I started working."

"Because you've become the absentminded professor."

Suze laughed, spewing out bits of quiche.

"Absentminded and basically a slob, obviously." She grabbed a paper napkin and brushed off the front of her shirt and pants, wadded up the napkin, and tossed it on the far edge of the coffee table.

Van smoothed it out and stuck it under one of the tins.

"Unlike some people I know."

"I like things neat."

"Which is why you're so good at what you do. I'm just the opposite. If I had the money, I'd hire you to organize my life. Especially when I'm so totally stressed about the grant money. Makes me even more absentminded and sloppy."

"You need money?"

"Van, I live on a professor's salary. Do you know what untenured professors make?"

Van shook her head.

"Peanuts. But enough about my grantless state, my bad habits, and your good ones. Eat up. Because one of us is going to have to tell Dorie that Harold has gone off—again."

Van shrugged, considered. "I bet she knows."

"Like I said—clairvoyant."

"No way. Though I wouldn't put it past her to orchestrate his departure."

Suze chewed her quiche, her face registering a comical mix of innocence and surprise. "I hadn't thought about that."

Van groaned. "This better not turn into *The Big Chill Jersey Shore Edition*." There was still time to follow Harold's example and run. Maybe Suze would like to go with her.

Chapter 4

Van accepted a second half glass of wine. It wasn't that she was afraid of becoming an alcoholic. It was just she didn't like being out of control. She'd done that once with disastrous consequences.

Already she could feel her control slipping, not from the wine but from just being back in Whisper Beach. She'd been crazy to think she'd never have to confront her past or her past relationships. Even when she decided to come to the funeral, she thought she could get in and out without too much discomfort. But she'd been wrong on both counts.

She hadn't cut her ties as she'd thought these last twelve years. They were just as strong; maybe they'd grown stronger while she'd been ignoring them.

Van heard the front door open, squeak on its hinges, a sound that was still so familiar that it caught her off guard. For a second, she was eighteen again, and Dorie didn't have those lines of age and worry on her face.

Suze did a backbend over the chair arm until she could see Dorie. "We've red, white, and white zin. And we helped ourselves to some of the funeral food. Hope you don't mind."

"We'll pay you back," Van said without even thinking.

Dorie snorted. "You think I can't afford to replace a few measly crab puffs? Eat up, girls, then we'll send out for some real food. And not from the Blue Crab, either."

She looked over her shoulder as if she heard something. But there was nothing— or more accurately—no one there.

Suze cleared her throat. "Uh, we saw Harold when we got here."

Dorie nodded.

"He was . . ." Suze shot an agonized look at Van.

"Carrying suitcases," Van finished.

"Oh?"

"You knew he'd be gone, didn't you?"

Dorie came into the room. "Suspected. That man's like clockwork. You almost get a decent chunk of time out of him and he gets the wanderlust."

Harold had always been a philanderer. Van would have kicked him to the curb years ago if she'd been married to him. The Listers had kids, but Van had met only two of them and that had been years ago.

"Picked a hell of a time to run off, though. Now I gotta find somebody or -bodies to help me close up for the winter." Dorie gave them an over-the-top innocent look.

Van frowned at her. Suze might still be here to help, but Van would be long gone when it came time to close the restaurant. She might be able to spare a weekend here or there.

Suze unfolded herself from the chair and stood. "What'll it be? White zinfandel?"

"Sure, that's good."

While Suze went to get the wine from the kitchen, Dorie sat down in the other chair facing Van and reached for a cube of cheese. "So where do you want to begin?" She finished with an expression that Van recognized all too well. As teenagers they had quailed beneath that look. Well, everyone except Harold, who would just slap her on the butt, call her babe, and get the hell away.

Van didn't think she'd be able to escape so easily. "How about with Clay Daly's death? How did he die and what's going to happen to Gigi and the kids? She has a couple, right?"

Dorie nodded distractedly as she looked over the remains of their snack. She finally decided on a mini egg roll and popped the whole thing in her mouth, wrinkled her nose. "I'm thinking Italian. How long are you staying?"

Taken aback by the abrupt change of subject, Van said, "At least through tomorrow. I promised Gigi to come see her in the morning—maybe a week. If that's okay."

Dorie's eyes flew heavenward. "All right then. Since Gigi will try to color it pink, I'll give you the real facts. She and Clay were one of the families on the bay that got flooded out when Sandy hit." She raised her voice. "Hey, Suze, look in the cabinet next to the coffeemaker and bring those take-out menus."

"So the *Reader's Digest* version is, they got flooded, they screwed up the FEMA papers, cause Mr. I-Don't-Need–No-Help Daly tried to do everything himself.

"They moved in with Gigi's mother and father. But Clay got it in his head looters were going to steal everything from the house and moved into the RV in the driveway. If you ask me, Clay had just gotten enough of Amelia.

"Then he lost his job 'cause the damn machine shop where he worked closed up and never reopened. Then his unemployment ran out, and he started acting crazy. Sitting out front with a shotgun at night. Hammering and sawing like he was going to rebuild the house himself, which he couldn't do because, besides the fact that it had been condemned for being structurally unsound, it was growing killer black mold.

"Last week, he climbed up on the roof, God knows why. Roof gave way and he fell and broke his neck. You know the rest."

Suze came back with a glass and corkscrew in one hand, the bottle of white zin in the other, and a stack of menus wedged under her chin. As she put the bottle and glass down, the menus slid out from under her chin and cascaded for the most part to the coffee table.

"Damn." She leaned over to retrieve the ones that were on the floor while Van cleaned off the ones that had landed in the artichoke dip.

Conversation was put on hold while Dorie and Suze flipped through the take-out menus, settled on a local Italian place, then spent the next few minutes deciding what to order. Van didn't join in; she'd eaten a couple of crab puffs, and a piece of cheese, and her second glass of wine sat untouched on the coffee table. None of it was sitting well in her stomach.

"And what about Gigi? Does she have a job?"

"Did," Dorie said. "Suze, hand me your phone so I can call the take-out place."

Suze handed her the phone.

"Worked at Gifford's Furniture. Stopped though when she got pregnant. Another one of Mr. No-Wife-of-Mine-Is-Gonna-Work Daly's pronouncements.

"I swear, I think the men in this town were dropped down by some unfriendly alien space ship just to make stupid decisions."

Suze barked out a laugh. Even Van smiled. She had to admit, it felt good to be here with Dorie; she never pulled her punches and had an opinion—most of them totally un-PC—about everything.

Dorie called their food order in and spent a couple of minutes commiserating over the demise of Clay Daly with whoever was at the other end of the conversation. Then she turned off the phone and gave Van her full attention.

"So does she have a plan?" Van asked.

"Who?"

"Gigi."

"Ha. Has that girl ever had a plan?"

Once, thought Van. Once she'd wanted to go to nursing school. But she'd given Van her college savings so she could get away. And even though Van had paid Gigi back and more, she must have given up on the idea by the time it was all repaid.

Van sat still on the couch as the familiar tendrils of hurt wrapped around her throat. She tried to breathe it away. It was stupid to react like this. It wasn't her fault that Gigi hadn't gone to college, or that she'd married a man who sounded like a Neanderthal.

Was it?

"Who paid for the funeral?"

"Nate and Amelia; they paid for everything."

"Catering, too?"

"They'll pay me back, someday. So enough about Gigi. What I want to know about is you."

Van shrugged. "I'm doing great. I own my own business. A lifestyle management service. It started out as a glorified cleaning service. Something I learned working at the hotel and the restaurant all those summers."

"Ha," Suze said. "It developed into much more than a cleaning service. It's a total organization service for rich Manhattanites.

Apartment living the Van Moran way. She takes your messes, your schedules, your laundry, your bratty children and makes them run smoothly. Down to recommending a nanny.

"She's been featured in the *New York Times* and *New York* magazine."

Van held up her hands. "Thanks for the endorsement. I should hire you to do advertising, but I don't think Dorie is interested in the daily grind of it all."

"I am, I am," protested Dorie. "But first I have a question."

Van knew immediately that it wasn't going to be about her business. She reached for her wineglass with an unsteady hand. "What do you want to know?"

Dorie pulled the magnum of zinfandel over and filled her glass to the brim. "Why don't you start with why you left and where you went? I can't believe this was all because you and Joe Enthorpe had a lovers' spat."

Even though Van had expected Joe's name to come up sooner or later, hearing it out loud was a shock, and she bobbled her wineglass. Put it down.

"It wasn't Joe's fault." Not exactly. The fact that he'd turned into one more disappointment in a life of disappointments had driven her over the edge. He was the last person she had totally trusted. And he'd betrayed her.

"Or was it because while you two were broke up, he and Dana had a little fling? Not that he ever cared a whit for the likes of her."

"How did you know that?"

"Gigi told me."

Van was appalled to feel tears spring to her eyes. She was thirty years old, and a teenage crush could bring her to tears? She looked away, trying to pull herself together.

She saw a white tissue appear in front of her nose. Recognized Dottie's Aren't You Something red polish.

"Because if it was that, I have two . . ." Dorie counted on her fingers. "Three words for you. Get. Over. It."

"It wasn't," Van said, and sniffed. "Nobody carries a torch for a high school sweetheart for all this time."

"Then what was it?"

"It's what happened after . . . the spat."

Van was aware of Suze's arrested attention. Dorie leaned forward. Here it was. Dorie deserved an explanation. And now that it was time, Van looked forward to getting it all out. Sort of. She took a breath. *Just start.* She had no doubt the rest of the story would pour out. It had been bottled up long enough.

"I got pregnant."

Suze looked down at her wineglass.

Dorie narrowed her eyes. "And for that you left town and were never heard from again until today?"

"Um, Dorie?" Suze said.

Dorie waved her away. "Don't you think that's a little melodramatic? Even for an Irish girl? Joe woulda done right by you. You know he would."

Van and Suze exchanged looks. "It didn't matter. I lost the baby."

"Lost or . . . ?" Dorie left the end of the question unasked, but Van knew what she was saying.

"I miscarried. Ask Suze."

Suze nodded confirmation.

Dorie turned on Suze. "You knew about this and didn't call me? Of all the—"

"I couldn't. I had my hands full at the time. I nearly called." She stopped to give Van an apologetic look. "Van almost died.

She waited so long before she called that by the time I drove to Manhattan and got her to the hospital, she'd nearly bled to death."

"But I still don't see why you had to run in the first place. Did you even tell Joe?"

Van shook her head.

"Because of Dana? Gigi told me you caught them going at it. But that didn't last long enough for her to get her clothes back on. He loved you. We all thought you two would end up getting married. You could have been married before the baby came."

Van stood up abruptly. Walked to the window. The old anger, hurt, and humiliation overflowed into the present. When the words came, they were harsh and louder than she'd meant. "It wasn't Joe's baby."

She stood facing the two women, defiant. At least it was out. That part was out at least.

"Well, hell," Dorie said, her voice subdued. "Are you sure it wasn't Joe's?"

"Positive."

Dorie looked at her hard. Raised her eyebrows in question.

Van shook her head and Dorie let out a big sigh. Evidently still not convinced, she asked, "You and Joe never . . . ?"

"No."

"And the father?"

"I don't know. I don't remember his name. I'm not sure I even knew it then. I just had a knee-jerk reaction and . . ." She ended with a shrug.

"You always were so responsible."

"And the one time I wasn't, look where it got me."

"Did you tell your father?"

Van nodded. "I don't know what I was thinking. I wasn't thinking. He was yelling at me about something else, and I just blurted it out." After all these years, knowing that his words could still hurt was appalling. "He told me I was a whore just like my mother and to get out. So I did."

Dorie took a couple of deep breaths, let them out. "Just as well, but you could have stayed with me."

"I knew you would take me in and don't think I don't appreciate knowing that. But what would have happened then? I'd just finished high school. Had no job except at the Blue Crab, and how could I work and take care of a baby, while watching Dana and Joe together, when I had just screwed up my whole life."

"So you would have kept the baby?"

"Of course." Because God knew when she'd called Suze for help she had been too far gone to care about saving herself.

The doorbell rang and they all jumped.

Dorie levered herself from the chair and went to answer it. She came back carrying a pizza box and a large paper bag.

"I'll get plates and stuff." Suze practically ran out of the room.

Dorie pulled containers out of the bag and placed them on the coffee table. Finally she looked up.

"I don't mean to sound uncaring. But that was all a long time ago. Why are you still holding on to it?"

"I'm not. I never even think about it. I'm a different person now. It's just being here . . . I don't know. I'm successful. I make enough money to live comfortably in Manhattan. I have friends." *When she had time for them.*

"No significant other?"

"Not at the moment." *Hardly ever. For significant reasons.*

Van saw Suze hovering in the doorway, plates clutched to her middle like some kind of armor.

"Hurry up," Van said with forced enthusiasm. "I'm starving."

Suze passed the plates over.

While Suze opened containers, Dorie slid a slice of pizza onto a plate and handed it to Van.

But when Van reached for it, Dorie held on, studying her face.

"What?"

"Nothing. But someday I hope you'll tell me the whole story."

Dorie stood at the sink letting the water run. She'd insisted on doing the dishes, not that there were too many, and leaving the girls alone. Seems like she had a bunch of broken people on her hands. At least Harold was out of the way, and with any luck he'd be gone long enough for her to see things through.

Suze had called her months ago. She wanted to rent a room for a few months. She said she needed a quiet place to work for the winter. She had a year off to write some paper on some poet Dorie had never heard of. Of course, Dorie's knowledge of poetry consisted of Rod McKuen and limericks she heard down at the pub.

Dorie would be glad to have her, and there was no way she would charge her rent. But what the hell was Suze doing, staying in a stuffy room in an old beat-up house, when she could live in a mansion with a whole suite of rooms two miles away? It didn't make sense.

Then there was Van. Van worried her. She might be successful. Hell, Dorie knew she was successful, but she didn't seem happy. Not by a long shot. And that just wasn't right.

Gigi's life was in tatters way before Clay fell to his death. She hadn't been right since Van left twelve years before. It's like she just gave up. She'd always talked about being a nurse, but suddenly she was marrying Clay Daly instead and working at the furniture store. Now she was alone and back home with Amelia taking care of the children. Nate and Amelia didn't have a clue as to what to do. Dorie thought the girl needed a big dose of therapy, though she wouldn't dare suggest it.

And then there was Joe. Dorie had never believed in broken hearts until Van left town and she'd watch that boy pine away. Everybody commiserated for a while. Then made fun of him and he laughed, too, like it was a good joke that he'd get over. But it seemed to Dorie he just never got over it. Her. Never got over Van.

Sometimes you saw two people together and you thought, *Wrong, wrong, wrong*. But sometimes, you knew that two people were right for each other, righter than they could be with anyone else.

And if ever two people were meant to be together, it was Joe and Van. After Van left, Dorie had watched Joe go out with one girl after another, never sticking with any of them for very long. Then she'd worry about him when he'd go weeks, months, without even showing up at the pub or the Crab; he was living and working on the farm. He told the boys he didn't have time for fun.

That was no way for a man to live. He was thirty-three now. That summer he'd been twenty-one and home from college helping out at the dairy and driving the dairy's delivery truck. He saw Van, and his eyes popped right out of his head like one of those cartoon characters. Love at first sight.

Hell, watching the two of them together was better than going to the movies. And then one little fight and she disappeared. It had never made sense. After all she'd endured, to run off over something like that.

Now Dorie knew the real reason. Or part of the real reason. She hadn't dealt with kids for years without being able to tell when one of them wasn't telling her the whole truth. Van was holding something back, and maybe it wasn't Dorie's business. Maybe it just wasn't her damn business. Still . . .

She'd thought Clay's funeral would be the perfect time to see what might happen. But for some reason Joe hadn't even come to the funeral. Couldn't be because he wanted to avoid Van. Nobody knew she was coming, including Dorie. And Van didn't even ask about him.

Maybe she'd been wrong. Maybe it was too late for them, too much heartache, too much time, too much water under the bridge. And she was a fool for stirring up things better left alone.

It was late when Joe walked through the door of Mike's Pub. He hadn't meant to come back, the same way he hadn't meant to stop by this morning. But here he was, standing just inside looking around the room before making his way to the bar. Mike had good enough food, but Joe had really come to hear about the funeral.

There was an empty stool between Jerry Corso and Hal Daniels. They motioned him over.

"Why the empty seat?" Joe asked as he sat down. "You guys fighting or something?"

"Nah," Jerry said. "Vinnie was here, but he had to get over to Pep Boys before it closed."

Mike pulled a beer for Joe and slid it toward him. "You eating?"

"Burger and fries."

"Medium, got it." Mike snagged a waitress and sent her back to the kitchen.

"You at the funeral today?" Hal asked.

Joe shook his head and took a deep drink of the beer. It was cold, and after sweating all day at the marina, he felt like he was being frozen from the inside out.

"Didn't think I saw you." Hal went back to peeling the label off his beer bottle.

"Damn," Jerry said. "Thirty-seven years old and phhhht. Gone. Just doesn't seem right."

"No, it don't," Hal agreed. "But he'd been having a hard time of it for the last few years. Still, it was stupid to try to fix a roof by himself. Anybody taking up a collection for Gigi and the kids?"

"Down at the station," Jerry said. "Clay's brother, Jack, organized it. He made sergeant just this spring, and I think he's feeling bad that he didn't help Clay out more when he was still alive. All of us are pitching in what we can, but nobody's got much extra cash these days."

"True." Hal lifted his beer. "How come you didn't go to the funeral, Joe?"

Hal's question caught Joe off guard. He shrugged. "Had a hire. Can't afford to turn down work, even for the dead." *Especially for the dead,* he thought.

Hal swiveled his seat around, started to stand, changed his mind, and swung back around. "Hell, Dana's heading this way."

"Hey, boys." Dana Mulvanney squeezed in the opening between Hal and Joe. "Started without me? Or you been drinking since the funeral let out?"

On Joe's far side, Jerry contemplated his beer.

"Pretty much," Hal said, and he called out to Mike for another round. "Whatcha drinking, Dana?"

"Dirty martini."

"Didn't see you at the funeral, or the get-together afterward, Joe." Dana leaned against him, a routine she went through nearly every night that she came to the bar. Mike's was a local hangout. Everyone showed up at least a couple of times a week, and some dropped in just about every night. Joe came in at least twice, mainly for dinner when he didn't feel like cooking.

Dana came in sporadically. And it spelled trouble when she did.

"I couldn't make it," Joe said and turned to face her. "You want to sit down?" He started to get off the stool, but she put up a hand and stopped him. Then she let her fingers splay across his chest and linger there. Slowly she walked her fingers lower—and would have kept going if Joe hadn't caught her wrist.

She laughed and dropped her hand. "You're no fun."

"Afraid not." Joe glanced up and wished he hadn't. He was close enough to see the bruise that she'd attempted to cover with makeup. She'd pulled her spiky dark hair over her cheeks, but it only called attention to what she wanted to hide. "Dana—"

She turned away. "How about you, Hal? Has Mary Kate let you out for some fun?"

"Mary Kate would have my fun and serve it to me on a platter," Hal said. "Go on home, before Bud finds you in here."

"Oh, Bud's over there flirting with a table of tourists." Mike put three beers and a martini on the bar. Dana plucked the glass up and began fishing the olive out of it. "I really just came over to talk to Joe here. 'Cause I know he's dying to know who I saw at the funeral today."

"I'm sure a lot of people were there today. Clay was a popular guy."

Dana smiled slyly. And Joe knew what she was going to say. He'd been waiting for it, expecting it. He'd prepared for it—maybe even hoped for it, but he couldn't stop the shot of emotion that went straight to his gut.

"Well, don't you want to know?" The coy expression she'd perfected in high school looked a little tired on her thirty-year-old face—her thirty-year-old bruised face, he added. They should be doing something for Dana; it was too late for Clay Daly.

"This better be good."

"Oh, it is, sweetie. It really is."

Chapter 5

DANA PLACED HER MARTINI GLASS ON THE BAR, SLOSHING some of the liquid over the rim. Obviously not her first drink of the evening. When she let go of the glass, her hand drifted down to Joe's knee.

Joe turned his head to give her a friendly reminder of her boyfriend who was probably watching the whole scene. And met her face inches from his. He managed to pull back just as she pursed her lips in an exaggerated pucker.

"Dana, cut it out. You're just asking for trouble."

"Trouble's my middle name."

"No," Hal said. "Trouble's your boyfriend over there. He's looking this way and he ain't happy."

Dana turned away from Joe long enough to take Hal's chin between two fingers and plant a kiss on his lips.

"That's it." Hal slid backward off his stool, grabbed his beer, and went to stand on the other side of Jerry.

Dana pouted as she watched him walk away.

Joe shook his head. "Dammit, don't you have any sense of self-preservation?"

"Aw, c'mon, Joe. Can't a girl have a little fun?"

"Not when it leads to a shiner like the one you're trying to cover with makeup."

Dana's fingers went reflexively toward her cheek, before she realized what she was doing and snatched her hand down. "We just had a little tiff. That's all."

Dana had stopped pretending that her bruises had come from accidents a long time ago. Now she didn't even bother to deny it.

The fire had just gone out of her. It started after Van left, but she really spiraled down when she hooked up with Bud.

Bud Albright was a cop with anger management problems. He'd been censured a couple of times for rough handling of a detainee, but somehow he managed to stay on the force. Probably by taking his anger out on Dana instead of his collars.

"All right, you were going to tell me who all was at the funeral."

"Not all, babycakes . . . But one particular person."

"Fine, but you'd better get it out, because Bud is headed this way."

"I'm not afraid of him."

"You should be."

Dana smiled. "Your girlfriend, that's who."

"Dana, I don't currently have a girlfriend. Can we just cut to the chase? My dinner's here."

Mike put his burger in front of him and reached below the bar for ketchup and mustard. "Let the man eat in peace, Dana."

Dana made a face at him. Mike began scrubbing the counter, ignoring her.

Joe reached for his napkin.

"Van's back."

Joe flinched even though he'd steeled himself not to react. But Dana had waited for his one moment of distraction before going in for the kill. The girl had black widow instincts.

"Thought you might be interested."

"Well, Gigi *is* her cousin. Stands to reason she might come to the funeral."

"After twelve years? Are you serious?" The seductress and the syrupy singsong voice were gone; the old Dana stood before him, angry, belligerent, and spoiling for a fight.

Joe would have welcomed the change if it hadn't come in tandem with Van Moran's reappearance.

He didn't know why Dana was still so angry after all these years. Nothing had happened to her. She'd managed to break him and Van up with her stupid flirtations.

Van should have known he'd never take Dana seriously. He was a guy. A young guy and he enjoyed the attention, but he loved Van. He'd been pissed at her, but he'd always meant to make up with her. Then Van just up and left without a word, and he'd never heard from her again.

And life went on.

He'd gotten over it. He couldn't figure out why Dana hadn't. She still had her life, her friends; it was Van's life that had changed. Van was the one who left, the one no one heard from again. Dana just went back to what she did best, flirting. And then Bud came along; but it still hadn't stopped her—she reveled in causing trouble.

She couldn't seem to help herself.

Joe had once asked why she kept at it. She'd just looked at him and said, "Guess God just made me cute, sexy, and mean as a snake."

She'd missed on all counts.

At least in Joe's mind. She was too hard-edged to be pretty, and her in-your-face come-on was anything but sexy—at least to him. And it didn't get any prettier with age. And though she might not be hiding a heart of gold beneath her bitchy exterior, she wasn't nearly as badass as she wanted people to believe. And that's what kept getting her in trouble. She was like a bad kid, acting out for attention.

He reached for the ketchup and shook some out on his fries. Screwed the cap back on, put it on the counter. Picked up his burger . . .

Dana's fingers walked up his thigh. "You'd have hardly recognized her."

He put the burger down.

"Listen, Dana, I know you enjoy drawing this all out. But I'm hungry and tired; can you just please say what you're going to say and be done?"

Dana's dark eyes flashed with interest or anger, he couldn't tell. Nor did he care.

"Well, if you really want to know. She's totally sophisticated. Sle-e-e-ek." She drew the word out. "And totally full of herself. Probably wouldn't give any of us, including you, the time of day. In fact, she just came to the funeral, made a scene afterwards and left without even acknowledging anybody. Still the stuck-up bitch she always was."

"You know better." Joe reached for his burger; this time it made it to his mouth.

"Well, she was and still is," Dana said, knowing his mouth was full and he couldn't defend Van.

"That's so much horseshit and you know it." Hal leaned over

the bar so he could see Dana past Joe. "She was always nice. And if she didn't have much time to party and get in trouble, it's because she was working all the time to support her dad."

"Oh, and an angel, too. I forgot that part. All you boys thought so, didn't you? Just because she wouldn't put out for any of you. Except maybe for Joe."

Joe swallowed. "Okay, that's enough. You've had your moment. Now it's over. Van was here and I assume she left again after the funeral." As a hint it wasn't very subtle, but his patience was hanging by a thread.

"Wouldn't you like to know?"

Joe dropped his head in exasperation. Did Dana have any idea how silly she sounded? Like she was still in high school instead of a grown woman.

Calloused fingers wrapped around Dana's arm. She twisted in reaction.

"She wasn't doing anything, Bud," Joe said.

Bud scowled at him; his eyes had the glazed-over look of too many beers with a bit of bully thrown in.

Joe turned back to his burger.

Bud pulled Dana toward him, practically lifting her off her feet. Jerry started to stand. Joe put out a warning hand. Mike would kill them if they started a brawl. He'd just finished refurbishing the place after the last one.

Bud pushed Dana behind him.

She just laughed and peered around his side. "Maybe she'll decide to stay for a few days. Maybe you should go ask her to."

"Shut up, Dana. Get in the truck," Bud said.

Dana reached out and snagged her drink. Gave Joe an air kiss and sashayed across the room.

Bud didn't follow.

"Give it a rest, Bud. You know she's just being Dana."

"Yeah, but I got something else to say to you."

Joe glanced at his rapidly cooling burger. "Mind if I eat while you talk?"

"It won't take long. You're letting those poachers use your mudflats to catch crabs and clams. It's a restricted area. If you don't stop them—"

"Look, Bud, I told you. I don't own that property. I'm just working there for the season. They're not my mudflats. And it's not my responsibility to stop them."

"But it is your responsibility to call the police when they trespass."

"I don't ever see them trespassing." Joe picked up his burger and took a bite.

Bud stared at him for a couple of extra seconds then finally walked away.

Hal slid back onto his stool. "Arrested development, the two of them."

"Yeah," Joe said. "Kind of like being back on the playground."

"Or wandering into a bad western."

"He was always a bully, long as I can remember," Jerry added. "Just never grew out of it. At least you guys don't have to work with him."

"Heard he got censured or whatever the cops do for roughhandling people he picked up."

"Yeah. We all figure it's just a matter of time till he goes bonkers. You feel like you're always walking on eggshells around him. He's supposed to be going to these anger management sessions."

Hal snorted. "Well, if they're using my hard-earned tax dollars, tell 'em to quit. It's not doing any good, far as I can see."

"Doesn't look like it." Jerry agreed. "Sure hate to see what's happening to Dana, though. If she had any sense, she'd dump his ass and find a decent guy."

"When pigs fly." Hal slid off the stool. "Well, I gotta get going. Promised Mary Kate I'd take the kids to Six Flags tomorrow. Hello crowds and junk food, good-bye paycheck." He plunked some bills down on the bar and looked at Joe. "So are you going to see Van while she's here?"

Joe shrugged. "Don't know that she's still here."

"Oh yeah, she is. Mary Kate was at the funeral. Van and that other girl, remember the rich sorority one who hung out with them?"

"Suze?"

"Yeah, her. Well, Mary Kate says they came to the funeral and then to the pub afterward. And that someone heard they were gonna stay with Dorie for a few days while they try to shore up Gigi."

"Good luck with that," said Jerry. "Gigi would do better just to cut bait and start over."

Hal nodded and headed for the door.

Jerry leaned on the bar. "Not for nothin' but you oughta watch it with those diggers. I know they aren't doing any harm. Water's fine . . . at least enough for eating shellfish, just not for selling shellfish."

"Like I told Bud—"

"Yeah, I know. Not your responsibility. And it's not like the Shellfish Commission is policing the waters. But if you see them, you might want to warn them that Bud's out to get them. He's been on his good behavior, but it won't last. It's just a matter of time until he takes it out on somebody besides Dana. I wouldn't want it to be any of those poor suckers. And I wouldn't want it to be you."

He stood. "I gotta get going. I have the early shift tomorrow. Then three night shifts in a row. I need my rest."

After Jerry left, Joe finished his dinner, paid, and went out to his truck. Maybe he could catch up on some *z*'s himself.

And he almost made it home. He was approaching the bridge that would take him to the marina when the light turned red. As he sat there waiting for the light to turn again, something just shifted inside him. When the light changed to green, he made a sharp turn toward the shore, leaving the bridge behind.

He drove a block, two blocks, telling himself he was a fool. Three blocks. A real fool. And an idiot. Four blocks. But what harm would it do? It wasn't like anyone would ever know.

He'd just cruise past, see if there was a light on. Dorie would have closed the restaurant by now. She'd be at home, but it was late; she'd probably be in bed. He wouldn't stop. Just drive by.

Luckily for his self-esteem, he would never be able to get a parking place on the street, especially on a Saturday night.

A car pulled out of a space just ahead of him. He slowed even further. A parking place. No yellow paint that he could tell. No fire hydrant. There was nothing stopping him from parking and getting out.

He drove past. Saw headlights in his rearview mirror. He slammed on the brakes; backed up and into the space. He only made it halfway. But he waited until the car passed by before he pulled out again, aligned the truck properly, and parked.

And sat. Ten hours ago he'd been doing the same thing. Sitting in the bar. Waiting. And for what? Why was he even doing this? It's not like they would have anything in common now. But hell, after all these years, he just wanted to know.

Dorie's house was dark. The Caddy was gone, but there was a car he didn't recognize parked on the grass. Van's? Suze's? Someone else who'd come from out of town to the funeral and needed a place to stay?

He drummed a tattoo on the steering wheel, watched the door. But for what? Who did he expect to walk out in the middle of the night?

A thousand times he'd wondered why she had left town. It wasn't because he'd been flirting with Dana. Van wasn't that volatile. She couldn't afford to be.

He'd seen her come into Mike's and saw her expression before she let him have it. And before Mike escorted her to the door with the warning to stay out. She was only eighteen.

Joe should have gone after her. But the guys were all ribbing him and he was embarrassed. But even as Van's features dimmed in his memory, her expression remained. He'd thought she was pissed, but he knew now that it was hurt.

He'd hurt his best friend. The girl he loved.

After a few days he gave in. Tried calling her, but the phone had been turned off. He asked people about her. She was around, but steering clear of him. He'd planned to be patient, wait for her to come around. Explain to her that it didn't mean anything.

Several weeks passed, but she stayed away. No one knew where she was, or at least they weren't telling him. Desperate, he even went to her house. But her father just yelled at him and said she was gone and good riddance. Joe could have killed him right there. Van had spent every day after school and summer vacation working to make money to keep a roof over their heads. And her father was glad she was gone.

Joe never saw her again. No one had. She left town without telling anyone. And never came back. He remembered it like it was yesterday.

He'd meant to marry her and take her away from her father and all the stuff that made her unhappy, but he had a scholarship to study dairy management and he'd let it slide. He thought he had plenty of time.

He wasn't ready to get hitched then. He thought if she could just hold on a little longer. But . . .

There was speculation that she'd died. An accident or by her own hand, but Joe didn't believe it. Van was tough. Had to be after what she'd been through. But not hard like Dana. Van had managed to keep her compassion and her ability to love intact. She was sensitive and artistic and thought she might like to go to art school someday. They made plans. But that all ended when she disappeared.

Everyone blamed him and Dana, and it hadn't mattered how much he said nothing happened; Dana was close behind him implying that it had.

The tattoo turned to a drum. At least Van had made a life for herself. He followed her career on the Internet. But he hadn't once tried to contact her. He didn't know why. Maybe it was fear that she'd reject him or that she'd totally forgotten him, or maybe he just didn't want his memory of how special she was to be tarnished by reality.

And now he was sitting in a parked truck like a stalker.

He reached for the keys. He'd go home. Ignore the diggers. Try to sleep.

Dorie's front door opened. At first Joe thought he was imagining things. Or that he'd stumbled on a burglar.

But the dark figure came down the steps, paused at the sidewalk, then turned and walked toward the beach.

And he knew who it was. She was a mere silhouette; there was nothing discernible except the way she walked. And he knew just as if it were broad daylight and she was staring him in the face.

He grabbed the keys and opened the truck door. Was careful to close it quietly. Because he was really crazy.

Really crazy and pitiful, he thought as he started after her, moving slow, hugging the shadows. If a patrol car passed by, he'd be spending the night in jail. 'Cause he looked guilty as hell.

He followed her for the block and a half to the boardwalk. Stood back when she crossed the street. It was pretty quiet. A few stragglers walked by, but the Blue Crab had closed earlier, and the serious drinkers had moved on to the bars up the beach or in town.

He didn't cross the street but kept parallel to her movements. She was headed toward the Blue Crab, but she walked past the restaurant, and he lost her in the shadows. It didn't matter. He knew where she was going. Whisper Beach.

As soon as she disappeared over the side, he crossed the street.

He didn't think she should be alone on the beach at night. Especially one so isolated. God knew who might be down there. He crossed the street, moving slowly until he was at the boardwalk railing.

She was standing on the sand, facing the sea. She looked almost otherworldly.

Then she raised her arms and turned. Saw him and stopped. He slid back from the rail and into the shadows.

What had he been thinking? He didn't stop to see if she would follow but crossed the street and, ducking his head, quickly walked way.

VAN COULD SWEAR someone was watching her. And yet when she turned, no one was there. She was alone with the tide and the sand and the night. Above her the clouds drifted across the stars, blocking out the sliver of moon, only to pass on like a theater curtain, leaving it center stage.

She'd missed this. The expanse of open space, the dark unencumbered blankness of it all. Life in Manhattan was never totally dark, lights were always on somewhere, and the only panoramic view you got was from the roof of a penthouse, where you could see Queens stretching into Long Island. Or walk through Riverside Park to look at the lights of New Jersey across the Hudson. But it wasn't the same as looking into deep dark that might go on forever.

Now there was too much Manhattan in her to feel completely at ease in the dark. Hence that prickling feeling that made her alert, defensive, ready to run or protect herself. From what? There was no one there. Or if there had been, it must have been another poor insomniac who'd come to be lulled to sleep by the waves.

Van felt calmer now, but she wasn't ready to go back inside, so she walked to the water, her sandals in her hand. Splashed at the edges of the surf. Reveled in the cool water that lapped over her ankles.

Maybe coming here was just what she needed. A little downtime. Not like the scene at Rehoboth. She'd been working hard for a long time. For as long as she could remember. Even on the weekends, she was always planning for the next week or analyzing the last. Because it didn't pay to leave anything to chance. She'd learned that a long time ago, and she wasn't about to forget it now.

But she wasn't stupid. She knew her body and mind both needed a rest. Time to uncoil from the tension of running a successful, demanding business.

And if Whisper Beach wasn't her resort of choice, she was here, she had friends, and maybe confronting the bugaboos from her past would finally set her completely free.

She reached the point where the river spilled into the sea. People used to fish there. She wondered if they still did. She turned and retraced her steps, her footprints already washed away by the tide. As she walked, her footprints disappeared behind her.

A car engine revved in the distance. A door slammed somewhere on the street, then silence and just the *shush shush* of the surf as it swirled beneath the pier—the sound that gave Whisper Beach its name. When they were kids, they all thought that if you stood beneath the pier and whispered the name of the boy you wanted to marry, it would come true.

But Van had always loved the old legend more. The one of poor Melody Kilpatrick, who stood at the water's edge, hushing her baby as she waited for her pirate lover to return. *He never did, but if you come to the pier at night and listen closely, you can still hear her hushing her fatherless child at water's edge.*

Van smiled into the night. She used to be fanciful like that. But fanciful had been torn from her years ago. And she ached for that girl who, even with the horror that was her father, still managed to find some joy.

Chapter 6

It was nearly ten before Van padded, yawning, into the kitchen the next morning. She'd showered and dressed, but she still felt tired.

Suze and Dorie were sitting at the table with a plate of pastries occupying the space between them; a trail of crumbs led to Suze's plate.

Van crossed to the coffeepot and poured herself a cup.

"Sleep well?" Dorie asked.

"Like the dead." Van pulled out a chair and sat down.

"I heard you go out," Suze said. She shrugged. "I'm having a little trouble sleeping myself these days."

"I heard you, too." Dorie half smiled and Van couldn't tell if she was trying not to smile or couldn't manage a decent one.

"I wasn't sneaking away if that's what you were afraid of."

Dorie looked at the ceiling. Suze took a huge bite of a jelly donut. The jelly oozed onto the plastic tablecloth.

"I wasn't," Van said.

"I know. I watched you from the window just to make sure you didn't try."

Van coughed out a laugh. "What were you going to do if I was leaving? Throw yourself under the wheels of my rental car?"

"Nothing so drastic." Dorie rummaged in the pocket of her housedress and tossed a set of keys over to Van. "You'll need these if you're driving over to Gigi's this morning."

"You stole my keys?"

"I believe the word is *appropriated*."

"Some things never change," Suze said and ran her finger over the jelly spill.

"When?"

Dorie dusted the crumbs off her fingers. "When I walked past your purse on the way to bed last night. I'm smooth. Had lots of practice taking them away from drunk teenagers."

Van snatched them off the table; then, realizing she didn't have her purse and her capris had no pockets, she put them back on the table.

"I gotta get going over to the Crab. Dairy delivery this morning."

Van didn't miss the surreptitious look Dorie shot her.

Van sighed. "Okay. I'll bite. Is it still the Enthorpe Dairy?"

"Hell, no. They sold the dairy years ago. The year after you left I think, maybe two."

"Wow." Van was stunned. "That's been in the family for generations. What happened? None of the kids wanted to take over?"

"You know that isn't true." Dorie said. "They'd been losing money for years. Couldn't compete with the prices the corporate dairy business could sell for."

"That's a shame. A real shame. Did they sell the land? What happened to the family?" Van thought she'd asked that with complete disinterest, but she didn't fool Dorie for a second.

"Sold a big chunk of land to a developer. Nearly broke old Joseph's heart. But they made a bundle off the sale, so at least they're not hurting like a lot of folks around here."

Van waited.

Dorie waited.

Van could win this battle of the wills. She did it every day with recalcitrant clients.

"So where's Joe?" Suze asked, unwittingly ending the standoff.

"He's working over at Grandy's Marina."

"What?" Van blurted out before she could stop herself.

"Yep. Looking after the place during the season."

Van shook her head. "Why? How did he go from studying dairy management to pumping gas and scraping barnacles?" But she knew all too well. Dreams were made and sometimes crushed in Whisper Beach. Just look at them all.

"Maybe you should go say hello."

"I don't think so." What was over was over, and Van saw no need to travel down that path again. Besides, she wanted to remember Joe as a boy with a plan, not some poor slob who had given up.

"Suit yourself." Dorie pushed herself out of her chair. "Now I really gotta get going. Don't have time to sit around and schmooze unless you start getting up earlier."

"Dorie—"

"Don't make me take your keys away."

Van sat back, resigned. "Fine."

"Fine." Dorie shuffled out of the kitchen. It was the first time that Van noticed how stooped she'd become. Dorie was getting old, and it hit Van with a sharp pang, before it was superseded by another thought. Was Dorie just playing to her sympathies? She hadn't been stooped and shuffling last night.

It was all an act. Wasn't it?

Suze stood and carried her plate to the sink. "I better get to work."

"Oh, no, you don't. Don't think you badgered me into hanging around and then think you can hole up in your room. I'm sure Gigi would love to see you, too. Just like old times," Van said. "Won't that be fun?"

"Minus Dana," Suze said. "And, Van, sarcasm doesn't really make it this early in the morning."

Van sighed and put her head down on the table. "Please?" She tilted her head to gauge Suze's reaction. "Pretty please?"

It took another cup of coffee and several more minutes to convince Suze to go with her to see Gigi. Suze didn't want to cramp their reunion. Van didn't want to face Gigi alone. They finally compromised. Suze would come if she could have the afternoon to work.

"Deal."

"But I have to wait for the mail to come."

"Suze, it's Sunday."

"Oh." Suze slumped against the chair back.

"Are you expecting mail?" Van asked only half jokingly.

"Yes."

"What's going on?"

"What do you mean?"

"I mean you're having your mail delivered here? Are you planning on staying awhile?"

Suze reached for another pastry, chose one, and pushed the plate toward Van.

Van shook her head. "Suze?"

"Yeah. I'm thinking about staying here for the fall."

"The whole fall? Why? You didn't lose your job or anything?"

"No."

"Then why here? You have a great apartment on campus and your family lives in the next town."

"I need a fresh environment. And if I go to my parents, they'll try to set me up with promising men for the duration. And insist on buying me my own apartment and a car and—"

"So what's wrong with that?"

"Because it all comes with strings attached."

Van nodded. It would be nice to have a family who wanted to buy you things, make your life better, but she wouldn't want the expectations that accompanied the Turners' generosity any more than Suze did.

"You want to go to Rehoboth with me?"

Suze snorted and ended up in a fit of coughing.

"You shouldn't eat and snort at the same time."

Suze waved at her and finally got her breath. "I can't afford Rehoboth."

"I've already paid for the room and everything."

Suze gave her a look.

"Hey, no strings attached."

"Thanks, but I really have to get some work done. If I don't get this paper finished and published, I'll be looking for work down at the marina. You've heard the expression publish or perish?"

"Yeah."

"Well, it's true. But I need this grant money to be able to afford to take off from teaching."

"They don't pay you to publish?"

"Ha. Part salary. But not enough to do all the research, have time to write, and still eat."

"Wait, they make you write this stuff to get tenure but don't pay you to do it?"

"It's complicated."

"When's the deadline for the application?"

"It has to be postmarked by next Monday. I've done the preliminary and this is round three. Several others are vying for the same money." Suze laughed ruefully. "Cutthroat competition behind those ivied walls."

"Well, come on, let's go to Gigi's. We'll take her out to lunch if she promises not to break down and bawl in the restaurant and then you can come back and work. I promise to be quiet and not bother you."

Gigi's parents lived near the parkway. Not beach property and not exactly the suburbs. The houses looked caught somewhere in between. Most had been refurbished with new siding, or paint. The lawns were fairly manicured, and some were still green even though it was late August.

Nate Moran was Van's father's brother, but unlike her father, he'd taken responsibility for his family, made a comfortable home for them. He'd added on to the house with each new baby, and it was now a rambling ranch.

Several cars were already parked in the driveway.

"This was a really bad idea," Van said. "I just assumed Gigi would be alone." She took a breath. "Well, hell, what do I care."

Van parked on the street.

"For a quick getaway?" Suze asked.

"Yeah, so when I give the signal, don't hesitate, head for the door."

"It won't be that bad."

"It might be. Aunt Amelia never liked our side of the Moran

family. Plus I really screwed things up yesterday. That's so not like me. If I hadn't been so ambivalent about coming, I would have come to the wake on Friday and skipped the funeral altogether; I could be sitting on the beach today."

"You can still sit on the beach today. It's only a block and a half away."

She gave Suze a look and rang the doorbell.

It opened so quickly that Van took a step backward. Gigi stood in the opening. Hopefully she hadn't been standing at the window all morning, because they hadn't hurried to get here.

"Hi." Van gave her cousin a quick hug and stepped into the house, avoiding any repeats of yesterday's sob fest.

It was dark inside, and Van had to blink a few times before things came into focus. Too much fabric was her immediate response. Too much stuff in general. She took another step into the room and nearly tripped over a plastic pull toy. Kids. Right. Gigi had two.

"Come on back. Everyone's in the family room."

Everyone. Oh, great.

They followed Gigi to the back of the house to a long wood-paneled addition with windows across the back. Several couches and chairs of various vintages were clustered together in front of a huge flat-screen television, muted to a Phillies game. A wall air conditioner rattled and pumped a stream of tepid air at their heads.

"You remember my brothers, Pete and Kirby?"

"Of course I do. Hi, guys," Van said, then added to the one girl in the room. "Is that you, Jane?"

"No, I'm Leslie. Jane's gone to Mass with mamma."

"Wow. I won't say how much you've grown." Especially since she'd grown out as well as up.

Leslie laughed and heaved herself out of the recliner. "Please don't." She patted her butt and went over to a table where a variety of funeral food had been laid out. "You and Suzanne get yourselves some food and have a seat."

"Thanks, but we just had breakfast."

Suze sat at one end of the couch. Van reluctantly sat down next to Pete. He'd been in his early twenties when Van had left. Now in his thirties, his head was shaved, hopefully to camouflage his receding hairline and not denoting his political affiliation. He'd grown pretty thick around the middle.

"How are things?" Van asked him.

"Besides Clay croaking? Pretty good. Got my own place now." His eyes drifted to the ball game.

About time, Van thought. "Nearby?"

"Down the street, renting the apartment over old man Dooley's garage."

"How is Mr. Dooley?" Van cast a help-me-out look at Suze. She'd go stark raving mad making small talk with Pete all afternoon. She hardly remembered Kirby, who had been a gawky preteen when she'd left.

"Oh, he died years back. His widow rents out rooms. Got me a good deal, too."

"Ah." Van's eyes strayed to the end tables, Depression veneer but polished to a shine. The doily would have to go. She resisted the temptation to at least straighten it where the lamp resting on it had twisted it out of shape.

Gigi squeezed in between Suze and Van. "Mother will be back any minute now. I know she'll want to see you."

Van smiled. She was sure Amelia Moran could go a lifetime without seeing Van. Things couldn't get much more stilted. How long would they have to stay? With all the funeral food sitting around, she doubted they could get away on the pretense of taking Gigi to lunch. It was going to be a long afternoon.

"You back for long? Yes!" Pete jumped to both feet. "What a play! Wow!" He threw himself back on the couch, pumped his fist in the air, and reached for his can of soda. "Damn! Did you see that? Yeah!"

A baby cried from another room. Gigi stood. "Pete, you woke the baby." She scowled at her brother and left the room. In the family room, silence reigned while Leslie ate, and Pete and Kirby fought over the remote.

"Can't even enjoy a game around here anymore. You have kids, Van?"

"No."

"No husband, either?"

Van shook her head.

"Well, what are you waiting for, girl?"

Van was saved from answering by Gigi's return. She was carrying a blond curly-headed girl, still half asleep, who rubbed her eye and hid her head in Gigi's shoulder when Van smiled at her.

"This is Amy. Amy, can you say hi to Van and Suze? Van's your cousin."

Amy shook her head against her mother's shoulder.

"She's a little shy," Gigi said and handed her off to Leslie, who moved her plate aside, then gave the little girl a piece of cheese.

A car door slammed.

"Mom-mom," Amy squealed as she slid off Leslie's lap and toddled toward the door.

Gigi went after her. Suze slid closer to Van. "Isn't there another one?"

"I think so."

There was the sound of general bustling, and Van braced herself for her aunt Amelia. If yesterday was any indication, she wouldn't be met with open arms. The first to arrive was a boy about four or five years old. He headed straight for the table of food and grabbed a cookie in each hand.

"Clayton Nathan Daly, you put those down until after lunch." Gigi made a beeline for the boy. He managed to shove one whole cookie into his mouth before Gigi confiscated the other one.

Lunch. That would be a good excuse for them to leave. No way would Van sit down for that meal. Not that Amelia would invite her.

Van stood with a double purpose, to show deference to her aunt and prepare for an exit. She shot a look toward Suze who looked more than ready to go.

"Aunt Amelia," Van said. Her aunt looked pretty much the same as she had before Van left, a little wider in the butt. But then Amelia had always looked middle aged, even when she was younger.

"Well, it's about time you came home and let everyone know what happened to you," Amelia said. "Even though it took a funeral to do it," she added under her breath but loud enough for everyone to hear. She scrutinized Van from head to toe.

Van stood still for the inspection. She had nothing to worry about. She was wearing a pair of black slacks and a gray silk shirt. She was the only one who'd even made a nod to the solemn occasion.

"You'll stay for lunch."

"We really can't—"

"Your uncle Nate wants to see you. He had to stop by the hardware store after Mass."

This is why she'd never come back. She was a nonperson here.

Someone to be talked at, shoved around, and generally ignored until she did something that they didn't like; then she was maligned and cast out.

Families. This was what families were. And she wanted no part of it.

Except for the Enthorpes. They had never treated her that way; they'd been loving and strong, and had cared about her. They had always made her feel welcome the few times she'd gone out to the farm with Joe. Would they welcome her now? Probably not.

"Jane, come help me set the table."

"I can't stay. I've got the three o'clock shift at the hospital," Jane, who had just entered the room, said. "I have to get home and fix Tom and the kids lunch."

"You'll take some of these leftovers," Amelia said, and the two women went off to the kitchen together.

"I'm not staying either, Ma." Pete pushed to his feet. "I gotta help Wally Phelps with his car."

"And Pete's giving me a ride," Kirby said.

"Gigi, we really can't stay for lunch, either," Van said. "Maybe we can come back later this afternoon or tomorrow."

Gigi grabbed her wrist. "You can't go without seeing Dad. He wondered why you didn't stay longer at the repast."

Van stood helplessly while all the old feelings—the sense of being trapped, being stifled, being ignored—rose up and threatened to paralyze her. It was like she had never left. She had to get out. She'd been crazy to have come in the first place.

"Please."

Suze had come to stand by her side. "I really need to get some work done," she said apologetically.

Gigi looked so disappointed that Van began to give in. Just

like she always had. Only now she resented the feeling. It was something that she hadn't done in years—backed down or felt resentful. She didn't want to start again now.

But just as she and Suze got to the kitchen to make their apologies to Amelia, the back door opened and her uncle walked in.

Nate was her father's brother but as different as two brothers could be. Her father was tall, wiry, angry, and a mean drunk. Nate was tall and robust, enjoyed a good joke—even if they were off color and politically incorrect—and still athletic. He drank, but not to excess. And he was never mean. At least as far as Van knew.

"Well, look at you," he said and held out both arms.

Powerless to resist, Van walked into his hug. "Hi, Uncle Nate." She pulled away. "Sad time."

Nate shook his head. "Sure is." He held her at arm's length. "You're looking real New York. Aren't you something?"

"Van says she can't stay to lunch," Amelia said.

Nate winked at Van. "I'm sure she needs to see lots of people while she's here. How long you staying, Van?"

Van shrugged, her mind suddenly blank for a real excuse. "I'm not sure. Long enough to spend some time with Gigi. I'll call you tomorrow. Maybe we can get together. Maybe get her out of the house." She glanced at her aunt. "If that would be appropriate."

"Better than her moping around here." Amelia turned back to the sink.

"Good, good," Nate said. "I'll walk you out to your car."

Gigi didn't want them to leave, but with the distraction of the kids and Amelia wanting her to help in the kitchen, Nate managed to maneuver Van and Suze out the front door.

He closed the door behind them with a sigh. "Never a dull moment."

"Sounds like you could use one," Van said sympathetically.

"I don't mind so much. Gigi's had a rough time of it, but it's been a strain on the whole family. Amelia's just about at the end of her rope."

He slowed down, and Van slowed with him. Suze made no pretense of holding up but went ahead to the car and got in.

"Clay was a good enough guy, don't get me wrong, but they had no business getting married. He couldn't support a family and little Clay came along in less than a year and Gigi had to stop working.

"Then with that damn hurricane . . ."

"Dorie told us some of it last night."

"Hell, I woulda helped them, but Clay was just a stubborn cuss. When the looting started, he moved into the RV with a shotgun. Then last week he climbed up on the roof to do God knows what. The whole place was condemned. And that was that.

"Now she's a widow with two kids, no insurance, and living at home."

They stopped at the car. "It must have been hard on her and the kids with Clay living away from them," Van said.

"Hard on everybody. There were tears and fights, and I think she feels guilty for not being able to make him come stay with us. There was room. But like I said—stubborn. And now it's too late.

"We love having her and the kids live with us, but it isn't healthy."

Van nodded.

"I sure would be grateful if you could talk to her. Maybe give her some ideas about what to do. She just seems stuck."

"Uncle Nate, I don't really know what I could do to help."

"Just talk to her. She always looked up to you. She still talks about you. She could use a friend right now."

"All right. I'll see what I can do." Maybe she owed Gigi that. Her uncle hadn't said anything, but he must know about the money Gigi gave her. At least he hadn't pulled the after-all-she-did-for-you card—yet. "Maybe Suze has some ideas. Tell Gigi we'll call her tomorrow."

"Thanks."

Nate opened the door for her but held it before she got in. "One more thing, Van."

She waited.

"You ought to go see your father while you're here. He won't have anything to do with us. But maybe—"

She shook her head.

"Oh hell, Van. I know he was a bastard. He was an unhappy man."

"He was a monster."

"Maybe it seemed that way to you."

"He killed my mother."

"What? Nonsense."

"He was too drunk to pick her up from her job at the hospital, so she had to walk home."

He shut the car door and faced her. "And if he had picked her up she wouldn't have gotten hit by the car?"

Van blinked furiously. She didn't want that all dredged up. "I offered to help Gigi out, not get a lecture about family."

"I beg your pardon. But remember this, and you're old enough to hear it. There were any number of people your mother could have called to pick her up. Even more at the hospital who would have gladly given her a ride home. But she didn't ask. She was mad at your father and had to play martyr.

"There are two sides to every story, Van. Takes two people to have a fight. Now that's all I'm gonna say. If you decide you want to see him, I'll let him know. If not, well . . . that's your choice."

He opened the door again, and Van got in.

"Uncle Nate?"

He stopped. "Yeah?"

"Don't be mad. But you don't understand."

"I'm not mad, but think ahead to how you'll feel when he's dead."

Happy. That's what she wanted to say. She'd be happy when her father was dead. "I should have been your daughter," she said at last.

Nate chuckled. "Nah. You got all your father's good qualities. He didn't start off to be bad, no more than Clay started off to be a failure. Just think about it." He shut the car door.

Van drove to the corner. Stopped at the stop sign. And screamed.

"Geez," Suze said, covering her ears.

"Sorry, but these people are . . . are . . ."

"Your relatives?"

"Ugh. Don't remind me."

"The Morans really know how to push your buttons. What did you promise to do?"

"Stay and help Gigi get her life together."

"That all?"

Van sighed. "I'll give her three days. Actually . . . there might be something else I can do." Van turned abruptly to look at Suze.

"What?"

"Do you mind if we make a little detour? It won't take long."

Chapter 7

"DOESN'T LOOK LIKE ANYBODY LIVES HERE," SUZE SAID.

"No." They were sitting at the curb of a white wood house. A beach cottage really, though it was several blocks from the beach. The white paint had grown a little dingy, the shutters a little grayer, but the lawn was cut. The windows were intact. There were even curtains, the same curtains that had been there the day she left. But it looked deserted. Of course it would; no one had lived in it for years.

"You grew up here?"

"Yep."

"What happened to your dad?"

"My father? Not a clue. Nor do I care. He moved out right after I did. Evidently he's still alive."

"So why are we here?"

"Because I own it. My grandmother left it to my mother, who left it to me."

"You mean you could have kicked him out after your mother died?"

"I was a minor. If he'd left, where would I have gone?"

Suze sighed. "There is that. Are we getting out?"

"I don't know." Van didn't want to get out. But she couldn't really keep paying taxes while the property fell to ruin. She could get a good price for it; several real estate agents had called her with interested buyers. She should have let it go. It could be sold, she would be richer, and there would be nothing to hold her here.

And yet here she was.

How many nights had she come home from work, tired from going to school all day and working the afternoon and night shift at the Blue Crab—feet hurting, back aching, with homework still to be done—only to get hit with the pungent beer and cigarette smell that permeated the room? Her father passed out on the couch, the guests and hosts of a late-night talk show blathering away on the television.

At first after her mother died, when her anger at her father subsided a bit, she'd try to get him to bed. But that didn't last long as her anger rekindled and settled in her gut. There were nights when she thought about killing him while he slept.

But something held her back. It wasn't fear. It wasn't morality. She was just too tired to care. So she'd pick up the worst of the mess and go to her room. Close the door and try to concentrate on her studies.

She'd graduated. Not with great grades, but not bad for someone who was hanging on by a thread. She began hiding her tips from work; her father was too far gone to notice that she wasn't bringing in as much as before.

She thought she would have enough after the summer season

to move out, find a room somewhere, or even move to a different town. But it all blew up in her face; it—

"Van. What are you doing? You're either spaced out or comatose, and neither is appropriate for the situation. Plus you're scaring me."

"Huh?" Van turned to see Suze's face a foot from hers.

"Are you all right?"

Van blew out air. "Yeah. I've been planning to sell it. But now . . . I'm thinking maybe I could let Gigi and the kids live in it until she gets her life together."

Suze unfastened her seat belt and turned in her seat. "What makes you think she's going to get her life together, especially if people keep giving her excuses not to?"

"You thinking loaning her this house is enabling her?"

"Uh, whaddaya think? She wasn't even living with her husband the last couple of years, but back at her parents', where I bet you money, her mother takes care of the kids, does the laundry, and the cooking. And Gigi doesn't have to pay for a thing."

"Well, she's been going through rough times."

"Like you haven't? Like any of us haven't?"

"You don't seem very sympathetic," Van said.

"Me? Of course I am. It's just, I don't know. I only knew her that one summer, but she always seemed so vapid. And perfectly willing to let other people take responsibility for getting things done."

"I guess, but she was so . . . I don't know. Everyone loved her. She was always sweet, scared, or crying."

"Well, we saw crying and sweet already. Do you think she's scared?"

Van barked out a laugh. "If she's smart, she is."

"Maybe she's smarter than you think."

"How so?"

"Maybe she wants everyone to take care of her. Poor, sweet Gigi."

"Well, she *was* sweet. Never said anything bad about anybody. Never did anything scandalous."

Suze groaned. "I remember. She even made excuses for Dana. Who, by the way, I saw at the funeral repast."

"You did? I didn't. Did you talk to her?"

"Hell no. She saw me and headed for the opposite side of the room. I don't think she'll be making overtures anytime soon."

"Well, as long as I don't have to deal with her, I guess I can't begrudge a few days of shoring Gigi up while I decide what to do about the house. I suppose I'll have to call the lawyer to make arrangements for getting inside."

"WELL, IF IT isn't Joseph Enthorpe." Dorie placed a menu in front of him. "Haven't seen you in a while."

"Been busy."

"So I hear."

She stood there grinning at him, and Joe knew he hadn't fooled her. Dorie always did know what was going on.

"What are the lunch specials?"

She told him, her smile didn't waver.

"How's Harold?"

"He's off on one of his trips."

"Oh. Well, if you need any help closing up for the winter—"

"But don't worry that I'll be lonely."

She was baiting him. Why didn't he just go ahead and ask? It was natural to ask about someone you hadn't seen in a while and who was back in town.

"That's good to hear." He gave her his order.

She didn't go away. "Don't ya want to know why I won't be lonely?"

God, did he ever. "I'll have a Guinness with that."

She coughed out a laugh. "Guess you already know why I won't be lonely. And I thought you were here for my crab cakes." She took his menu. "I'll be back with that Guinness." She walked away.

Joe should just get up and leave before he embarrassed himself further. What was wrong with him? He was thirty-three. Had never been shy or marble-mouthed. Women liked him. And yet he couldn't bring himself to admit that he cared about how Van's life had turned out more than he should. And more than he had any right to ask.

It had been twelve years. Couldn't they just pretend that all that shit hadn't happened? Couldn't he just ask about an old friend without it being a big deal?

He'd bite the bullet and ask Dorie when she came back with his beer.

A young waitress came with his beer. He thanked her, grinding his teeth.

He played with his beer glass until the same waitress brought his meal. Ate his crab cakes. They were delicious as always, but he hardly tasted them waiting for Dorie to reemerge from the kitchen.

She didn't.

He glanced toward the kitchen door. No sign of Dorie.

He speared the last roasted potato wedge. Brought it to his mouth, chewed slowly. Swallowed. This was stupid. He caught the waitress's eye. She hurried over to his table.

"Is there something I can get you?"

"Yes. Could you ask Dorie to come out here?"

A flicker of anxiety flashed in her face. "Is there something wrong with your meal?"

"No. I'd just like to talk to Dorie. We're old friends."

"Oh." The girl visibly relaxed. "I'll get her." She practically ran for the kitchen.

It seemed like ages before Dorie sauntered back out, wiping her hands on a white dish towel, and letting the door swing closed behind her.

"What? You have a problem with my crab cakes?"

"They're delicious as always."

"Oh, for a minute I thought I had lost my touch."

"Is Van staying at your house?" There, he'd asked.

"Who wants to know?"

"Cut it out, Dorie. It's hard enough to ask without you giving me grief."

"Hang on a second. I got to tell Cubby to watch the kitchen." She flashed him a smile. "I'll be back."

She was going to make this difficult. Joe guessed he deserved it. He hadn't handled things very well—okay, he'd botched things—all those years ago. If he'd known things were so desperate, he would have asked Van to marry him. Live with him in Syracuse while he finished school and then come back to run the dairy farm.

But it all blew up in his face. Van. The farm. Everything that mattered to him. He'd recovered from most of it. Instituted a plan to work what was left of the land. And if his mother was on him about grandchildren, hell, she already had a few and there was still plenty of time, if he could just find the right woman to share his life with.

Dorie came back, sat down across from him. "Now where were we?"

Joe sighed. "We were at the place where I asked about Van and you ran off to the kitchen."

"Oh yeah." She frowned, patted her hair, a newer, blonder version of her last trip to the salon. "Well, she came back for Clay's funeral. Stayed over last night, then was going to see Gigi today. Noticed you weren't at the funeral."

"Van did?"

Dorie shrugged. "How should I know? I just know that I noticed that you weren't there."

Joe huffed a sigh. "I had a job."

"Ah."

"So is she still here?"

"She better be. I told her she better not try to sneak off without saying good-bye."

"So you don't know if she's planning to stay for a while?"

"Nope. Though I expect she won't. She was on her way to Rehoboth Beach for a vacation."

"Rehoboth? Why would she—" He caught himself. Of course she would never come back here for a vacation. He was surprised that she'd even come back for a funeral.

"Why don't you call over to the house and ask her yourself?"

"I don't think so."

Dorie looked out the window and back at him, then jumped to her feet. "I gotta get back to work. I'll tell her you asked about her."

"Dorie, wait a minute."

"Gotta go." She didn't even slow down, and before he could even consider going after her, she'd disappeared back into the kitchen.

Well, now he knew. That would have to do. But it left him feeling depressed. He finished his beer. Left a tip and carried his bill to the cashier.

He was being stupid; he should at least make contact. Maybe they could be friends. But that was a joke. When he dreamed about women, they always were Van. Even when he was with women, he often was thinking about her.

He was making way too much of Van's return. It was probably from hanging out at Mike's in the evenings. It was like stepping back in time. He'd grown up with half the guys who hung out there.

And the women. It was kind of depressing. He'd be glad when Grandy was back to take over the marina and he could go home to the farm.

He lifted a toothpick from the dispenser, nodded to the cashier, and paid his bill.

"Over there." Suze pointed to a minuscule parking space near the Blue Crab.

"I don't know why we just didn't park at Dorie's and walk. We could use the exercise the way we're eating."

"Speak for yourself. Anyway, she said to hurry. The word got out that she was making crab cakes today. There was a rush at lunch, and she's having a hard time saving any for us."

Van squeezed the car into the space.

Suze jumped out and Van ran after her. "The things you'll do for food."

"Not all food. Just Dorie's crab cakes."

"Then it's a good thing we were in the car and only a few blocks away." Van followed Suze diagonally across the pier to the entrance of the Blue Crab. It looked a little run-down in the daylight. But it was still a popular place. She could see people at the tables by the windows.

They stepped inside to a blast of air-conditioning. Van couldn't remember if that was something new since she and Suze had worked here. Or whether that had been another reason waitressing at the Crab had been such a plum job.

It took a minute for Van's eyes to accustom themselves to the low lighting; it was too dark for her taste. On the edges of the large dining room the sun glared through the windows but cast everything else in between into dark relief. Some nice bamboo shades would prevent the patrons from having to wear sunglass in the morning and late afternoon.

"Our gang's old table?" Suze asked. "It's free."

"I guess."

They stepped past the hostess desk just as a man who had been paying his check turned around.

Van stopped.

He stopped.

"Oh shit," Suze said and walked away.

Behind him, Dorie burst through the kitchen door and stopped cold.

Van had a wild urge to laugh. But it would hurt too much.

She tried for a friendly smile. He didn't bother.

"Van."

"Joe," she said, trying to sound pleasant, as if seeing him hadn't just knocked her on her ass.

"I heard you were back."

"For the funeral."

A muscle in his cheek jumped. "How have you been?"

"Great. You?"

"Fine. I— Fine."

"Well, good to see you." Van stepped away. A few feet away Dorie threw her head back, mouth open, eyes to the ceiling. Van glared at her.

She heard, "Yeah, good to see you, too." But when she turned back to Joe, he was walking out the door.

She turned on Dorie. "If there is a God, Dorie, you're not going to find him in your ceiling."

"Not God. Only the saints. But I swear even the saints can't help you. What's wrong with you, girl?"

"Nothing. Why should it be?"

"He loved you. The least you could do is be civil. You know you're not the only one who's had a hard life."

"I was civil."

"Ha. If that passes for civil in New York, you'd do best to come back to Jersey and learn some manners."

"Stop it. He caught me by surprise, that's all." Van narrowed her eyes. "You planned this, didn't you?"

"For Chrissakes," Dorie said. "He would love you again if you'd make the least little effort."

"I don't want him to love me. We were kids. It ended. Period. No fond memories. No rekindled flames. Over and done with."

Van stalked away. Ran into one of the tables that cluttered the large rectangular room.

The Blue Crab could use some organization, Van thought, clutching her bruised hip bone. It didn't really hurt that bad, but she needed something to concentrate on while she forced angry tears from her eyes and tried to keep her mind off her utter humiliation. How dare Dorie set her up like that. She didn't think Joe had been in on it. He seemed completely stunned to see her. And not at all happy.

He still looked good. A man now, filled out, strong. And just as heart-stopping. She squelched any inclination to think further than that. Did Dorie think she was so pitiful that she needed help getting a boyfriend?

She found Suze sitting in her old spot at their favorite table. Van hesitated, frowning at the table and at the three empty chairs. Van had usually sat across from Suze by the window and next to Joe. She sat down in his spot instead, as if to eradicate his memory.

"That was weird," Suze said.

"No, that was planned. I'm going to kill her."

"She just wants you to be happy."

"By dredging up the past? Were you part of this?"

Suze held up both hands. "Not me. She said crab cakes and I came running."

"Good, because I'd hate to have to kill you, too."

The crab cakes were good, the potato wedges crisp and not too salty. Dorie had disappeared into the kitchen and it looked like she wouldn't be coming out again anytime soon. Just as well. Van was pretty mad, and either Dorie knew it or Dorie herself was mad at Van.

"Are you sure you don't want to go to Rehoboth with me?" Van asked.

Suze looked up from her plate. Her mouth was stuffed with crab cakes, and there was a dab of ketchup on her polo shirt.

Van couldn't stop the smile of affection as she took in her

friend's hopelessly messy appearance. The woman was a scholar, smart, sensitive, creative—and a slob. Already her room at Dorie's was piled with books and papers and clothes hanging on every piece of furniture.

And they had only been there one day.

Suze swallowed and took a sip of water. "Why are you in such a hurry to get to Rehoboth? If it's a hot cabana boy, you'll do fine without me. If it isn't, having me along won't help. Damn." She'd spotted the ketchup, grabbed a napkin, and begun scrubbing at the stain.

"You need a keeper," Van said.

"Not you. You'd drive me stark raving mad. Tell me you've never spilled ketchup on your shirt."

"Of course I have. Only I don't make it worse by rubbing it into the fabric."

Suze dropped the napkin, pulled her shirt front out so she could view the front and groaned. "I do need a keeper. It's just that my mind starts thinking about something else and I forget to pay attention to what I'm doing."

"What are you thinking about? And don't tell me Joe Enthorpe unless you're planning to wear the rest of your dinner on your head."

"No-o-o. Actually I was trying to find a relationship between Nabokov's Lolita and the Wife of Bath and the misogynist writings of the fourteenth century."

"Say what? No wonder you didn't notice that ketchup. I don't even know what you're talking about, though I did read the juicy parts of *Lolita*."

"And I love you anyway because it's a topic that can really kill a conversation. And flirting? Doesn't happen."

Van pulled her eyes from the spreading ketchup stain. "Yeah, but you could flirt, with a little practice. You used to have the boys falling all over themselves to ask you out."

"That was then, and, besides, I think it was because I came from a rich family."

"Bull. It was because you were hot. Still are except for the ketchup. You should wear more black. It covers a lot."

"But shows chalk."

"You're something else, you know that?"

Suze made an exaggerated frown. "How well I know it."

By the time they finished eating, the memory of that uncomfortable meeting with Joe was fading, and Van felt a lot better. She and Suze ordered dessert and coffee.

Dorie hadn't made another appearance, but Van didn't know whether it was by design or because the restaurant had become crowded.

"I think we better go," Suze said, looking around. "They could use our table." She pushed her chair back, started to stand, and exclaimed, "Oh Lord," before sitting down again.

"What?" Van felt panic rising and, along with it, her strawberry cheesecake. She didn't dare turn around.

"It's . . . oh, you know . . ." Suze frowned.

Van risked a glance behind her. A trio of police officers were headed their way. "Oh Lord. It's Bud-Whosit."

"Albright," Suze said. "And I think that's Jerry Corso, isn't it? I don't recognize the other one."

"Maybe they won't recognize us."

"Or maybe they will," Suze said. "Put a smile on it."

The group slowed as they passed the table.

Jerry stopped, squinted at Suze, looked at Van. His eyes widened. They went back to Suze. "Suzy? Suzy Turner?"

"Hey, Jerry."

The other two turned their attention to the table. Bud half smiled at Suze then switched his gaze to Van. Van forced a smile to her lips. She'd never liked him. He was a bully in high school.

Bud's eyes widened, and a not very nice smile spread across his face. "Well, hell. What are you doing back here?"

Van kept her smile, though it hurt her teeth. "Clay Daly's funeral."

"You sticking around?"

"Leaving in the morning."

"Huh." Bud nudged the others away. "I'll tell Dana I saw you. She'll be sorry she missed you."

Van and Suze watched the men walk to the back of the restaurant.

"Bud certainly has perfected his bully swagger," Suze said.

"Is that what it was? I thought he was trying to keep his pants up."

Suze started to laugh. Stopped herself. "Dana? Do you think he and Dana are . . . ?"

"Married? Going out? BFFs?" Van said. "Sounds like it. But I wouldn't wish him on my worst enemy, not even on Dana."

"Snark. You're not really leaving tomorrow?"

"No, but Bud doesn't need to know that."

"I don't get it."

"Do you want him knowing where you are?"

"Eeww." Suze brushed crumbs off her lap. "I wonder if Bud has ever written anything?"

"Besides a ticket?"

"Yeah."

"I doubt it. Why?"

"Because I could add him to my work on misogynist literature."

"Guess you don't like him either."

"Never did. Still don't. And I can't imagine what Dana sees in him."

"He's a guy, isn't he? Dana was never very particular."

"Sorry, Van. I didn't mean to bring up . . . you know."

"Not your fault. But do you see why I didn't want to come to Whisper Beach? All roads lead to Dana and Joe."

"Well, at least it means she and Joe didn't stay together."

"I don't know what it means. Nor do I care. We're grown-ups now. Are you ready to go?"

As they stood up, two waiters collided on their way to the kitchen. Plates, cups, saucers, and glasses slid off their trays, and clattered on the floor.

Everyone in the restaurant turned to gape.

"Looks like Dorie could use some good advice about organization," Suze said.

"Tell me about it. At least the trays fell away from the two tables that someone placed right in front of the swinging door."

Dorie appeared in the doorway to the kitchen. Shook her head.

Van and Suze waved and went to pay their bill.

Chapter 8

Dorie stood at the front window of the Crab and watched Van and Suze cross the street to Van's car. She was a little annoyed that her plan hadn't worked better. It was a perfect setup; boy meets girl after all these years, instant romance. The two of them had been as useless as a couple of wooden statues. They might as well have been standing in front of a cigar store.

What was wrong with them? Besides twelve years and God knows what. But whatever it was, Joe was still single. He'd never really gotten over Van. The fact that he was thirty-three and still not married attested to that.

She didn't know about Van. She was successful, sophisticated. Hell, she'd gotten so polished, you would never know she was raised the way she was. Maybe she'd gotten too polished for Joe.

Dorie snorted. Thought she could get away and people wouldn't find out about her. Did she think that none of them knew how to use the Internet? Really, the girl needed to lighten up, loosen up, and have some fun. And not the kind that she could find at Rehoboth Beach.

Van needed somebody she could trust, somebody who could love her and had enough good qualities that she could love him back.

What Dorie needed here was an intervention, but besides kidnapping the two of them and holding them hostage until they saw what they were missing, she didn't have an idea.

"Whatcha looking at?"

Dorie let out a yelp. "Jerry Corso, don't you sneak up like that on an unsuspecting woman."

"Sorry." Jerry grinned at her.

"You're no more sorry than spit. What do you need? We're a little busier than I thought we'd be today. Got people overworked now we lost the summer staff. I'll send someone over to take your order."

"Nah, I just wanted to say hi. And I just . . . Well, how long are Van and Suzy planning to stay?"

"I don't know about Van. She has vacation plans somewheres else. But Suze is planning to stay for a couple of months at least. Needs a quiet place to work. And I hope you didn't call her Suzy when you saw her."

"Why not?"

Dorie threw her hands open and looked at the ceiling. "She's a college professor."

"So? What should I call her? Prof?"

"Maybe you should just stay away from her until you can locate your brain. I'd start looking south and work your way up."

Jerry blushed. "Man, Dorie, you know how to get to a guy."

"If that were only true," said Dorie, and she wandered back to the kitchen, shaking her head.

Joe didn't go back to the marina but drove west. A thousand times in the past, he'd practiced what he would say when he saw Van again. After a while, it became *if* he ever saw Van again. And then he'd just stopped thinking about it . . . for the most part.

But now that it had actually happened, he'd been totally unprepared. Anything he might have said ten years ago, even five years ago, seemed stupid now. They'd both gotten on with their lives; they had nothing in common, and that had been obvious by the way she had reacted to seeing him. He could have been a total stranger for all the warmth she showed.

Either she hadn't forgiven him, or she'd forgotten all about him. He didn't like the idea of the first, but he didn't like the second choice even more.

He was still beating himself up over his inept social skills when he pulled onto the two-lane road that led to the farm. He drove past the two metal posts that had once held the sign for Enthorpe Dairy but had held nothing but air for the last decade.

Maybe it wasn't too early to have a new sign made up. ENTHORPE VINEYARDS. But he didn't want to jinx the project. He should get a novice crop this fall, but the vines wouldn't start producing at full volume for at least another year. And in the meantime, he had plenty to do.

Well, actually that wasn't true. He *should* have plenty to do, but his business plan was in pretty good shape. He would need to start advertising but not for a while. The day-to-day operations would be a different thing. But for now, his father and brothers and the foreman he'd hired could oversee the work. And Joe would be back full-time in a week.

He stopped the truck in front of the white farmhouse he'd grown up in. These days the windows and doors were kept shut because of the air-conditioning. All was quiet but for the hum of the compressor around the side of the house.

Joe didn't miss the heat, but he missed the sounds of the farm—the dogs, the roosters, the lowing of the cows as they were herded in to be milked, the kids playing on the swing set out back. They'd lost a thousand sounds along with the acreage.

As he walked to the kitchen door, an old bird dog scrambled to his feet and padded over to him, tail kicking up a breeze.

"Hey, Duffy." Joe leaned over to scratch the dog behind his ears. As soon as Joe straightened up, the dog returned to his place in the shade and lay down again.

Joe opened the door and stepped into the kitchen. There were pots on the stove and the kitchen was warm. He heard voices from the other room and realized they were all at dinner.

He should have come here to eat, and then he wouldn't have run into Van. But if he hadn't gone to the Crab, he wouldn't have run into her and wouldn't have come here.

He laughed. He was a mess.

"Joe, why didn't you tell us you were coming? I'll get you a plate." His mother was already pushing her chair back.

"Thanks, Mom, but I already ate." He leaned over and gave her a kiss.

She smiled up at him. Gave his hand a squeeze.

"Come out to check on the vines?" His father sat at the other end of the table, still robust even though he'd been retired for the last ten years.

Joe pulled up a chair and sat at the corner of the table.

"No, just came to see my family."

"River stench finally get to you?" His grandfather squinted down the table at him.

Joe nodded. "I'm getting pretty tired of it."

His mother offered him the breadbasket and he automatically took a warm dinner roll. "Well, you'll be home next week."

His grandfather cackled. "Too bad he gave his house to Renzo and his family."

Joe had heard this argument before. "Granddad. We need someone on-site who knows vineyards so you and Dad don't have to stand out in the broiling sun digging weeds and trimming the vines."

"What did we send you to that expensive school for then?"

For dairy management, Joe thought. *But you sold the dairy while I was gone.*

"He just enjoys giving you a hard time," his mother said. "He's the first one up every morning going out to look over the grapes. Aren't you, Dad?"

"Just making sure Renzo ain't taking advantage of Joe while he's gone."

"Thanks, Granddad." This was an act his grandfather loved to put on. Actually, he and Renzo had already become fast friends.

"He can't have his old room back," Matt said. "I just finished painting it."

Joe groaned dramatically. "What god-awful color this time?"

Matt grinned at him. "You can come see for yourself after dinner."

"Be warned," Dave said. "He's got a lava lamp."

"Lava lamps are back in style." His mother handed Joe the butter and a knife.

"Hippie nonsense," Joe Senior said.

Dave laughed. "Oh, Granddad, you never saw a hippie in your life."

"A lot you know." He cut a look at Joe Junior.

"No," cried Matt. "Dad, you were a hippie?"

"I led a double life," Joe Junior intoned in a deep radio voice.

Joe sat back in his chair and ate his roll, glad of the change of subject and the familiar banter. He felt better than he had the whole weekend.

After dinner, Joe and his father walked out to the vineyards. Joe felt the same twinge of excitement he always felt when he looked over the land, only now it was grapevines instead of dairy cows.

The rows of vines trailed green and thick along the trellises. The bunches had been thinned, and the grapes looked plump and firm. They would be ready in another four weeks or so.

"Looks like you might have a pretty good crop this year," his dad said.

"I think we will. At least enough to experiment with."

It had been a long time to wait for the land to start paying again. But it was a price Joe was willing to pay. Because he would not, could not, let it slip away from the family.

He and his father stood looking over the nascent fields, not talking. And if not totally in agreement over Joe's methods of farming, they felt the perfect camaraderie that farming brought to both of them.

"Van's back."

Joe felt his father look at him, but Joe just looked ahead.

"Ah, come back for the funeral?"

"I guess."

"Have you talked to her?"

"I ran into her at the Crab. I think Dorie manipulated it."

His father chuckled. "Sounds like something Dorie would do. How did it go?"

"Not well." Joe exhaled slowly. "I was stupid with surprise. She didn't seem glad to see me. Didn't get past 'good to see you,' and that was it."

"Maybe she was surprised, too."

"I guess."

"Well, was it good to see her?"

At first, Joe didn't answer. He wasn't even sure what he was feeling. A mixture of pleasure and pain, hope and despair. "Yeah. I guess."

"So what are you going to do about it?"

Finally Joe turned to look at his father. "I don't know."

His father slapped him on the back, his form of a hug. "Well, don't wait too long to figure it out."

They took their time walking back to the house.

It was dark when Joe finally left the farm. He met a steady stream of day-trippers leaving the shore for the day, but there wasn't much traffic going in his direction.

He'd be glad to be back on the farm near the vineyard. He was glad he could help Grandy out, but it was beginning to wear on him. He wanted to be home with the grapes.

Grandy had actually asked him if he wanted to buy the marina. The same thing was happening to him that happened to the dairy farm. Grandy's couldn't compete with the big, exclusive marinas going up along the shore. Eventually he'd sell out. It was a shame, but Joe didn't want it.

It wasn't too late, and Joe considered going to Mike's for a beer, but he wasn't really in the mood. When he came to the marina, he pulled in.

The tide was going out. In a few hours the clam diggers would creep onto the mudflats, looking for their family's next meal. Yeah, the river was polluted, but nobody had died of river shellfish that he'd heard of. And it helped stretch out budgets that were already stretched close to snapping.

He went inside, poured himself a glass of coastal cabernet, and took it over to his desk. Lights lined the opposite side of the river. Headlights of cars made a steady stream over the bridge in both directions. It was one of the perks of living at the marina, the constant light show out the big plateglass window.

Nothing fancy. Just a rectangle of glass. The window air conditioner rattled away behind him. It didn't do much toward chilling the place, but it kept the worst of the heat away.

He sat down, dug his reading glasses out of the drawer, and opened *The Principles of Vineyard Management*.

It was almost midnight before he stretched, tossed his glasses onto the open book, and went to look out the window.

Across the water the buildings were dark, and the flow of headlights had trickled to a few. Joe yawned, stretched his arms out again, and watched the shadows of the clam diggers move along the flats beyond the marina.

Not his job, and if the harbor patrol didn't care, neither did he. But just as he turned from the window, he saw a sudden flurry of movement out on the flats. Grabbing buckets and shovels and whatever they could carry, the clammers headed silently for the woods. And like shadows, they slipped into the darkness of the tree-covered bank.

Moments later, two squad cars pulled into the marina parking lot.

The poachers must have a lookout.

Car doors slammed. Heavy-duty flashlights were turned on, and arcs of light bounced along the riverbank. Joe wished he'd turned the lights off at the first sign of trouble, but it was too late. And he knew Bud would be out there leading the search. No way to avoid him; he might as well meet him head-on. Joe stepped out onto the porch.

It was only a few minutes before the officers returned, their flashlights bobbing along the ground in front of them. None of them were too interested in following the culprits through the mud and brush and who could blame them.

Vinnie Bukowski came to stand at the bottom of the steps. "Man, it stinks out here. We all think Bud has lost his marbles. He's still out there looking for some poor sod. Shit. Here he comes, and it looks like he's got one of them. Now we'll have to take the guy in, and the whole damn cruiser will smell like river mud."

Bud was half dragging, half carrying one of the diggers. The man was very small, and his feet stuttered along the ground as Bud yanked him toward the squad car. The guy didn't stand a chance.

"Damn," Vinnie said under his breath. "He's already been reprimanded twice in the last year for using undue force in an arrest. He better be careful or he'll find himself sitting at a desk if they don't get rid of him completely." He trotted across the boatyard to meet them, and Joe came down the steps.

Bud shoved the man to the ground. He hit hard and landed on his hands and knees. His cap fell off. A shaggy-headed boy cringed and covered his head with his arms. He was just a kid, not older than twelve, probably younger.

Bud growled something to his victim, yanked him to his feet, and ordered him to hold still. "Get my cuffs out of the truck."

"Ah, Bud, he's a kid. You don't have to cuff him."

"No-o-o!" The boy squirmed beneath Bud's grip.

Joe ran down the steps. "Hey. What are you doing?"

"Catching me a poacher."

The kid looked up with round frightened eyes.

"He's not a poacher. He works for me," Joe said. "He was on his way home and we saw the poachers. I told him to go run them off."

"The hell you did."

"The hell I did. You've been carping at me for weeks about them, so I was just doing my civic duty."

Vinnie wiped his face to hide a grin.

"Yeah?" Bud shook the kid, and his head snapped back. "What's your employer's name then?"

" Aw, Bud," Vinnie broke in. "Stop bothering Joe, here. Everybody knows he hired a kid to help out with the boats. Isn't that right, kid?"

The boy nodded energetically.

Joe stepped forward, put his hand on the kid's shoulder. He looked at Bud, who was slow in letting go.

"If I find out you're lying."

Joe pulled the kid closer and out of Bud's reach.

"Bud, give it a rest."

"I'm warning you."

The radio squawked. Vinnie and the two other cops returned to their cruisers. With another scowl at the kid and Joe, Bud finally strode back to his cruiser.

Joe waited until they had driven away, sirens blasting.

"Well, kid, it looks like you got yourself a job."

THE FIRST THING Van did the next morning after pouring herself a cup of coffee was call her office. It was only eight o'clock, but she knew that either Ellen, her ace office manager, or Maria, her executive secretary, would already be there. They were perfectly able to run things without her for a couple of weeks. Longer if need be. She had tried to resist calling them too early. That would be a sign of not trusting them. Though she suspected she wasn't fooling anybody. She had control issues.

They'd joked about it to her face and groused about it behind her back. But she couldn't help it. It looked like she was going to have a full day, and she had things to do; besides, she really wanted to touch base with the familiar. She just had to remind herself not to micromanage when Maria answered the phone.

"Elite Lifestyle Managers. How may I help you?"

"Hi, Maria. It's me."

Was that a sigh she heard?

"Everything is fine. You better be on the beach with a drink with an umbrella in it."

"There's been a blip in the schedule."

That was definitely a groan.

"I'm still in Whisper Beach."

"Fine. As long as you're on some beach. Having a good time. Don't call unless you need us to send cash or get you out of jail."

Van laughed. "I know you guys are capable of handling everything. I just wanted to—"

"Check in. I know. And we love you for it; now go have fun. Oh, and this should make your day. We just landed the Hallmark building account. So relax and have fun. I'm hanging up now."

"Wow, I wasn't sure they'd go for the group discount thing. How soon do they want—"

"We're taking care of it; go to the beach."

"Okay, okay, I'm putting on my bikini now."

"Hooray. Good-bye."

The line went dead. The Hallmark building. A biggie. Lots of apartments with overworked, harried families in need of organization.

Van sat down at the kitchen table and looked at her phone. Definitely too early to call the lawyer. Besides, she thought she might run her idea about renting the house to Gigi past Dorie. She didn't want to enable Gigi to not deal with her life. But she knew Gigi wouldn't get on with her life until she was out from under her mother's thumb.

Suze wandered into the kitchen holding a huge coffee mug.

"Morning," Van said. "Did you just get up?"

"Been up for hours. Trying to concentrate on my paper while waiting for the mailman to come." She poured herself a cup and sat across from Van. "What are you doing today?"

"I'm going to try to get the key from Mr. Pimlico and go take a look at the house. If you'd like to go."

"Thanks, but I have to get some work done. Why don't you do that this morning, and after lunch, we'll go to the beach. Or maybe we'll take Dorie to lunch."

The outer door opened, and Dorie came in carrying two filled grocery bags. "Take me where?"

"To lunch or something."

"I thought you were calling Gigi."

"Oh, right, I forgot. I will." Van made a face. "But first, I wanted to consult you about something."

"Let me put the eggs in the fridge, and you can hit me with it." Dorie slid the carton of eggs in, along with lettuce and tomatoes and a few other things, then poured out the last of the coffee and sat down. "Shoot."

"I'm going to see the lawyer about the house."

"Well, it's about time. I don't guess you're planning to live in it?"

Van gave her a quelling look.

"So you're going to sell it?"

"I was thinking maybe Gigi and the kids could live there. It's small, but big enough for them—if it's in decent shape or at least doesn't need a lot of work. I don't want to put any real money into it."

"And you would be doing this why?"

"I think Uncle Nate and Aunt Amelia have had enough. And I don't think Gigi's going to move on until she has her own place, and since her own place is foreclosed on and since my house is sitting there unused, it makes perfect sense."

"Enabling," Suze said from the bottom of her coffee mug.

"What do you think, Dorie? Is it enabling?" Van asked. "I thought it might give her the impetus to pull herself together. I know Nate is worried about her, and I got the feeling he would love to have his house back."

"I don't know. Why don't you take a look at it before you make any decisions."

Which is just what she did.

Van met the lawyer at his office at nine fifteen and drove over to the house with his set of keys. She parked at the curb and sat, feeling a sudden lethargy that kept her in the car. Lethargy or anxiety.

She didn't know what shape the cottage would be in, what she would feel, if anything. Would memories crowd around her like soul suckers in a sci-fi film? Or would it just be another empty house? One thing was for sure. It wasn't going away.

Van got out of the car and walked up to the front door, noticed that her hand shook slightly as she pushed the key in the lock, turned it. The door opened on a squeak of hinges.

She automatically reached for the light switch. Of course the electricity had been turned off years ago.

She walked into the dim living room, groped her way to the windows and pulled back the drapes, setting off a cloud of dust. She stood in the center of the room and looked around. The light coming through the window barely reached into the gloom. Just enough to show the same old furniture untouched and covered by a thick layer of dust.

Van stepped through to the kitchen; the counters were bare, the laminate faded and cloudy. There was a water stain in the corner and the blackish mold that grew around it. That would have to be removed. A spray of TSP should do it; it didn't look widespread.

She opened a cabinet. Mismatched plates and glasses; a drawer, cooking utensils, another drawer, the aluminum flatware Van had bought on sale for her mother's Christmas present one year. Everything was like she remembered it, only dusty.

Back through the living room to the other half of the house; the two bedrooms and bath. She went through to her bedroom first. Opened the closet and saw the clothes she'd left behind, still hanging there. On the desk a pile of schoolbooks that had never been returned. A green stuffed frog that Joe had won at the boardwalk in Ocean City.

She didn't pick it up, didn't even touch it, just walked past it, the dust and mold tickling her nose and throat. She coughed, sniffed, pulled open the top drawer of the bureau, where she found underwear and pajamas neatly folded. The second drawer held T-shirts and jeans, just as neat. The bottom drawer, empty. She couldn't remember what had been there.

She moved to the bathroom. Everything was gone from the windowsill except a bottle of shampoo and conditioner, the brand that she had used in those days, maybe the actual bottles she had used. The medicine cabinet had been cleaned out. A hand mirror and a glass of makeup brushes sat on the back of the toilet. Everything was just as it had been when she'd left twelve years ago.

She left the bathroom, hesitated, then stepped into her parents' room. Her father's room after her mother's death. Still the white Battenburg runner on the dresser, a picture of the three of them at the beach. It had sat there ever since the summer it was taken when Van was seven.

They'd been happy then. Van picked it up. At least Van had been happy. But looking closely at her parents' faces, she understood now that something was already deeply wrong.

The way you could almost feel her father bending away from her mother. Her mother's frantic eyes caught perfectly by the camera. Van was smiling between them, oblivious. He'd even left that behind.

It takes two to make an argument, Nate had said.

But it didn't take two to make a drunk. The photo had been taken before her father started drinking heavily. Van remembered he'd go to work every day. Come home and they would eat dinner together, then he would take a beer to the easy chair, turn on the television, and pick up the paper.

It was like he couldn't do just one thing at a time; he had to be doing it all at once. And remembering this, Van wondered if it was him building a barrier through which neither she nor her mother could travel.

Later, tired turned into blitzed. He stopped eating with them, would grab something to put on his plate, and take his plate and beer down to the basement where he'd installed a second television; it was where he lived when he wasn't at work or at the pub, and where he slept on an old sagging couch he'd found on the curb one day.

Van shivered. There was nothing of him left in the house. Not a forgotten razor in the bathroom, not an undershirt or a pair of socks in the dresser. Not one book that he kept by the bed for when he went to sleep sober enough to read. Nothing but empty hangers in the closet. And Van knew if she went downstairs, it would be empty, too.

It was like he'd never existed. Anger boiled up inside of her. He'd taken himself and his possessions away and left *them* behind. Everything that had been Van and her mother lay rotting in these few rooms. And nothing of him.

Bastard, she thought. He couldn't wait to get away. Well, good riddance. Good riddance, good riddance.

But why? What did we do that was so bad that you needed to erase us?

Van backed out of the room. She'd have to hire a service to cart the stuff away and then cleaners. Everything would go. Everything. If Gigi wanted to live there, Van was sure she could scrounge some extra furniture from her parents.

And if Gigi didn't want it? Well, Van would put it on the market before she left.

Chapter 9

Gigi was standing on the sidewalk when Van pulled into Dorie's driveway. She was wearing shorts, had a beach bag slung over one shoulder, and was holding a stack of papers that looked like the mail.

"I was going to call you," Van said, getting out of the car. She'd hoped to have a few minutes with Dorie and Suze.

"I just thought I'd come and surprise you."

"Oh, good. Let's go inside. I need more coffee."

"In this weather? Ugh."

As they walked toward the front door, it opened and Suze stepped out. She zeroed in on Gigi and then her hand. "Is that the mail?"

"Yeah, I ran into the mailman when I got here."

"Great." Suze gently extricated it from Gigi's hand and started back toward the house as she riffled through the envelopes.

Van and Gigi followed her inside and got to the foyer just in time for Suze to drop the mail on the table with a "Dammit."

"No luck?" Van asked.

Suze shook her head. "I don't know why this is taking so long. I need coffee." Suze headed for the kitchen.

"Was she expecting something important?" Gigi asked.

"Yes. She's up for a grant and the deadline for the final round or whatever is looming, and they haven't sent her the forms she needs."

"Oh. Why is she having her mail sent here?"

"I think she's planning to spend the fall here, at least if the grant comes through. You should ask her."

Suze was gloomily nursing a mug of black coffee when they reached the kitchen.

Dorie was at the sink. "What's in the bag?"

Gigi held up her beach bag like it was show-and-tell.

"My beach towel. I'm wearing my swimsuit under my clothes. I thought Van and I . . . and Suze could go to the beach today. Like the old days. Dad said it would be all right as long as we minded our own business. And I didn't call attention to myself. I brought my sunglasses."

Suze snorted, but turned it into a sneeze. She quickly covered her mouth and said, "Excuse me, need a tissue," as she fled from the room.

Dorie rolled her eyes and turned back to the dishes, leaving Van to wrestle with the smile on her own face.

"Do you think sunglasses will keep people from recognizing you?" Van asked.

"I guess. Besides, nobody will be at the beach. It's a weekday."

"Good point. Well, Dorie, if you don't have anything for us to do, I guess we're going to the beach."

"Have fun."

"I'll just get changed," Van said. "Back in a flash."

She went upstairs and knocked on Suze's door. A muffled answer came from the other side, so she walked in. Suze was sitting on the bed, red faced, and for a second Van was afraid she'd been crying. But she saw Van and said, "Sunglasses," and broke into suppressed laughter.

Van closed the door. "Shh, you'll hurt her feelings."

"I'm sorry, but is that the most ridiculous thing you've ever heard?"

"Pretty silly. You are coming to the beach with us, aren't you?"

"I need to work."

"I respect that, so let me phrase it a different way. 'If you don't come to the beach with us, I'll sneak in and hide all those musty tomes you have stacked on the desk.' "

"I took yesterday off."

"I know and ordinarily I wouldn't beg, but ple-e-e-ase."

"God, you sound like Gigi."

"Did it work?"

"Okay, for a couple of hours, and then I'm locking myself in here and do not want to be disturbed."

"Deal. Get changed."

From downstairs, Gigi's voice called, "What's taking you two so long?"

Suze and Van exchanged looks. Surely this wasn't normal recently widowed behavior.

Van went across the hall and pulled her suitcase up to the bed. She hadn't bothered to unpack. In her mind she was still thinking four-star luxury hotel. That's what her vacations should be these days. Upscale luxury, not sleeping on a sagging single bed surrounded by faded florals and Depression-era furniture.

She rummaged in her suitcase, pulled out the little—and she did mean little—bikini she'd bought for the beach at Rehoboth.

It was a shame to waste it on Whisper Beach, but it was the only one she'd brought. Actually it was the only one she had.

Van slipped it on and put on a pair of denim cutoffs, which she'd bought at a Fifth Avenue boutique and fit wonderfully, though she was still having trouble reconciling the price for something she used to wear when she was too poor to even afford Kmart.

Life could be funny.

She slipped on her new, gauzy cover-up. Unfortunately she'd been depending on the hotel to provide soft, thick beach towels. She took the threadbare towel she'd dried off with after her shower.

She didn't have a beach bag. She wouldn't need one. She could take her laptop. The news that they'd won the Hallmark contract was an itch she was dying to scratch. But one big wave could destroy her entire digital life. She could take one of the paperbacks on the tiny bookshelf under her window.

Or she could bite the bullet and just pay attention to Gigi. And what was so hard about that? They'd always gotten along. And Gigi needed friends at this sad time. That had been obvious yesterday when Gigi fairly disappeared around her boisterous family.

This was supposed to be Gigi's day, though Van would rather spend her time with Suze than her cousin. And she felt a little guilty.

Suze stuck her head in the door. "You ready?"

"As I'll ever be." Van unzipped her toiletry bag and retrieved a pump bottle of sunscreen. She looked at Suze, still dressed in her khaki shorts and polo shirt from breakfast. "You sure as hell better tell me there's a swimsuit under that safari outfit."

"It's there, but I'm not walking to the beach in it."

Gigi was waiting for them at the bottom of the stairs. "Dorie went to get us some beach chairs out of the storage shed."

Van nodded. She guessed Gigi hadn't thought to help. She wished Suze had never mentioned that Gigi let everyone take care of her, because it made her *über*aware of it now. If there was ever a time Gigi needed to be taken care of, it was now when she was reeling from the death of her husband, but to Van's mind it was also the time she should take charge of her life. Maybe it was just too early. Hopefully, it wasn't too late.

They went out the front door where Dorie was hosing off three aluminum beach chairs. A huge umbrella was propped against the steps.

"Dorie, are you coming with us?" Van asked.

"Thanks, but I have to get over to the Crab. Have the crew, what's left of it, coming to do some cleanup before the weekend."

"You should have told me," Van said. "I'll be glad to help. I'm kind of good that way."

Dorie grinned at her. "I may take you up on it, but go and enjoy yourself this morning. There will be time to work later. You girls have fun."

Gigi put a straw hat with a huge floppy brim on her head.

"Where did you find that?" Van asked. Van thought it was more likely to attract a few strange looks than hide Gigi from prying eyes.

"In the closet. Dorie said I could wear it."

Van didn't dare look at Suze.

"I packed up the cooler," Gigi said. "Dorie said to help ourselves. So I did. I picked things I thought we would all like. And I brought our beach passes." She sighed. "Since hardly anybody's gotten a chance to use them this summer."

For some reason, Gigi's benign personality was really rubbing Van the wrong way. She wanted to shake the girl and say, *Your husband just died, your children need you, go get a job, move out of your parents' house. Make a home for you and your kids.* Or maybe dealing with kids all day, she'd begun to treat other people like children, too.

Of course, Van had no right to make judgments one way or the other. She wouldn't know what to do with a kid if the stork dropped one in her lap. Which she guessed would be the only way she'd be getting one.

The thought put a momentary pall over her spirits. But today was about Gigi; maybe for once her cousin actually needed some pampering herself.

"I've got beach towels. Also compliments of Dorie." Suze hiked a stuffed beach bag over her shoulder and picked up one of the beach chairs that Dorie had propped against the steps. She handed it to Gigi, gave one to Van and took one for herself. "Let's get this over with. I've got work to do."

Van grabbed the giant beach umbrella and they set off on foot for the beach.

Gigi led the way down the sidewalk until the spray from a lawn sprinkler forced them into the street. After that, they walked three abreast down the middle of the street.

A few cars were parked along the side, but it was Monday and it was nearing the end of the season. Already the streets were less congested.

They stopped at Ocean Avenue while they waited for several cars to pass. Suze said, "Look at us with cooler and umbrellas and bags. We look like three shoobies on a day trip."

Gig swiveled her big hat around. "You two are—these days. Come on."

They crossed the street and headed up the boardwalk. Below them the beach was covered in a legion of colorful umbrellas. But not nearly as many as there would have been only a week before.

That was fine with Van. She got enough of crowds taking the subway every day.

Gigi walked right past the stairs that led down to the beach.

"Not there," Gigi said. "I thought we'd go to Whisper Beach. Like we used to do."

Suze traded a look with Van. "What's wrong with down here?" she asked.

Gigi looked at Van. "Oh, does it make you sad?"

"It doesn't bother me in the least," Van said. "I was just thinking that if Uncle Nate wants you to keep a low profile—" Van had to stop to compose herself. It would be impossible with Gigi wearing those sunglasses and floppy hat. She could hear Suze's adenoidal breathing behind her. She was trying not to laugh.

"It's more likely people you know will be at Whisper Beach than out there."

"It's a weekday; there won't be anybody there."

"I'd really like to stay on the big beach," Suze said. "I'm, uh, on the lookout for some cute guys."

Van had to stop herself from doing a double take. But she knew what Suze was doing, and she gave her friend a grateful smile. Going to Whisper Beach by herself at night had been one thing, but sitting for hours and reminiscing about the past would drive her right back to Manhattan, where she was beginning to realize she really belonged.

Suze started down the steps to the beach, walked a few yards across the white sand, and stopped. "How about here?"

"Okay by me," Van said.

"Fine," Gigi said.

Suze dropped the bag with the beach towels onto the sand. Wrestled with her beach chair and finally adjusted it to nestle in the sand. Van snapped her beach chair open, put it down next to

Suze, and positioned it facing the sun; then she realized Gigi was still standing, holding her chair and looking at them.

"What? Open your chair and sit down."

"Oh, okay." Gigi opened her chair and slowly put it down next to Van's.

Van wondered if maybe she was on tranquilizers or some other medication. She seemed so lethargic.

There were a few minutes of readjusting chairs to catch the best rays, taking off cover-ups, and lathering on sunscreen before they were all sitting, legs stretched out on the sand, heads back, eyes closed, worshipping the sun.

"This is great," Gigi said, sounding not at all like a grieving widow. But not sounding content, either.

"Hmmm," Van said.

"Hmmm," Suze agreed.

"Do you think it's wrong of me to be sitting on the beach when Clay was just buried?"

"Nuh," Suze said.

"Nuh," Van agreed.

"It's not like I've gone out shopping or throwing a party. But I never get to do anything for myself. Is that selfish? The kids are always wanting me, and Mother needs help with the house. She's babysitting today."

"That's nice of her," Suze said.

"Hmmm," said Van.

"But usually I don't get any time off . . . ever. Is it so bad to want just a little time to yourself?"

Van sat up. "Gigi, you wanted to come to the beach. We're here. But it's stupid to stay if you're not going to enjoy it."

"I am enjoying it." Gigi turned her head and lifted her sunglasses to look at the other two. "But is it wrong?"

"No," growled Suze.

Van just sat back and closed her eyes.

"I was just wondering." Gigi lowered her glasses and stretched out again.

Van and Suze turned their faces toward each other. They didn't have to take off their sunglasses to know what the other was thinking.

A few minutes went by, with the sun beating down and the waves rolling onto the shore. Van felt a sheen of sweat break out on her midriff, trickle down her neck. She was getting antsy. She looked over at Suze. She'd brought out a big book and was reading. It was impossible to tell if Gigi was awake or asleep behind her big glasses.

Van should have brought a book or something. She could be spending time on accounts, except, she reminded herself, she was on vacation. Lying in the sun was boring. She thought longingly of Dorie's air-conditioning. Her laptop . . .

This is for Gigi, she reminded herself.

She pulled a beach towel out of the bag and spread it on the sand. Lay down on her stomach.

Stayed there for as long as she could. Moved back to her chair.

She pressed a finger to her thigh; the sunscreen was working. She'd never get a tan at this rate.

Suze turned her head toward Van. "Would you hold still? You're supposed to be relaxing. It's a vacation, remember?"

"I could sit here all day," Gigi said with a sigh.

Van would be having more fun helping Dorie at the Blue Crab. She had a few suggestions that would improve efficiency, and what better time to institute them than when they were cleaning up, throwing out, and planning for the coming weekend?

"I think I'll go for a walk."

"Looking for sea glass?" Gigi asked, looking out from half-lowered glasses.

"What?"

"Sea glass."

"Why would I look for sea glass?" Why was the mention of sea glass ringing a distant recognition?

Gigi sat up; the glasses came all the way off. "Gee, Van. How could you forget? Suze, you remember, don't you?"

"Remember what?"

"That Van always used to collect sea glass and draw those tiny little scenes on them. Remember? You used to sell them in the hotel gift shop and at the Blue Crab and some other places. You can't have forgotten."

But Van had. Now she remembered. Out early in the morning after a storm or a high wind, filling a burlap bag with flat pieces of smooth glass that had washed to shore. Cleaning them in the backyard tap, rubbing them to a polish, and then—

"Oh right," Suze said. "I do remember. You did these miniature paintings on the surface. You were really good."

"You all made fun of me."

"Did not."

"We didn't," Gigi agreed. "They were beautiful."

"Yeah, you did."

Suze said, "Maybe just a little, but I still have one in my keepsake box." She straightened up. "All literary people have keepsake boxes . . . and spinsters in Victorian novels," she added.

"Ah," Van said. "Good thing to know."

"Do you still paint them?" Gigi asked.

Van grimaced. "Kinda hard to find sea glass on the Upper East Side of Manhattan."

"You can find anything in Manhattan," Suze countered.

"Right. I'll be back in a bit." Van slipped on her beach cover-up and snagged her sandals and carried them toward the water. She wouldn't have sea glass if Tiffany's was giving it away. She had forgotten all about her secondary-income scheme. She'd spent the winters collecting the glass and hoarding it in a box in her closet, taking it out on weekends and school vacations and whenever she had spare time between school and work and dealing with her family.

She'd made a decent profit on the painted sea glass since the sea glass was free and she'd found some brushes in an old case once when her mother made her clean out the basement as punishment for staying out all night. She'd been fourteen at the time. Amazing she hadn't gotten into trouble sooner than she had.

As Van walked along the shoreline heading north toward the pier and the Blue Crab, she found herself searching the sand for a glimmer of color. But when she realized what she was doing, she jerked her gaze away from the sand and stared out to sea.

It had been a lucrative business, once she got the hang of condensing scenes into an inch- or two-inch-long surface. She was good at it, too. In demand. Sometimes so in demand that she had a hard time keeping herself in glass or finding the time to give to the intricate designs.

Then one day it came to an end, like all good things her father touched. She was in her room with her work spread out before her. A row of finished pieces was drying on the open windowsill. More painted ones were spread across the table. She was spraying them with a fixative that the guy at the art supply store had shown her.

She heard the front door slam and knew it was her father home early from work or wherever he went during the day. She hurriedly closed the spray can, rolled it under the bed, opened the window, and tried to fan the fumes away.

It was futile. Her door banged open. Her father stood swaying in the doorway. "What's that smell?"

He roared the question, his face so full of rage that she was afraid he was going to kill her. She backed up until she was against the window, part of her wondering if she could get out and away before he caught her. But he stopped at the table, leaned over it, and nearly fell. He grabbed the edge to steady himself, then with a howl, he toppled the table. The glass pieces bounced to the floor; Van hurled herself through the open window and ran, the rage of that ungodly sound echoing after her.

Van didn't come home for two days. That was the first time she'd shown up at Dorie's door. It wasn't to be the last. When she finally went home a few days later, the glass was gone, the brushes, the paint, the finished paintings, all of it gone. The only thing he'd missed was the aerosol can of fixative that rolled under the bed. Van threw that away herself.

She never collected another piece of sea glass or painted anything again.

Van hiccuped as the memory of her father's wounded cry echoed in her mind. Strange. She'd forgotten the sea glass, but she would never forget the sound he made as he lunged for that table and those little pieces of glass.

She reached the pier and turned toward the street, climbed the steps to the boardwalk, where she rinsed off her feet and put her sandals on. Then, looking down the beach and seeing Gigi and Suze still stretched out on the sand, she turned right and walked across the pier to the Blue Crab.

She knew the front door would be locked since the restaurant wouldn't be open until the following weekend. She went around to the far side to the delivery door.

The kitchen faced Whisper Beach, and when Van looked down, she realized Gigi had been right; it was completely deserted. A couple of fishermen stood on the opposite side of the river, but that was all.

They could make it a public beach, but they couldn't make people come to it. It was like an invisible line had been marked in the sand. No trespassing.

IT WAS GOING to be a scorcher, Joe thought as he held the hose on Bill Cassidy's Starcraft. Bill had hardly been down to use the damn thing all summer, but he paid Joe to clean it once a week whether it needed it or not.

So here he was barefoot and shirtless, showing the young poacher, whose name turned out to be Owen, the tricks of scrubbing a boat. Joe hadn't expected to see the kid again, but he'd been sitting on the steps, ready to work, when Joe got up that morning.

He was a pretty good worker, except for the habit of turning the hose in the direction he was facing instead of keeping it aimed at what he was cleaning. Consequently, Joe was soaked from trying to give the boy instructions. He'd finally given up and sprayed him back. A short hose fight was waged before Joe reminded him he was on the clock.

But he had to laugh. It was the most fun he'd had since he'd offered to help Grandy out during his hospital stay. He and Grandy were friends, and Grandy was going through treatments for some serious cancer. Joe had Renzo to look after the vines, but Grandy had no one, so Joe had been living at the marina for the last month and a half until Grandy could come home.

This way, Joe could help out a friend, make a little extra money, and try to figure out what to do about his personal life now that he had a new business in the making.

So far he hadn't gotten far with the latter. At least not until Van Moran came back to town. And that had sort of worked out too. He went weeks without coming into Whisper Beach, and yet here he was when Van returned to town.

Crazy that someone you haven't seen in years could give you that same whoosh of breath that left you feeling wrung out and, at the same time, hyped like crazy.

She, on the other hand, had been totally cool. *How are you? Good to see you.* Hell, he thought he deserved a little better than that, even if they had sort of broken up before she left.

He'd finally convinced himself that her leaving had nothing to do with him, but that had made him feel even worse, because if she couldn't come to him for help, what kind of relationship did they have anyway? So mostly he just stopped thinking about her. And that had been working out okay for him. He'd thought.

Until Saturday. He really wanted to talk to her. Just talk. Like old acquaintances. This would probably be his only chance. She was way out of his league now; she wouldn't be back anytime soon. She might already be gone.

"Hey, Owen, think you can finish up rinsing her off without me?"

Owen nodded.

"After that you can go on home, but Owen . . ."

Owen turned and sprayed him with the hose.

"Sorry."

Joe shook his head. "Do not go out clamming again, okay? That policeman is out for blood. In fact, I would tell the others to be very careful, maybe move upriver for a while. Capisce?"

Owen nodded.

"I mean it. Don't make me a liar. You work here until further notice."

Owen saluted. Joe didn't really know what to make of the boy; he didn't say much, even less when Joe had asked him about his family.

Joe went inside, jumped in and out of the shower, and threw on jeans and a clean T-shirt. Then he rummaged around for a decently clean pair of running shoes and shoved his bare feet in before he turned over the Closed sign and headed for his truck. He paused only long enough to tell Owen he'd locked up and he'd see him in the morning, then drove toward the beach.

The same car was still parked in Dorie's driveway. It might be Van's. He pulled onto the lawn next to it and ran up the porch steps to ring the bell.

Waited. No answer.

Dorie would be at the Crab doing her regular postweekend cleaning. If Van was gone, at least Dorie could tell him where she was.

Yeah, joker, and what are you going to do, drive after her? And then what?

And then he was going to ask her why the hell she'd left without bothering to explain to her family and friends why, or at least to let them know she was okay. That was his story, and he was not going to look more closely than that at his motive for finding her.

He thought he deserved at least that. She was evidently talking to Suze, and Dorie and Gigi, probably others, why not him? Yeah, he at least deserved something more than *Fine, how are you?*

He ran back to the truck, drove to the Crab. There wasn't one damn parking place. A car pulled out of a space going the other way. He checked his rearview then made a U-turn into the space. Yanked his keys out of the ignition and headed for the restaurant.

He went straight around to the kitchen.

Was he acting kind of crazy? Probably. Did he really care? Not really.

He could imagine Dorie's face when he asked her whether Van was still here. She'd be smug as all get-out. She'd tried to get him to go to Manhattan for years until she'd finally given up.

But no way was he going to follow some girl years later like a lovesick hound. Of course Van wasn't some girl; she was Van.

He stopped at the door. Below him, Whisper Beach lay empty. Not one solitary soul walking or lying out or anything. They should call it Ghost Beach instead of Whisper Beach.

He could hear the banging of pots and pans, someone giving orders. He huffed out a breath and opened the wooden screen door.

The kitchen was a warren of activity; workers were carrying stacks of dishes; pans and boxes were being dragged out of the storage area, and the dishwasher was going full blast. Dorie stood in the middle of the room, hands on her hips watching the activity.

But the voice Joe heard giving orders belonged to Van.

And he smiled.

She was standing on a stool, barefoot, wearing a soft, white see-through thing over a very tiny bikini.

She looked good.

Dorie noticed him and came to stand by him.

"She's still here," he said.

"Well, obviously. Is that why *you're* here?"

Joe thought about making up some story, but what was the point? "Yeah. I wanted to talk to her for real before she took off again."

"Good, but do not interrupt. She walked in off the beach, suggested several ways to improve the kitchen's efficiency, and is in the process of doing it. The woman's amazing. They should make a reality show of what she does."

"They should." Joe had read her website, and the articles in the magazines, but it wasn't until now, watching her in action, that he began to understand. And though he might not have the right, he was proud of her.

She'd always liked things to run smoothly, because her home life was always in chaos. So she'd taken that need and made a career to fit. Just like her to do something like that.

"If I were you," Dorie said, breaking into his thoughts. "I would wipe that goofy grin off my face before she thinks you're having randy thoughts about her."

"Was I smiling?"

"Yup."

"I just wanted to talk to her. See how she's doing."

"Uh-huh."

"Okay, that's a start," Van said, totally unaware of Joe and Dorie watching her. "See how much shelf space you freed up by that one change?"

She was thin and fit and supple, things Joe had been too gobsmacked to have noticed yesterday. But he noticed them now, and he prayed she would turn around as ardently as he hoped she wouldn't.

"Cubby, come give me a hand down." Van reached out her hand, but Cubby, instead of taking it, lifted her by the waist and set her on her feet. She laughed. "Thanks." The smile they exchanged made Joe hurt inside.

She sounded so happy. Content. Satisfied.

"Maybe I shouldn't have come."

Van turned. "Dorie, what do you think about moving the—"

"Too late now."

Van had just sort of stopped. She didn't move forward or back or say anything.

"She doesn't want to see me," Joe said and started to back away.

"She doesn't know what she wants." Dorie clamped bony fingers around his wrist. "Don't make me embarrass you."

Before he knew what she was doing, Dorie dragged him over to Van. "You two talk. Van, you owe him at least that."

And suddenly she was gone, and he was left looking at Van. She didn't move at first and he drank her in. The dark hair she used to wear long was now cut short, severe. Her dark eyes were wary. Of him? Or because she thought he would cause a scene?

He was aware of Dorie quietly herding the others into the dining room.

"I . . ." he began, ". . . was too surprised to really say hello yesterday. I didn't want you to think I wasn't interested in hearing how you are."

She shook her head. "I didn't. It's okay. Don't worry about it."

"I do want to hear about what you've been up to. What you're doing now. I want . . ." *To find out why you left and why I can still feel like this after twelve years.* "Would you like to go for coffee or something?"

"Now?" She looked down as if she suddenly became aware of what she was wearing.

He had been very aware of it since he'd first stepped into the kitchen.

"I'm wearing a swimsuit."

He smiled. "We're at the beach."

She hesitated, like she was trying to decide.

"Just talk, catching up like frie— people who used to know each other do."

She looked around the room. It had cleared out completely. "I guess I have a few minutes."

She walked past him to the door. He could feel her bracing herself. Preparing herself. He'd seen her do it in the past. When a customer complained. When they'd stayed out late and he'd dropped her off at a dark house. He didn't want her to feel that she had to protect herself from him.

She seemed distant. Almost untouchable. Could this possibly be the Van he had known and loved?

Chapter 10

She waited for him at the pier railing, the backside of the restaurant with the garbage cans and the delivery crates. And he thought how she deserved to be surrounded by something nice, someplace beautiful. The boardwalk was hardly that place.

"Why is it empty?" she asked, looking out over Whisper Beach.

He came to stand beside her. "I don't know. Maybe it's too isolated for the tourists. They prefer the big beach, where all the action is maybe. And the locals . . . most of them don't have time to hang out at the beach like they used to."

"That's sad. It was always such a special place."

He wanted to ask if that was why she had come here the night of Clay's funeral. To see the beach, maybe to remember.

"Doesn't mean we can't go down."

"I— Sure."

Impulsively, he ducked under the rail and jumped to the sand. Reached back to help her down, slid his hands around her waist as Cubby had done. But when he lifted her down, she stayed rigid in his arms. Not the laughing girl who had flirted with Cubby.

They walked across the beach to the retaining wall that kept the river from washing the sand away and stood side by side looking at the water rushing backward up the river. The tide was coming in.

What were they doing standing here? It did more to separate them than a table at a crowded café.

"Van?"

She turned toward him, steeling herself, he thought. For what? Did she think he was going to heap recriminations on her head, a decade plus later?

"I'm glad things turned out well for you."

She half smiled. "Thanks. I've done okay."

Another silence.

"Dorie said you sold the farm."

"Yeah. Dad did. We just couldn't compete with the big guys. I wanted to go organic, but they were just tired out."

"I'm sorry. How are they?"

"My grandmother died a couple of years ago. But everyone else is okay. Granddad moved in with my parents. Maddy got married, nice guy she met in college. They live in Ohio."

"Wow, do you ever see her?"

"They came last Christmas. She and Mom talk on the phone a lot. Skype." He laughed. "The modern family."

That half smile again. Maybe he shouldn't mention families. He'd thought—they'd all thought—that she'd be joining theirs. Instead she left without a word.

He wanted to ask her why. Tell her there was nothing between him and Dana. Ever. But it seemed so silly now. And maybe it hadn't even been about that. Maybe she left because she didn't want to get stuck with him.

He heard her sigh, looked at her. She was smiling. "I don't think I should ask what you're thinking."

Here was his chance. Just blurt it out and get it out in the open, then maybe they could start again. Start again? Was he nuts? She was leaving. He didn't even want to start again.

Why am I even here? Van wondered. Why was he? And could things be more awkward? Should she mention the past? Get it out of the way? Tell him it was all cool and not to give it another thought.

Maybe he wasn't even thinking about the past. And it wasn't cool. Just standing next to him made all her old anger rise up again. Not at him. But at the way life was then. They had nothing in common now, so she should be happy that she hadn't found herself stuck on a failing dairy farm.

These days the mere idea of her as a farmer's wife brought a smile to her lips. But she liked him, standing there looking down at the river like it could answer the questions he obviously wasn't asking. He was a good guy. And she was glad of that. Because it would have been really bad if she'd run away because of someone who turned out to be a jackass.

"So how long are you staying?" He didn't look at her, just kept staring at the water.

"I'm not sure. A few more days at least. Gigi is a little lost. And I have some legal stuff to take care of."

He looked at her now.

"I still own the house, but it's stupid for me to keep paying taxes on it. I might as well put it on the market. Listen, I'd better get back. It's really good to see you, but I've torn Dorie's kitchen apart, and I want to make sure they put it back the way I want them to." She laughed softly. "It's what I do for a living. Organize people's living spaces and their lives. Ironic, isn't it?"

He moved, like he might take her in his arms and comfort her and tell her he would take care of her always like he once had. And for the briefest instant she wanted him to. But she wouldn't—couldn't—go down that road again. Besides, she was probably misreading him.

She wanted them to part on good terms. It shouldn't matter. Maybe ultimately it didn't matter, but still . . . it mattered. "Want to walk me back?"

This time she made sure they took the stairs. She'd try not to think about his hands around her waist. The strength of him; no, it wasn't that. It was the unexpected fact that for that brief moment, she'd felt safe. And that was so not the strong self-reliant woman she'd become. It rattled her, and she'd had to steel herself not to react.

She'd stopped being mad at him long before she'd left town. Before she knew she was pregnant with a drunken frat boy's baby. Her stomach burned at her stupidity. How one moment of irresponsibility had changed her life forever.

She didn't want him to know that. Just that she hadn't left because of something he'd done. Nothing could be further from the truth.

It had been something that she'd done.

They were back at the kitchen door.

"It was good to see you," she said, her throat burning.

"You, too."

Impulsively, she put her hand on his arm. "I know it was a long time ago. But I didn't leave because of anything you did."

"Then why?"

"I just had to. And it's worked out well for me. And you, too."

He looked like he might try to argue, and she couldn't hold on to her emotions for that long.

"I've really got to go. See ya."

"Yeah . . . see ya."

She grabbed for the door and went inside.

She walked straight through the kitchen and out to the dining room.

Dorie was awaiting with her hands on her hips. "Back so soon?"

Van could see Joe pass by the restaurant windows, cross the street, get into his truck.

Van nodded, it was the best she could do.

Joe sat in his truck outside of Mike's. He didn't much feel like company, but he sure didn't want to be stuck with himself. He'd even settle for Owen, but he'd be long gone by now.

He couldn't believe they'd parted with "See ya." Both of them. "See ya."

See ya? They wouldn't be seeing each other; she was selling her house, not that she would ever want to live there. But at least that was one tie to Whisper Beach. When that was gone, she wouldn't even have to come back for legal reasons.

Maybe she'd come for another funeral? Whose? His?

He looked around the parking lot. The last people he wanted to see today were Dana and Bud.

It looked safe.

He got out of the truck and went inside.

"Playing hooky today?" Mike asked.

"Just came in for lunch. Too hot to cook at my place."

"Burger?"

"Sure, why not?"

"We do make other things."

"A burger's fine, and put a salad on the side."

"You got it." Mike went off to the kitchen.

As soon as he left, Joe began to wish he hadn't come in. He was too restless to sit over lunch. But he'd have to get over it. Might as well start now.

Mike came back. "You want a beer?"

"Iced tea."

Mike filled a glass with ice and then poured tea into it. Placed it on the counter.

"So did you see Van while she was here?"

Joe nodded. When did his business become everybody's business? Stupid question. It was the way of things in Whisper Beach.

"Uh-oh, here comes trouble."

Joe didn't even have to look around to know who had just come in.

He sighed. "Make that burger to go, Mike."

Mike nodded and headed for the kitchen.

Dana sidled up to Joe and deposited herself on the stool next to him.

"Saw your truck outside."

Next time he would walk. "What are you up to today?"

"I don't know. Bud's working a double shift. Guess I'll just hang here for a while. Wait for Bud to get home. You working?"

"Yeah, just stopped by to pick up some takeout."

"Did you get to see Van before she left?"

None of your business. "Yeah, I just saw her a little while ago."

"What?" Dana spun around to looked at him. "Bud said she left already."

"Well, she's still here. Why? Were you were going to call her for a lunch date?"

"Funny. No, but I'd like to give her a piece of my mind."

"Oh, give it a rest, Dana. She never did anything to you. And everybody's gotten about as much mileage as they can from the brief reappearance of Vanessa Moran."

"Don't we sound grumpy."

"Just not in the mood."

"So the son of a bitch lied to me."

"Dana, don't start."

"That—"

"Leave it."

"I wonder how long she's staying."

"Dana, do not think about making trouble."

"Moi?"

"You," Mike said, putting a Styrofoam carton on the bar. "Go get a hobby or something. Take up crocheting. Or wait—news flash—get a job and leave Joe here alone."

Dana pulled a long face, pouty lipped. "I'm not bothering him. Am I, Joe?"

"Actually, Dana, yeah. I've got to go."

He slipped off the stool away from Dana. Reached in his pocket for his wallet.

"I'll put it on your tab," Mike said. And lifted his chin toward the door.

"Maybe I'll go see her."

Joe stopped. "Leave it alone, Dana."

"I'm sick and tired of everybody blaming me for her going away. I didn't do anything,"

Mike groaned. "Grow up, Dana. Nobody even thinks about it anymore."

"Maybe not before, but trust me, as soon as she walked into that party room, all dolled up and looking like a million bucks, speculation started and they all looked at me."

She seemed close to tears.

"You're delusional," Mike said.

"I gotta go." Joe started for the door.

"Are you two getting back together?"

Joe sighed. "Dana, what reality are you living in? It's not high school anymore."

"Don't I know it. I'll have a dirty martini, Mike."

"Dana, go on home; you don't want to start drinking at lunchtime."

"You want to take me home, Joe?"

"No, Dana. I want you to get out of this god-awful funk you're in. Go get yourself a job and your own apartment. Or you gotta get better makeup. 'Cause it's not covering the bruises anymore."

Her hand went to her eye.

"Better still, go stay with a friend. You've got to get away from this relationship."

"If I had a friend I would."

"Oh stop, you have friends."

She smiled. "You?"

"Not me. Sorry." He went out the door and back to the marina. Owen was gone, and he'd done a pretty good job on the boat. Joe stayed long enough to put up the Closed sign and dump his burger in the trash bin.

He'd had enough of hamburgers, Whisper Beach, and its crazy

inhabitants. He got back in the truck and drove straight to the highway and home.

Dorie shooed Van out of the kitchen an hour later. "You're on vacation."

"But I'm just getting started."

"You'll have plenty of time to get your ideas in place if you want. Now, go to the beach and hang out with your friends."

"I don't think it's in my constitution to do nothing," Van said.

"Then it's a good thing you decided to stay here instead of going to that fancy hotel. You'd be on your way back to Manhattan by now."

"Would I?"

"Oh, hell, I don't know. But I want you here. I know it sounds selfish. But I wasn't just trying to make you feel guilty saying I was lonely. I've missed you girls. These days, nobody wants to work. Just party. You all worked hard and partied hard, but pretty much didn't confuse the two.

"These new kids. Christ. They're just bodies marking time until they can get off and go out. They all want to make a fortune without doing anything. Then they wonder why they don't get big tips."

Van smiled. "Bet they still show up at your house."

"Not so much, but mainly because I don't want them. They don't call it the entitled generation for nothing."

"Dorie," Van said, surprised.

"Can't help it. No camaraderie anymore." She sighed, slapped her cheek. "Damn, I sound like an old fart."

Van laughed at that. "Why don't you come sit on the beach with us?"

"Har. And make this bag of skin even more wrinkled than it is already? But I will make dinner if you're not planning to go out."

"Do you want to make dinner or are you trying to find out if I'm going out with Joe?"

"Both. So?"

"We're not going out. But we were nice to each other."

Dorie threw up her hands. "Oh Lord, what is this world coming to? Now, they want to be nice." She zeroed in on Van. "Is that the best you could do?"

"I think it's important not to have any bad feelings."

Dorie heaved an exaggerated sigh. "Looks like I'm making dinner. Now go on down to the beach."

On her way back to the beach, Van called Suze's cell.

"Where are you?" Suze answered in a chipper voice totally unlike herself.

"I was at the restaurant, but I'm on my way back. Just wanted to make sure you guys were still there."

"Oh yes, but I'm getting burnt to a crisp and Gigi is already a tomato."

"Then I'll come get my beach chair and we can go back to the house."

"Oh, don't worry, we'll bring it. We'll meet you there."

Van hung up. Suze sounded so bright that Van decided she must be pissed at her for abandoning her with Gigi. They were supposed to be helping her cope with her recent loss and Van had wandered away.

She'd just meant to work out the fidgets, not end up at the Crab reorganizing shelves, and certainly not going to the beach with Joe.

And maybe it would have been better if she hadn't. She didn't even know what to think, except that somehow the thing that broke them up wasn't important anymore. Maybe hadn't been important then except for the way it played out. For her anyway.

She wondered if they could be friends, cut through some of that awkwardness. Though maybe she'd gotten what she deserved, and this was a reminder to leave it alone.

She beat Suze and Gigi back to Dorie's. She sat down on the porch to wait for them. They showed up a few minutes later and she went out to relieve them of the beach chairs.

"I'm going up to take a shower," Suze said and disappeared.

"I guess I better get back to the house. Mom's had the kids all day, she'll probably want a break by now."

"Well, I'm glad you came," Van said. "Sorry I wandered off. I stopped by the restaurant, and then Joe came—"

"Oh, you saw Joe?"

"For a few minutes."

"So are things back on with you two?"

Van frowned at her cousin. "No. We're different people, and, besides, I won't be around to see where it might go. Or not go."

"When are you leaving?"

"A couple of days. Are you tired of me already?" Van meant it as a joke but Gigi teared up.

"No, of course I don't want you to go. Why would I?"

"Well, not to worry, I'm going to offer some suggestions to Dorie about streamlining the Crab and then I'll probably continue on down to Rehoboth for the rest of my vacation. I'll see you tomorrow if you can get away."

"I'll see."

Van stood on the porch until Gigi got in the car, waved as she drove away.

"Whew," Suze said behind her.

"Sorry," Van said. "Didn't mean to desert you. I just started doing stuff at the Crab and one thing led to another. I think Gigi's upset."

"Uh-huh. Boy, did I get an earful."

"She ragged on me?"

"No, just asked a lot of questions. You and Joe, you and me, but strangely she didn't mention dead husband or kiddies even once."

"Strange, isn't it? Maybe she's past the 'Why me? Life will never be the same' stage and has moved on to the next."

"What are you talking about?"

"The stages of grief. I don't remember what they are, but I think there are five or six."

"Well, don't look at me. In Shakespeare, they grieve and then they die."

Van shuddered. "On a happier note, Joe came and we walked over to Whisper Beach and talked for a minute."

"And?"

"He came over, we talked a little bit, and he left." Van looked at Suze. "But . . . oh, I don't know."

"Okay, that's it. I'm declaring the rest of this day as shot to shit and opening up the pomegranate martini mix. And then you're going to tell me about the 'I don't know' part.

"Go change out of that little bikini; you're making me feel matriarchal. I'll go look for the little umbrellas."

Dinner was just the three of them, and they talked and laughed like the years hadn't passed. They even reminisced. At first Van kept up her guard, determined not to wander into territory that might set off her carefully buried demons. But after a while she relaxed, and they sat on the porch not really talking, just hanging out.

And Van wasn't bored at all.

And when they climbed the stairs for bed, she stopped Dorie on the landing. "I'm glad I came."

But sleep eluded her. She would start to drift off and some random thought would pop into her head.

Like Gigi standing on the sidewalk looking helpless and anxious to please. Then her terse "I'll see" before she left.

Van turned over, punched her pillow, dozed.

Joe's face when they bumped into each other at the restaurant. Dorie saying, *he'd love you again if you'd let him.* Seeing him again that afternoon and knowing that it was true.

She looked at the clock. Midnight.

Suze smiling when she saw Jerry Corso at the restaurant. She'd always liked Jerry.

Walking into her childhood home, not a home at all.

Uncle Nate saying *You should see your father.* Her father dashing her sea glass to the floor. Her father sobbing over her mother's coffin, not even sober for the funeral.

He'll die soon enough.

He'd love you if you'd let him . . .

Publish or perish.

A lonely old woman.

Don't you ever go to the beach?

When are you leaving?

See ya. See ya.

Three o'clock. Still dark outside.

She could just get up and go downstairs, make some tea, get some work done. Maybe being back wasn't such a great idea.

She'd carefully trained her new self. Inside out. Gotten an education, purged shore slang from her accent. Polished her manners, her look, took control of her world. Built her business and her image and she swore she would never run from anything like she had so long ago.

But, boy, would running back to Manhattan be easier than facing all the demons she'd left behind but were somehow crowding into her mind tonight.

At least the room was cool. Not like when she was a teenager. This had been her room then, too. When she was afraid to go home. When she worked too late. When she just needed to regroup. Only then it had been sweltering, barely cooled by an oscillating fan and an open window. So much nicer now. And quiet.

Something banged, and she was jerked back from the edge of sleep. Banged again.

She couldn't make out where it was coming from. Maybe trash cans being overturned.

More bangs, too early and too insistent to be garbagemen. She sat up, heard a door open across the hall.

The door. Someone must be banging on the door downstairs. Harold? Coming back and lost his keys? Wouldn't that be a reunion with her and Suze there.

Van grabbed her sleep shirt off the chair, pulled it over her head, and went out into the hall just as Suze's door opened.

"What's going on?" Suze asked, yawning.

"Don't know."

Dorie came out of her room at the end of the hall. "Did you hear something?"

"The door I think."

Dorie breezed past them; Van and Suze fell in step behind her.

The banging continued, more frantic now. But not the front door. The three of them turned as one toward the kitchen.

"Dorie, don't open it until you know who it is," Van said as they hurried to the back of the house.

Dorie didn't answer, just strode across the kitchen, and flung the door open.

A woman tumbled into Dorie's outstretched arms.

"I'm sorry. I didn't know where else to go."

Van and Suze moved closer together.

Van couldn't see the woman's face, but her nails were painted purple, and one fake tip was missing.

Then she pulled away from Dorie in surprise, clutched her side. One eye was swollen shut; blood had dried on her lip and chin. And one cheek was scraped and turning blue. But Van recognized her. She hadn't changed much, just gotten older.

"Dana?"

Chapter 11

DANA STAGGERED BACK, DUCKING HER HEAD AND BRINGING her hand to her face as if she could hide it from the others. But it was too late.

"Good God," Suze whispered.

Van just stood frozen.

"I shouldn't have come," Dana said through her swollen lip. "I didn't realize— Sorry." She tried to turn away, but Dorie grabbed her arm and held on.

"You're staying right here." Dorie flashed Van and Suze a look that dared them to say anything.

"No. I thought— I didn't know anyone would be here." She tried to pull away. "Dorie. Let me go."

Van could barely look at her; it made her stomach lurch. "Dorie, maybe we should take her to the hospital."

"No. No. I can't."

"We should call the police," Suze said.

"No!" Dana shot Dorie a panicked look.

"No police," Dorie said. "Who do you think did this?"

"The police?"

"One policeman," Dorie said. "Right, Dana?"

"I— He—"

Dorie sighed. "Don't even try to explain. Come. Sit down and we'll get you fixed up in a jiff. Then I'll take you upstairs. You're staying here with us. Suze, get my supply box out of the hall closet. Van, get some of that brandy out of the pantry. Van!"

Van jumped, moved numbly toward the pantry. She found the bottle of brandy and set it on the table. Got a tumbler down from the cabinet and poured an inch into it.

Dana just stared at the floor, expressionless. Van, against her will, felt a pang of compassion.

Suze returned with a shoebox, the top dusty and broken at the corners and put it on the table. It didn't look very sanitary, but Van kept quiet. Dorie seemed to know what she was doing, and Van thought it might not be the first time girls—women—like Dana had come to her for help.

Dorie pulled out a chair facing Dana, lifted her chin at the other two, silently telling them to leave. Van was more than ready to go. And evidently so was Suze. She stepped on Van's heels as they slipped out of the kitchen.

But once they'd gotten into the hall, they stopped. And on tacit agreement, turned back to listen, face-to-face, ears to the door. They heard nothing at first, then Dorie's voice broke the quiet. "I'm not going to give you what-for, tonight. But you're not doing yourself any favors when you keep going back to that son of a bitch."

"Don't." Or at least that's what it sounded like through Dana's swollen lip. "It's not his fault."

Suze rolled her eyes in disgust, made a sharp twisting motion with her hand that let Van know what she would do to Bud

Albright if he laid a hand on her. Van was thinking a big kitchen knife would do the trick.

Suze began tiptoeing down the hall toward the parlor. Van followed and when Suze rummaged in the liquor cabinet and brought out the bottle of cabernet they'd opened the night before, Van nodded and sat on the couch. She could use something to settle her nerves.

She was rattled. Well, who wouldn't be to find an abused woman on your doorstep. And to know that woman and know who did it to her. *Not his fault*. Hell, if she wasn't already angry at Dana, that would have pushed her into it.

"What a stupid, stupid— Ugh."

Suze handed her a glass and sat down beside her on the couch. "Well, as much as Dana's pissed us off in the past, that's hard to see."

"I know. Man, I thought if I ever saw her again, I'd want to scratch her eyes out, but tonight, ugh, I just feel horrified." Van took a sip of cabernet. "And actually thankful that I got out of here, even if it took a disaster to drive me away."

"We used to be friends with Dana." Suze looked over the rim of her glass at Van.

"I'm still mad at her."

Suze nodded.

"It's her fault . . ."

"That Bud beats her?"

Van shook her head. "No, of course not. Though if she didn't stick around, he wouldn't be able to. That's *her* fault."

"That's harsh."

"Is it? Would you stay with somebody who did that to you?"

Suze didn't answer.

"Well, would you?"

"I don't know. Until you've walked in somebody's shoes—"

"Oh, come on."

"Van, be a little compassionate. How long did you stay living with your father? He may not have beat you, at least I hope he didn't, but . . ."

Van shook her head. "But I did get out."

"I know."

"Though I didn't have a choice. He kicked me out."

"Oh, Van, is that what happened?"

Van shrugged. "I would have gone anyway. I couldn't stay around here. He called me a whore and said I was just like my mother. And to go get whoever knocked me up to take care of me. Let me ruin *his* life. God, I hated him." She shuddered. "Sorry, I really haven't thought about that in years."

"Like the sea glass."

"Yeah. Whoever said 'You can't go home again' sure the hell knew what he was talking about."

"Thomas Wolfe."

"Huh?"

"It's the name of a Thomas Wolfe novel, about a writer who becomes successful and goes home, but everyone resents him so he—"

"Well, he was right. I should never have come back."

It was almost four when Van and Suze heard Dorie take Dana upstairs. Dorie came down to the parlor a few minutes later.

"I gave her something to help her sleep." Dorie collapsed into the armchair. "Damned if I know what to do with her. She didn't want to stay. I think she was embarrassed for you two to see her that way."

"How long has this been going on?" Suze asked.

"A couple of years. Though I have to say, she provokes him. She pokes and prods at him, flirts with every man she comes in contact with. I think she enjoys provoking him."

"Even when she knows what will happen afterwards?"

"A sad case. I'm going to try to get her to stay here for a few days." Dorie paused. She seemed to be waiting for feedback.

Finally Suze said, "Of course."

"None of my business," Van said. "I have a hotel reservation in Rehoboth for tomorrow. I think it would be better if I took it."

"Better for whom?" Dorie frowned at her with one of her penetrating looks that could make you feel guilty even if you weren't.

"You'll have Suze as backup."

Suze shook her head. "Don't think you're going to dump her on me. I have to work."

"You say you have to work as much as I say I have to go to Rehoboth."

Suze just stared at her. "Maybe you're right. You *should* go to Rehoboth."

"Suze, I'm sorry— I—"

"In fact I'd better get to bed, if I want to get any w-o-r-k done at all."

"Suze."

Suze ignored her and climbed the stairs.

"Are we having fun yet?" Dorie said

Van stood. "I'd better get to bed, too."

"Sit down."

Van sat.

Dorie pulled her chair closer. "You know the world is an effed-up place sometimes."

"Tell me about it."

Dorie tilted her head. "I'm not going to beat this dead horse."

"Good."

"But you have unfinished business here, and it's high time you took care of it."

"What's this infatuation everyone has with finishing unfinished business? I have plenty of new business to keep me more than busy. Why can't I just leave it unfinished?"

"Is that one of those rhetorical questions or do you want an answer?"

"You've got an answer?"

"Yeah. It's sort of like making sourdough bread."

Van leaned back. "This I've got to hear."

"You damn sure do. So you got this starter and if you keep it alive, then when you add your other ingredients to it, you get a nice raised tasty loaf."

Van crossed her arms. "Uh-huh."

"But if that starter goes bad, and you try using it to make your bread, you ruin the whole batch."

"Ergo, if I don't deal with everything that I left in Whisper Beach, I won't be able to organize other people's apartments."

Dorie narrowed her eyes. "Don't be gratuitously stupid, Van. Twelve years is too long to be fettered by your past."

"I'm not."

"The hell you aren't. You can't sit on the beach for a half hour before you have to be doing something. And don't think I'm not grateful, because the Crab has gone to the dogs in the last few years, too much turnover, the prices—but that's not what we're talking about."

"What *are* we talking about?"

"You walked out on your friends and your family all because

you were pissed at Joe and Dana. And you left everyone's life missing a little piece."

"I don't believe this. My father kicked me out. Joe made his choice. I should have said good-bye to you, I'm sorry, but I wasn't thinking all that clearly. And I did say good-bye to Gigi. So . . ."

"What's between you and your father is one thing. But Joe—"

"I talked to Joe today. And I paid back the money Gigi gave me years ago with interest and more." Van made two checks in the air.

Dorie raised one eyebrow, an expression Van remembered well.

"Sorry, but it's over. I've moved on."

"But Dana hasn't."

"And I'm sorry Dana's life is messed up, but that's not my fault."

"Of course it isn't." Dorie huffed out a sigh. "I don't know why you girls can't let things go. What happened is over. Has been over for a long time. Done."

Van felt her bottom lip tremble; she bit it to quiet it. "It isn't over. Not for me."

"What do you mean it isn't over for you?"

"It's not important."

"Did I ask you if it was important?"

Van shook her head, inhaled. It seemed that that her lungs had been sucked closed, then they suddenly opened and she swallowed air. She'd been here before, pouring out her heart to Dorie and Dorie ready to comfort. Though Van was beyond comforting. Maybe she just didn't care anymore.

"You want to know? And then it will be finished, okay?" She hesitated. Was she really going to do this? "I lost more than a boyfriend. More than that baby when I miscarried. I lost any chance of having other children."

There, she'd said it out loud. She'd never told anyone, never. Except Suze, and they never talked about it after that night in the hospital.

The room grew completely quiet; not even a car passed outside on the street. Van wished she could just get up and leave. She was afraid she might start sobbing and not be able to stop. Why had she blurted out the truth? It was so much easier to live with when it was buried.

"Well, that sucks," Dorie said. "Does that make a difference to you? I mean, do you want children?"

"Not really. It was bad at first. I decided I didn't deserve kids. But then I just got busy and wouldn't have had the time for them anyway. They're just not a part of my life."

"And men? Are they a part of your life?"

"Sure. I've had relationships, just not significant ones. So it doesn't really matter." Van shrugged, attempted a smile. It didn't matter what she wanted; she'd met men who said they didn't want children, but as soon as you confessed that you couldn't have their children, they had a way of becoming the past. It didn't matter. "No biggie really." She breathed in. "So that ties up one more loose end."

"Which one?"

"The future. Joe always wanted a large family. We even talked about it. Check three."

"I think he'd rather have you than kids, even now."

Van shook her head. "Dorie, he hasn't seen me in years, and I haven't thought about him. So don't keep thinking that things will—" Her voice cracked. "Change. It's all fine so don't feel sorry for me. Now I really have to get to sleep."

She stood, made it to the base of the stairs before Dorie spoke again.

"And your father?"

"Not happening."

"They say he's a changed man."

"Well, whoop-de-do. It only took killing my mother and getting rid of me to make him happy. I was over at the house today. All my mother's things and mine were there all neatly put away. Stuff on the dressers and the bookshelves. Even the makeup in the bathroom. It's over a decade old. Nothing had been moved.

"But he took everything that was his with him. There is nothing, nothing there to show that he ever existed. Like he just erased himself from our lives."

"Or he felt he had no right to what was yours."

"Well, he's right there. The keys to the house are on my dresser. Tell Gigi I'm sorry, but I had to leave. If she wants, she and the kids can live in my house until she can get on her feet. If she doesn't want it, ask her to return the keys to my lawyer. He'll put the house on the market for me."

"Gigi doesn't need for you to give her a house; she needs you to light a fire under her. Everyone else is already enabling her to do nothing."

"I think it's too late for her to change. I'll send you some ideas for streamlining the dining room at the Crab. Should be a fairly simple fix. And tell Suze . . . well, I'll apologize to her before I leave."

"Vanessa Moran."

"I've loved being here with you and Suze, even seeing Joe again, but the rest of it— I thought it would be good for me, but it isn't. Don't ask me to stay. It's just too hard."

"Okay, leave if you must. But at least go say good-bye to Joe. You left him once before; don't do it to him again."

"I already told him it was nice to see him. We didn't make

plans to see each other again. It isn't his fault that I left. I was pissed at him and Dana. But I overreacted." She paused to take a breath. "The only time I ever just reacted without thinking of the consequences, and look what happened. I did it to myself. My responsibility, not Joe's, not Dana's."

In one movement, she turned and ran up the stairs. Closed the door to her room and leaned against it, no longer able to hold back the tears she'd held in for so long.

She didn't make any noise, didn't shudder or gasp. She'd learned early on not to let anyone know how much she hurt. Not her mother, not her father, and now, not even Dorie.

MAYBE SHE WAS getting too old for this, Dorie thought as she stood in the hallway between the three guest rooms. She had a full house again. She hadn't had one of those in years.

There had been a time when the girls and the boys would come to her for shelter in whatever particular storm they were going through. Dorie never turned them away. Even if she had to sleep some of them on the floor with a blanket and a couch pillow for their heads.

Harold took it all in stride. Of course, Harold liked having the girls around. In those days, he had a roving eye, and an occasional roving hand, but he never compromised a young woman as far as she knew. It was later that the real philandering started.

But to love Harold, you had to love the whole man. The man who built (with her help) a successful restaurant from nothing. The man who put their entire savings into shares of the hotel only to have it go belly-up a few years later. He sold his shares to the new owners for a song. But that had been years ago, before the hotel became the favorite place to stay and before Sandy ended its reign and wrecked the foundation beyond repair.

Maybe it was working in the shadow of that hotel year after year, knowing he'd almost owned it, that he was the man who almost made it, that gave Harold wanderlust. Not just for women but for adventure.

Though his idea of adventure was sometimes just weird. Scuba diving in the Keys—surely a young thing in a bikini accompanied that one. An immersion course in Hungarian? He came back from four weeks in Budapest emaciated with walking pneumonia.

Did that stop him? No. Vegas to study poker, dealing not gambling. He could just as easily have learned in Atlantic City. Definitely picked up a woman or two in Vegas. Stupid old man. He was a good ten years older than Dorie, pushing eighty.

Still going like the Energizer bunny.

And still coming back when he got tired or ran out of money.

Dorie didn't begrudge him his travels or his women, though if they were getting any more than an arm to hang on she'd be surprised. She wasn't even jealous. Never had been.

They had three kids. All moved away and more or less successful. Dorie was alone a lot, but she didn't really mind, did she? She looked at the three closed doors. Well, she wasn't alone now.

This was all the adventure she needed. And if she helped out a few people along the way, gave them a place to be safe for a minute, well, hell, it's what she did. Let Harold go out and search for whatever he was searching for. She had everything she needed or wanted right here. She just wished she had the money to keep it going.

It was much later than Van had intended when she bumped her packed suitcase down the stairs the next morning. She could smell coffee and bacon of all things and heard the murmur of conversation coming from the kitchen.

She rolled her suitcase to the front door. She'd have to come back for her printer and laptop. She knew her eyes were puffy and not just from lack of sleep, but there was no help for it. She'd just have to brazen her way through the good-byes.

Quick and gracious, optimistic plans to keep in touch and then she'd be on her way to her vacation.

Her vacation. Maybe she should just go home to Manhattan.

She wiped her hands on the front of her new shorts and strode down the hall to the kitchen.

They were sitting around the table, Dorie, Suze still in her pajamas, and Dana, wearing what had to be Dorie's bathrobe.

Conversation stopped. Van stepped inside.

"Hey, just wanted to say a quick good-bye before I take off."

She got no response.

Van came farther into the room. Gave Dorie a one-armed hug and stepped away. "Thanks . . . for everything. Suze, let's get together."

Suze frowned at her and stood up. "I'll walk you out."

Van turned to Dana, who was looking down at an untouched cup of coffee.

Her lip was so swollen it was hard to imagine her being able to get the liquid in her mouth. Her eye was swollen, surrounded by deep purple. And something Van hadn't noticed the night before, her chin was scraped, like a child who had fallen on the sidewalk.

Van's stomach lurched; she nodded, gave Dana a tight smile.

That was the best she could do. Her emotions were pushed well back inside. She wouldn't take the chance of reacting to Dana's injuries and having her own feelings tumble out again.

"Tell Gigi I'll call her." She headed for the door to the hall. Heard chairs scrape; she kept walking, faster now.

She reached the suitcase, pushed the handle down, and picked it up. It would be faster than rolling it across the lawn.

"No, Van." It was Dana and she was alone. "I'll go. I had no business even coming here. I just didn't know where else to go."

Van forced herself to look at that bruised face. "So if you left now, where would you go?"

Dana shrugged. "Back to Bud. He doesn't mean—"

"Dana, stop right there. Do not go back. You don't deserve to be treated that way."

"I don't?"

"No. No one does. And I'm not leaving because of you."

"Then why?"

"It's complicated."

Suze moved forward.

Van quickly turned away, opened the front door, and walked straight into Gigi.

"Oh!" Gigi exclaimed and jumped back. She was dressed in beige cotton slacks and a pin-striped blouse. She was balanced on two-inch heels and was incongruously holding a beach bag in one hand. She held a pile of mail in the other.

Van tried to bypass her, but there was no way it was going to happen. Resigned for more tears, hopefully only on Gigi's part, Van said, "Oh, I'm glad you dropped by. I wanted to say good-bye before I head out."

Gigi seemed to notice the suitcase for the first time. "But . . . where are you going?"

"I'm on vacation, remember? I have hotel reservations starting today, and I don't want them to think I'm not coming and give my room away." Van smiled brightly. It was so fake that not even Gigi the naive could mistake it for a real.

"I thought— Why can't you spend your vacation here?"

Suze efficiently relieved Gigi of the mail and began rifling through the envelopes.

Momentarily distracted, Gigi asked, "Is she still waiting for those forms?"

"Yeah. And she's staying here for a while to write, so you guys can hang out together."

"But you promised."

Van stared at her. "Me? Promised what?"

"You said you'd stay."

"No, I didn't."

"Yes, you did. After the funeral when we were at Mike's. I said I knew you didn't want to stay, and you said you did."

"I meant for the day and I stayed over yesterday just to see you."

Suze had stopped shuffling through the mail. She dropped it onto the foyer table.

"Nothing?" Van asked.

Suze shook her head.

"I thought you and Suze and I could go to the beach today. Like we did yesterday."

"I can't." Van leaned forward to give Gigi a quick hug.

Gigi latched on. "Please. Just for a few days. We're family."

And family was one of the big reasons Van was in a hurry to leave.

The change in Gigi's expression was so quick and so stormy that Van stepped back, right onto Dana's foot.

Gigi's eye widened almost comically. "What's she doing here?"

Dana rested her chin on Van's shoulder. "Girls' weekend away. Too bad you missed it."

Dana was back in Dana form; bruises and all, she was going to tough it out. Van dug her heel into Dana's toes. Dana pushed her from behind. Not strong, but enough to let her know she was a force to be reckoned with. Not that Van had any intentions of dealing with her in any manner ever again.

"This is all her fault!"

"No, Gigi, it's just my schedule."

"No, it isn't. You said you would stay, then she came and now you're leaving." Gigi glared at Dana. "Why don't you just go away?"

Dana crossed her arms, cocked one hip, feisty and belligerent regardless of her battered face. "Why don't you?"

Gigi's lip quivered.

Damn, Dana. She never knew when to leave things alone. Van could walk out the door now, leave the others to sort things out among themselves. She could be in Rehoboth in a few hours, lie on the beach alone, have her meals alone, drink at the bar alone, then go to bed alone— What kind of vacation was that?

Or she could have the problems that hounded her here instead. But then what kind of vacation would staying here be?

Gigi smiled tentatively. "Please?"

"Yes, for crying out loud, please," Suze said under her breath. "You really can't leave me and Dorie like this."

"You're welcome to come with me," Van said just as quietly.

"Plé-e-e-ease," Suze whined in a parody of Gigi. "I promise not to mention work if you promise not to say Rehoboth."

"Suze, don't ask—"

"I'm dying," Dorie blurted out.

Chapter 12

THE OTHER FOUR WOMEN STARED AT HER.

Then Gigi started crying.

Van put a comforting arm around her. "Dorie, if this is your idea of a joke, stop it."

"I'm not joking. Well, I'm not dying, either. At least I hope I'm not."

"Not funny!" Dana yelled. "Not funny, Dorie."

"Chill. Look at you all. Suze is totally balled up over the mail. Dana, you act like you're mad at the world, when you're here with people who care about you. Van can't wait to get away. Gigi, I don't even know what to say about you. You just stopped growing somewhere along the line."

"I'm going upstairs," Suze said.

Van reached for her suitcase.

"Stop! All of you."

Van stopped, Dana crossed her arms and glared at them, Suze

looked down on them like the wrath of the almighty college professor.

"Would you have stayed if you thought I was dying?"

No one answered.

"You're all so caught up in your own problems or agendas or whatever that you don't even see what's in front of you."

"And what would that be?" Dana asked.

Dorie looked them over, long enough to make Van squirm.

"You know, life is short. Before you know it, you're looking back on it and wondering what the hell happened.

"And it's too late to fix the things you didn't fix, or really enjoy the things that you didn't even pay attention to."

"But you're not really dying, are you?" Gigi asked, her voice trembling.

"When you get to be my age, you're always dying."

"Oh, horse twaddle," Suze said, coming back down the stairs.

"Okay, here's the truth. I'm not dying, but the Crab is. Harold has totally cleaned out the operating money not to mention the joint bank account, and if I don't figure out how to do things more efficiently, I'm going to lose it."

Van narrowed her eyes at Dorie. Her confession sounded sincere, but Dorie was clever that way.

"You're serious this time?" Van asked.

"Dead serious."

Still Van hesitated. She didn't like to be manipulated. But if Dorie needed help with the Crab, Van could turn it around. And it would be more fun than sitting on the beach by herself.

She looked at Suze and could see she was thinking the same thing. Gigi looked hopeful. Dana just looked pissed off. But then Dana only had two looks: pissed off and her version of sexy.

"And when were you going to get around to telling us this?"

"I was hoping I wouldn't have to. But . . ." Dorie shrugged. "What little was left, left with Harold this week."

Suze cut a look toward Van.

Van hesitated.

Dana and Gigi both turned to look at her. Then Dorie.

"Oh, what the hell. I'll call the hotel and cancel my reservations. But Dorie has to make pancakes."

Van hauled her suitcase back upstairs. When she got up to her room, she called the Rehoboth hotel and canceled her reservation. If things got too complicated, she'd just go home to Manhattan.

When she came downstairs again, Suze and Dorie were bustling about the kitchen. Gigi sat at the kitchen table across from Dana, watching her like a terrier at a rat hole. Though what she expected Dana to do was anybody's guess.

Van walked over to the stove. "Can I do anything to help?"

"You can make some more coffee."

Van got down the coffee and filled the coffeemaker. Suze passed by with a stack of plates. Van gave her a quick look and then glanced toward the table.

Suze shrugged.

They set the table, and poured more coffee, brought butter and syrup from the fridge and still Gigi and Dana hadn't moved. Dorie brought over a towering stack of pancakes, surrounded by bacon strips, and Van and Suze took their seats.

"Mmm," Suze and Van said together.

Dorie had always made the best pancakes, the best crab cakes, the best lasagna, the best of a lot of things. And it wasn't fair that she was having trouble with the restaurant because of Harold's low-life lifestyle.

Restructuring the Blue Crab would be a challenge; Van

mainly did apartments and office buildings. But she'd met enough people in the business to know who she could call for advice if she needed it.

"I'm stuffed to the gills," Suze said, when the pancakes and every morsel of bacon were gone, and the dishwasher had been loaded.

"Which is why we're walking into town for supplies," Van said.

"What about my work?"

"You can work this afternoon while I go over to the Crab and make some sketches."

"You coming, Gigi?"

"Sure."

Van steeled herself. "How about you, Dana?"

"Dana will stay here with the doors locked, so take a key," Dorie said. "She's keeping a low profile for a while. I'm going to run down to the Crab to pick up some supplies for dinner."

"Right. Do either of you need anything? We're just going to Main Street."

For a moment Van thought Dana was going to make a request. But she just shook her head.

Van, Suze, and Gigi started off toward town. It was only four blocks and even though the sun was already heating the air, enough trees lined the streets to making walking bearable. Which was better than trying to find a place to park in the three-block strip of trendy stores.

"We probably should be paying to stay at Dorie's," Suze said. "I planned to pay her rent anyway, but every time I bring it up she puts me off."

"She won't take any money," Gigi said. "At least she never did before."

"Maybe we can put some toward the Crab renovation. But first

I want to make sure that Harold can't get his slimy hands on it."

"Absolutely," Suze said. "We would never have known she was in such trouble if you hadn't tried to leave, Van."

"Rub it in," Van said.

"No, I mean it; it was a good thing. And I'm sorry I bitched about Rehoboth."

"Same for me about your work."

"What are you guys talking about?" Gigi asked.

"A minor spat," Van said. "I haven't been thinking straight this morning. Like I hope it's all right for you to be seen in town, Gigi. Should you have stayed at Dorie's? I just have to pick up some graph paper and pencils."

"It's okay, I guess. It's not like . . . It's—"

They stopped on the corner, waited for a car to pass, then Van and Suze started to cross. Gigi stayed behind.

"Gigi?"

"Don't you wonder why Clay was living in a trailer at our house and not with me?"

"Uh, because he was protecting the house from looters?"

"Because he didn't want to be with me."

Van blinked, took a quick look around. "I'm sure that isn't why."

"Of course it is. Nothing went right for him after he married me. He bought the house with money he'd saved to open up a machine shop. But I didn't want to live with his parents or mine, so we bought that house. Then the storm came and wrecked everything, and then Clay lost his job.

"Everything we tried to do failed. And he blamed me."

"No, I'm sure he didn't," Suze said and shot a panicky look at Van, and they both hurried back to the curb.

Why Gigi decided to bare her soul while standing on a street corner right downtown, Van couldn't guess. She only knew she had to stop it, before someone overheard and it got back to Gigi's mother.

But what could either she or Suze say? They had no idea what had actually transpired.

Van was acutely aware of the tears about to fall. She pulled Gigi back from the street. "Stop this. You're grieving and not seeing things clearly. Just give it time. Try to just hang in; come shopping and try not to think about it until you have some distance on things."

Gigi nodded. "But I think he climbed up on that roof on purpose."

"To fix some shingles, Uncle Nate told me."

"No, to jump off."

"What?" Van asked, nonplussed.

On the other side of Gigi, Suze looked worried.

Van took a breath. "Gigi, people don't jump off two-story roofs on purpose. At best he would break a leg or collarbone." Only in Clay's case it had been his neck. "Besides, there are better ways to go if that's what you mean."

"Oh, no. It worked perfectly well." Gigi sniffed. "Is it too early for ice cream?"

Van stared at her cousin. What kind of gear switch was that? From her husband's possible suicide to ice cream.

"Yes," Suze said. "We just finished breakfast, and I for one don't have room for more. Let's do a little shopping first; there are some great little boutiques here."

"I can't afford boutiques," Gigi said.

"Neither can I," Suze said. "But we're going to window-shop and pretend." She took Gigi by the elbow and practically dragged her across the street, shooting a look to Van over her head.

Van followed, speechless and beginning to really worry. Is

this what made Gigi seem so fragile? She thought her husband killed himself because of her? And yet, how could she talk about suicide in one breath and want ice cream in the next? It didn't make any sense. They stopped at the window of an antiques store.

"You have lots of money," Gigi said to Suze.

"My parents have lots of money. I am living on a professor's salary."

"Professors don't make a lot of money?"

"In a word, no."

"Then why don't you get something that pays better?"

"Because I like what I do."

They moved on to the next store, a dress boutique.

"Aren't you married?"

"No."

"Do you want to get married?"

"This looks interesting. Shall we go in?"

"Sure." Van opened the door, and Suze walked in but not before cutting her a look that begged her to help out.

"Well, do you?" Gigi continued, following them in.

"Gigi, that's enough. Let's look at the earrings."

They managed to distract Gigi for a few minutes while Van bought a pair of seagull earrings for Dorie.

"They're really expensive," Gigi said as they returned to the sidewalk.

"Well, maybe a little. Is Untermeyer's still here? I need to pick up some graph paper."

They crossed the street to Untermeyer's Five and Dime, a relic from before Van was born that had managed to stay alive by adding upscale skin products, high-end beach toys, curios and jewelry to the cards, candy bars, and sundries.

Van felt a momentary pang. She'd once sold her sea glass paintings here. Right in the display case over there, now filled with handcrafted curios with price tags that would have made her rich back in the day.

She wandered to the back of the store past the cards to the office supplies, picked up a few things. Most of her work she did on computer, but she liked to get a hands-on sense of the space she was working with.

She took her things to the counter where an older woman rang up her purchases. "Why, Gigi Daly. Is that you?"

Gigi jerked around. "Mrs. Untermeyer. How are you?"

"I'm just fine, but I should be asking you how you are? Though it looks as if you're doing fine, too."

Van caught the undercurrent of disapproval in her voice. "Gigi was very kind to keep me company while I picked up a few things I needed," Van said. She leaned over and said confidentially, "And Amelia wanted us to get her out of the house. So sad."

"Yes, it is." Mrs. Untermeyer studied her curiously. "You look familiar. But I'm afraid I can't place you."

Van smiled. Considered. Decided what the hell. "I haven't been back in a while. I'm Vanessa Moran."

It took a few seconds for Mrs. Untermeyer to assimilate the information. "Oh my goodness, and here we were all thinking you were dead."

"Rumors of her death have been greatly exaggerated," Suze quoted.

Van shot her a quelling look.

"Well, I'm so glad they weren't true. Are you here for the art festival this weekend?"

Van had noticed the posters in the stores they passed and hadn't thought much about them.

"Uh, no, just here for Gigi. I don't paint anymore. Not since I left." Her artwork belonged in the past with all the other things that hadn't worked out.

"Oh, that's too bad. Well, you still might enjoy the festival. So nice to see you."

Van paid for her purchases, and they said good-bye to Mrs. Untermeyer.

"I forgot you sold your glass art at Untermeyer's," Suze said when they were back on the street.

"So had I. Okay, let's get ice cream and get back to Dorie's."

They walked three abreast past a real estate office and an art gallery.

"Hey, look," Gigi said. "That's a picture of the Blue Crab."

Van had to look twice. A large oil painting was displayed in the window. It was definitely the Crab, but in former days, just as funky but more colorful. The painter had managed to catch the spirit of the old hangout. "Maybe we should see how expensive it is; it would look great in the entrance, wouldn't it?"

But when they went to the door, a sign read CLOSED FOR INSTALLATION.

"Oh, well, we can come back Saturday," Suze said.

"Why Saturday?"

"The art festival." She pointed to the blue-and-white poster in the window. "Saturday, nine to six. Sounds like fun," Suze said. "Maybe we'll find some paintings on velvet."

Van laughed. "Do they even make those anymore?"

"Sure they do," Gigi said. "I have one of the sunset, and it's so pretty."

Suze shook her head. "Oh, Gigi."

"What? It's one of the few things I saved from the hurricane."

They came to the ice cream shop, another throwback to a simpler time, but like Untermeyer's, it had upgraded—to the six-dollar scoop with designer flavors.

They ordered, then took their cups out to the sidewalk and sat on one of the wooden benches that lined the street.

Van hadn't thought about art in years. She hadn't had time. She never went to museums and only went into art galleries to pick up something for a client. It was amazing the things people would pay for. And how much of their lives they would entrust to a virtual stranger. Van would come in to organize their living space and end up organizing their day-to-day existence.

"This is really good," Van said, licking mango gelato off the plastic spoon.

"Hmmm." Suze's chocolate chip dripped onto her shorts. "Damn."

"Aren't you supposed to be working on your thingy today, Suze?" asked Gigi.

"When we get back. Besides, it's hard to work on something when you don't know if you're going to have the money to do the research. And if I don't get it, it will be useless to kill myself trying to get the research finished.

"They're supposed to send the final round of the application here. I hope they don't screw this up. The deadline for returning it is next Monday."

"You should call them," Van said.

"I did."

"So if you don't get the grant, what happens?" Gigi asked.

"I have to stay in Princeton and teach and try to write at the same time."

"And if you do?"

"I take a year off and can write it anywhere I want. I'm thinking about spending at least the fall, maybe the winter with Dorie."

"Here?"

"What about you, Gigi?" Van asked. "Is it too early to make plans for your future?"

Gigi shrugged. "I'll have to find a job, I guess."

"What about your old job?" Suze asked. "At the beach yesterday you said the furniture store where you'd been working would take you back."

Gigi nodded. "But I want something with a future."

Suze nodded. "What did you study in college?"

"I didn't go."

Van felt the world shift. "Why not?"

Gigi shrugged. "I don't know. It just cost too much money."

Van bit her tongue. She'd sent back the money she'd borrowed within the first year. She'd sent extra after that. More than enough to go to the local community college.

"And then I married Clay and the kids came along. Besides, Clay didn't want me to work, just stay home with the kids. Only it hasn't worked out so well."

"Well, I'm sure something will turn up," Van said.

"Mr. Micawber," Suze said.

Van and Gigi both looked at her.

"Oh, right," Van said, laughing. "Dickens. What book was he in?"

Gigi looked confused.

"It's a character in *David Copperfield*. He's always saying something will turn up."

"And does it?" Gigi asked.

"Yes," Suze said. "Yes. It does."

"This is really fun," Van said. "I can't remember when I last sat on a sidewalk bench and ate ice cream."

"We used to do it all the time," Gigi said. "Don't you have any friends in New York?"

"Sure I do," Van said. "Just no time." And not that many friends, real friends, friends who would give you the last of their money or drive two hours to take you to a hospital.

"Except, in the city, it's coffee bars and bistros," Suze said as she scraped the last of her ice cream out of the cup. "That does it for me. You guys can stay and play, but I really have to get back."

"We'll all go; I'd like to get a jump on plans for the Crab."

They were a block from Dorie's when a police cruiser sped by.

"Idiot," Suze said. "He could take out a whole family driving like that."

The cruiser stopped in front of Dorie's.

"Uh-oh," Van said and started walking faster.

"Do you think Dorie called him?" Gigi asked. "Is something wrong?"

Van grabbed her by the arm. "Whatever it is, let Dorie handle it."

Van looked at Suze. Suze nodded.

"What?" Gigi asked. "Why are you two looking like that?"

"Because there's a good chance that they're looking for Dana," Suze said.

"Good, they can have her."

Van nudged Gigi to the side. "No, they can't. Let Dorie do the talking. And don't you dare say a word. You don't want to be responsible for Dana going back to Bud. Understand?"

Gigi reluctantly nodded.

"Or better still, just go into the house and get out of sight."

"Why?"

"Because," Suze said, "you could never tell a lie worth shit.

Didn't you ever wonder why we put you in back whenever we had to think up a story fast?"

"I thought you were trying to protect me."

Suze rolled her eyes upward; it was becoming a group habit. "Just don't say anything."

They were stopped at the sidewalk by Bud Albright.

"Anything wrong?" Van asked.

"You tell me. The door is locked, and nobody's answering."

"Probably because Dorie is out. We're just getting back from town." Van held up her packages as evidence.

Suze wedged herself in front of Gigi, just in case she was inclined to blab.

Another officer got out of the passenger side of the patrol car.

Jerry Corso nodded to Van, smiled at Suze. "C'mon, Bud. Dorie's not here and we have rounds to make."

Bud ignored him. "Are you staying here?"

"Yes," Van said.

"Is Dana here?"

"Dana? Why would she be here?"

"Is she?"

"I don't think Dorie would invite Dana to visit with me here. Do you?" Van slathered on the sarcasm.

"Guess she did sort of screw up your life, didn't she?"

Van felt Suze move closer to her. She didn't need to. Van knew how to handle bullies. She had spent her first months in New York pretty much on the streets, and she'd been a fast learner.

"Yeah, she did. So I don't think you'll be finding her anywhere around me."

"If you see her, tell her I need to talk to her."

"Sure."

Bud strode away. Jerry nodded and followed him. Van waited until they drove away, then went up the walk to the driveway and around to the side door. It was locked. Van felt around under a flowerpot and found the key that Dorie had always kept there.

She opened the door, stood while Gigi and Suze went inside, then came in and relocked the door. She looked at the key, then put it on the kitchen counter. "I don't think we'll be leaving this outside for a while."

"I can't believe you talked to him like that," Gigi said.

"I was perfectly polite," said Van.

"Well done," Suze said, and she and Van began to laugh.

The door to the hallway opened a crack. "Is he gone?"

Dana stood in the opening, looking black and blue and colorless.

"Yeah. But I wouldn't stand near the windows; he might get it in his thick head to cruise by again."

Dana's lips tightened. She nodded abruptly and left the room.

"She didn't even thank you," Gigi said.

"She had nothing to thank me for," Van said.

"You lied to Bud for her."

"I didn't lie."

"I don't know why she's still here," Gigi said. "After all she's done. I mean I'm sorry she got beaten, but . . . Oh, what am I saying, I'm terrible. I'm sorry for her."

"It's all right, Gigi, you don't have to like her," Suze said.

"And you don't have to be angry at her on my behalf," Van said. "It's all water under the bridge."

"I'm going upstairs." Suze stopped at the door. "I'll be down for happy hour."

Van was itching to get to work on her plans for the Crab, but she couldn't very well leave Gigi sitting in the kitchen by herself any more than she could tell her it was time for her to go home. Besides, she wanted to make sure Bud was truly gone.

Chapter 13

Dorie returned around five o'clock, loaded down with plastic shopping bags. Suze and Van were sitting on the front porch sipping pomegranate martinis. Suze was reading, and Van was sketching some designs that she thought might work for the dining room at the Blue Crab. Gigi had gone home. Dana had declined to join them, even though Van had made a point of knocking on the door to her room. There was no reason to continue holding that particular grudge.

"Why didn't you call?" Van said as she hurried to take some of the bags from Dorie. "I would have picked you up. What's the point of a rental car if you don't drive it?"

They carried the groceries into the kitchen and began unpacking them.

"Holy cow, are you expecting an army?"

"No, I just thought I might as well start stocking up for the winter."

Suze peeked into one of the tins. "Yum, ravioli with vodka sauce." She put the container down.

"Where's Gigi?" Dorie asked.

"Had to go do something with the kiddies."

"Do you girls want to invite her for dinner?"

"Maybe we should," said Suze. "I think she is feeling a little left out."

"She spent hours with us today," Van said.

"I think it's the 'us.' I may be wrong, but something she said while we were at the beach yesterday made me think she's afraid I'm replacing her as most favored nation."

"What?"

"In illiterate terms, she's afraid you like me more than you like her."

Van hesitated. Gigi was right. She and Van had been like sisters when they were younger, but now Van couldn't find even a spark of what had once held them so close. She was much more in tune with Suze, even though they had different professions, lived in different cities, and hardly ever saw each other.

"Am I particularly dense?" Van asked. "Should we be worried about her? She burst into tears this morning in the middle of town, said Clay didn't want her, that he fell off the roof on purpose and it was all her fault."

"Her husband just died way too young," Suze said. "She's bound to be fragile—and maybe just a little guilty for what she perceives as something that she should have done or would have done. It's a classic reaction."

"Shoulda, woulda, coulda."

Suze shrugged. "Maybe. Dorie?"

"She's had a lot on her plate for the last few years, but I doubt if Clay meant to kill himself if that's what she's thinking." Dorie handed Van the bag of food. "Put that in the fridge, will you? Suze, could you pour me one of those red drinks?"

"We ran into Bud on our way home," Van said as she put the food away.

"Close encounter of the worst kind," Suze agreed as she poured Dorie a martini.

"Where?"

"On the sidewalk in front of the house."

"Where's Dana?"

"Upstairs," Van said. "I asked her if she wanted to come down for happy hour, but she said no . . . through the door."

"I know she's not your favorite person, but Gigi isn't the only one around here who could use a friend."

"Van has tried, we both have . . . a little," Suze said. "Dana just doesn't make it easy."

"Well, put yourself in her place."

"I'd never let a man or anyone do that to me," Van said.

"Don't you think Dana thought the same thing, once? Nobody goes out and plans to be abused," Dorie said.

Or to be treated the way Harold treats you, Van thought.

"So she comes here, not for the first time, and instead of finding a soft place to land, she runs into you and Suze. Both successful and sophisticated."

"Me?" Suze barked out a resounding laugh. "I'm changing to wine; this sweet stuff is making me hear things. Where did I put that corkscrew?"

"Well, you are when you aren't distracted," Van said. "Which is hardly ever. It's right where you left it last night. On top of the bread box."

Suze stuck out her tongue. "But of course."

Van smiled. "See, very sophisticated."

Dorie put both hands on the table and frowned at them.

"Van, you ran out of town because of something you think Dana did."

"Something she and Joe did."

"Whatever. You left town, and no one hears anything about you for over ten years. Then suddenly you come back all dressed to the nines, sophisticated, manicured and saloned to near perfection.

"And Dana shows up at the door wearing cheap clothes and beaten to a pulp. She's bound to feel humiliated and just a little defensive."

Van tried to feel remorse, but she just kept thinking the words *white trash*. Except for Suze, they'd all come from pretty much the same background. Working-class families. They'd all had to work summers. Van and Dana also worked part-time after school.

Van had gotten out and made something of herself. Gigi had a family even if she was going through some bad times. What did Dana have? Would she still be getting made up and going to Mike's to come on to the barflies when she was forty? Fifty? Van shivered. "Does she even work?"

Dorie nodded. "Now she works part-time at the Blue Crab."

"You gave her a job?"

"She lost her job at the nail place because the clients complained about the bruises."

"That's awful, but you can't really blame them. What about the diners? Those bruises and cuts could definitely put you off your food."

"She's been working in the kitchen, but she'll have to move out front this weekend."

Suze came back to the table carrying the corkscrew but no wine bottle. "Why doesn't she get help?"

"I've tried. I know Joe has tried." She shot a look at Van. "And it's not what you think. He's just a friend."

Van waved her statement away.

"We've all got our lives to live. It helps if you've got some folks around you who want you to succeed."

Yeah, Van could have used a few of those when she was creating a new life for herself in New York. But then she had, hadn't she? Two of them were sitting right here at the table.

Dorie went upstairs to ask Dana to join them; she was gone for a while.

Suze set the table while Van got the food out of the fridge. "Think I should set four places in case Dorie talks her into coming down?"

"I guess. If she does come down and there are only three places, she'll get all bent out of shape."

Suze pointed a handful of forks at her. "You're determined not to cut her any slack."

"I told you, I'm not holding a grudge. But I'm not going to act like one big happy family, no matter what Dorie wants. I take full responsibility for what I did, but it doesn't mean that I forgive them for what they did. Though in a way I'm glad I found out just how faithful Joe would be before I ended up milking cows as a way of life."

Suze shrugged. "I wonder what's taking Dorie so long?"

"Old age," Dorie said, banging through the door, just like she was at the Blue Crab during the dinner rush.

"Guess you didn't convince her to come down?"

"She's having some pain. I gave her a couple of aspirin."

They sat down to dinner. The fourth place setting sat empty while they ate; the symbolism wasn't lost on any of them.

As soon as dinner was over and the dishwasher was loaded, Suze went upstairs to "do some research" and, Van thought, probably worry about the forthcoming grant. Dorie went to check on Dana.

Van sat on one of the porch chairs, nursing a cup of coffee even though the night was muggy and hot and the citronella candle did little to chase away the mosquitoes.

Life was weird. Here was Suze, from an *über*rich family, wanting to live at Dorie's old beach house on her own earnings. Gigi was back living at her parents' house with her children. Dana was hiding out at Dorie's.

And Van herself? She was supposed to be on a vacation that she hadn't wanted to take and at a place she'd picked at random. And here she was, spending her time off in Whisper Beach to work on revitalizing the Blue Crab.

Inside, the telephone rang. Van heard Dorie answer it, talk for a few minutes.

Dorie stuck her head out the front door. "That was Amelia. She wanted to know if Gigi was making a nuisance of herself."

Van sat up. "Did she really say that?"

"You know Amelia."

"All too well. What did you tell her?"

"That Gigi needed to be with her friends."

"And?"

"Well, Amelia has always been the one who knows best . . . about everything . . . but she finally conceded that Gigi had been showing more life in her since—well, let's not say since the funeral—but since you and Suze came."

"Great. Make me feel responsible."

"Anyway, I suggested she let Gigi come for a bit during the day, and she agreed as long as she got home to put the kids to bed."

"Wait a minute," Van said, turning fully to look at Dorie. "Why does this sound like a playdate?"

"Because Gigi is not thinking straight these days. She's fallen into a stupor. We've all been there, where you just couldn't get motivated."

"Dorie. When were you ever not motivated?"

"There've been times," she said vaguely. "And if you haven't gotten to that point yet, I hope you don't ever. I'm going to bed now. I'm beat."

"Dorie?"

"Uh-huh?"

"I can help streamline your business if you want. Not the financial and ordering but organization of the kitchen and front of house. But it will take some work, and maybe some things that you won't agree with."

"I'm counting on it. Hell, if it works, I'm for it."

Van grinned. "You are a piece of work, you know that?"

"And proud of it. But are you going to be around long enough to do it?"

"It won't take long, but we'll need bodies. I'll try to enlist Suze and Gigi, but I need a few strong guys."

"I've got 'em. Are you sure you want to spend your vacation working?"

"It's not work to me. And, besides, I have some other stuff to do here."

"Oh?"

Van automatically held up her hand. "I'm not going to renew old acquaintances, or go dredging up the past, if that's what you're thinking. But I have to decide what to do with the house." A little twist of pain clutched her gut as she remembered how spotless the house was and how empty of any bit of her father's presence. "Whether I offer it to Gigi or sell it, it has to be dealt with. I don't want to be responsible for Gigi refusing to take charge of her life, or to keep her dependent on me or anyone else."

"Gigi has always been dependent on her family and friends."

"Things didn't change when she married Clay?"

"Evidently not; seems she just transferred her dependence to him."

"Is that what happened? She—I don't know—acts like she's still a girl."

Dorie cackled. "Honey, you're all still girls. Just wait till you see what's waiting for you down the pike. Gigi is not your responsibility, but you do what you feel is right for you about the house." She yawned. "If anybody needs me, I'll be watching the *Late Night News* in my room."

"Good night." Van stretched back on the cushion, tucked her feet up under her, and listened to the sounds that floated up from the beach. The distant hush of waves. The thread of music from the pizza joint that stayed open most of the year. A shouted greeting. But it all sounded far away.

Van felt a strange kind of calm. She didn't trust it. Was it true calm or just the calm before the storm? She didn't think she'd ever be able to fully relax or feel comfortable in Whisper Beach again. Always a memory, or perhaps a living person, was waiting to ambush her.

All the more reason to deal with the house. That would be her last real tie to the town. Dorie and Gigi could always come to the city. She might even phone them now and again. Suze was just a train ride away. But that was it. The others—her father, Joe, and Dana—would become part of a distant and blurry past.

But first she would reorganize the Blue Crab, as a gift for all the things that Dorie had done for her.

The front door opened.

Van glanced up, expecting Suze or Dorie.

It was Dana. She didn't say anything but sat down on the chair across from Van.

The silence stretched, but since Van didn't know why Dana had come out or why she'd sat down, she waited.

Dana finally cleared her throat. Maybe it was hard to talk. Maybe Bud had tried to strangle her. "You know, you were my best friend."

Van was sure she must be hearing things.

Dana as best friend? None of them had even really liked her that much. She could be fun, and she knew where to buy liquor and find the rich boys, but none of them really trusted her not to forget them when she found something or someone more interesting. Leave them stranded when she suddenly got a chance to leave a party with some guy who had a car.

Best friend? Was Dana rewriting history? Or was she setting Van up for another sucker punch? How could she trust Dana after all she had done?

"I know you probably don't believe me. And you probably didn't even like me, even then, but you were the only person who was nice to me. I mean really nice."

And look what it got me, thought Van.

"I know you hate me, I don't blame you. I don't like myself much either."

Van was tempted to say that was obvious since she let Bud beat up on her like she did. No woman with any self-respect would let that happen. Though maybe Dana didn't have self-respect. That would account for a lot.

"It wasn't my fault. What happened."

Van sat back. "I was wondering when you'd get back to that. Whose fault was it, Joe's?"

"No, yours."

"Oh, that's rich."

"You got mad at him for flirting with me. I flirted with everybody. No big deal."

"Look, I don't want to talk about it. It's over. I've gotten on with my life. I have a good life. So let's just leave it at that, okay?"

"You shouldn't have given up on him so easy. He didn't want me or anyone else. Just you."

Van surged to her feet. "Okay, that's enough. It's ancient history. Let's just call it done and start over from here."

"You mean it?"

"Yeah. Truce. Okay?

"Okay. Thanks."

"I'm going to bed." Van headed to the door, looked back long enough to say good night, and went inside.

Best friend. Gigi was her best friend, at least had been. But Gigi, for all her clueless ways, was no dummy. She'd picked up on the fact that there were things between Suze and Van that brought them closer, and that left Gigi out. So maybe Suze was her best friend now. Though that seemed odd since they never saw each other or even talked. But Van was too busy with work to go out and find best friends. She barely had time to see associates and clients. Some of them were friends. Acquaintances.

But Dana? Best friend?

A ridiculous idea from the woman who had been the girl who'd stolen her boyfriend and started Van on a downward spiral that . . . that had actually turned out all right—more than all right—in the long run.

Most of it, anyway. Part of her should thank them for driving her into the larger world. But the rest wasn't so silly. It may not have been Joe and Dana's fault, but she wasn't ready to completely forgive and forget.

Part of her would never be whole again.

"Jerry on duty tonight?" Joe asked Hal Daniels as he slid onto a stool at Mike's.

"Yep. I just stopped in for a quick one on my way home."

"Well, you sure are gracing our establishment a lot these days," Mike said, placing a beer in front of Joe. "Think I've seen you in here more this last week than I have all summer."

Joe took his beer. "My cupboard is bare. And frankly the marina apartment is getting a little claustrophobic."

"Not to mention the stench. I can smell it all the way up here," Mike said. "Makes old beer smell like perfume."

"Guess you'll be glad to get back to the vineyard," Hal said.

"Yeah, I really will. Sort of."

"You seen any of Van since she's been back?"

Mike leaned over the bar, listening.

"I've talked to her a couple of times."

"Talked? That the best you can do?"

"Well, yeah. We haven't seen each other in years, and she's dealing with a lot of stuff right now."

"Like what?" Mike asked.

"Like just being back here," Hal told him. "Some serious shit went down between her and Dana and Joe."

"Do we really have to rehash all that ?" Joe asked.

"No, but speaking of Dana." Mike stopped to wipe a glass.

"What?" Hal and Joe said simultaneously.

"Bud was in here earlier looking for her."

"That all?" Hal went back to his beer.

"Did he find her?" Joe asked.

Mike shook his head. "Nope. Guess she's done a bunk."

"Well, good for her," Joe said. "I hope she stays away."

"Me too," Mike said. "'Cause if Bud finds her . . ."

"Do you know where she is?"

"I ain't seen her. And I don't want to. He's nuts tonight."

Joe nodded. "He's nuts every night."

"Well, more so tonight. He was looking for you, too."

"Me?"

"He thinks you encouraged her."

"I did. I always do. Don't you?"

"I'm just the bartender," Mike said.

Hal shook his head. "Man, I'm not touching that one. My wife doesn't even like me coming down here. But, hell, a guy needs to hang with his buddies."

"You know where she is, Joe?"

"Not me." Though he had some ideas. "She's an adult. It's not like she doesn't know what she has to do. She'll find a place to stay if she's smart."

"Well, I'm staying out of it," Hal said. "Next thing I know he'd be stopping me for speeding, or rolling through a stop sign or whatever. I don't need that kind of aggravation. But, Joe, I'd watch my back if I were you."

Joe sighed. "Yeah, we never got along, but I'm getting a little tired of him being in my face all the time about those poor dumb clam diggers out by the marina."

"I think he's just using it as an excuse to stay in your face, Joe. He keeps harping on Dana about what she's doing with you."

"She's not doing anything with me, and contrary to popular opinion, she never has, and never will."

"Yeah, we know. But the truth don't mean shit to Bud. He gets something in his head and just lets it grow till he cracks."

"Well, at least he's on duty tonight," Hal said. "Though I don't know how Jerry stands him."

"No, he ain't," Mike said. "Leastways, he wasn't in uniform when he came in awhile ago." He leaned on the bar. "So Joe, what are you going to eat?"

"Not another burger. How about a chef's salad if the lettuce is fresh."

"Man, you sure know how to get a guy where it hurts. My lettuce is always fresh."

"Okay, I'm convinced. Salad."

"Oh shit."

"What? You're out of salad?" Joe asked.

"No, I got salad. But Bud just walked in, and he's headed your way. I don't want no trouble, Joe."

"You won't get it from me. I just came to have dinner."

Joe didn't turn around. He didn't have to; he could feel Bud stride across the floor, people stilling as he passed them like a cowboy in an old B western.

"Must've seen your truck outside," Mike said under his breath.

"Must have. You'd think I had the only gray truck in town."

"Maybe you should start walking from now on."

Or just move back to the vineyard and eat at home.

Joe steeled himself for the confrontation. This was not how he wanted to eat dinner, but he was prepared when Bud's beefy fingers closed on his shoulder.

"You son of a—" Bud whirled Joe around to face him. "Where is she?"

"I don't know what you're talking about."

Mike appeared at the bar. "Okay, Bud. She ain't been here. Nobody knows where she is. So just go on home now."

Bud ignored him. He was fixated on Joe and looking for a fight.

Joe held both hands out to his side, fingers stretched in full view of the others. "I'm not going to fight you."

He saw Bud wind up, saw the fist coming. Joe was still seated, and there was nothing he could do to stop it.

Chapter 14

A SLEDGEHAMMER RAMMED INTO JOE'S GUT, KNOCKING THE air out of him and driving him back against the bar.

"Hey, stop that." Hal started to get off the stool, but Bud round-armed him and knocked him to the floor.

Joe had managed to get to his feet. "Stop it, Bud. If you want to fight, let's go outside."

Bud backfisted him and as he fell to his knees, Bud got off a kick to his gut that knocked Joe to his side before Hal and another man pulled him away.

Someone across the room threw a punch at the guy next to him. He fell against a table and knocked it over. The two people there joined the fray.

Fighting had broken out throughout the bar. It was going to be a free-for-all.

Joe was half aware of Mike running around the bar.

"Mike," Joe yelled. "We'll handle this. Call the cops."

That's all Joe heard before Bud grabbed for him. He dodged to the side, and Bud crashed into the bar, rattling mugs and overturning glasses and bottles.

He spun around, sending bottles and glasses flying. "Where is Dana?"

"I don't know where she is," Joe yelled. "I don't care. I'm not interested in her."

"You're lying." Bud knocked Hal aside and threw his full weight against Joe. Joe felt something give in his ribs. Bud outweighed him by twenty or thirty pounds. Two men and Hal pulled Bud away but Joe was having a hard time getting on his feet.

"Okay, dammit, that hurt."

"Where is she? I gotta tell her."

But it was too late.

Joe pushed away from the bar, but Hal pulled him back. "Don't do it. Stay cool, man, this is exactly what he wants."

Joe hesitated, gulping in air and trying to get his temper under control. But Bud broke away from the other men and lunged for Joe's throat. Joe ducked and came back with his best right hook. Bud's head snapped back, and blood gushed from his nose

Sirens rent the air, and people rushed to the doors.

Joe could hear Mike cursing over the rest of the din. "I'm pressing charges, Bud. Don't ever show your face in here again."

Joe sat back in the closest chair, as the police rushed in and began rounding up anyone still left in the bar.

"Tell me I'm seeing things and you didn't start this." Joe looked up to see a slightly blurry Jerry Corso standing over him. "Oh man, why did you have to come to Mike's tonight. Come on." He pulled Joe to his feet.

"It wasn't his fault," Mike said.

"I'm sure he didn't start it, but the captain said to bring everybody in. I think Bud just hit strike three. Are you okay, Joe? You look like shit."

"Sorry, Mike," Joe said as Jerry helped him to the door.

"Not your fault," Mike said. Then the door closed, and Jerry pushed him into the back of a patrol car where Hal was waiting.

"Mary Kate is going to kill me."

"Tell her it was my fault."

Jerry leaned into the door opening. "I doubt if the captain will hold you. Mike said he'd vouch for you two if need be."

"Where's Bud?" Joe asked.

"They took his ass away right off the bat. Sure glad I'm not Bud tonight." Jerry shut the door.

"Or any night," Joe said under his breath. He leaned back against the seat and closed his eyes. He was beginning to hurt everywhere.

"DANG IT ALL to hell," Dorie said and groped for her cell phone. "So help me, Harold, if this is you needing money, or a ride or wanting to home come before I'm ready to let ya, I'll do something awful."

"Hello," she barked. "What? Uh-huh. Oh Lord, is he okay? I'm on my way. Thanks." She turned to Van and Suze who were sitting on the couch. "I need you to drive me somewhere."

"Sure." Van grabbed her purse. "Is everything okay? Is someone hurt?"

"I won't know until we get there. You too, Suze."

"Me?" Suze asked, but she got up and slid her feet into her shoes.

They hurried out to Van's rental car.

"Suze, you sit up front." Dorie climbed into the back.

"Where are we going?" Van asked as she backed out the drive.

"The police station."

"Really? I can't believe you're still bailing kids out of jail."

"Some kids. And not usually this one."

Van headed for the station. She knew where it was, though she'd never been taken in herself.

She parked in a visitor's parking place. "Want me to come with you?"

"No, you just stay put." Dorie hurried up the sidewalk to the entrance of the station. Jerry Corso met her just outside, then escorted her inside.

Van sighed. "Things just don't change in Whisper Beach."

Suze agreed. "Only now Jerry Corso is upholding the law instead of breaking it. Go figure."

Dorie was gone for a long time, and Van grew impatient.

"Do you think it's a kid? Or maybe Harold? I could do without him," Suze said.

"Me, too."

Finally the front door opened, and Dorie and Jerry came out, propping up a man who was barely managing to stand on his feet. "He better not be drunk," Van mumbled. She would be pissed as hell if he threw up in her rental car.

She tapped the steering wheel. He didn't even look like a teenager. Too big for Harold. For one blinding nanosecond, fear seized her and she could hardly breathe. But he was too young to be her father.

She had just whooshed out her breath, when the man looked up. It was almost as horrible as having to see her father.

Joe Enthorpe looked out at her from a face that rivaled Dana's for battered and bruised.

"Oh my God," Suze gasped.

"My exact thoughts," Van said, trying to banish the utter sadness she felt to see how far he'd fallen. Jerry ran around to the passenger side and opened the back door. He helped Joe inside. Dorie climbed in after him.

"I'm pretty sure he's not going anywhere tonight. Still, call my cell or the dispatcher if there's any trouble."

Obviously Jerry was continuing a conversation. Van had no idea what he was talking about, unless he was afraid Joe was going to cause more trouble. Her stomach turned. She was the one who was in danger of throwing up in her car. How had this happened to someone like Joe?

"Don't worry about us," Dorie said. "I've got my shotgun."

Oh good God, Van thought. As much as she thought she had divorced herself from her past, it just kept coming at her. She lived in Manhattan and didn't know anyone who carried a gun.

Jerry wagged a finger at Dorie. "You know you don't keep that gun loaded, and so does everybody else in town."

"I'll load it tonight."

Jerry didn't bother to argue. He leaned in to the back where Joe was barely sitting upright. "You. Keep your head down."

"Thanks," Joe said.

"Put on your seat belt." Jerry pulled out the belt and reached across Joe to buckle him in.

Joe hissed between his teeth.

"Hey, Van. Suze." Jerry looked grim. "Are you having fun yet?"

Van didn't bother to answer. Jerry nodded and shut the door, watching them until Van had pulled out of the lot.

"Where are we taking him?"

"Marina," Joe said.

"My house," Dorie said.

"Marina. I'll walk." He reached for his seat belt.

They took him to the marina.

No one spoke for several blocks. Van had moved past surprise, shock, disgust, to curiosity.

"Barroom brawl?" she asked, keeping her eyes on the road.

Joe grunted. "Tripped."

"Uh-huh."

Dorie had been quiet in the backseat. Now she snorted. "Tripped into Bud Albright's fist."

"Really?" Van said, exasperated. "You and Dana should try staying away from him."

"Pretty impossible if you live here."

"Well, I don't, thank God."

After that no one spoke, and Van didn't bother to try to make conversation. Not even with Suze, who looked straight ahead.

Things didn't change. Except when she'd left town, Joe hadn't been a fighter. He didn't drink much. And he certainly wouldn't have gotten into a fight with Bud Albright. He'd had real plans for his future.

Van guessed she should feel lucky that things had turned out the way they had for her. It hurt like hell at the time and for a long time after, but on the other hand, if it hadn't happened, she might be stuck living at the old marina with a drunk for a husband—just like her mother had.

Still, she felt a stab of disappointment for the way things might have been. She shoved it away. She had a real affection for some of the people in town, but no way did she want to be like them.

"My truck," Joe said as they passed Mike's Pub.

"The girls will come back for it," Dorie said.

The girls, thought Van. She didn't bother to point out that she and Suze were adults.

She knew the way to Grandy's Marina. She'd spent many a

night there, drinking beer with the local kids and dangling her feet off the end of the pier. It was tucked in a bend in the river with a few berths for larger fishing boats and a handful of pleasure cruisers, most of which had seen shinier, cleaner days.

Still, she almost missed the turnoff in the dark. Not a light was on to mark the entrance to the marina. The office as well as the attached apartment where the watchman stayed were dark.

She turned into the lot, pulled around back, and stopped at the steps up to the door of the wooden shack. There were smaller boats on racks in the yard. Several on trailers were waiting to be launched or put into dry dock.

Joe was living here?

Joe fumbled with his seat belt. "Thanks for the ride." He opened the car door, gingerly got out, then leaned back inside. "Thanks, Dorie. You didn't have to come for me, but thanks."

"Who did you think would come for you? You gonna call your ma or grandpa to come get you? Or did you think staying in jail overnight is going to make things different?"

"Well, thanks."

"I'm coming in with you. Give me the keys to your truck. Van and Suze will bring it back over here. Won't you, girls?" Dorie grinned at them.

Suze took the keys. "You have to sympathize with Ichabod Crane when she grins like that."

"I thought the horseman was headless."

"He carried it under his arm."

"Ugh." As Dorie helped Joe up the rickety stairs to the marina office, Van turned the car around and backtracked to Mike's. "You know how to drive a truck?"

"No," Suze said. "I'll have to drive your rental."

Van took the keys and got out. Suze moved to the driver's seat and waited for Van to start up the truck. Then she followed Van back to the marina.

But when they got there, Suze refused to get out of the car.

Van trudged up the steps. Knocked. When no one answered, she went inside.

"Yeah, and I'm gonna keep her as long as she'll stay. Now get some rest. And stay out of trouble."

Great. This was about Dana. So maybe things weren't over between them. Van wrestled with an unexpected pang of jealousy. Squelched it. Decided it was annoyance and not jealousy at all.

"Here are your keys." Van dropped them onto the counter where Dorie was cleaning Joe's face with a washcloth. She'd meant to leave but got a look at his face.

"Maybe you should go to the hospital."

He shook his head slightly.

"You might have internal injuries," Dorie said.

"If I start coughing up blood, I'll give you a call."

"Hey, show some respect."

"Sorry."

"I'm not sure you should be left alone," Dorie said. "What do ya think, Van?"

"Go ahead and stay, Dorie. Suze and I will pick you up in the morning. Maybe Joe has an extra toothbrush you can use."

Joe pulled the washcloth away. "I'm fine. Thanks. You don't need to stay, Dorie."

Van really wanted to get out of the small, claustrophobic room and the pervasive stink of beer that was emanating from Joe. The smell from the river was almost as overpowering. She couldn't believe that he'd stooped to living here.

Then she saw the wine bottles lined up across the back of the table. And she understood.

More wine bottles were lined up throughout the room, like he was keeping count. Other were placed in groups or sometimes stood alone. Wherever he put them down.

She sighed; the disappointment and sadness she felt was much deeper than the realization called for. Her father did the same thing. Didn't even bother to throw them in the trash. And Van had cleaned up after him, night after night after night.

"Maybe you should lay off the vino and stay out of the pub for a while."

"Wha—?" He followed her gaze to the bottles. "No. You don't understand."

"Van—" Dorie's voice warned her to be quiet.

"Save it. I'm not interested in excuses. Been there, done that. Good night."

She felt Joe staring after her as she turned and almost fled the room.

"You're wrong," he called after her.

She didn't slow down, but she heard the scrape of the stool and his footsteps across the floor.

"You think you're the only one of us who isn't a failure. Well, you're not."

"Fine."

"Oh hell, what's the point." His voice cracked and he slammed the door.

Van reached the car and threw herself into the passenger seat.

"I guess that means I'm driving," Suze said.

"I never thought Joe would turn out like the rest of them, but he did. There were bottles everywhere." She slumped in her seat and covered her face with her hands, but she couldn't block out the memory.

"That's a shame," Suze said, and then they were quiet.

Dorie finally came back to the car. Got in the back.

Suze started the car and backed out.

"Maybe Joe's a little right about you," Dorie said from the back.

Van turned to face her. "What does that mean? That I'm somehow deficient because I don't approve of guys who brawl in bars. Who have empty wine bottles on every available surface? Thanks. But I don't have any sympathy. I could have spent a lifetime without ever seeing him like that."

"Do you know why he has all those wine bottles?"

"Trash day isn't until Wednesday?"

"Sarcasm doesn't become you, Van."

"Okay, why does he have wine bottles everywhere? The answer seems pretty obvious to me, but go ahead and tell me. I really need to hear the excuses. I know them all."

Van's teeth sank into her lip, creating a little specific pain to take her attention away from the pain in her heart.

"Because he's started a vineyard. He's studying the competition, deciding on labels, the design, working on a logo, and, yes, probably running some taste tests. But it's research; didn't you notice all those big reference books?"

Suze almost missed the turn, screeching into a left turn at the last minute. "Sorry."

Dorie groaned. "Don't kill the messenger."

"What big reference books?" Van hadn't seen any books . . . There had been big books lined up along the shelves. She'd assumed they were logs and tide charts.

Not tide charts; reference books. "Oh God. I'm an idiot."

"Pretty much," Dorie agreed.

"That still is no reason for him to get arrested for fighting with Bud Albright."

Dorie snorted a laugh. "Start thinking of something more than idiot to describe yourself. He wasn't arrested. They took everyone down to the station. Bud Albright started it. Joe refused to fight him. That's why he looks the way he does. Bud came looking for him tonight because Joe's been trying to talk Dana into leaving him. We all have been. So Bud's got it in his head that Joe is a rival for Dana's affections."

"That's so quaint."

They reached Dorie's. Suze pulled into the driveway and turned off the ignition.

"Don't get out. I'm not finished."

Van burned with embarrassment. She sat back to hear the rest.

"So what you saw was the effects of a man sticking up for a friend."

"Then why didn't he call his family to come get him instead of you?"

"He didn't want to worry them. And he didn't want them down at the station. And he didn't call me. Jerry did. Joe was just going to sit there until he came before the judge, bruises and all. He wasn't too happy that we went and got him."

"But why is he even working at the marina if he's got a vineyard to take care of?"

"Oh, hell, Van, he's helping out a friend. That's what friends do, in case you've forgotten."

"You make him sound like the golden boy of Whisper Beach."

"No, just an ordinary man, who cares about his family and helps his friends and has been a lifesaver to this old hen more times than I can count."

Dorie reached for the car door. "So maybe you should think about hustling your butt over there tomorrow and apologizing."

She got out and slammed the door.

"I am such an ass," Van said.

"Pretty much," Suze agreed.

"I just saw those bottles and went a little nuts. I was so angry, so outraged."

"So disappointed?"

"Yeah. He accused me of thinking they were all failures, because I had run away and made something of my life. And he was right."

And she was so wrong. "Whisper Beach obviously brings out the worst in me."

"Nah, the situation tonight just pushed all your buttons."

"It did," Van admitted. In Manhattan, she was just a normal person going about building a business, but here in Whisper Beach, she felt how tenuous her escape had been. Could still be. And it brought out the worst parts of her.

"I wish I had never come back."

"No, you don't. You're just smarting under the long lash of Dorie's whip. But she's right. You're going to have to man up and go apologize."

"I'll write him an I'm sorry card."

Suze snorted out a laugh.

"What?"

"You really think that's an adequate apology?"

"What do you suggest, I crawl across the mudflats and grovel at his feet?"

Suze frowned at her. "No, you act like a responsible adult who can admit she was wrong and apologize to a man who deserves your respect."

"I can't. I don't want to see him again."

"Tough." Suze tossed her the keys and went inside.

Chapter 15

DORIE AND DANA WERE WAITING FOR THEM IN THE KITCHEN. Dorie nodded and sat down at the table. "Getting too old for all this excitement."

"I didn't mean to cause all this trouble. I'll pack my things." Dana started for the door.

Dorie smacked her hand on the table. "Between you and Van I've never seen two people in such a hurry to leave a place and people who want them to stay. And I got three words for the both of you."

"Get over yourself," chorused Suze, Van, and even Dana who spoke the words under her breath.

"So was Joe okay?" Dana asked.

"He was until Van finished him with a one-two punch."

Dana shot a look at Van. "You didn't."

"I didn't hit him," Van said. "I just . . . we had a little misunderstanding."

"All on Van's part," Dorie said.

"Yeah, okay, all my fault. I'm going to bed." Van didn't wait for anyone to protest. She was pretty sure no one would.

Van didn't sleep all that well for obvious reasons. She'd jumped to conclusions and hurt someone she cared for—*had* cared for. Who according to all accounts was a good person. And it was because of her own insecurities and preconceptions.

Okay, so she was a bitch. She'd apologize. She'd even go and apologize in person. That would be better than having to listen to Suze moan, Dorie chastise her, and God only knew what Dana thought. Probably glad Van had made a fool of herself.

And there it was. She might as well admit it. She was petrified of appearing anything but completely put together, the happy, educated, professional success story.

Was her success so tenuous that it couldn't withstand a few honest mistakes? Would it fall in shambles if she forgave people who had also reaped the consequences of their, and subsequently her, actions?

And if the life she'd carefully built could fall apart so easily, why was she holding on to it so tightly?

THINGS DIDN'T LOOK much better when Van came down to the kitchen the next morning. She felt even more embarrassed, and she was dreading the apology she would have to make.

Dorie set a cup of coffee down at her place. *Her place.* Funny how after a few days, they already had their own places. She sat.

"Before you go apologize to Joe, will you drive Dana over to pick up some clothes? I'm getting sick of seeing that red T-shirt."

"She doesn't have to,"Dana said.

"I'll be glad to," Van said, resigned. She was determined to try to be at her best today.

"Could you drop me off at Thirtieth, or is it too far out of your way?" Suze asked.

"Of course," Van said. "Have you been summoned by les parents?"

"La mother. For lunch. I'm sure she thinks she can entice me back to the manse to work on, as Gigi called it, my little thingy. But, Dorie, don't you dare think of renting out my room. Not only is it a great place to work, but the rest of the time it's like living in reality TV."

So after a breakfast of eggs and toast that Dorie made and refused help for, Van dropped Suze off in the next town over and drove Dana across town to get her things.

Dorie had just taken the wash out of the dryer and was folding sheets when the doorbell rang. She hadn't heard Van's car return, and she didn't think Suze had been gone long enough to have come back already.

She tossed the sheet on the top of the dryer. The bell rang again before she could get down the hall to answer it. She peered out the side window.

It was Gigi. Dorie let her in.

"How come the door was locked?"

"Because we had a Bud Albright alert last night, and I decided it was better to be safe than sorry. Come on in."

"Where's Van's car?"

"She had to drop Suze off at her parents' house."

"Is Suze leaving?"

"No, she'll be back after lunch."

"So when is Van coming back?"

"I asked her to take Dana over to pick up some of her things. She's going to stay here for a while. Come on back while I finish folding the clothes."

She led Gigi back to the laundry room. Dorie saw a volatile situation on the horizon. She didn't know Gigi that well. She'd hung out at the Crab with the others and had joined them in a few of their less outrageous escapades. Even stayed overnight here a few times. But not because she was in trouble. It was more like a sleepover to her.

"Help me fold." Dorie handed one end of the sheet to Gigi. "How are the kids?"

"Fine. Did Van say when they'd be back?"

"No." Dorie made the last fold, but held on. "Are you thinking about going back to work soon?"

"I have to." Gigi's voice cracked. "I don't see why Dana doesn't go home and take care of herself."

"She isn't in a place where she can really take care of herself right now." *And neither are you.*

"Because everyone else is taking care of her."

Dorie took Gigi's end of the sheet. "It may seem that way, but everyone has to take care of themselves. Look how well Van has done, and she only had herself to rely on."

"I would have helped her. I gave her money."

"I know and she was appreciative. But there comes a time—"

"Did you hear that?"

"No. What did you hear? You don't have to worry about Bud breaking in."

"I'm not worried about him."

Gigi stressed the "him," but Dorie was at a loss as to why. There was no reason why she should be worried about Bud or anyone else.

The more Dorie saw of Gigi, the more she realized that her family and friends had done the girl a disservice. Always one of the "good" girls, that goodness had led to something close to total apathy. And to make it worse, she seemed incapable of standing on her own two feet.

"Shall I carry these upstairs?"

"Thanks. The linen closet is just outside the front bathroom."

That was a good sign. Trying to be helpful. She'd get Van to put her to work helping to restore the Crab. Maybe that would push her out of this awful lethargy.

Dorie sat down and poured herself a cup of coffee. Well, life certainly wasn't dull with these girls around, though she'd better stop thinking of them as girls. They were women, had been for a while. But hell, they still came to Dorie when the chips were down.

Gigi came back into the kitchen a few minutes later. "I put the linens away. The mail came. I put it on the hall table." She frowned. "Still nothing for Suze. I wonder what's going to happen."

"Don't you worry. Suze will take care of it—if she has to drive to the grant committee and wrestle them into giving her another chance."

"But the deadline."

"Yeah, that's a problem. I guess we'll just have to wait and see."

Van and Dana didn't talk much, except for Dana giving her directions to the apartment complex where she shared an apartment with Bud. Dana didn't invite her in, and Van didn't offer to help her pack. She waited in the car looking at the two-story strip of apartments that must have been converted from an old motel. It was pretty depressing.

"Are you sure Bud isn't going to waylay us?" Van said.

"Jerry called. He's still in jail. I guess he tried to call me to get him out, but I had my phone turned off." Dana smiled; her face was less bruised today, and she'd pretty much covered it up with makeup that she had borrowed from Dorie.

Van didn't comment. She'd forgotten how much people got into fights here. And how often it escalated into worse. "You wouldn't have gone to get him?"

Dana shrugged and got out of the car.

She was gone so long that Van was beginning to worry that she wasn't coming out again. Horrid things began to go through Van's mind: Bud had gotten out of jail and was waiting for Dana upstairs; Dana had given in to despair and was guzzling a bottle of pills.

Van was just about to go up and knock on the door when the door opened and Dana lugged out a heavy duffel bag.

Van got out to help her down the stairs. They hoisted the bag into the backseat.

"You rival Suze for heavy suitcases."

"She's planning to stay for a while, isn't she?"

"I know she'd like to. I guess it's dependent on her getting this grant. If she doesn't, she'll have to go back to Princeton to teach and try to write at the same time."

"That doesn't sound too bad."

"I guess, though I can't even imagine trying to write anything more than an apartment prospectus. Hell, even a grocery list is sometimes beyond me."

"Me, too," Dana said. "I'm not going back this time. I'm really not."

"Good for you."

"But I feel bad."

"Good God, why? He beats you, and he gets drunk and beats other people. You should have seen Joe last night. Your boyfriend is a gorilla." Van sucked in her breath. "I'm sorry. I shouldn't have said that."

"He's not. Okay, maybe he is, but he had an abusive childhood. His father was a bully."

Now, there was an excuse. Van's father was a bully, a drunk, and just plain mean. But she didn't go around beating people up.

"I thought— Well, I thought he would change."

"But he didn't," Van said, trying to sound sympathetic. Actually, she guessed she felt sympathetic. Though she didn't understand how Dana could love someone like that. Of course her mother had loved her father. Hadn't she?

Now that she thought about it, she could only remember her parents fighting. And her mother had yelled just as loud as her father. Van pulled to the curb.

"What? You want me to get out?" Dana's hand was already reaching for the door handle.

"No. No! I just freaked out for a second. Just sit. It's not about you. Well, it's sort of about you. And Bud."

"What? I'm pitiful, aren't I? I know it, and I keep going back for more. I don't know how to get him to stop what he's doing, so we just fight." She stopped, then said more quietly. "It's what we do best together."

Van turned to look at her. Really looked at her.

"I know it's no good. But I don't want to lose him."

"Why?"

Dana took a long time to answer. "I love him?"

"Is that a question?"

Dana buried her face in her hands. "I don't know. I feel sorry for him, and he knows it. And I think that's what makes him crazy."

"Well, I can understand that, because who would want someone to stay with them just because the person feels sorry for them? But I don't accept the hitting-you part."

"I know. I'm so screwed up."

Van sighed. She didn't have a word of encouragement. She had no idea what to say, more so because suddenly she began to understand what Dana was talking about. "I think there are therapists who can help."

Dana snorted. "Sure, just try to get Bud to go to one."

"What about you?"

"Me? Why would I go to one?"

"I don't know. Maybe because it takes two of you to make an argument."

"You don't know Bud."

And Van was glad she didn't. "When is he going to stop, Dana? When he breaks your bones, when he kills you?"

Dana finally looked up. "Joe says the same thing, but Bud wouldn't kill me, would he?"

"I have no idea. I lived with an abusive father, but he stopped at yelling at my mother. I don't think he ever hit her. I never was aware of it if he did."

"You told everybody that he killed her."

"Well, he did in a way. She wanted him to pick her up from work, but he was drunk and told her to get a ride. She walked home instead. It was rainy, the streets were slick, and a car slid into her when she was only two blocks away. She almost made it home." Van sucked in air as the pain of that night filled her.

Dana stared. "That's it?"

"You need more?"

"Why didn't she just get a ride?"

It was Van's turn to stare. It was just what Nate had said. And for the first time in her life, Van asked herself, *Why hadn't she gotten a ride home? If she had . . . if she had, what?* Life would have gone on, all of them miserable and trapped in a cold, unloving family. As it was, the family dissolved. She didn't know what had happened to her father, and she didn't care.

Her mother's death had driven Van and her father apart. They struggled along for a couple of years, living in the same space, ignoring each other. Instead of being happy that the wife he didn't love was dead, her father spiraled down to a place that Van couldn't imagine, locking his bedroom door and not communicating. Van went to school and work, came home, and left the money she made on the kitchen table.

Then the rest of her life fell apart, and it was the best thing that had ever happened to her.

"I think you have to leave him permanently, Dana."

Dana nodded, and Van looked away as the tears started to fall.

She pulled back into traffic and drove back to the beach. She was totally out of her area of expertise. She might not have helped Dana, but she'd made things clearer for herself. No more expecting the worst—from people or from life. She'd drop Dana off and then go to the marina and apologize.

Van stopped at Dorie's and went inside. She knew it was stupid, but even though she was just going to the marina long enough to apologize, she didn't want to look thrown together. A little light makeup was in order.

She stuck her head into the kitchen before she left.

"I'm going to apologize, Dorie. When I get back, if you want, we can start going over some ideas for the Crab."

"Okay. Just so you know. Gigi was here."

"Oh damn, I forgot about Gigi."

"I told her Suze was out for the day and you had business to take care of and we'd see her tomorrow. I think we could all use a break. And, besides, I think we should have a little chat about her. But it can wait. Get going. And don't hurry back."

Van gave her a look that made Dorie shrug innocently.

She arrived at the marina much too quickly. She had tried to think of a way to apologize that would sound intelligent and sincere, and that she would still come out unscathed. She wasn't having much success.

She saw Joe standing on the bow of a fishing boat, giving instructions to another person. They were laughing. Joe's rich baritone and a higher tenor.

She couldn't see the other person, and for one mortifying second she was afraid she'd interrupted something she shouldn't.

Then a head appeared from the cabin. It was a young boy. He tossed some rope to Joe. Joe reeled it in and climbed down to stow it in the utility hutch. The boy leaned over, looking in, and Van could tell Joe was explaining to him how to keep the coils from tangling.

And the image burned into her heart. This is the way she had always imagined Joe, his son beside him working at the dairy or, she guessed now, the vineyard, with her inside with dinner ready, waiting for their return home.

But that had been then. And here he was with a child. What about the wife? She hadn't thought that Joe had been married. Surely someone would have mentioned it.

There was a cold, rapidly growing pit in her stomach. She wished she could just back up and drive away. But she knew she couldn't until she'd apologized.

Joe looked up and saw her car. Said something to the boy, who had stopped to look, too.

Reluctantly Van got out. She wasn't sure of her reception. She watched Joe say something else to the boy, who went back to work, then Joe jumped to the ground and started toward her.

She met him halfway across the yard.

"Hey," he said.

She looked past him. "Who's your helper?"

Joe looked back. "Owen. And I'm not exactly sure what his story is, but Bud caught him clamming one night; the others got away."

"Leave it to Bud to pick on a kid."

"Yeah; anyway, I told Bud that he was working for me. He didn't believe me but there wasn't much he could do. And damn if the kid didn't show up the next day, ready to work."

"Lucky kid."

Joe shrugged.

"No, really. This was always such a great place to hang out."

"When the tide was in," he said.

"When the tide was in," she agreed. They had all sat on the old pier with sodas, sometimes beer, waiting for a breeze, or for the next round of friends to show up.

Sometimes they'd pile into someone's truck or walk down to the Dairy Queen.

"It's gotten a little shabby. Well, a lot shabby. Grandy's been sick."

"Dorie told me. Is it serious?"

"Yes, but things are looking better now. He's coming back next week. And I have to get back home."

She nodded. "Joe, I'm sorry about the way I acted last night. I jumped to the wrong conclusion. It was a stupid thing to do. It was just . . . I . . . preconceived ideas . . . stupid . . . uncalled for."

He was smiling at her.

"What?"

"I don't think I've ever known you to stumble for words."

"Especially last night, you mean."

"Well, appearances did lean toward your analysis. It just happened to be wrong."

"Well, I'm sorry. Truly. That's all." She turned to go.

"Wait."

She stopped.

"You didn't give me my turn."

She turned resolutely around. She should have known she wouldn't get off this easy.

"I'm sorry I lashed out at you. I just got so angry that you would think— Well, I take those words back. If I can."

"No need. I know I'm an uptight bitch. Well, not a bitch most of the time. But I like to be in control."

"You always did."

"Because there was so much that I couldn't."

"I know. I always admired that about you."

There was a pause in the conversation, a perfect time for Van to turn around and leave. But she didn't. "Dorie says you've planted a vineyard."

"Hence all the wine bottles. They're local wines that I've been studying."

"Why wine?"

He shrugged.

Standing face-to-face, Van finally took the time to look at Joe. In spite of his bruises from the previous night, she could tell that he'd matured well, filled out but not too much. He was trim and fit and still had his hair as far as she could tell. Close shaved. Even with all that dark hair, he'd never had much of a beard when they were young. And he'd grown into the determined jawline and the sun-crinkled eyes of the older Enthorpes.

"I needed something that could compete with other farms when I only had twenty acres to play with."

"Is that enough to compete?"

"Well, I decided to go organic. That was the best chance we had of turning enough profit to, you know, to live comfortably. Plus, I like the idea of organic. Get the real flavor of the wine, not just the additives.

"I should be able to hold my own if the vines are productive and barring any disasters.

"Sorry, your eyes are probably glazing over. It's something that I don't get to enthuse about too much. The guys at Mike's aren't exactly connoisseurs."

"I think it sounds fascinating. Really. I was just wondering . . . how you went from dairy farming to vintnering. Is that what it's called?"

"Viniculture. Growing grapes for wine. When Dad and Granddad sold the dairy farm, I looked around for some way to make the land productive. Actually, first I got really angry. I'd just spent three years learning how to streamline the dairy. Then it was gone."

"Oh, Joe, I'm sorry."

"Yeah, well, I was pretty pissed, there were a few scenes, then I packed up and left home."

"You? Left home?"

"Well, I packed up and went back to school. Where I began studying viniculture. I'd already taken some courses. It's kind of fascinating."

"So you learned how to grow grapes and came home and planted them?"

"Granddad and Dad thought I was crazy. There were a few rough years. So I went to work at a New York State vineyard. Learned the ropes. Spent a year and a half in California, same thing. I even went to France and Italy."

"You're kidding."

"I know; crazy, right? Joe Enthorpe in Europe."

"Not crazy. Did you learn the language?"

"Sure I did." He smiled. "*Tres bien* and *arrivederci*."

She punched his arm.

"Well, I did learn a bit more than that. By the time I came home, they were willing to listen. I think my mother had something to do with it."

Van smiled. Mrs. Enthorpe was quiet and never even raised her voice, but she ruled the roost in that household.

"That's so great, Joe. When I heard you'd sold the farm, I was afraid—"

"That I had gone to work at the marina, became a drunk, and started fights in bars."

She blushed.

"It's okay. If I had been more coherent last night, I could have explained. You want to see the vineyards? I have photos on my computer upstairs."

"I'd love to." Awkwardness and disappointment had morphed into a kind of comfortable familiarity.

They went up the steps and Joe opened the door for her.

"Sorry about the mess. All my stuff is living on top of Grandy's stuff."

The room was definitely crowded. Last night Van had only been aware of Joe and all the wine bottles. In the daylight without the drama, the room appeared just as it had years ago. The counter. The shelves of fishing gear and emergency angler and boating supplies. A case of new and used rods and reels. A wall mount of fishing nets, bags of lures, hooks, coils of nylon rope, plastic containers of wax, oil, and sealant, and a display of candies and chips that looked like they might have been the same ones from years ago.

To that Joe had added a desk and chair that abutted the glass window, a bookshelf filled with books. An easy chair had been shoved into a far corner. He must sleep in the tiny office whose door Van could see over the counter.

Joe led her over to the desk where his laptop was set up. "Have a seat."

He closed the book he must have been reading, tossed it to the side, then turned the desk chair toward her. She sat down. Joe dragged a plastic molded chair over and sat beside her, rummaged through some papers on the desk, and found a pair of horn-rimmed glasses.

She looked over to him and smiled. "You wear glasses?"

Joe held them up and looked at them as if this was a surprise to him, too. "For a few years, for reading." He put them on.

He reached across her and opened a file. The screen was filled with rows of lush green grapevines.

"Is that your land?"

"Yep. Renzo, that's my foreman, just sent these photos over a few days ago. This is our third year, so the vines are producing their first real crop."

He clicked through a few photos. "Here's what they looked like when we first planted them."

Van leaned closer to study what appeared to be little sticks rising up from the plowed earth.

"And this is the next spring." He brought up more photos.

Straight rows of wire trellises supported by evenly spaced metal posts. The area between the rows neatly mowed. And the fledgling vines, trained to grow up and along the wires.

"They've really grown," she said enthusiastically. Then shrugged. "At least it seems that way to me."

"They're doing well. Knock wood." Joe knocked on the desk, and so did Van. This gained her a smile from Joe. They looked at each other until Joe pulled away. "And here's last fall."

Another photo at another angle, some close-ups, then one with a young man and woman with a little girl.

"Is that Maddy?" Van asked.

"Yeah. They were back visiting for Thanksgiving."

"They? Is that her family?"

"Yeah. She and her husband and little girl, Josephine—we call her Josie. Three Joes and a Josie all in the same house for the holidays is little confusing, but hey. They live in Ohio. They're expecting another kid pretty soon now."

Van smiled, but she suddenly felt very sad. And that was something new for her. She'd long ago accepted that she would never be a mother, nor a part of this boisterous family.

"Are you doing this by yourself or did your dad finally come around?"

"Drew and Brett decided to invest. We made a chunk of change on the land we sold. And a big chunk of it was divided up among the kids.

"Dad retired, but the Enthorpes have never been a family to sit back and do nothing. He was alternating between watching television and walking out to look at the condos where the pastures used to be. Granddad was cranky and . . . well, they were driving Mom crazy. Since they've gotten involved they still make fun and complain, but they're happy as two clams."

He changed the photo again. An aerial shot of the acreage planted in grapevines.

Van could see the stream where they sometimes fished and swam and that edged the planted land. She remembered the fun they'd had. And eating early dinner with the family, a loud raucous crowd, who had opened their home to her. As Joe spoke she could see them all as if she were back there again. And she realized that those dinners and afternoons had been the bright spots in her life and she'd forgotten them in the overpowering memory of unhappiness.

"Thanks."

Joe frowned at her. "For showing you photos of our vineyard?"

"Yeah." *And your enthusiasm, your family and your love for them, and for being an anchor for me when I didn't even appreciate it. Didn't even know I should appreciate it.*

"If you'd like to see it, I mean up close and personal, I'd love to take you out there. I'm sure everyone else would love to see you. Dad was just asking about you the other day."

"Thanks. I'd like to see it, but I— I'm only here for another ten days and I promised Dorie I would help streamline the Crab.

It hasn't come into the twenty-first century. She's trying to do it all herself, and she's got overlap, and inefficiency, and well . . . It could take me some time."

"Is that why you're back? To help Dorie?"

"No. I was on my way to— I'm on vacation. I stopped to attend Clay Daly's funeral and the rest as they say is history."

"Dorie suckered you into staying?"

"Pretty much. I didn't see you at the funeral."

"I couldn't make it." He clicked out of the file; the screen went dark.

Van wondered about the abrupt change in mood.

"You do restaurants, too?"

"Too?"

Joe shrugged. "I've seen your website."

"Yeah. I own and operate a sort of glorified cleaning, housekeeping, scheduling service. You know, for busy Manhattan families that don't have time to do it all, and aren't organized enough to do what they do efficiently."

"Basically you fix people's lives."

"You mean since I didn't do such a great job with my own?"

He lifted her right out of the chair, held her arms, and looked directly into her eyes. "You did a great job with what you had. I always admired that. If you— I understand that you had to get away, but I'm sorry if I was the thing that drove you to it. I'm still not sure what I did, but if it was me, I'm truly sorry."

"Joe, it was just circumstances. Better left in the past where it belongs."

"So you aren't going to tell me?"

"Joe, I don't—" What could she say? She didn't remember? That was a blatant lie. And he would see through it; he'd always seen through her. That had been what she loved most about him; he saw through her and still liked—loved—what he saw.

She shook her head, suddenly having trouble trying to talk. She took a breath. "It's all good. And I'm so glad things are working out with the vineyard. But I have to get back."

They both seemed to realize that he was still holding her in place. He let go, she stepped back.

"So you're staying at Dorie's."

"Isn't that a kick?"

"Suze, too?"

Van nodded. Reluctantly smiled. "And Dana, too, though please don't tell Bud."

"How do you think I got these bruises?"

"Not a drunken brawl."

"Well, I can't speak for Bud and the other bozos that joined in, but last night I was wearing all those beers, not drinking them."

"I just—"

Joe put his fingers over her mouth. "Jumped to the wrong conclusion. I know. It's okay, as long as the next time you jump, give me the benefit of the doubt."

"Deal."

"So it's like a weeklong slumber party over there, huh?"

She gave him a look that made him laugh.

"That is so you. I'm glad to see that hasn't changed."

"Unlike the rest of me?"

"The rest of you seems fine, too. I just wasn't at my best last night."

"Neither was I." Van walked to the door.

He opened it for her. "So if you finish up with the Crab and change your mind about going out to the farm, or if you just want to have coffee or something, give me a ring."

"Okay. Thanks." She stood there for a second, indecisive. Did she just walk away? Shake hands? Give him a quick hug?

He walked down the steps ahead of her, and she followed him. He opened her car door and she climbed in, smiled at him before he closed the door.

And she drove away.

Chapter 16

Is that your girlfriend, Joe?" Owen got up from where he was sitting on an empty boat trailer, reading a comic.

"She used to be."

"She's really pretty."

"Yeah, she is."

"How come she's not your girlfriend now?"

"I'm not really sure," Joe said.

"Man, that's stupid. I think you oughta get her back."

"Thanks for the advice, man. You finish untangling those dock lines?"

"Yeah."

"Then what do you say to some lunch?"

Since Joe didn't keep food in the marina office, they drove into town to a local place known for its homemade pasta and thin crust pizza. Ordered enough food for three grown men.

Owen dug in with enthusiasm.

Joe thought about Van.

He'd left it in her court, whether they would see each other again or not. Maybe not the smartest move he ever made. But he wasn't totally sure he wanted to see her again.

No, that was a total lie. If the glimpse of Van he'd had today was the real Van, then he absolutely wanted to see her again.

But if this was just her on good behavior because Dorie had made her come apologize, something he wouldn't put past their old friend, then he should let it go.

He didn't want to open up only to be shut down again. He sure didn't want to go through that kind of heartbreak again, and he doubted she did either.

So he'd wait and see. He had plenty to do, maybe too much, to embark on reawakening their relationship. As intriguing as the idea was, his work came first.

Next week he'd shut down Grandy's for all but the regulars who could fend for themselves. Grandy would be home from the hospital by then, and though he wouldn't be able to run the marina, he'd be able to oversee the daily operations. Maybe he could get Owen to come after school to help.

The kid was a good worker and needed the money. From the little Owen had said, Joe knew he lived with his mother and two younger sisters. And that he'd started going out with the clam diggers to help stretch the limited food budget.

Labor intensive, illegal, and too late for a kid to be staying up if he planned on getting to school the next day. He could be a big help to Grandy.

Joe would move back to the farm, concentrate on the vineyards, get the grapes harvested. Start the fermentation process. Then he'd start planning for the next leg. Tasting room and possibly a store. He'd have to run the numbers. And of course it was dependent on the success of the crop.

He wondered if Van could help him with the setup of the winery. Then he dismissed the idea. She had her work in Manhattan, which she was probably anxious to get back to. He doubted she would be interested in a little winery and vineyard.

Then again, she was helping Dorie fix up the Crab.

But would she be interested in helping him? And would he want her to? There was a time when he thought he'd spend the rest of his life with her, but that was a long time ago. He hadn't found anyone since that he'd felt as strongly about, who he could share everything with—until today. The first couple of times they'd met this past week, it was awkward and she was definitely standoffish, but today . . . today it had almost been like before. Her enthusiasm fueled his. He'd fallen into an energy he knew so well, so quickly, that it was kind of scary. And she had, too.

Was it worth it, just to see where it would go? Was he totally self-destructive to take the chance? Was this a temptation that was bound to fail?

"Are you going to eat that last ravioli?"

Owen had finished his spaghetti, and a slice of pizza. Joe pushed his plate across the table. The kid would make himself sick eating so much, like a feral puppy afraid his next meal might not come.

Joe motioned to the waitress, a woman he'd known in high school, and ordered a large spaghetti and meatballs to go.

Dorie looked around the kitchen of the Blue Crab as she sipped a cup of coffee. The whole thing needed upgrading. But she didn't have the money to do it right. Hell, she didn't have the money to do squat. If Van really did take on the Crab as a project, Dorie would have to pay her on time.

At least she'd put aside enough money to keep going for a while in spite of Harold's sticky fingers. He had his shortcomings, but, hell, he'd never raised a hand to her.

Dorie chuckled. She'd like to see him try. Harold wasn't so bad in the scheme of men. But it seems the older he got, the more discontented he got. She kept thinking he would run out of steam, but no.

Though she had to admit, she'd rather have him running around than sitting around after work watching television and doing nothing. They suited each other.

But the kitchen, on the other hand, had fallen to an all-time low. It was clean—hell, she didn't need health department problems—but the appliances were old. And she'd accumulated so many utensils and God knows what, she wouldn't even know where to begin sorting and organizing them.

But Van did. She'd walked right in wearing that little bikini, taken one look, and started moving things around. The kitchen already looked less cluttered, and with a little effort they would uncover enough counter space to accommodate an extra food prep station or two.

Yep, the Crab could be hopping again instead of hanging on by its pincers, crowded in the summer, closed down in the winter. Most people were still willing to wait for a table, wait for the food. Dorie had kept prices down by hiring a young waitstaff, giving work to a few kids during the summer while keeping her costs down.

But she should have been giving them more training. And she should have kept a few regulars on for the transition between seasons, not have to hire new staff at the end of the summer.

The waitress-busboy collision in the restaurant yesterday was one of many.

Dorie crossed to the fridge and pulled out two boxes of frozen lobster ravioli. Another large container of her vodka sauce. It was homemade; she knew because she'd made it herself. The ravioli weren't, but they were from a local market who made them.

She tried to buy local when she could. She chuckled. She always had. Now it was something called "artisan." Restaurants charged an arm and a leg for some of the same food Dorie served for a song.

But local markets were becoming scarcer with the loss of one family business after another: Whitaker's poultry farm, Fratelli's bakery, the Enthorpes' dairy farm. She'd been through three different vegetable markets and finally had to move to a wholesaler for most of her produce.

It couldn't be helped, but it wasn't the same. Maybe she should let Van go on to her vacation and call it quits.

Van had thought she would apologize and leave, and that would be that, one more loose end tied up. But she didn't feel like she'd tied anything up, except maybe tying the past more firmly to the present, and maybe her feeling for Joe tied firmly to the man.

For a few minutes looking at the photos of the vineyard, it was almost like she'd never left. So much so that she was almost surprised when she stood up from the computer and they were in the present again, both a decade older.

Dangerous, she told herself. Dangerous to pretend that things could be the same again. Besides, it was impossible. Why was she even thinking like this?

Dana was sitting at the kitchen table reading the newspaper when Van returned to the house.

"Back so soon?"

"It's not so soon." Van gave her a sour look, though she wasn't even annoyed, more amused than anything. "Catching up on current events?"

Dana held up a pencil. "Looking at the want ads."

"Any luck?"

Dana returned Van's sour look. "Same old, same old."

"Dorie said you studied to be a manicurist."

"Yeah. Dumb work, looking at other people's fingers for a living. But better than waitressing where you're on your feet all day."

Van thought she should be thanking her lucky stars to even have that, instead of grousing, but that was Dana, through and through.

"Suze back?"

"Nope. But Dorie said if you're interested, she's over at the Crab."

"Great. Want to come?" Van asked as an afterthought.

"No . . . thanks." Dana went backing to perusing the want ads.

Van went upstairs to get her notes, then headed over to the restaurant.

She found Dorie standing in the middle of the kitchen, not exactly a queen surveying her kingdom, but close.

"You're back. How did things go with Joe?"

"Okay."

"Just okay?"

Van went over to the coffeepot. "They went fine, but don't get any ideas. How old is this coffee?"

"Fresh. What kind of ideas?"

"You know the kind where Joe and I fall madly in love again like some Hallmark movie."

Dorie snorted. "I wouldn't be so naive. But did you get along?"

Van poured herself a cup of coffee. "Yeah, actually we did." She sat down, looked across the table at Dorie. "It was kind of freaky," she admitted. "For a few minutes it was like it always was. He showed me photos of the vineyard. It's amazing, he's amazing. He just reinvented himself when the dairy farm closed."

"See, you still have a lot in common."

Van raised her eyebrows. "Reinvention."

"Are you going to see him again?"

Van shrugged. "He said if I'd like to go out to the farm and see the family, to call him."

"That boy." Dorie heaved a huge sigh. "Are you going to call?"

"No. I mean, it just seems like something that doesn't need to be done. I'll be leaving in a few days, and that will be that."

"And is that how you want to leave things? 'That will be that'?"

"Dorie, I left things long ago. It's senseless to revisit them or open up any old wounds."

Dorie stopped. "Yours or his?"

It took Van a second to respond. "Both, I guess."

"Huh."

"I— I still like him, I think. He's growing grapes. I know he must have been pretty devastated when they had to sell the dairy farm. It's all he ever wanted to do. Run the family farm. But he figured out what he could do and did it. You have to admire that."

"Yes. you do. What about the rest of him?"

"The rest of him?"

"Don't be dense."

Van smiled, though she didn't want to. "That's nice, too. It always was. Now do you want to talk about the Crab or not?"

"Hit me with it."

"I've made some notes, mainly about traffic patterns and cosmetics. Come out to the dining room."

Dorie pushed open the swinging door.

"First problem. Do you know how many near misses you have every time a new order comes up?"

"Don't tell me. I just cross my fingers and hope for the best."

"That is not a plan. We'll have to look at a few options and choose one to implement."

"I don't have a lot of money to spend on upgrades—or to pay you for your expertise."

"Really, Dorie? After all you've done for me, you think I'm going to let you pay?"

"Damn straight you are. But the other . . ." Dorie trailed off.

"We'll come up with a compromise. Now here is another major problem, but an easy fix. I was working from memory, so this is not exact." Van showed Dorie the schematic of the dining room she'd gridded out on the graph paper. "I know you're strapped for table space in the summers, but you have to lose at least one of these tables by the kitchen door. You'll save on glasses and china. It's just a matter of time before someone trips and dumps food all over the diners sitting there. If we move this one and reroute waitstaff and bus staff, we should be able to . . ." Van explained her ideas for making the transporting of food more efficient.

"Why didn't I think of that?" Dorie asked as she stood at Van's shoulder comparing the drawing to the current arrangement of tables.

Van grinned at her. "Because then you wouldn't need me."

Dorie laughed. "What else?"

"I've got a lot of suggestions, but we won't be able to implement them until after this weekend when I mean to watch the staff in action."

"That makes sense." Dorie turned on her. "You're not going to get everything discombobulated, then leave me before it's done?"

"No, of course not. We can get the major points accomplished next week. Then there are some other long-range projects you can start at your leisure, if you even want to do them."

"Like what?"

"Well," Van said, hedging, "those of us who have been coming here forever love the 'ambiance.' But if you were serious about staying open off-season, you'll need to appeal to a wider demographic."

"English, please."

"If you want some high-class diners to come here, you might want to dust the plastic flowers or even put fresh flowers on the tables.

"You can spiff things up without losing the old feel of the place. I mean, when was the last time you painted?"

"Painted?"

"That answers my question. The wood trim is fine, dark—and rich if given a good oiling, but you need to move out of the dark-doesn't-show-dirt restaurant mentality and brighten the place up at bit. Small things but a big difference. Then with the table rearrangement, there will be several clear paths to the silverware and condiment station, which you can camouflage with a decorative screen or something; that will give you a lot more space out of sight of the diners. I mean, do people really want to look at trays of mustard and ketchup while they 'dine'?"

"Nobody's complained yet."

"And they won't, because it's all fine, but you're the one—"

"I know that I said I wanted to save this old albatross. And you're right. I'm not going to make it on the cops coming in when they get off their shifts. Or the old regulars who come once a week if I'm lucky but usually only a couple of times a month.

"Hell, I wish there was a way to predict if it will be worth the bother."

Van dropped her clipboard and put her hands on her hips. "What do you want?"

Dorie wrestled with a smile. "Oh, all right. I said I wanted to upgrade the joint. What else do I have to do?"

They spent the next few hours studying the restaurant from front door to kitchen. Dorie telling Van what she envisioned for the Crab, and Van making a list of ways to achieve it. They argued about several things. But they were minor, like redesigning the paper placemats or whether they could dispense with them altogether by refinishing the tables.

But Van didn't want to get too carried away or she might find herself back in Whisper Beach on weekends. *Not that it would be so awful,* she thought. Especially if Suze would be staying over the winter. Actually, it sounded sort of relaxing.

"What?" Dorie asked.

"I was just thinking."

"About what?"

"You wouldn't want to know."

They finally called it a day when Suze phoned to say she was back and complaining about starvation and the absence of happy hour.

"Uncork the wine," Van said. "We're on our way."

"I can't find the corkscrew," wailed Suze.

Van thought. It had been on the toaster, then Suze had used it last night and put it on the . . . "It's next to the kitchen telephone."

"You're brilliant. Hurry up."

Van hung up. "She's hungry and couldn't find the corkscrew."

"Gotta love her," Dorie said.

Van packed up her papers and put them in her carryall. "Did Suze tell you that she's thinking about staying for the winter?"

"Sure. We talked about it weeks ago. I'll be glad to have her."

"And did the two of you plot to get me to come back for Clay's funeral?"

"My, my, you do think you're the center of our universe." Dorie headed for the door.

Van hurried to catch up. "No, I don't. I just—"

"Stop being so prickly. I bet you dollars to donuts you don't act this skittish around your other clients."

"You're sort of more than my client, Dorie."

"Well, that's good to know. But no. I called her after I e-mailed you. And told her what I'd done."

"So you coerced *her* into coming."

"Not really; she was coming anyway, but not until after she got the grant. Come on, we can walk and talk at the same time."

They locked up and crossed the street. There weren't many cars today. They might get a few more weekends of foot traffic, but there wasn't much else around here to draw in crowds during the off-season.

"I'm an idiot." Van turned around and looked back toward the beach and the ocean stretching out to the horizon. "You're one of the few restaurants right on the water."

"So?"

"Is the Crab weatherized?"

"Yeah, from back when the hotel was open three seasons."

"Oceanside dining. It would appeal to the trendy set, I bet. I'll make a couple of calls and get a second opinion. It could stay the beach joint for the season, then streamline in the off-season to accommodate people in the know. It might work." Van looked at Dorie. "If you think you really want to put that much work into it."

"Can I charge higher prices off-season?"

"I bet you can; that's one of the questions I'll ask."

"I'd need it to make a profit enough to support me. Between

you and me, Harold has spent everything. There's nothing left for our retirement money. Harold has spent it all on one scheme or another."

"Dorie, why do you let him spend your money? Why do you let him keep coming back?"

They were walking shoulder to shoulder down the sidewalk. Now Dorie slowed.

Dorie shrugged. "We're a pair like salt-and-pepper shakers, different as different, and yet we go together."

Van thought she sounded an awful lot like Dana.

"He's still looking for that pie in the sky. And if he finds it, I know he'll share it, he always did.

"Worse comes to worse I'll turn the house into rentals, or maybe I should just sell the damn thing."

Van did a double take. "The house?"

"The Crab."

"You'd consider selling?"

"I've gotten some pretty hefty offers."

"And?"

"And? For one, what would I do with myself? And two, I know Harold would manage to blow it all and then where would I be?"

Van hoped that was a rhetorical question, because she didn't have a clue. For a wild second she thought, *Silent partner.* She'd been planning to expand her business into another city. But she could invest in the Crab instead. And have Harold steal her money, too?

No, Dorie would just have to do the best she could, with a little help from her friends.

When the two arrived back at Dorie's, Suze was sitting in the parlor, an open bottle of white wine on the table, and the air-conditioning going full blast.

"How was your day?" Van asked.

"Hmmph," Suze said.

"Oh dear, not going well."

Suze threw herself back into her chair, one hand over her forehead like a melodrama heroine. "Nothing's going well. The work is fine, but I still haven't heard from the grant people. What is so hard about returning one of my fifty calls?"

"Can we just drive over and pick up the forms? I have a car."

"To Cincinnati? Scholars from all over the country have applied for this money. I worked my butt off to make it down to the finalists, and for what." Suze groaned and switched hands. "But that's not the worst."

"There's worse?" Van wasn't sure she wanted to hear any more bad news.

"My mother is having a 'drinks' party on Sunday."

"Oh."

"She just never lets up. She did her down-the-nose thing at me staying here at Dorie's. Really got frosty when I told her we were having a reunion."

"I'd hardly call it that."

"It is sort of, and besides I was being gratuitously ornery."

Van laughed. "I like that—'gratuitously ornery.' I'm going to remember to use that with a few of my clients. So you had a fight?"

"One doesn't fight with my mother. She just hands down edicts. Like my attendance at the 'drinks' party."

"That seems a small price to pay."

Suze rolled her eyes. Van swore they were all turning into Dorie. "She wants to take me shopping so I won't embarrass her in front of her guests."

"She didn't say that."

"No, she said there would be single men there and she wanted me to make a good impression."

"Ouch. So are you going shopping?"

"No. I told her I was bringing a date."

"Really? Who?"

Suze slumped back in the chair. "I thought maybe I'd call Jerry and see if he was available."

She gave Van such a bland look that Van burst out laughing.

"I know. Fish out of water. Do you think he'll do it?"

"Call and see, but are you sure you want to put the poor man through one of your mother's cocktail parties?"

"I guess it wouldn't be fair, would it?"

Van shrugged. "But it would be very interesting."

"I just might do it. I'll warn him, of course. It wouldn't be fair to let him enter the lion's den unprepared."

"Poor Jerry."

"The other alternative is for you to go with me."

"Thanks, but let's try Jerry first."

Chapter 17

The first thing Van did the next morning was call the office, but not to check up on them; they'd be doing fine. The good part of setting up something efficiently was that it practically ran itself. The problem with it was . . . It practically ran itself.

"I'm not calling to check up on you," Van told Ellen before she had a chance to complain. "I need your expertise. I need the names of . . ." Van explained what she wanted.

"This does not sound like lying on the beach to me," Ellen said.

"A friend of mine owns a restaurant here. She just needs some advice about restructuring. I thought maybe she could get in touch with somebody who has experience. What was the name of the guy in the penthouse on Sixty-Eighth? He's a restaurateur. We just restructured his second bedroom into an IT center, remember? Thought he could help my friend to restructure her restaurant."

"First promise me that you're having a good time."

"I am." Now that she had something to do.

"And you're meeting hot men."

"That too."

"Pinky swear?"

"Pinky swear."

"Okay, his name is Milo Duchamp. Here's his e-mail and cell."

Van took down the information. As soon as she hung up, she called Mr. Duchamp and left a message for him to call her.

She went downstairs to get a cup of coffee. Suze and Dana were there. Dorie had gone to the Crab to wait for deliveries.

"What's on the agenda today?" she asked.

"Working and waiting for the mail," Suze said.

"Reading the want ads," Dana said.

"No luck yet?"

"No," both said.

Van sat down to drink her coffee and look over her plans while she waited for Duchamp to call her back.

He did a half hour later. He remembered her very well. He loved his home office. She explained what she was doing and what she needed to know. He agreed to look over a prospectus once she had a better handle on the situation.

After they hung up, Van went online and began looking at restaurant supplies. Storage bins, tables, chairs. She made notes and took screen shots.

She had a week left. She knew she could turn the environment and organization of the Blue Crab around in that time. But retraining the staff would be Dorie's responsibility, and Van wanted to oversee her inauguration of that effort. Dorie ran the Crab on the laissez-faire principle. If she wanted to jump to the next level, she'd have to be more labor intensive.

A week left. It would definitely take that long to set up a long-range plan for the Crab. She also had to decide what to do with her house, which meant she'd have to talk to Uncle Nate.

And she wanted to see Joe again. Which was probably crazy. She should leave well enough alone. But she wanted more. But how much more? To solidify their friendship, get to know him better? For what reason? Have a chance to say good-bye and good luck?

All that and the restaurant, too? Absolutely. She was revved. This was her idea of a vacation.

She jumped when there was a knock at the door.

Suze stuck her head in. "Gigi's downstairs. I told her you were working, but you'd be right down."

"Damn, I forgot." She'd called and made plans last night before they went to bed. And then forgot all about them in her excitement about talking with Duchamp. "Tell her I'll be right down. Does she have her swimsuit?"

Suze nodded. "And her sunglasses. And don't look at me. I'm staying in my room until further notice."

Van sighed. She was not looking forward to a day on the beach. It wasn't Gigi; it was the doing nothing. She changed into her bikini, slipped her notebook into a carryall, just in case she had a minute to study it, and went downstairs.

"Sorry I took so long," Van said when she reached the foyer where Gigi was waiting. "I was just finishing up some things I need to get for reorganizing the Crab."

Gig sighed. "You're not starting today, are you?" The disappointment on her face was pathetic.

"No. Have you had lunch? I'm kind of hungry. I can't even remember having breakfast."

"I ate already." And she didn't look like she wanted to wait for Van to have lunch.

"Let me just grab us some waters and a snack and we'll go." Van needed fortification if she was going to really sit down and talk with Gigi, encourage her to get on with her life and whatever else Nate expected her to do.

She grabbed a couple of apples, some grapes, and two bottles of water. Put them in her carryall with her notes and went out to get Gigi.

"Isn't Suze coming?" Gigi asked.

"No. She has to work. It's just the two of us. Is that okay?"

Gigi shrugged.

Van tried not to feel impatient. Gigi wasn't happy when they were all together, and she didn't seem happy to have Van all to herself. Closets and kitchens—even nannies—were so much simpler to understand.

She was all too aware of the divide between Suze and her and Dana and Gigi. She didn't think she was being snobbish. Well, hell, that was absurd. But she was independent, and Suze was a respected scholar. Dana hadn't seemed to have moved past teenage flirt. Gigi was a widow with two children and still living with her parents. Well, maybe Van could help remedy at least the latter.

She just wished the idea of sitting in the sand all day didn't feel like such a chore.

At least it would give her time to let Gigi talk. Find out what was really going on in that mind of hers. Blurting out that your husband didn't love you in the middle of Main Street didn't qualify as a heart-to-heart.

And what about her children? How were they coping through all this? Gigi had barely mentioned them. Were they in school? Who was taking and picking them up? Amelia? Van hadn't even asked. Well, she'd ask about them today.

Gigi was waiting outside. She'd already gotten the beach chairs out of the shed. She picked hers up as soon as Van reached the porch. It was like she couldn't wait to get to the beach. Or away from the others? Was Van missing some subtext that Suze had picked up on?

When they got to the beach, Gigi led the way down the steps, but instead of stopping on the sand she kept walking toward the pier, then passed underneath it. The air immediately became fetid and dense. It would have felt clammy if it had been colder, but as it was, it was just uncomfortable.

Gigi was determined to go to Whisper Beach. That was fine with Van. One small group was sitting beneath a bright beach umbrella. The rest of the beach was empty.

They set up their chairs and put on sunscreen.

As soon as she sat down, Van's mind wandered back to the day she and Joe had talked out here looking at the river. She would like to see his family. His vineyard.

She smiled thinking about the two of them sitting over the computer.

"What's so funny?" Gigi asked.

"Oh, nothing. Just happy to be out on the beach." Van put on her sunglasses. Tried to think of something to talk about. She didn't understand why it was hard. She and Gigi had always told each other everything.

"So tell me the names of your children again."

"Clay Junior and Amy."

"Are they in school?"

"Clay Junior is going to kindergarten next week. Amy is only three. Mom says I should put her in day care and go back to work, but I don't know. Clay didn't want me to work. Said children needed to have their mother around to give them proper guidance."

"Most of my clients with children either send them out or have a nanny."

"Send them out? You make them sound like laundry."

"Did I? I didn't mean to. I like children."

"What happened to yours?"

"What?"

"You were pregnant when you left, remember? That's what you told me. Why you had to leave."

Of course Van remembered. It wasn't the kind of thing a person could forget even if she tried. "I miscarried."

"Then why didn't you come back?"

How could she tell Gigi that Whisper Bay held nothing for her? That she'd tried to forget living here. Tried to forget her family, and Joe and all of them. Because it was the only way she could pretend to look toward the future instead of being dragged down and strangled by her own abiding fear that she would turn out like her mother had.

That in Whisper Beach she wouldn't be strong enough to say what she wanted to be. That she couldn't be anything here. That she was afraid if she did come back she'd end up like Dana or Gigi.

She hated herself for thinking that way. Because there were some really good people here. But Dana hadn't changed. And Gigi? Gigi had done what girls from their neighborhood did, gotten married, raised a family; she'd done what everyone expected and now she was alone with two kids.

Except she had a large family to buffer her from the world. Van wouldn't have had that.

"I don't know. I just couldn't. But what about you? I know it's early days yet, but do you have an idea of what you want to do?"

"I'll have to get a job, I guess."

"Is there something you'd like to do?"

"No."

"You always wanted to be a nurse and help people. What if you went back to school?"

"No."

"Why?"

"It doesn't matter."

Van twisted in her chair, tucked her legs up, and tried to read her cousin's expression. Gigi's statement had sounded totally without rancor or even sadness. Van didn't understand how she could be so apathetic.

Her husband was dead, her house was lost, and she had two young children to support. Van didn't understand why Gigi didn't do something, but maybe she was just overwhelmed.

Was that what coming to sunbathe was all about? Maybe Gigi was just trying to reconnect with something that made sense, like friendship. People you could count on. Who wouldn't let you down.

"Gi, I know you feel that way now, but—" She was about to deliver a cliché and she didn't even know if it was true. She tried a different approach. "When I left Whisper Beach, I felt like my life was over, that I had no friends—"

"But you did have friends."

"Yes, and I am so grateful to you and Suze, but it took me a long time before I could start building a new life for myself."

"It was Joe and Dana's fault. I don't know how you can be nice to them."

"Me? You always saw the good in people, not me. I always expected the worse."

"Maybe you were right."

"No. I wasn't. It's better to be like you."

"There's nothing worse than being me."

This made Van sit upright, then drop to her knees next to Gigi's beach chair. "You're a great person, and you have two wonderful children and parents and siblings who love you. And friends. I know it must be so hard to lose your husband and I wish it hadn't happened. But there is still good stuff out there for you. There really is."

"Easy for you to say." Gigi closed her eyes. "Now, can we just lie here and pretend the world doesn't suck? Just for a little while?"

Van sat back in her chair. Gigi had effectively ended her attempt at consolation. Not that Van could blame her. She hadn't done a very good job of showing Gigi the bright side.

But she hadn't expected such lack of spirit, even in Gigi. For as much as Van could reorganize offices and bedrooms so that traffic flowed smoothly, so that everything was just a fingertip away—schedules could be tweaked that made everything fall into place . . . city life crisis management, one of her clients had called it—she didn't know anything that could help her cousin.

Van was good at her job, able to fix just about any external mess. But she couldn't begin to understand a family's dynamic; she could recommend places to find the best nannies, but she couldn't give advice about child rearing. She could pretty much tell if a person was unhappy, but outside of making her daily schedule less stressful, she was at a loss. She couldn't help a woman regain her self-esteem or tell her how to deal with a job loss or heartbreak.

And clients asked her things like that. Things they wouldn't even tell a bartender, they told Van. Came to her seeking advice about everything from which cabinet to fill with Tupperware to whether a wife should leave a husband who was having an affair.

And Van would have to tell those clients she couldn't help. Not because she didn't want to fix everything, even their personal lives, but because she had no experience to draw from. Her childhood had mostly been a nightmare. She'd had no significant other since Joe. She watched families interact and wondered if it was a trick done with mirrors, a fake façade to keep people from seeing the dark underbelly of their lives.

She was the last person to advise Gigi. And yet here they were.

They sat quietly for a while, then Van stretched her towel out on the sand and lay down on her stomach. It was a few minutes before she realized that Gigi had changed seats and was sitting on Van's chair watching Van.

Van turned to her side and looked at her cousin's intense face.

"Take me with you when you go back."

Van sat up. "Gi . . . you mean for a visit?"

"Take me to the city. You can help me get a job there. I can work for you. I know how to clean and stuff."

"Gigi, I don't think you could make enough to get an apartment large enough for the three of you and hire a nanny to watch the kids when you're not there."

"I can leave them with Mom . . . I mean, until I save up some money."

Van was floored—afraid to say anything and afraid not to say something. Had Gigi actually suggested leaving her children to move to New York?

And why was she so shocked? Women had to do that all the time, coming to the States to work and sending money back home to support their families. Some of those women worked for Van, and every one of them spoke of her children with longing. Most of them had no choice.

That wasn't the same thing, though. And Gigi's being willing to leave her children just didn't seem right.

But what did Van know about children and their mothers? She

tried to think back to her own mother. Van had been sixteen when she died; Van couldn't remember much before that but the fighting. And Van would never have children of her own to find out what that relationship might become.

Carefully choosing her words, she said, "Gigi, you wouldn't really want to leave"—what the hell were those kids' names?—"Clay and Amy, would you? Really? Who would tuck them in at night? Make sure they were happy? Help them with their homework?"

"What would you know? You got rid of your kid."

Van stared at her. "My—" Van shook her head. "I didn't. I miscarried. I told you."

"No, you didn't. Not then. You didn't tell me anything. I sat here day after day waiting to hear from you. And you didn't call or anything."

Because even in her delirium, weak from loss of blood, Van had called Suze. Not Gigi, not anyone from Whisper Beach who would judge her, blame her, tell her she'd gotten just what she deserved, but Suze, who she'd known for a few short weeks during the summers and who she'd trusted with her life.

"I sent you the money I owed you as soon as I could."

"It's not the same thing, Van."

"I know. I'm sorry."

"It doesn't matter. I always did what I was told, never caused trouble, was never mean to anybody, and look where it got me."

Van began to feel a little sick. She wished Dorie or Suze were here to help her out. But no such luck. And she was beginning to feel her sympathy fray. She knew she should listen to Gigi unload. It was probably her way of coping.

But Van would have done just about anything to have been on Gigi's side of the family, even have Amelia for a mother. Van was sure she would have loved her if she'd been her child. Gigi had had every comfort that they could afford. Now even as a widow, she had two children to brighten her days and a family to take care of her and them.

And even though Van knew in her heart that she'd never willingly trade Gigi's life for the one she had now, a tiny shard of jealousy pierced her heart. She didn't want Gigi's life, but she would have appreciated it more.

Gigi stood and began gathering up her things. "I have to go back. Mom says we have to take Clay Junior shopping for back to school."

Van stood and slipped on her cover-up, then gathered her own things and followed Gigi across the beach to the boardwalk. Gigi was upset, Van realized that, but she wasn't sure what she'd done to cause her cousin to abruptly put an end to their day.

Gigi didn't bother to change but got right into her car and drove away while Van watched from the sidewalk. Then Van went inside.

Dorie was just coming down the stairs. "Where's Gigi? I thought you two would be down there all afternoon."

"She had to shop for school clothes."

"So what's up? You look angry."

"I'm not angry. I'm perplexed."

"Gigi unload on you?"

"Yeah. How did you know?"

"It's been coming. Saw it the first day she was here. It's just part of the process. I imagine she can't say what she feels to Nate or Amelia or even her sister."

"Why? Why me? Someone she hasn't seen in years."

"Because you were always her confidante, weren't you? You always included her in things you were doing."

"No, I didn't. She was part of the group."

"You know for a smart person, you can be really dense. You remember yourself as an abused, downtrodden kid who barely survived."

"Well?"

"Well, you may have been all that, but you were smart and fun loving and creative . . ."

"Dorie, have I become hard and jaded? Is that what everybody thinks?"

"No."

"I just wanted them to be impressed at how I've succeeded. I needed to show them. I didn't mean to rub it in."

"You haven't even done much to show them how successful you are. You didn't stay at the funeral long enough for anyone to say hello." Dorie put up her hand. "I know why, but imagine you from the side of us."

"What?"

"You sweep into town looking glamorous and successful, make an appearance as if you were above the company. No, be quiet and listen. I know what you were thinking. You saw yourself as someone so unsure of yourself that you were afraid of being dragged back into what you perceived as you as a failure with no future."

"I— Wow. You saw all that?"

Dorie cracked a laugh. "How many kids have come through this house? How many people have I watched grow up? I've got it down. And I know firsthand about not wanting to come back and take a chance of regressing or even being reminded about where you started from. You don't have to look any further than my own children.

"Ever wonder why they visit so little?"

"They still don't visit?"

"Occasionally, but not much. They have their own lives now, and Whisper Beach is not a part of it."

"Do you visit them?"

"Not too much. I have a restaurant to run."

Van wondered if it would have been different if she'd had parents who had been happy together. But she would never know now. "Dorie?"

"Yep?"

"She said some really weird things. Like she begged me to take her to Manhattan with me. She was going to leave the kids here with Amelia. That sounds like more than grief, doesn't it?"

"It does sound extreme."

"I guess I'd better talk to Nate about her."

"Well, I expect they know something isn't quite right, but he could use a sounding board. Amelia will never accept the fact that her daughter is hanging on by a thread."

Van sighed. "Is Suze still upstairs?"

Dorie nodded. "There's another one on the brink, but for better reasons."

"She's really counting on this grant."

Van got out her cell phone. Called Suze. "Get your professorial butt down here. I'm declaring an early happy hour."

"Nothing happy about it." Suze hung up.

"Oops, that didn't sound good." Van and Dorie listened to Suze stomp down the stairs. She came into the living room but stopped just inside the door.

"What's up?" Van asked quietly.

"The grant people finally called back. They sent my papers last week to this address. The stupid post office. They said they would send them again, but they wouldn't budge on the deadline. I mean, what the hell kind of attitude is that to have? I asked them to e-mail them. They don't do that. It would be too easy to hack into.

"I just about told them what they could do with their security system." Suze deflated suddenly and slumped down into her chair. "I am so screwed."

"Well, did they give you any hints about what you have to present in the next round?" Van asked.

"That wouldn't be fair. Ugh." She lowered her voice. "To the candidates who received theirs in a timely manner. Are you kidding me? Like I'm responsible for the U.S. Post Office losing the damn thing."

"They should come into the twenty-first century," Van agreed. "Couldn't you call one of the other candidates and ask them what the project is?"

"Remember the perish part of academia? They'd rather see me crash and burn than help me to compete."

Van sighed. She was running out of enthusiasm. The situation looked pretty bleak for Suze.

"Even if they manage to get it out by tomorrow and overnight it, the deadline is Monday. I might as well start packing and try to get extra classes for the fall." She groaned dramatically. "I think I'll go for a walk."

Chapter 18

VAN AND DORIE SAT LOOKING AT EACH OTHER UNTIL THEY heard the screen door slam. "You're not having much of a vacation."

"Well, it certainly isn't dull, and actually I'm glad I stayed."

"Well, hallelujah."

"But I'm worried about Suze. Should I go after her?" Van asked.

"I think it's best just to let her work through her disappointment."

"You act like it's a fait accompli."

"If that means, she's up the crick without a paddle, yeah."

"There must be something we can do."

"Unless you can reorganize the whole postal system and find that grant packet before Monday, yep, pretty much a fait accompli."

In the silence they'd fallen into, Van heard footsteps over their heads. "Is that Dana up there?"

Dorie nodded. "She's another one. Been up there all day. I

don't know if she's afraid to go out or afraid to come downstairs and face you."

"Me? She has nothing to feel weird about. I told her to forget everything. It's so yesterday's news."

"Funny," Dorie said. "So yesterday and yet everyone's got it on their minds."

"I don't."

"Don't make me squirt this wine out my nose. You and Joe are dancing around each other like it was mating season."

"We are not. Besides mating season isn't an option."

"Are you sure? Did you have a hysterectomy?"

Van shook her head. She really didn't want to talk about it.

"Then what's the trouble?"

"I don't know. Scar tissue, compromised walls, and I don't remember the rest. They just said I couldn't get pregnant."

"When?"

"Dorie, do we really have to go through this?"

"Just humor me. When did they tell you this?"

"I don't know. In the hospital, again later on."

"Have you tried?"

"Tried? To get pregnant? Why would I? Why would I put myself through the disappointment?"

Van heard footsteps on the stairs; seconds later Dana stepped tentatively into the parlor.

"Come on in," Dorie said.

Van relaxed. She didn't think Dorie would pursue her medical history while Dana was present.

"Would you like a glass of wine?"

"No, thanks. I think I'd better cut down. Maybe quit drinking altogether."

"Excellent idea."

Dana sighed. "Now if I could just get Bud to quit, maybe we could—"

"Don't even go there," Dorie said. "You can't do anything for him. He has to do it himself. And quite frankly I don't have too much hope for that."

"He's not a bad guy," Dana said. "He's just . . ."

"Violent," Van finished for her.

"It's not his fault. His father was violent. Died in a bar fight."

Van shuddered. Bud was definitely following in his father's footsteps. She was just glad Joe had escaped with a few bruises and his life. "Well, it isn't your fault."

Dana shrugged.

Van gave up. *Why was it that everyone's life was screwed up but hers?* Dana's abusive boyfriend, Gigi's grief, Suze's missing grant application, Dorie being married to Harold and the failing Crab.

Van almost laughed out loud. She was probably the most screwed up of all of them, but at least she'd channeled it into a thriving business. That counted for something, didn't it?

It was late when Suze returned, accompanied by Jerry Corso in uniform. Van, Dorie, and Dana were still sitting in the parlor amid a large pizza and tins of salad and sautéed spinach that Van had insisted on. She was beginning to feel green depleted.

"OMG," Dana said. "Did you get arrested?"

"No," Jerry said, smiling. "I found her wandering the streets, so I brought her home."

"Thanks, Jerry," Suze said.

"See you Sunday night, then." Jerry nodded and left.

"Sunday night?" Dorie asked.

Suze glanced at Van. "I invited him to my mother's cocktail party."

"The poor guy," Dana said and grinned.

"We're taking you shopping first thing in the morning," Van said.

SUZE TURNED OUT to be a hard sell, but over eggs Benedict and coffee, with Dorie and Van and even Dana chiming in, she accepted defeat and went to get her purse. As soon as she came back, Van, Dana, and a recalcitrant Suze walked into town.

They'd gone a half block when Dana's cell phone rang.

"Aren't you going to answer that?" Van asked.

Dana shook her head. "It'll be Bud. He's called me about fifty times since I came to Dorie's."

"Why don't you just turn it off?"

"I might miss something."

Van let that one slide. This was Suze's day, and Van was determined not to let anything bring them down.

"I really ought to go out to one of those big box stores," Suze said. "And find something cheaper."

"To wear to your mother's cocktail party? Forget it," Van said. "You need dy-no-mite, not discounted."

"I need to watch my money in case I don't get the grant."

"You will, and it's the end of the season. There will be sales."

"Besides, you should support your local businesses," Dana said.

"Absolutely," Van agreed.

The first boutique was a bust. Mainly expensive size twos and not very well-constructed dresses.

"Well, we know why they're having a sale," Van said as they crowded out the door and back onto the street.

"Man, did you get a load of those prices?" Dana groused. Van had a suspicion that she secretly wished she could afford them. Maybe bringing her hadn't been the best idea, but Van was in an accepting mood this morning.

The second store was not much better. The third was some kind of import store that Suze suggested they go into. But after being berated for picking out a batik long gauze skirt, she gave up and gave in and followed Van to the place she'd wanted to look in from the beginning.

"Red," pronounced Dana, lifting a little shift away from the rack.

Suze shook her head.

"Oh, come on. You'd look great in this."

Suze shook her head.

"This." Van held up a black raw silk sheath, form fitting but forgiving, with a heart-shaped neckline, a low scooped back with a pleat at the hem. *And it wouldn't show food,* thought Van, *as long as she stays away from cream sauces and mustard.*

They picked out a couple of other choices, a purple wrap waist in voile, and a hand-dyed silk that flared from a high waist and looked like the sunset. Suze took all four into the dressing room.

"And we want to see every one," Dana called.

Suze mumbled something. There was the sound of grunting, thumping, an occasional mild expletive and Suze appeared wearing the purple.

Van and Dana both shook their heads.

Suze returned to the dressing room. More grunting and thumping and mumbling.

Suze came out in the red dress. It was too short and a little too tight.

"You look amazing," Dana said.

"*You* might look amazing in it," Suze told her, "but I look like a fire engine."

"Try the black," Van said.

When Suze was gone, Van turned to Dana. "I liked the red, but the black will be better. It won't show wrinkles or the occasional bit of food."

"Oh," Dana said as understanding dawned. "She doesn't pay much attention to what's she's doing, does she?"

"It's because she's so smart and doesn't bother with the mundane."

"Well, she should. Jerry has had some cool girlfriends. He's not just a local dumb-ass cop. Well, he is, but he's nice and not too dumb."

"Now there's a glowing reference," Van said. "But I don't think she's dressing for Jerry."

"No, then who?"

"Her mother."

"That's dumb. If she'd fix herself up a little, she could get lucky; and then it wouldn't matter what her mother thought."

Van let that one pass, and fortunately before she had to say something, Suze stepped out of the dressing room.

"That's the one," Van said.

"Yeah, it's pretty, all right," Dana agreed. "But you need to do something with your hair."

"First things first." Van moved over to Suze, checked out the back of the dress. "Go walk over there and turn around."

"And shoes," Dana said, as Suze's thongs flopped across the showroom carpet.

"Definitely shoes," Van said.

Suze came back and perused herself in the full-length mirror.

Turned to the back and looked over her shoulder. "It's expensive."

"You're worth it."

Suze half smiled at Van, but Van could tell she liked the dress and maybe liked how she looked in it.

"Oh, what the heck."

Dana fist-pumped the air. "On to shoes. I know a great place. Not that I've ever been inside, but the window is a beaut."

Suze paid for the dress, and they went down the street to Bijoux, a shoe boutique that made Van think twice. Fortunately, they were having a sale.

Suze picked up a pair of floral high heels. Turned them over, checked out the price, and put them down. "I could just—"

"No, you couldn't," Van told her. "No sandals, no ancient Mary Janes. You deserve a shoe for the up-and-coming young scholar."

"Sensible shoes," Suze said wryly.

"See if they have these in your size." They were basic black with a little gold link on the back of the heel. Conservative, but expensive looking. And on sale.

Suze sat down to wait for the saleswoman to return with her shoes.

"Yo mama, it's Cinderella," Van said when Suze stood up on wobbly ankles. "When was the last time you wore heels?"

"I wear heels at the faculty meetings, two-inch ones."

Van groaned. Dana rolled her eyes.

"Well, I don't want to be taller than my colleagues. They're very sensitive."

"And short, right?" Dana grinned.

Suze nodded. "And short. I'll take them."

"Good," Van said. "I have a bag you can use so you don't break the bank on your first outing."

"Thanks, Van. You, too, Dana. Ice cream?" Suze asked.

"Works for me," Van said. "But let's pop by that art gallery and see how much that painting of the Crab is going for. It would be a nice thank-you present for Dorie."

Dana and Suze followed her across the street and into the gallery.

"It must be some kind of opening," Suze said as they stood on the outskirts of a sizable crowd.

"Probably what they were installing when we were here the other day."

They slipped through the crowd of people standing outside and went inside.

There were quite a few people inside as well. Suze wandered over to the first display wall. "They're nice." She leaned closer to look at the display tag. "It's called *Beach*. Short and sweet. And, gee, only five hundred."

"Whew," Dana said. "You shoulda stuck with that crazy glass painting you used to do. You could be rich."

"Hmm," Van said, taking a closer look at the next painting. "Where is that? It looks familiar, but the title is *Beach 2*."

"Next to *Beach 1*?" Suze quipped.

"I think it's Whisper Beach," Van said.

They all peered more closely. It was definitely Whisper Beach.

"I guess it's a local artist."

They moved on to the next painting. More beachscapes, each different but all conveying a sense of power and yet peaceful. They came to the end of the panel and moved on to the next, which displayed a row of portraits.

"Wow," Suze said. "Didn't you used to have a dress like that?"

Van looked more closely at the seated young girl, her hair pulled back into a long braid. Something in her stomach twisted. She did have a dress like that. And she used to wear her hair like that.

"Too weird," she said and moved on to the next painting. This was a torso view of a woman standing at a window looking out at a meadow, or perhaps it was marshes. She didn't look at all familiar.

The next one was two children playing on the beach. The artist was good, capturing color and movement with minimal strokes. She looked more closely at the title plaque. *Children Playing on Beach.*

She thought it was funny that someone who could create such grace and feeling in their paintings couldn't come up with more inventive titles. She peered at the lower corner of the painting, but the signature was just a jagged brushstroke at odds with the subtlety of the painting.

"Hey, they have food," Dana said. She started off in the direction of the buffet table that was covered with trays of canapés and wineglasses. Suze and Van moved to the next painting.

"They're a little pricey; do you want to spend that much on the one of the Crab?"

"Maybe," Van said. "If it's under five, I would do it. Plus it's an investment."

"And it looks like Dorie might be needing some investments," Suze said.

"Exactly what I was thinking. But I really do like these. I wonder who the artist is." They came to the end of the row and there was a printed biography of the artist—Robbie Moran.

"Look," Suze said. "The artist has the same last name as you. Do you have any relatives who paint?"

Van stared. Managed to shake her head. "No. Just a coincidence. Someone with the same last name." And the same first name. But it couldn't be. Because she'd never even seen him draw a stick figure much less paint with oils and watercolors. Besides these weren't the work of a mere hobbyist. This painter had real talent and training.

Still, it was weird, and Van had an overwhelming urge to get outside. "Let's get Dana and go."

"What about the Crab painting?"

"I changed my mind. I'll wait for you outside." Van turned back toward the front door.

He was standing by the window talking to a man who appeared to be the gallery owner and a middle-aged woman with short-cropped hair. He was facing slightly away from Van, but she recognized him, in spite of the silver hair, in spite of the twelve years separating them.

And she couldn't get to the door without passing right by him. "Forget Dana; she can catch up to us later." Van began to edge toward the door.

She'd almost reached the entrance when he turned from the gallery owner. Somehow their eyes met. His registered shock and disbelief. For a moment they both froze, locked in an inescapable bond.

Father and daughter.

Then he took an involuntary step forward. And Van bolted.

Chapter 19

Van didn't stop until she was halfway down the block and only then because she heard Suze and Dana running after her. She slowed to a walk, then stopped altogether and waited for them.

Her heart was pounding so hard that she was afraid it might be the beginnings of a heart attack. And she kept saying over and over to herself, *No no no.*

She made herself turn around and stand still while she waited for them to catch up to her.

"Jeez," Suze said when she finally caught her breath.

Van could just shake her head. Suze took her elbow and turned her toward home.

"What the hell just happened?" Dana asked, holding a handful of crudité.

Van opened her mouth. Waited for the explanation to come out and finally said, "That was my father."

"Holy crap. Man, he doesn't look like a drunken louse. Actually, he looks pretty hot for an old guy."

"Dana, cool it." Suze steered Van down the sidewalk.

Van didn't protest. Now that she'd escaped, shock, real shock, had set in. She was shaking and felt cold even though it had to be in the nineties even under the trees.

"How could that happen?" she finally managed. "It just doesn't make sense."

"I'm afraid it's a case of 'for that which is fated and doomed,'" Suze said.

"Huh?" asked Dana.

"Shit happens," Suze said.

Van saw a bench up ahead and headed for it. She barely made it before her knees gave out and she fell onto the seat. Suze sat down beside her, and Dana sat on her other side.

"How is it even possible?"

"Did you know your father was an artist?"

"No. He hated art. He refused to help me with any project that required anything close to crafts or drawing. He threw out my last batch of sea glass paintings. I keep thinking I must be hallucinating. Those were his paintings, weren't they?"

"They were," Suze said. "No doubt about that. But it really makes no sense at all."

"Huh," Dana said. "I guess you won't be buying that picture after all."

"Not likely," Van said, trying desperately to pull herself together.

"You have to admit they were impressive. Beautiful and, as far-fetched as it seems, gentle."

Van looked at Suze like she'd grown horns.

"Don't you?"

Van shook her head. "I-I- . . . I can't assimilate it yet. Let's go back to Dorie's."

"Better hurry," Dana said. "Some woman I saw at the gallery is headed this way."

Van looked up. Saw the short cropped-hair. She'd been standing next to— "Let's get out of here."

Van turned away from her and started to walk.

"Vanessa, please. Wait."

Suze steadied her elbow. "It won't hurt to see what she wants."

"It might." It might hurt a whole lot. What could she possibly have to say that wouldn't tear Van to pieces? But it might be better to get it over with. She took a breath, turned to wait for the woman to reach them.

She felt Suze and Dana move closer to her, and she almost burst into tears. Shot them a silent thank-you. She'd thank them out loud later, when they were back at Dorie's.

"Vanessa. I'm Ruth." The woman smiled gently.

Van waited. She had no idea who this person was. Or what she wanted.

"I know you're surprised—no, shocked—to meet your father like this. We had no idea you were in town."

We?

"He would like to see you. I know you aren't ready. He's not a bad man. Not anymore."

Van just stared at her.

"He doesn't expect you to forgive him. He never meant to seek you out. He thinks he has no right."

He was right. For once he'd gotten it right.

"But I thought, hoped, that you might want to at least reconnect with him. There's a big hole in each of you that needs to be filled."

Van began to shake her head. What the hell did this woman know about any of it?

"Just think about it. I've written our address and phone number on this card."

Our.

"If you think you might want to talk. Or maybe just hear about him . . . I would welcome you."

She stuck out a card with a hand that trembled slightly. Her fingers were long and tapered. A model's hand.

Van just looked at the card. She didn't want it. She had no intention of ever seeing him or this woman ever again. *Our. Our?*

He'd killed her mother, made Van's life miserable, and as soon as she left, he moved out of the house lock, stock, and barrel, had taken up painting, and found happiness with another woman.

It was enough to make her want to scratch the woman's eyes out.

As if sensing Van was on the edge, Suze said, "Thank you," took the card from the woman, and guided Van away.

"Man, she's just standing there looking after us," Dana said, following after them. "Gives me the creeps."

They didn't talk for the rest of the walk back to Dorie's.

Dorie was sitting on the porch, drinking a glass of lemonade when the girls returned from town. "Well, how was the shopping spree?"

Van just kept going into the house.

Dorie lifted her eyebrows in question.

"Well," Suze said. "I got a nice dress and a pair of shoes. And we went into this art gallery, and Van ran into her father there."

Dorie put down her glass. "Robbie Moran in an art gallery? Don't believe it. She must have been mistaken."

"No mistake. They were having an opening. There was a painting of the Blue Crab and we went in to see if it was affordable. Van thought you might like to have it."

"And Robbie Moran was there?"

"Robbie Moran was the artist."

Dorie frowned. Why was that striking a chord? She shook her head, couldn't place it. But for a second . . . "So what happened?"

"Van got the hell out," Dana said. "And we went after her."

Suze looked toward the door, then sat down. "The strangest part was this woman, late forties, fifty maybe, came after her. And gave her this card." Suze fished in her pocket and brought out the card.

Dorie took it. Robbie Moran. Landscapes. Portraits.

"You sure this is the same Robbie Moran?"

"I only saw him once," Suze said. "Dana?"

Dana shrugged. "I knew him, uh, when he was always piss drunk, just like my old man. This guy looked like . . . I don't know . . . like you'd expect an artiste to look. And sober. Didn't he look sober to you, Suze?"

"Yeah, though I'm no expert."

"Well, I am. He looked stone cold. And shocked as hell when he saw Van. As soon as she got out the door, he kind of swayed, ya know? Like he was gonna pass out or something. That woman who came after us started fussing over him and I got the hell out, too. Man, those people are weird."

"I don't think there was any doubt in either of their minds," Suze said.

"Is she okay?"

Suze shook her head.

Dorie pushed to her feet. She had gotten them in this mess, the least she could do was see them through. "Give us some privacy for a few."

Dorie looked in the living room then the kitchen. She climbed the stairs feeling much older than her sixty-some-odd years. Van's door was closed, so she knocked. Lightly. When there was no answer, she rested her hand on the doorknob. "I know you might not want company, but I'm coming in."

And in she went.

Van wasn't curled up on her bed crying her eyes out or packing her suitcase, for which Dorie was really grateful, but standing at the window looking out on the roof next door.

Dorie walked up beside her. Glanced over to see how she was holding up. The girl wasn't even crying. Just looking out the window.

It was kind of spooky. She didn't even seem to be aware of Dorie being there. So Dorie just stood there, too.

"You know," Van said finally. "When I first left Whisper Beach, I never wanted to see him ever again. I prayed that he would die." Van breathed out a laugh that gave Dorie the willies.

"Then as time passed, I used to imagine what would happen if we ever met again, whether I would walk away like I didn't even recognize him, or spit in his face and then walk away." Another one of those unnerving laughs. "But since I never perfected the art of spitting, that possibility got eliminated. So I decided that I would just kill him.

"Not in a million years did I think I would ever see him in an art gallery, with some woman who said, 'visit our house.' Our house! How dare he."

Now she turned toward Dorie with such feeling that Dorie had to consciously not step back.

"He looked happy. Damn him. In that second before he saw me, he looked happy."

Now Van started crying. "How can he be happy?"

"Maybe it's time you asked him. Because you're never going to be free until you let go of all this anger."

"I'm not usually angry. I haven't thought about him for a long time. It was just the shock. I've seen him now, and I don't need to know anything more. I don't care."

"You're angry because he looked happy."

"Leave me alone, Dorie. I didn't do anything bad. Stupid maybe, but I've paid for that. So just leave me alone."

Dorie sighed. "You still coming to the restaurant tomorrow?"

"Of course I am. Why wouldn't I?"

"Just checking." Dorie crossed slowly toward the door. She opened it but didn't go out. "You know, Van, you fix other people's lives for a living. Don't you think it's about time to fix your own?" And Dorie closed the door.

"I HAVE FIXED my own." But instead of saying it to Dorie, Van was speaking to the closed door. *I have.* This time she spoke to herself. She had.

She'd worked her way through school, gotten a degree, had her own business.

Had no family, no real friends.

She had friends.

Not like the friends she'd had in Whisper Beach.

Well, she wasn't angry, not anymore.

Then why did she try to leave as soon as Clay's funeral was over?

She had a hotel reservation in Rehoboth.

Van sat down on the bed. "You didn't even want to go to Rehoboth. Ugh."

And now that she was back, and now that she had accidentally run into her father, there was only one person she wanted to talk to. The other person she hadn't wanted to see. She could always tell him what she was feeling. She'd given up that closeness when she'd lambasted him for flirting with Dana mainly because she was having such a hellish week at home.

And he'd paid her back royally.

Van could still picture him and Dana in that truck like it had been last night. But she wanted to talk to him. Work things out for herself while he listened—like they used to do. She'd always trusted him before that stupid night. Could she trust him now not to cut her off at the knees if she confided in him again?

There was only one way to find out. Maybe.

Van grabbed a windbreaker, took a quick peek in the mirror. She had her pride after all. Then she shoved her wallet and keys into her pockets and jogged down the stairs.

She heard voices coming from the parlor. Suze and Dana. She went down the hall to the kitchen.

Dorie was there chopping green beans.

"I'm going out. I'll be back."

"In time for dinner?"

"I don't know."

"Fair enough."

Van drove along the beach. Trying to decide what to do. There seemed to be a big hollowness inside her. *There's a big hole in each of you.* She did have an empty place in her. She knew it. The hole had always been there, but it had grown small over the years, almost like a pinprick, something she hardly ever noticed until a song came on the radio, or she turned the corner to see a lit Christmas tree in the snow. Walking into a stranger's apartment to the aromas of a stew slow-cooking on the stove. A school bus parked on the street.

That's what she had wanted at one time, what she'd thrown away. No, she hadn't thrown it away. She'd been jettisoned out of it and left broken.

She was fine now. More than fine. But she wanted someone to talk to. Really talk to. Not have to be the strong one. Not have to be the one with the answers, the plan; just the one with the hurt, and the indecision and the questions.

Was she asking too much? Probably. And if he turned her away, she knew she'd deserved it. But she wanted to go back, just for a second, like a drowning man knowing it was hopeless, still comes up for one last gasp of air.

Joe's truck was parked at the marina.

She stopped alongside it. Got out of the car before she could change her mind. Walked up the steps and knocked on the old wooden door. Waited. For a long time.

At first she just stood there, not able to believe she'd actually gotten up the courage to come and he wasn't even home. So par for the stupid day she was having.

Or maybe he was there. Maybe he was watching from the window. Saw who it was and decided not to answer. She didn't blame him. It had been a stupid idea.

She wouldn't even leave a note. He didn't need to know she'd come after all.

The door opened. Joe stood on the other side.

"I saw my father today."

"I JUST PANICKED and ran," Van said. She and Joe were sitting on the small couch near his computer desk.

"I mean, what are the odds? I saw this painting of the Crab and wanted to buy it for Dorie. I wanted to buy one of his paintings. How can that happen?

"How could a man like him paint those beautiful paintings. And they were beautiful. Serene. Gentle but with emotion. It doesn't make sense."

"Maybe he's changed."

Van shook her head. "People don't change."

"Don't they?"

Joe suddenly seemed too close. She didn't move back. It felt too close, but it also felt right. Joe hadn't changed.

No. Maybe some people, but not him. "I don't even know how to react. It isn't right that he got to live and my mom died because of his neglect.

"And then that woman he was with. Talking about 'we live' and 'our house' . . . I bet he doesn't treat her like he treated us. Did she actually think she could change my mind with all that smiley sweetness? Ugh."

"Do you think you'll go?"

"Not a chance. He has no right to find happiness with another woman. My mother didn't have that chance to be happy." And neither had Van.

"Van." Joe moved closer, turned her to face him, held her by both shoulders. "Look at me."

"Joe, he was so mean to her; always yelling, or worse, she would try to talk to him, and he'd just ignore her. If she turned off the television to get his attention, he just got up and walked out of the room. That was so hurtful."

"Maybe he was wounded, too?"

Van shook her head. It seemed to be the only thing she could do. The rest of her felt extraordinarily tired and heavy. Today when she first saw him, before he turned around, he seemed calm, filled with life, not the drunken shell of a man he'd been when he was her father. "He was mean, Joe. You know he was."

"I know. He hurt you and that makes me hate him. And I don't think you have to hear his version of what happened or his excuses. You don't need to forgive him."

"I'll never forgive him."

"Fine. But maybe you should ask someone how he got that way."

"Everybody says he started out bad."

"Nobody starts out bad."

Van didn't know what to say. As she thought back over the day, now with distance from that dreadful meeting, something shifted. If she'd seen him today for the first time, would she know what an awful person he was? And how could that woman, Ruth, seem to care for him so much, if he was?

"My mother never showed him any affection. I realize that now."

Joe sat, waited. It was so natural. Letting her work through whatever was bothering her. He'd heard it all before, and yet he sat patiently listening.

"If I had just gone on to my vacation after the funeral, this would never have happened."

"Maybe it was supposed to."

"That sounds awfully woo woo to me."

Joe shrugged. "I was never very woo woo, but I do believe some things happen for a reason."

Van shifted. He wasn't going to bring up the past, was he?

"You can wash your hands of him if you choose. But you can't walk around afraid you might run into him again."

"I'm going home as soon as I get Dorie's restaurant reorganized."

"Home?"

"Yes. I've made a place for myself in Manhattan. And it's not likely that I'll run into him there."

"Unless he shows his paintings in a Manhattan gallery."

"Oh God. I didn't think of that. Well, I just won't go to any art exhibits."

Joe chuckled. "Confront your demons, Van-kerie."

His pet name for her. He'd remembered.

Van bit her lip. Wouldn't it be best to shove her memories back into the dark where they belonged. What if she tried to exorcise them and they just devoured her whole? Her brain screamed, no.

"Can I at least convince you to come out to the farm before you leave? My parents heard you were back and asked about you."

Van hesitated, looked down at her hands clasped in her lap.

"If you're afraid they'll ask questions or judge you for running away, don't be. After you left, Ma said it was a shame, and Dad said I was a damn fool." Joe smiled slightly. "And I was."

"We were young, Joe. It doesn't matter anymore. We turned out all right. I have my business, and you have your vineyard."

"But we might have turned out all right together." He tugged at one of the short strands of her hair. Just as he did when they were young and her hair was long.

She looked up to see what he was thinking, and he kissed her.

Chapter 20

DANA'S PHONE BUZZED. SHE IGNORED IT AND TOOK A roasted chicken out of the fridge.

"How many times a day does he call you?" Dorie asked.

"I've lost count."

"Why don't you just turn it off?"

Dana shrugged and put the chicken on the counter. "Want to nuke this?"

Dorie looked up from the pan of boiling potatoes. "Not yet."

The phone kept ringing. Dorie wondered if Dana had really not talked to Bud in the last few days. If she had held out, there might be hope for her.

The ringing stopped. Dana let out a sigh of obvious relief. "Shouldn't we wait to eat until Van gets back?"

"I don't think so." Dorie speared the potatoes with a fork. "Done." She took a hot pad and carried the pot to the sink.

"Did she say where she was going?" Suze asked.

"No." Dorie began pouring out the water, holding a firm grip on the lid.

"Well, she couldn't have gone to see her father, because I have the address and phone number," Suze said.

"Maybe she went to Mike's. I like going there when I don't want to be alone."

"Dana. She's not alone here," Suze said, then to Dorie. "Do you think she's just driving around thinking? Maybe I should call Jerry and tell him to look out for her."

Dorie shook the potatoes. "Dana, come mash these while they're hot. And no. I think we'll just let her do whatever she's going to do and in her own time."

"But what if she's bolted," asked Dana. "Or—worse?"

Dorie sighed. "Dana."

"What?"

"Never mind. Start mashing."

Dorie began shredding lettuce for a salad. Maybe Van was just driving around. Maybe she had stopped at a bar to pour out her heart to an anonymous bartender, though she doubted it.

She figured Van either went somewhere to think things through—or to someone to talk things through, and Dorie was banking on the latter.

The doorbell rang.

"That must be her." Suze dropped the dish towel she'd been holding and headed for the hall.

The doorbell rang again, this time more urgently.

"Suze, stop. I don't think that's Van."

A fork clattered on the floor; Dana knelt to pick it up. "Sorry."

"You just relax. And don't even think about opening that door."

The three of them stood looking at one another.

There was silence from the front.

Just as they began to relax, the pounding started at the kitchen door.

Dorie jumped, but she recovered before Dana did. She was standing stock-still, staring at the shadow that filled the glass behind the curtain.

The doorknob rattled, and Dana whimpered.

"Dana, I know you're in there. Come on out, honey. I just want to talk."

Dana jerked, took a step.

"You aren't going anywhere near him." Dorie pushed her down into the nearest chair.

The doorknob rattled again. This time more forcefully. "Dana."

Dana jumped up. "He's going to break it. I better go see what he wants."

"You stay put. We know what he wants, and if you go now, it will never change. Is that what you want? To spend the rest of your life beaten and abused, until one night he goes too far and kills you?"

"Dorie," Suze began.

"You hush. You think I'm being harsh, but I'm just protecting her. You know that's what will happen, don't you?"

Dana nodded. Then covered her face with her hands.

"Suze, take her upstairs."

Suze reached for her shoulders, but Dana broke away. "Bud, Bud. Go away, please."

"Honey, I just want to talk. Come on, sweetheart. Just talk."

"No. You need help."

"I know. I know. Just come back, and you can help me."

"Hell, no," said Suze.

"Shhh."

"You need professional help."

"I love you, Dana."

"If you loved me, you wouldn't beat me."

"I won't. I promise."

"Get help, Bud. I'm not coming back until you do."

"Open this door." Bud pounded on the door, harder and harder until the frame shook.

"Stop it! Stop it!" Dana cried and ran toward the door.

Dorie grabbed her and pushed her into Suze's arms. "Take her upstairs and keep her there."

"But, Dorie, you can't face him by yourself."

"Oh, yes, I can." Dorie picked up the carving knife. "Take her upstairs."

VAN WASN'T SURE how she got back into her car. They'd been talking, and then they were kissing, and everything sort of winked out for a bit. Just like twelve years hadn't passed, only they were older; he was more experienced and so was she.

And it still had the force to make her forget the outside world. Fortunately she'd trained herself too well to fully succumb. But she had luxuriated in that kiss for as long as she safely could.

Then had drawn back. It had been hard to do. Part of her, most of her, wanted to just stay there, pretend that the world wasn't a hard-ass place ready to kick you to the curb if you stopped paying attention just for a second.

Van made a three-point turn and tried to keep her eyes on the exit to the street.

Joe was standing in the parking lot where her car had been, wearing the same smile he'd been wearing when they came up for air. The smile broadened as he raised his hand in good-bye.

Not good-bye. What he was really saying was see you later.

She vaguely remembered promising him to go for Sunday lunch at the farm.

But as she waited to turn onto the street, she began to make excuses. She needed to plan for the work at Dorie's they were starting on Monday. She had to . . . she ran out of excuses. Besides, now that the idea had been put in her head, she really wanted to see the family and the vineyard.

It was just Sunday lunch. *Like it had been just a kiss?* She pushed both thoughts away. She didn't want to think ahead, and she didn't want to look back. But something told her she would have to do both before she turned her back on Whisper Beach.

Van pulled onto the street. Back into the normal world.

But Van hadn't returned to the world she'd left. It had started changing way before the kiss. Maybe that afternoon seeing her father. Or earlier than that when she first saw Joe again. Or when Dana showed up at Dorie's kitchen door bruised and bloodied. Or at the funeral. Or even as far back as her decision to come to the funeral.

She and Suze had been worrying about the stage of Gigi's grief. Now Van realized she herself had been in mourning for the last twelve years. It had become such a part of her that she hadn't recognized it for what it was.

Until the day of Clay Daly's funeral, when she stepped out of her rental car and navigated the gravel of Mike's parking lot to the church. She'd felt it then. The pull back. She'd tried to ignore it. Tried to tough it out, joke her way out, just sneak away.

But she was still here. She'd seen her father. Joe had kissed her. And . . . she'd kissed him back.

Stupid, she told herself. *It was a kiss. You've been kissed plenty of times since you moved to Manhattan.* Countless times. She hadn't locked herself away from relationships with men. She had friends. She just didn't have much time for either.

A car honked and sped by. Van jerked the wheel, pulling the car back into her own lane.

Pay attention. She had no intention of dying on her way back to Dorie's all because of a kiss.

If she had the chance, she would go back to yesterday. Play this day over again in a different way. She'd have gone shopping with Dana and Suze but she wouldn't have gone into that art gallery, she wouldn't have seen her father, Joe wouldn't have kissed her.

Van sighed. She couldn't go back. And she knew now that she wouldn't go back if she could, even though she was off base, uncomfortable. Afraid.

There it was. She was afraid to face her father. Afraid that maybe she would start to hate him all over again, after she'd spent so many years trying to forget his existence.

And Joe?

She was afraid that it would be even harder to forget him this time around.

Ahead, the light turned red. She pressed heavily on the brake and stopped just beneath it.

She was afraid to see Joe again. Because despite the years and her attempt to bury him along with her father, they were still connected. She'd prepared for awkwardness. Even anger on Joe's part if they met again. Or total dismissal.

But the connection was still strong; that had become pretty obvious just a few minutes ago. She hadn't expected that.

But she hadn't been wrong when she intuitively went to him when she needed to figure out what to do. He sympathized. Understood. Let her talk and figure out things by herself. He didn't try to bully her into doing what he thought was right. Oh yeah, there was a connection all right.

And now she would see him again. She could call, say she couldn't make it, things were taking longer than she expected at the Crab. She could drive away without a word.

But she knew she wouldn't.

The light changed, and she made the turn toward the beach.

She knew she wouldn't, just as sure as she knew she wouldn't leave without paying a visit to the address on the card Ruth had shoved at her that afternoon.

She slowed as she came to Dorie's house. All the windows were lit up, making the old house look cheery, as if a huge family had gathered for dinner after a day at the beach. And Van knew she wasn't quite ready to return there, her absence made all the more acute by her reemergence. Dorie's words echoed in her head. *You think our world revolves around you?*

Of course she didn't think that, but still she needed a little more time, a tad more solitude. She drove on. Turned onto Ocean Avenue and parked. It was dusk; she'd spent more time at Joe's than she realized. The beach was almost empty, but the Crab was doing a robust business. Dorie must be inside.

Tomorrow, Van would spend the day watching the operations of the staff, scoping out the traffic patterns. Looking for glitches. Taking notes. But tonight. Tonight she wanted solitude.

She walked past the Crab and down the steps to the beach.

Down to the tide line, close to the water and the hush hush of waves beneath the pier.

"So THEY REALLY suspended Bud?" Mike asked.

"Yep," Jerry said. "They decided that starting a bar fight even off duty constituted strike three. So until he gets his shit together he's suspended—and get this—without pay."

Hal put down his mug. "Oh crap. Add humiliation to just plain mean, and he'll be worse than ever."

"They're making him sign up for some anger management program."

"Good luck. He'll probably trash the place if they even suggest he's over the top."

"I think it will take more than classes to break his drinking-beating habit," said Joe, who'd come to Mike's just to take his mind off how lonely the marina office was once Van had left.

"What do you think will happen with Dana?" Hal asked.

Joe shrugged. "If she has any sense, she'll move out of the area and start over."

"Like that's gonna happen," Jerry said. "This is her home. She has a job here with Dorie. Friends."

"And a boyfriend who beats the shit out of her," Joe said.

"There is that. Hell, what a mess. Well, on a brighter note, I got a date." Jerry grinned at the other two.

"Hell you say. Who with?" Hal asked.

"Suzy Turner. Only she goes by Suze now."

"Van's friend?"

"Yeah, she used to work at the Crab with Van and Gigi and Dana."

"You taking her to dinner? Maybe you should go somewheres besides the Crab."

"And somewhere classier than Mike's," Joe added.

"Hey," Mike called from down the bar. "I got class."

"There's that place that was written up in the paper, over in Asbury," Hal said.

"What place?"

"I forget the name of it. Google it. Fancy schmancy."

"Well, I might, but we're not going to dinner, we're going to a party."

"Who's having a party that we didn't hear about?"

"Suze's mother is having a cocktail party."

Hal laughed, laughed so hard he nearly fell off the bar stool.

Even Joe was amused.

"What do you think is so funny?"

"Where is it? At the country club? You can bet it won't be held in Mike's party room."

"At her parents' house."

"Oh Lord, that's worse. Wipe your feet before you go inside. They probably have white carpet to identify the wannabes from the elite."

"Give the guy a break," Joe said, fighting a grin. The idea of Jerry at Suze Turner's mansion was pretty out there. The idea of Jerry conversing with a Ph.D. in English was even more far-fetched. And the idea of Jerry in a room with a bunch of society people was downright daunting.

Hal recovered himself long enough to gasp out. "Don't ask for beer; they'll be drinking fancy wine. And don't talk with your mouth full of food."

"I know that."

"Don't let this Neanderthal give you a hard time," Joe said. "You've got a lot of class."

"Well, listen to Mr. Suave and Sophisticated here," Mike said.

"Aw hell, Joe, the only class I got is when I went to one at school. And that wasn't all that often. I probably shoulda said no, but hell, she's kinda hot, you know. And I always liked her, you know, just liked, but I thought what the hell."

"Don't listen to us," Joe said. "We're just razzing you. You'll be fine."

Mike scooped up their empty mugs and wiped the bar. "You got something nice to wear?"

"Like a suit?" Hal added.

"Yeah, my church suit, but it's got some mustard on it from the funeral repast."

Mike shook his head and slid them another round of beers, followed by an epithet that made the three of them turn around.

Bud was standing in the doorway.

"I swear if he starts something with you guys, I'm calling the cops and filing a complaint against all of you."

"Want me to sneak out the back door?" Joe asked.

"Hell, no. I want him to get a grip. Damn if he doesn't come in here every night looking for Dana. And every night I throw him out. Man, if she even stuck her nose in here, I'd tell her to run and keep running." Mike paused. "But she ain't been in. Just in case you're wondering."

Bud walked across the room, headed right for the three of them. Joe braced himself for whatever Bud was wielding tonight. This time if Bud punched him, Joe would go down and let him keep hitting him until somebody pulled him off.

Then Joe would file a complaint. It was time to get the bozo off the streets before he killed someone.

"You seen her, Joe?"

Joe slowly shook his head.

Bud looked from Hal to Jerry. "How about you two?"

"No, Bud," Hal said. "I haven't seen her."

"You know I haven't," Jerry said. "I've been on the same schedule as you have this week."

"She didn't come in, Mike?"

Mike shook his head. "Nobody knows where she is, and you sure as hell better not break up my place again, or you'll be looking at the world from the wrong side of a jail cell."

Joe shot Mike a look that said *don't provoke him*.

But Bud just huffed out a sigh. "I know where she is. She don't want to come back."

"Bud," Joe warned.

"I'm not gonna cause any trouble."

Yeah, right, Joe thought. He didn't want to deal with Bud and his problems tonight. He hadn't even wanted to be here, but hunger had done him in in the end. It was fast food or Mike's.

Maybe he should have gone for the fast food, but he'd been thinking about Van since she'd left and somehow thinking about her while eating a Big Mac just didn't cut it. He chose Mike's, had just finished a steak dinner, and was enjoying the feeling of a full stomach. And he would have been out of here and home by now, alone but thinking of Van and being sappy, if Jerry hadn't told them about his upcoming date.

Now he was stuck with Bud and his baggage. "Hey, Bud," Joe said as affably as he could muster. "Take my place. I've got to get going. Gotta close up the marina tomorrow." Too late he realized he shouldn't have brought up the marina. It was bound to lead Bud to the clam diggers. But Bud seemed oblivious.

"See you guys. Have a good time, Jerry, and for Godsake, make sure your tie doesn't have spots on it before you go."

"Eff you, Joe," Jerry said. "I'd win a fashion show over you any day."

Hal laughed. "I'd come out on top of both of you. Couple of slobs."

So while Hal and Jerry traded insults and Bud sat down, Joe got the hell out.

It was dark when Van finally returned to Dorie's.

"Where have you been?" Suze asked when she opened the front door.

"How come my key didn't work?" Van countered.

"Dorie had to throw the bolt. We've had such excitement." Suze opened the door wider and looked over Van's head out into the night.

"What kind of excitement?"

"'Cataracts and hurricanes have stormed our kitchen door.' I paraphrase. Shakespeare. Not really my period."

"That's fine, now tell me in commoner English."

"Bud was here looking for Dana. He was not happy. Dorie went after him with a kitchen knife."

"Please tell me you're kidding."

"Nope."

"Then please tell me he still has all his body parts."

"Yes, unfortunately. I was hoping for a display of barbaric punishment." Suze grinned. "Abelard and Heloise style. Come on in. We saved you some dinner and I'll fix you a cosmo. We're celebrating girl power with pink drinks tonight."

"I think I'll start with a glass of water and then you can tell me all about it." Van headed for the kitchen.

Suze followed her. "Want me to nuke you some chicken and mashed potatoes?"

"Sounds great, but I can nuke potatoes. One of my best cooking skills."

Suze relaxed. "So you're okay?"

"Of course. Why wouldn't I be?"

"Because you took off, but I, for one, wasn't worried that you might not come back."

"You weren't?"

"Hell, no; your laptop and complete schedule for the next eighteen months was open on your writing desk."

"I just needed to think things through." She glanced out the door to make sure they were alone. "I went to see Joe."

"Dorie said she thought you might."

"How? No, don't tell me. Clairvoyant."

"So what happened?" Suze asked, getting a plate of chicken out of the fridge. "Is that old black magic still there?"

"You better watch out; your classical literary allusions are slipping. 'That Old Black Magic' was a pop song."

"Ha. I have very catholic tastes. I mean that in the universal sense."

"Suze?"

"Uh-huh?"

"I think you should start practicing cocktail conversation, especially if you're taking Jerry Corso."

"It's going to be a disaster, isn't it?"

"Not at all. Well, at least not if you remember to stay away from Abelard and Heloise. People might think you're talking about a new face-cleansing system."

Suze snorted, and the chicken began to slide across the plate. Van grabbed the plate just in time to save the chicken from falling to the floor.

Suze sank into a kitchen chair. “I’m a mess.”

“No, you’re not. You’re brilliant and funny . . .”

“Please don’t say I have a good personality.”

“Never. I was going to say . . . gorgeous and—”

“Ne’er the twain shall meet.”

“That’s what I mean. You have to learn to stop talking about twains and just say, ‘Not my type.’ ”

“Not my type. Got it. Who’s not my type? Jerry?”

“That was a general example. Actually I think you and Jerry are cute together.”

“Ha. That’s one thing I’m not. Cute.”

“And thank God for that,” Van said. “Now let me nuke some food, and you guys can tell me all about the Bud sighting. And what Dorie did. And tomorrow after I observe the Crab staff in action, we’ll watch several hours of network television. I wonder if Dorie has Netflix. I have it on my laptop. We can cram the latest hip shows in your brain. Television is a great icebreaker.” Van stopped. “I guess they didn’t overnight your grant application.”

“Nope. My academic ship won’t be coming in this year, so I might as well watch some television. I’ll even come help you revitalize the Crab.”

“Don’t give up yet. You know what they say.”

“What?”

Van smiled. “Something will turn up.”

Chapter 21

Saturday morning Van, Dana, and Dorie woke up at dawn and walked to the Crab. Cubby and several other men were already there, unloading boxes of produce and breaking down empty crates.

"Ugh," Dana said and finished the sentiment with a jaw-cracking yawn. "I don't usually work the morning shift."

"You said you wanted extra hours. This is what I got," Dorie said.

"I know and I love you for it." Dana made smooching noises.

The sound caught the attention of at least half the guys on the loading platform. Dana tossed her head and waved at them.

"You behave. I don't want anybody falling off the platform or chopping off a finger while they're ogling you."

"Yes, ma'am. Maybe I should go buy me a granny dress. Unless you've got one I could borrow."

"I don't own a granny dress or anything close to. But I'm sure we could find something at the consignment store."

Dana stuck out her tongue and flounced past the guys on the loading dock and into the Crab's kitchen

"That girl," Dorie said. She shook her head, but her eyes were twinkling.

"As you might say . . ." Van lifted her chin and rolled her eyes at the sky.

Dorie burst out laughing. "Touché."

They went inside where the kitchen was already stifling hot with breakfast prep. Two cooks stood at the grills, and two more underchefs were busy cutting wedges of lemons, slicing oranges, and pinching off sprigs of parsley.

Van stood just inside the door, taking it all in. The room was large and square, but much of it was dead space, used for stacks of pots and pans that wouldn't be used until lunch and dinner. Some hadn't been used in years, maybe decades.

"You have a lot of stuff," Van said.

"Guess I do," Dorie agreed. "Seems like as the Blue Crab grew in popularity, so did the junk. Equipment and cookware, utensils and shelves, linens and stuff that nobody knew what it was but didn't want to throw away in case somebody needed it. Guess some of it will have to go."

"Uh-huh."

"Just check with me before you toss; I don't want to come in at the crack of dawn to make my lasagna and find my favorite pan missing."

"Uh-huh."

"Never mind. I can see you're already in the zone," Dorie said. "I'll leave you to it."

Van nodded as she busily scribbled notes and sketches into her notepad and began to get ideas for streamlining the room. She didn't know much about cooking, but she did understand workstations and traffic flow. Dorie's had gotten out of hand, one area spilling into or crowding out another.

There was no room to expand, and probably not the money if Dorie wanted to, so Van would have to make the best of the space they had.

The two shelves she'd cleared a few days before were already crammed with things that couldn't possibly be needed near at hand. And when she watched one of the waitresses stuff a stained apron on the top of a stack of paper bags, she knew it was going to take a reality-show-type showdown to get things up to efficiency and speed.

But it wasn't her job to police staff. She would make her suggestions, explain how best to implement changes, and let Dorie deal with retraining the staff.

She just stood out of the way for a good twenty minutes. Made a note to ask Dorie if it was the same staff and the same type of prep for the other meals. Some stations could do double duty if they weren't used continually all day.

Van moved on to the storerooms. They were worse than the kitchen, and it was hard to believe that they actually needed all this stuff. The shelving unit only went up to eight feet or so. They could add two rows of shelves above for overstock and store a stepladder in the corner.

That was something she and Dorie could discuss on Monday, the day they were planning on dismantling the space. That would give them three days to reconfigure and get everything up to speed by dinner on Friday when the restaurant would open for the weekend—and Van would be returning home to Manhattan.

They should probably wait until the Crab was closed for the winter, but Van could tell Dorie was worried, was afraid she wouldn't be able to reopen if something didn't change soon. Van knew how important the Crab was to Dorie, and she was determined to help if she could.

Besides, Van wasn't sure she would have the time to run down to help out once she was back in work mode. She smiled thinking about what she was doing at the moment. This was her vacation mode.

She made a mental note to get out in the sun as much as she could before she had to leave—Maria and Ellen would never let her live it down if she came back from the beach as pasty as when she'd left.

When she least expected it, the image of Joe watching her drive away from the marina popped into her mind. It was followed by Joe listening to her talk as the two sat side by side on the couch, Joe leaning in until she knew what was coming and didn't even attempt to stop it. She lingered on the memory longer than she should, enjoying it more than she had any right to.

Then she'd shake herself and work even harder.

The breakfast rush ended, and Van was still working on the kitchen and storage area when Suze came in.

"No luck?"

Suze shook her head. "I decided to come have lunch and help out."

"Sounds good to me. I didn't have breakfast. And every time I put my coffee cup down, someone whisks it away. At least they work hard. Let's go get a table and eat before the lunch rush begins."

Van poked her head into the small office at the end of the corridor where Dorie and Cubby, her manager, were going over accounts.

"Taking a break, boss," Van said. "Want to join Suze and me for lunch?"

"You girls go ahead. I'll join you in a bit if we get through these accounts."

"Want me to help?"

"No, you've been working all morning. Relax a little."

Van and Suze sat down at their regular table. A couple of minutes later, Dana sidled over, put two menus in front of them, jutted out a hip, and said, "What can I do for you ladies?"

She was smiling like it was all a big joke, but Van knew the sting of humiliation, and she bet anything that underneath her overly large grin, Dana was seething.

Suze saved the day by bursting out with one of her raucous laughs.

"Jeez, how do you take her anywhere?" Dana said.

"It's a cross I must bear," Van said.

Dana nodded sympathetically. "It's probably because she's so cute."

"Cute? Hey," Suze protested.

"So whaddaya want?"

"I hope that's not how you treat your other patrons."

Dana cocked her hip even more. "Sometimes I use a southern accent."

Now Van laughed. She'd forgotten how funny Dana could be, that sharp sarcastic kind of humor that sometimes tumbled into bitterness. But most of the time she'd kept them in stitches.

Suze ordered a western omelet and Van a BLT. Then she watched Dana walk back across the room and deposit the menus on top of the stack that took up valuable counter space. Van opened her notebook and scribbled a note to order a menu rack of some sort.

"Why don't you use your iPad for that?"

"Because it doesn't fit in my pocket. Plus I can throw this down anywhere and don't have to worry if—" She cringed as a busboy came through with a crate of clean plates just as Dana started through the door in the other direction—"If *they* happen to it. Stay to the right. That should be easy enough."

Suze snorted. "We never did."

"I know. It's amazing we ever got food to the tables."

Dana returned with their meals. Suze's omelet was fluffy and filled the plate. She immediately dug into it. Van's sandwich had crisp bacon, the tomatoes were definitely Jersey, and the lettuce was fresh.

"Dorie said to bring you these, since they were your favorites."

A platter of cheese fries. Van hadn't had cheese fries in years. Didn't eat food like that. Didn't eat any of the kinds of foods they'd been eating since she'd arrived.

"She said to let Suze have one, maybe two if she begs." Dana tossed her head and went to wait on another table.

"She used to be fun," Suze said, as she reached for a fry.

" I remember . . . now. But this is the first we've seen of the old Dana."

"As long as we don't see her dark side, we'll be fine."

Van nodded and bit into a cheese-drenched french fry. It was good. The fry was crunchy, which kept the cheese from making it soggy. And the cheese, though Van knew it probably wasn't even cheese, was like a little piece of happiness. The ultimate beach-town comfort food.

They stuffed themselves and discussed whether it would be tacky to leave Dana a tip. They decided she'd be pissed if they didn't and went to pay their bill. Of course it was already paid by Dorie.

"Okay, put me to work," Suze said as she followed Van to the back. "Preferably something physical so I can work off some calories. I don't want to get too fat for my new dress before tomorrow afternoon."

Van sent Suze and Dorie to inventory the back closet since it turned out nobody really knew what was in it. Then she took a few minutes to explain to the staff that she wasn't a spy or watching their every move for mistakes, but analyzing patterns and ways to make the restaurant more efficient. She welcomed concerns and constructive criticism.

"But no bitching and moaning. Remember I used to work here."

After that Van plunked herself in a chair at the table where the extra condiments were kept.

Three hours later she had several pages of notes, several sketches of the current situation, and a two-page list of areas of concern. A bit more formidable than a one-bedroom Manhattan apartment or even an office. But conquerable.

At three o'clock she went in search of Dorie and Suze. The storeroom looked like a different room.

"Fantastic," Van said. "Now the key is to make sure everyone keeps it that way. And no more stuffing dirty aprons in any old unoccupied space."

"Guess I'll have to do a little training session."

"Afraid so," Van said, "and probably some refresher courses along the way."

"I say we call it a day," Dorie said. "Cubby can finish up what we've done so far."

Dorie rounded up the staff to tell them that Van would be working on spiffing the place up and asked if anyone could come in on Monday for a few hours to do manual labor. "No tips," she said with a grin, "but regular hourly salary will apply."

She had a number of volunteers, including Dana. Nobody was interested in turning down extra money.

Dorie gathered up some perishables to take home for later. "You might as well come home too, Dana. If you're planning to do another shift tonight, you'd better get off your feet for a while."

"Works for me." Dana pulled off her apron, scrutinized it for stains, then folded it and put it on top of the pile already on the shelf unit by the corridor.

Another thing that can be streamlined, Van thought.

Outside there wasn't a cloud in the sky; the sun beat down mercilessly on the people on the beach, and heat rose from the planks of the boardwalk.

"I didn't really notice the air-conditioning in the Crab," Van said as they crossed the street.

"'Cause you're not paying the bill," Dorie said. "Hey, watch out for pedestrians," she yelled as a carload of teenagers and a loud muffler shot past them. "I can tell you, as much as I miss the income, I'm looking forward to a little quiet time at the shore. Seems like they stay later and later every year."

"And I'll be looking for a job," Dana said under her breath.

"Well, keep your weekends open. If Van can figure out a way to make this old shack profitable during the winter, I'm going to give it a try."

"That would be great," Dana said with what appeared to be real enthusiasm. "People need more than pizza, hot dogs, and Mexican food until the next season rolls around."

"There are plenty of real restaurants around," Dorie said.

"Too expensive and not on the beach with an ocean view. People like to look at the water in the other seasons, too. And nobody has a view like the Crab."

Dorie and Van exchanged looks. "Not too shabby," Dorie said under her breath as Dana sidled up to Suze.

"Do you want me to do your nails for the party tomorrow? I have some of my stuff from . . . my old job."

"I don't really have any." Suze stuck out her hand for Dana to see and tripped over an upended square of pavement.

"You are such a klutz."

"I know. I'm hopeless."

"You wouldn't be if you'd pay attention. And I know things that Jerry likes. I'll give you a crash course on motorcycles, bass fishing, and capital punishment so you won't get stuck talking about dead authors. I'm not sure he reads all that much."

"It's going to be a disaster," Suze said.

"There's Gigi's car," Van said. "I wonder how long she's been waiting."

They climbed the stairs to the porch, Dana explaining to Suze the difference between sport, trail, and supersport.

They all squeezed into the air-conditioned foyer in time to see Gigi coming down the stairs.

"Hey, we were over working at the restaurant. How long have you been here?" Van asked.

Gig shrugged. She didn't look happy. "About a half hour."

She was holding a manila envelope.

"Is that for me? Did they send it special delivery?"

Suze started up the stairs, her hand held out.

Gigi clutched the envelope to her stomach.

"It's for you, but they didn't send it special delivery."

"What do you mean. How did you get it?"

All four of them had stopped in the foyer, looking up.

Gigi shrugged.

Van got a bad feeling.

"Gigi?"

"I was hanging around, and I saw there was clean laundry, so I thought I'd help out and put it away like I did the other day."

"Gigi, what does my mail have to do with you putting away laundry?" Suze's voice was almost shrill. Something Van had never heard.

Van stepped forward. "Gi, where did you get the envelope?"

Gigi glanced up and over her shoulder. "I feel terrible."

"Just give it here." Suze started to climb the stairs, but Dorie held her back.

"Are you saying you found it upstairs?" Dorie asked.

Gigi nodded. "While I was putting away the laundry." She took a shuddering breath.

"Where?" Dorie asked.

"I'm sorry."

"Where?" Suze repeated.

"I was putting things away, and I opened Dana's underwear drawer and saw it. Stuck under her panties."

"The hell you did," Dana yelled and started after her. Dorie and Van both grabbed her.

"I'm sorry. I was just trying to be helpful."

"Oh, you were." Suze turned on Dana. "You were going to teach me about motorcycles and give me a manicure, and all this time you had my grant packet when you knew it means everything to me."

"I didn't. I don't know how it got in my drawer. If it even got there. Maybe she's making the whole thing up."

"I'm not. I'm sorry, Dana, but why did you do it?"

"I didn't." She turned to Suze, then to Van, her face twisted in anger. "You bitches. You probably planned this together."

"Don't be stupid, Dana." Van could hardly control her voice.

She'd actually begun to like Dana, to forgive her for past transgressions, to sympathize with her problems with Bud. "Tell us how it ended up in your underwear drawer or why you took it. Something to make sense."

"I don't know, I didn't take it, and I don't expect you bitches to believe me, so to hell with you."

Dorie reached for her. "Dana, calm down."

"You calm down; I should never have come here." She broke away and ran up the stairs, jostling Gigi as she passed by.

Suze grabbed the envelope and opened it. "This was postmarked a week ago. She must have taken it out of the mailbox while she was here. I don't understand. Why would she do that?"

"I don't know," Van said. It seemed gratuitously cruel even for Dana.

"What did I ever do to her?"

"I thought things were going well," Dorie said. "I don't understand it any more than you do. I'll go talk to her in a minute."

"I feel awful," Gigi said, coming down the stairs. "I was just trying to be helpful and now . . ."

"Not your fault," Van said. "Thank God you did look in her drawer. It's not too late to get it out, is it, Suze?"

"No, if I work on it tonight and tomorrow. Oh damn, there's Mother's party."

Van gave her a squeeze. "Then get to work. If you need anything, let us know; food, library, dictation, just yell. Other than that, we won't bother you. Get going."

Suze turned to Gigi. "Thanks. I owe you big time."

Gigi waved her off. She'd started to cry.

Dorie and Van exchanged looks, and Suze hurried up the stairs.

"Now what?"

"I don't know."

Van didn't either. How could Dana go shopping with them and joke around with them when all the time she'd stolen Suze's mail?

"I'm sorry."

"Gigi, it's not your fault."

"Come on, Gi, Dorie's right. Your finding the envelope will at least give Suze a chance."

"It isn't too late?"

"I don't know. I sure hope not."

"I think it's about time I had a little heart-to-heart with Dana." Dorie marched up the stairs. Van didn't envy Dana. Not only had she lost their trust, Dorie didn't cut thieves any slack. So, besides sabotaging Suze, Dana may just have cost herself a job.

"Come on, Gi. Let's go sit down." Van took Gigi into the living room. She didn't know what to do. Gigi had done a good thing, but it seemed like everything made her cry. She'd always been a little like that, but the death of her husband had really done a number on her psyche.

Since talking with Joe, Van had decided to ask Nate about her father. It was time to deal with it once and for all. Now she would have to add Gigi's state of mind to that talk. Because this couldn't be natural grief.

So she sat with Gigi while Gigi explained again what she was doing looking in Dana's drawer. "I knew the underwear had to be Dana's because it . . . well, it was, you know, kind of sexy." She put her hand to her mouth and lowered her voice. "And cheap. I just opened the drawer to put it in and saw the corner of the envelope sticking out.

"I really wouldn't have looked at it if Suze hadn't been making such a big deal about her grant application. So I just took a peek. And then I knew."

Van nodded and made soothing noises until she heard Dorie

descending the stairs. "That was quick," Van said. "I wonder what happened."

Dorie stormed into the living room.

"What? Is everything all right? Is Dana still denying that she stole it?"

"She's gone."

"Gone? What do you mean gone?"

"Packed her clothes and climbed out the window."

"She's ruined everything. Just like the old days," Gigi murmured.

Yep, thought Van. *Just like the old days.* Only this time Suze was the one suffering because of Dana's betrayal.

Chapter 22

So do you want to go look for her?" Van asked Dorie.

Gigi sniffed. "Why would you want to do that? She messed up everything."

"I guess," Dorie said. "I'm not sure if I even want her in this house. But I would like to know why she did it. She's many things, a lot of them not very likable, but I've never known her to do something this wicked."

Van and Gigi exchanged looks. Van could distinctly remember another time when Dana had ruined everything. And Gigi remembered it, too.

"But I don't want her going back to Bud. I guess we have to look."

"After what she did?" Gigi asked incredulously.

Van searched Gigi's face. This attitude was so not like the old Gigi who was all forgiveness and compassion. Life hadn't been easy for her, but it hadn't made her stronger, just more defeated.

"Dorie, can you call her?" Van asked. "Not that she'll answer. She's been ignoring Bud's calls all week, but it's worth a shot."

Dorie rummaged in the bag she'd thrown on the floor. "I keep all my staff, even part-timers in here." She found the number, waited. "Dana, pick up. At least call me back. I'm not going to accuse you of anything. But don't do anything stupid because you're angry. Do not go back to Bud's. Call me."

She hung up. Shook her head.

"Can you text her?"

"If you want to watch me grow old." She handed the phone to Van. "You do it."

"Okay; what should I say?"

"That I'll kick her butt if she goes back to that—"

"Could you be a little more concise?" Van asked, her thumbs hovering over the phone.

"'Come back.' No wait. 'You'd better show up for work. I'm counting on you. If you don't care about me, think of the money.' Concise enough?"

Van finished entering the text, pressed send. "Yes, if only she'll bother to read it."

"I'll try Mike's." Dorie took the phone back, but Mike hadn't seen her. "He said he'd call if she comes in and try to keep her there until we can come get her." Dorie frowned. "I know you're all pretty mad at her. I am, too. Disappointed really. But we can't give up on her. Not now when she finally made an attempt to get away from Bud."

"I understand," Van said. Dorie just didn't give up on people. Van respected her for it, even though she didn't think Dana deserved it. She hadn't thought she'd deserved it when she left all those years ago. She'd come to Dorie and she'd done a bunk, just like Dana. Of course Van hadn't stolen anything, but she was just beginning to realize that she had a lot to answer for.

"I think I'll just take a spin around the neighborhood and see if I can catch up with her."

"What are you going to do to her?" Gigi's expression was comically alarmed.

"Nothing bad. I probably won't even find her."

"I'll come with you."

"Thanks, but you stay here and keep Dorie company." She shot a quick glance toward Dorie.

Dorie picked up on it immediately. "Yes, please, Gigi. I really feel like some company right now. Would you mind staying for a little while?"

"Of course I'll stay," Gigi said. "Why don't we go back to the kitchen? I'll make some tea or coffee for you." She took Dorie by the arm as if Dorie were an old lady, and they tottered down the hall.

Van grabbed her bag and ran for her car. She spent the next hour driving up and down the streets of Whisper Beach. She started close to home, hoping she might catch Dana as she was walking somewhere. Van gradually spread out into the adjacent beach towns since she had no clear idea of where Dana might go.

She checked the Crab, but no one had seen her. She was afraid Dana might go back to Bud's, and if she did, there was nothing much they could do about it. But if she didn't go there, where would she—

Van stopped searching the streets and drove straight to Grandy's Marina. Of course Dana would go to Joe. He wouldn't turn her away. And in Dana's mind, it would be putting the screws to Van once more. So be it.

She would make sure Dana was safe and she'd walk away.

Dana was sitting on the steps of the marina when Van drove into the parking lot. She stood up, started to go into the house, changed her mind, and stood defiantly with her arms crossed while Van got out of the car and crossed the parking lot.

"Dorie is worried about you," Van said without preamble.

Dana just gave attitude.

Van gritted her teeth.

"Did she send you to look for me?"

"Actually it was my idea. I figured even someone who would do something like you just pulled deserved not to have to go back to an abusive relationship."

"As you can see, I didn't." Dana glanced back at the door. "Joe's been trying to get me to move in with him for ages. I really like Bud better, but what the hell. Joe's almost as good in bed as Bud." A sly smile slid across her face and was gone. "Oh, but you wouldn't know if he's good or not, would you?"

"Dana, cut it out. You can't hurt me, and you can only make yourself look pitiful."

"Eff you. If you came to see Joe, you can't. He's in the shower." Another of her insinuating smiles.

Van got it. She didn't know whether to believe it or not. She clamped down on the next thought, that Dana would of course come to another man. And she tried to convince herself that it wasn't her business what they did, and that she didn't care.

"I wasn't looking for Joe. I was looking for you. Dorie wanted me to tell you that she wants you to show up for work tonight." Though Van couldn't understand why.

Dana sighed.

"And I'm telling you that you'd better not leave her in the lurch. Not after all she's done for all of us. You can hate Suze and Gigi and me, but Dorie doesn't deserve anything but your loyalty. So get your butt over to the Crab and waitress tonight. Besides, as Dorie pointed out, you'll need the money."

Without waiting for an answer or a snide remark, Van turned on her heel, walked straight to her car, and drove away. She made it all the way to the first traffic light before she screamed several epithets that she would never use in hearing distance of anyone.

She did care. All right, there it was. Ever since seeing Joe again she realized that she still cared for him. She wasn't sure how exactly, but Dana had just put an end to any possibilities. And Van had no right to complain. She'd left him and that was that.

She wasn't sure she would even welcome the opportunity to get closer to him. For that matter, she didn't know if Dana was just trying to hurt herself. Even with the distance of time, Van didn't see Joe as someone who would be interested in Dana as anything but a friend and possibly . . .

She wouldn't think about it. It had nothing to do with her. The light changed; she sped off. To hell with both of them. She'd done her duty, found Dana, told her to go to work. It was over.

Now all she had to do was finish her plans for the Crab, buoy Gigi up for a few days . . . deal with her house, which meant she would have to talk to Uncle Nate. See her father? Maybe. And then her vacation would be over.

Having a wonderful time. Wish you were here . . . Wish you were here instead of me.

Joe was drying off and looking out the window when a car pulled out of the parking lot and swung right toward the bridge.

He'd seen that car before. He'd ridden in that car. The night of the brawl at Mike's.

He got a rush of expectation followed closely by a rush of anger. Van had probably come looking for Dana.

Maybe Van had only come to make sure she was okay. And finding that she was, she left. But he doubted it was that simple. Nothing with Dana was that simple. The woman was so self-destructive, she was hard to be around. But he'd be damned if she'd bring him down with her.

He wrapped a towel around himself and strode out to the front door.

Dana was standing on the top step, looking toward the road, but she turned around when she heard him open the door.

"We-e-ell," she said at her most vampish.

"Cut it out; was that Van who just drove away?"

"Yeah, she just came to tell me to come to work."

"And what did you tell her?"

"That you were in the shower." She gave him one of her come-on smiles. It turned Joe's stomach. "And you sure are a temptation, standing there in that skimpy little towel."

Joe instinctively clutched the towel tighter. "Why the hell did you do that? God, you just couldn't help yourself, could you."

"Because she just assumed I came running here to get laid or something, so I let her think it."

Dana stepped up to the threshold and grabbed the towel. Joe grabbed her wrist so hard that she squeaked. He let go.

"Bastard."

"Sorry, but you just don't let up."

She pouted at him. "She's going to leave you high and dry—again."

"Stop it. You screwed up things between me and Van before,

and you're determined to do it again. Why? What did we ever do to you?"

Dana's bottom lip quivered, and Joe thought, *Please don't start crying.*

"Because you were happy," she spat.

She brushed past him, all the seduction drained from her. She grabbed her duffel and purse.

"Where are you going?"

"Back to Bud. He at least loves me. And in case you're wondering, I didn't steal that stupid letter. One of them did and put it in my room. You think they're so great? Screw you."

Joe grabbed the duffel and wrested it out of her hand. She lunged for it and Joe almost lost hold of his towel. He let the duffel go instead. "Stay here. I'm getting dressed, then I'm taking you to the Crab. It's probably time for your shift. And then you're going back to Dorie's until we can figure out a permanent solution.

"But I'm taking your duffel, and if you run, I swear I'll call the cops and have you thrown in jail."

"You wouldn't."

"Don't test it."

She was sitting on the front steps when he came out again.

He carried her stuff outside. They got in his truck without speaking.

"I'm only letting you do this because I need the money."

"Fine."

They drove in silence. Joe parked the truck by the Crab's kitchen entrance. "Dana, you're not a bad person. I don't know why you have this need to keep pissing people off. But it really needs to stop. And don't say you can't help it. You can. But you have to stay away from Bud until he gets help. Maybe even then.

Because one day he will go too far and kill you. And I don't think even you want that."

She scowled at him, got out of the car, and slammed the door. She walked into the restaurant without looking back.

He'd done what he could. He washed his hands of her. Now he needed to go explain things to Van.

He parked in front of Dorie's. Van's car was there. So was Gigi's. He sat for a minute trying to decide how to get Van out without going through her front guard, Dorie, Suze, and Gigi.

He could call Van's cell, but if she saw caller ID, she might not answer. He made the call. It went to voice mail. Maybe she didn't hear it. He called again. Still no response. He left a message. "Please call me."

He sat for five minutes. No return call. Fine, he'd just sit in his truck until she came out.

Twenty minutes went by. Someone tapped on his window, and he nearly jumped out of his skin.

Van's face appeared on the other side. She was frowning.

He didn't bother to open the window, just opened the door and slid out.

"Why are you sitting out here? Dana didn't go back inside, did she? Dorie already left for the Crab, and Suze will draw blood."

"Where were you ? I called you twice."

"I was out taking a walk. I left my cell in my car."

"Feel like taking another walk?"

"Why?"

"Because I need to explain about Dana."

She rolled her eyes; she couldn't help it. Dorie's influence.

"There's nothing going on with us. There was never anything going on with us. She just likes to cause trouble."

"Tell me about it."

"I will if you'll just walk with me."

"That was just an expression. Your life is your business. That's okay. Everything's okay."

"Maybe for you but not for me."

"What's wrong?" She looked closely at his face; he seemed tired but not sick or anything.

"You dumped me."

"What?"

"You dumped me, and I never knew why."

"Oh, come on, Joe, it's ancient history."

"It doesn't feel ancient to me. Or maybe it does. But I'm here and you're here, so I thought maybe you could just tell me why."

Van looked at him. Why did it even matter? Why did he care that she think he wasn't sleeping with Dana?

"You want to know? Okay, I'll tell you. I saw you with Dana."

"I don't get it. You didn't believe whatever she told you today. I know she tried to insinuate that something was going on, but it isn't."

"Joe, you don't have to answer to me. Your life is your own."

"Of course it is. But I'm a tenacious sort of bastard and just want to know. I thought we were going to spend our lives together and you caused a scene and disappeared. I figure it won't kill you to tell me why."

"Did I cause a scene?"

"They're still talking about it down at Mike's." He smiled. "Well, it wasn't that big a scene, but it was so out of character for you that it got everyone's attention."

"It's hard to remember what happened. I remember things were really bad at home, and I was just kind of straddling the lunatic fringe. You know?"

"Yeah, and I didn't help."

"You did, Joe. Never doubt that. You were my rock."

"So why didn't you forgive me and come back?"

She shrugged. It was all so long ago, and she didn't really want to remember. "You could have come after me."

"I did, but you had already hooked up with that pretty boy. I got pissed, then I figured you'd come back once you got bored with him or he went back to school. I'm tenacious, but I was stubborn. I was also stupid."

"We were kids. We were supposed to be stupid."

"You were a kid. I was almost out of college, about to take over the family business."

"That must have been a shock, to lose the farm."

"That they sold out from under me. Maybe you were smart to run. We wouldn't have had much of a life without the farm."

They'd been walking slowly toward the beach, but now Van stopped him. "But you do have the farm. And you made it happen. You couldn't have learned all you learned and gone the places you did if you were stuck with a child wife at home."

He smiled slightly. "You've become very wise since you left."

"School of hard knocks." She hurried on in case he thought she was complaining. "But it was worth it."

"You've had opportunities that you wouldn't have had as a farmer's wife, that's for sure. But you still haven't told me why you left."

They had come to the boardwalk, but instead of turning north toward the Blue Crab, they turned south, away from memory.

Of course, memory followed right along with them. Maybe it would be better just to get it all out, then they could both go into the future unfettered by regrets.

"Okay, let me lay this out as well as I can remember it, then we'll call it done and move on from there. The truth between us. And no ties left."

"That sounds harsh."

"Do you want the truth or not?"

"Yes."

"Okay, I went out with pretty boy once. But I came back to you."

He stopped again. She kept walking.

"I came back and saw you with Dana."

"I don't even remember talking to Dana after that blowup. I pretty much told her to get lost, that she'd ruined everything. I wasn't very nice."

Van sighed. "Men and their selective memories."

Joe just looked at her. "I don't get it."

This was taking forever, and she didn't think she could get through it if he kept interrupting. For even though it had happened years ago, and she'd put it behind her, now those old feelings were bubbling up again. And they hurt all over again.

"I saw you."

"And you threw a fit, and Mike threw you out of the bar."

"After that. Later, days later, I realized that I was being stupid and that I should have 'claimed' you and not let Dana do that to me, but it was too late."

"No, it wasn't."

"Joe, I came to the restaurant and I saw you and Dana in your truck out back."

Joe frowned. "Dana in my truck? She was never in my truck."

"Oh, don't act so innocent, you know exactly what I'm talking about. You didn't come after me. You didn't try to get me back, and then you had sex with Dana. You cheated on me. In a truck for Chrissake."

"Dana? Me and Dana? I never had sex with her. Never even contemplated it; she was trouble on a plate. Still is."

"I saw you. And I just freaked. And the rest as they say is history."

"But you were wrong. I didn't— I— Oh shit." The color drained from his face, leaving a shadow of a tan. "It wasn't Dana."

"Oh, come on, Joe. It doesn't matter anymore. Neither of us would be thinking about it, if you hadn't insisted."

"It wasn't Dana."

"I don't need to know. None of my business."

"It was Gigi."

He went out of focus for a second. There was a roaring in her ears. "Gigi? Gigi? You expect me to believe that?"

"Yes, but nothing even happened."

"I don't believe you. Gigi would never. No."

"Well, she did. She seduced me. Or tried to at least. She jumped in the truck when I was leaving one night. She said she was sorry about us breaking up, and all this other stuff that I don't remember and probably didn't even hear, because she started taking off her clothes.

"She said she wanted to make me feel better. She climbed on top of me and started . . . well, at that point I wasn't unwilling. I mean you were going out with that other guy and—"

"Spare me the details; this was my story."

"No, I won't. She tried, but it didn't work. And here's something that a guy never wants to admit. I was upset and angry and horny as hell, but I couldn't get it up. The more she tried, the limper I got." He laughed, shook his head. "I couldn't do it. Because she wasn't you."

"Gigi? No, Gigi wouldn't do something like that."

Joe looked at her long and hard.

"Gigi?" Van was having a hard time believing that Gigi would ever do something like that.

"She was humiliated, and I was humiliated at first. It lasted all of two minutes. Then she started crying and hit me a couple of times before she jumped out of the truck, ran off into the night. I figured she'd tell everybody what a wimp I was. But she never said a word.

"After that, you disappeared. I went to your house, but your father threatened to kill me. I went to Dorie, but she wouldn't tell me anything.

"Then I heard you left town. But that wasn't like you, Van. You were such a fighter, a survivor. I figured it must have been me, and you were just using Dana as an excuse to get rid of me. I never even thought that you might have seen that stupid comedy in my truck. It didn't last five minutes."

"Gigi? Damn her."

"If you'd only said something. You didn't have to leave."

Van shook her head. Closed her eyes. Pressed her hand to her stomach. "That's not why I left."

"Then why?"

Van swallowed. The words were stuck somewhere inside her. She knew that she had to get them out and be done with it. She was almost at the end of her tale. Then it would be done. She would go back to Manhattan and go on with her life. And Joe would stop wondering what might have been.

"I was pregnant."

He stopped. Stared at her. Shook his head slightly. "But we never—"

Van saw a bench up ahead and made for it.

"No. Pretty boy, God, I can't even remember his name, took me to a party. I got drunk. Something I never did, even then. But

I did that night. I was so out of it, I hardly knew or remembered what happened—until it was over." She had to stop for a breath. "It was my first time, and I paid the price."

Joe slipped his arm behind her, let it rest along the bench, still supportive even in this. "Van."

"Let me finish." She drew breath. "I went to my father, thinking he might have some pity for his only daughter. He called me a whore and threw me out."

"Why didn't you go to Dorie?"

"I did. At first. But I couldn't tell her what happened. I was too ashamed."

She ran her hands down her face. "All these years I've hated Dana for no reason. No wonder Gigi forced that money on me. She was feeling guilty."

Joe sighed. "More likely she wanted you out of the picture. I don't know why she was so persistent. Why me?"

Van was beginning to think she knew. A perfect example of what jumping to conclusions got you. Something she didn't often do but had been doing ever since coming back to Whisper Beach. And something she had done at least twice with Joe.

Chapter 23

NEITHER OF THEM SPOKE FOR A WHILE, JUST LOOKED OUT TO sea, together but not together. And never would be now.

"So Gigi gave you money to get away?"

Van nodded. "The money she'd saved for college. Almost two thousand dollars."

"She never told me. I don't think she told anyone."

Van started to say because she was loyal, but now in view of what Joe had just told her, it was probably to get Van out of the way and make sure she wouldn't be found.

"I just can't believe she did that. She never even intimated that she was interested in you."

"I was clueless, that's for sure. But at least the money helped you get on your feet."

"Her entire savings. I was so exhausted, mentally and emotionally wrung out, that I fell asleep on the train to Manhattan." Van laughed at the irony of it all. "When I woke up, the money was gone."

"Someone stole it?"

Van nodded.

"You went to the city with no money?"

"I had twenty dollars in my pocket."

Joe closed his eyes.

Van nudged him. "It turned out all right."

"So where do we go from here?"

"Well . . . You go raise grapes, and I go back to organizing people's lives."

"Stop it, Van. You don't have to be strong and solitary around me."

"Really, Joe? You think that seeing you would turn me into some weak, helpless female who can barely put on her own mascara?"

Joe flinched. "No— I— Jeez. Where did that come from? You know I don't think that. I never thought that. You're the strongest person I know."

"Sorry. I don't know where that came from. Just too many crazy things have happened to me this week. Most of them pretty hard to swallow."

"Including me?"

She smiled at him. "No, thank God. You seem like a really nice guy."

Joe barked out a laugh. "Well, thanks, but I'm talking about the chemistry between us. You have to admit it's still there."

"Do I?" She did. She felt herself moving closer to him, drawn almost without her will, and she knew that she would still fit right in that place on his shoulder. She needed Suze here to tell her that quote about going the way that caused madness. Because she would be crazy to let attraction derail her carefully built life.

"Yeah, you do. I feel it. And I'm pretty sure you do, too. That didn't change over the years. Or we wouldn't be sitting here."

"We're sitting here because you wanted an explanation for why I left, and I thought you deserved to know."

Joe gave her a look, the look. He didn't believe her; she wasn't even sure she believed herself.

"If you'd let down all that protective shit you've thrown up around you, you'd feel it. We'll always have it no matter where you run or how long you stay away. It's there."

Van stood. "Stop it."

"You don't need it, Van. You're just as strong as you ever were. More so. You won't dissolve if you let your control relax just a little."

"I let my control relax once, and I nearly died from it. I do just fine the way I am."

"Died?"

"Didn't you wonder what happened to the baby? I miscarried. Okay? Suze barely got me to a hospital before I bled to death."

"I'm sorry."

"So go find yourself some nice woman—"

"Look, I haven't been pining for you all these years. I haven't even thought about you except occasionally when something specific recalls the past. And for your info, I've met a lot of nice women."

"Good for you."

He shrugged. "I just didn't want to marry any of them."

"I have to go."

Joe smiled. Then laughed. "I can see the wheels in your brain turning a mile a minute. Stop thinking, Van. Stop worrying about the past, stop holding on to everything but the present. And don't you dare run out again. This time it won't be so easy to hide."

"Please don't make this hard."

"I don't mean to. Just see where we go from here. It might

be our separate ways." He laughed. "But not until after Sunday lunch. Mom expressly invited you."

"Joe, really . . ."

"You wouldn't want to hurt her feelings. Or Dad's or Granddad's . . . would you?"

"Joe, before you start making plans, there's something else you should know."

"Okay. You have a boyfriend? You're secretly married?"

"I can't have children. I got all messed up with the miscarriage. So— So just put that on your family tree."

She saw his face fall. Her heart ached, it really did, and her lungs were so tight, it was hard for her to breathe. Because suddenly it mattered to her, too.

Then he smiled again, not as humorously as a few seconds before, but it was a smile.

"Sunday lunch. No strings. No expectations except the best pot roast you've had in years."

Van had to turn away, because her mouth had twisted, and if he looked at her, she would break down. As it was, she couldn't stop a tear or two falling.

Joe brushed it away with one finger.

"They should change the name of Whisper Beach to Cry Baby Beach."

He put his arm around her. "Lot of tears over at Dorie's?"

"Bunches. But some fun times, too. Now I better get back and report on the Dana sighting so everyone can stop worrying."

"Yeah, I have to finish closing up Grandy's. Owen's coming to help. He's turned out to be a pretty good worker . . . and a big eater." Joe smiled, and Van's heart hurt.

They walked back to Dorie's, Joe's fingers stretched warmly against her back. "So I'll pick you up at noon. Don't dress up."

Van didn't answer. She suddenly wanted to see all the Enthorpes, the people who had accepted her into their family because she had no functioning family of her own. She supposed it would be rude not to see them. And Mom Enthorpe did make the best pot roast she'd ever tasted.

Joe's hand slipped down to her waist, pulling her slightly closer to him as they walked.

When they got back to Dorie's, Van stopped by his truck.

"You're not going in?" he asked.

"I don't think I'm ready to face Gigi right now. I might scratch her eyes out."

"That's my girl."

Van started to say *I'm not your girl,* but she wasn't sure of anything right now. Not even that.

"Get in the truck, Joe."

"Noon." He got in and drove away.

She watched until he got to the end of the street, then got her cell out of the car and called Suze. "Hey, where are you?"

"In my room."

"Alone?"

"Yeah. Dorie went to the Crab, and Gigi's downstairs waiting for you to come back."

"Do you have time to take a break?"

"Yeah, actually it's turned out to be easier than I could have hoped for. What's up, where are you?"

"On the corner."

"What are you doing there?"

"Avoiding Gigi. Can you get out of the house and meet me without her knowing it?"

"Sure, but I'm not going to climb down any fire escape. If she catches me, I'll tell her I'm going out to get some air and think."

Suze showed up a few minutes later.

"She was watching television, doesn't even know I'm gone. Now spill."

"First, who said that thing about the way that madness lies or something like that."

"King Lear. That way madness lies. Why? Are you about to do something stupid?"

"When have you ever known me to do something stupid?"

Suze shrugged. "Once?"

"Yeah. I just want to make sure I'm not about to make it twice."

"Oh Lord, let's go somewhere we can sit. I don't want to make any life-changing decisions standing on a street corner, though that would be an appropriate piece of symbolism, if a little trite."

"Suze!"

"Sorry, you set me off with the King Lear thing."

They started walking toward town.

"So?"

"A lot of stuff."

"Then it's a good thing I brought my wallet," Suze said.

It was happy hour, but they opted for ice cream on a bench instead. Already the crowds had thinned out. Day-trippers were on their way back home to beat the traffic. People never learned you just couldn't beat the traffic leaving the shore. Ever.

"Okay, start," Suze said, lifting a spoonful of butter pecan to her mouth.

"I'll just tell it in the order it happened."

Suze nodded and kept eating.

"I went looking for Dana, thought she might have gone to Joe's. And of course she had. Joe was in the shower, or so she said, and she insinuated they were an item and she was staying with him."

"That is such a lie. He would never."

"I know, but I sort of had a knee-jerk reaction and left. When I got back here and saw Gigi's car, well, I just didn't feel like talking so I went for a walk."

"And I was upstairs oblivious to everything but my own problems. Sorry."

"No. I called you, and you dropped everything to come down, didn't you?"

"I guess. So go on."

"When I got back, Joe's truck was here, and Joe was in it. We went for another walk and I told him everything about what happened and getting pregnant and seeing him and Dana in his truck."

Suze stopped with her spoon halfway to her mouth. Ice cream dripped down the front of her shirt. Van moved her hand, so that it dripped back into the cup.

"I know, I know, but you shouldn't hit me with this stuff when I'm eating. But don't you dare stop now."

"It wasn't Dana."

Suze looked up, pushed her spoon into the ice cream, and gave Van her full attention.

"It was Gigi."

"Whaaa?"

"It was Gigi. He has no reason to lie about something like that. I guess she had come to assuage his—"

Suze snorted.

"You've got a dirty mind. His wounded feelings. When I saw them, it was getting dark; I just saw naked skin and jumped to the wrong conclusion. But I guess she didn't manage to assuage his feelings or anything else."

"You mean they ended up not doing anything?"

Van shook her head. "Evidently. Unfortunately, in my hurry to get away, I missed that part."

"Oh Lord. So all that followed was for nothing."

"Well, I did get a new life out of it."

"Of course. I didn't mean that."

"I know what you meant. No, the question is . . ."

"What do we do about Gigi? Are you just going to pretend you don't know or call her on it?"

Van shrugged. "I don't see that it matters anymore. But with Dana it might. Because now I'm wondering if Dana really did take your grant application."

"You think Gigi set her up?"

"It's hard to believe, but Dana seemed genuinely surprised."

"Or surprised that she was caught."

"Or wanted to be caught. Who steals something then puts it somewhere it could be easily found?"

"Maybe she thought no one would look. It was in her underwear drawer."

"There is that. I don't know. Suddenly things are not making sense. Gigi tried to seduce my boyfriend twelve years ago, but she didn't succeed." Van leaned into Suze. "He couldn't get it up."

Suze's eyes widened. "You lie."

"No, but don't spread it around."

"I'm guessing he doesn't have that problem now?"

"I wouldn't know. I'm pretty sure he doesn't, but how humiliating for him."

"And for Gigi," Suze added. "She steals her best friend's boyfriend and he doesn't even want her. That's the stuff of black comedy. Do you think Gigi is still acting in reaction to that?"

"I don't know. I think I should talk to Uncle Nate. There's something not quite— I don't know."

"Not quite stable about Gigi," Suze finished.

"And I'd like to talk to Dana first."

"Even though she tried to make you think Joe was boffing her?"

"I think she did that because she was hurt. Like we were all getting to be friends again, then wham. We were all ganging up against her."

"But that initial getting close might have been enough motive for Gigi to steal my grant papers out of the mailbox and implicate Dana. I'd have to go back to Princeton, Dana would become persona non gratis, and Gigi would have you all to herself." Suze sighed.

"Except that I'll be going back to Manhattan, too." Though Gigi had begged Van to take her with her. God, she had been so dense.

"I guess we weren't very sympathetic. Her life is falling apart and we were trying to have fun."

"I think her life fell apart way before Clay died; that's another reason I want to talk to Nate. See if lending her my house will help or make it worse. I know having her and the kids living with them is taking its toll on Amelia and Nate, both. But I'm not sure Gigi can take care of her family without help."

"You'd still let her live in your house after all she's done? Well, we only know that she tried to seduce Joe, bless him. But we'll have to ask her about the other. She can't get away with those kind of things.

"Excuse me if I don't feel any sympathy for her. She may have just killed my chances of getting that grant."

"What do you have to do for it?"

"Write several analyses of texts. Fortunately I've done something similar already for other situations, so I lucked out. But I'll still have to spend the weekend working."

"Except for your mother's party."

"Except for that. And Monday I'll send it off and hope for the best. So what do you want to do?"

"Talk to Dana."

"Is she still at Joe's?"

"He dropped her at the Crab."

"And Dorie's going to take her back?"

"Dorie gave express instructions to get her there. She has faith in all of us."

"Well, let's go."

"Us?"

"You don't think you're going to confront her without me ?"

"The early birds are probably out already; it will be too late to talk to her," Van said.

"Better to take five and clear the air than to let it fester."

"Is that a quote?"

"Not that I know of."

Van looked back toward the house. "But what are we going to do with Gigi?"

"We could take her with us and make her confess."

Van shook her head. "If I'm wrong, it might push her over the brink."

"Then let's go straight to the restaurant."

As they passed Dorie's street they looked down the block. Gigi's car was gone.

"I guess she gave up waiting for us," Suze said.

"I guess I was pretty rude."

"I guess you're right."

"I just feel—"

"Stop right there. If you're about to say you feel sorry for her—"

"I was," Van said. "Old habits."

"You were always taking care of her, we all were, we all cared that she didn't feel bad, made sure she didn't get in trouble, and she let us. But guess what? She could take care of herself. Witness how quickly she went after your boyfriend. She used us all the time. And I bet she's using us now. So stop feeling sorry for her."

"Okay, Professor, I get what she did with Joe. But why steal your grant application? You never did anything to her?"

"Neither did you. But we're friends now, and Gigi is extremely jealous. I noticed it right away; that's why I've been trying to keep a low profile."

"Why didn't you say something?"

"I did."

"Ah. Most favored nation."

Suze nodded.

"Sometimes I'm a little dense. Come on. Maybe we can catch Dana on her break."

VAN AND SUZE stood in the back hallway while waiters and busers rushed by, waiting for Dorie to bring Dana back.

Dana put her hands on her hips and scowled. "Dorie's taking my tables, and probably my tips. You've got five minutes."

"Let's go outside where it's quiet."

Dana didn't move. "Are you back to ream me some more for something I didn't do? 'Cause I've just about had it with you people."

Suze pushed her. "You're about to get vindicated . . . maybe."

"What the hell is that? I didn't do anything."

"We came to apologize. Now get outside." Suze gave her another push. This time she went.

Van led the way onto the boardwalk and down the steps to Whisper Beach. It seemed like the appropriate place to clear the air.

Dana stopped as soon as they were on the sand. "Can you get to it? Some of us have to work for a living."

And then Van got it. She and Dana were more alike than she'd like to think. Not the flirting and the sharp tongue and the overly sexy clothes. But the fear. Dana wouldn't make the first move. Ever. It was amazing that she'd gotten herself to Dorie's that night when she'd shown up bloody and beaten. And Van bet she wouldn't have gone if she'd known that Van and Suze were there.

It was all protection, that hard-edged attitude. Joe had nailed it that afternoon. Van had her own protective shell. She had needed it first starting out. It kept her alive and made her successful. But she had survived and thrived, and she didn't need it anymore. Until she came back to Whisper Beach; and she didn't even need it here.

"I'm an idiot."

"I coulda told you that without you dragging me all the way out here."

"Oh, just be quiet," Suze said.

"Okay, I'll make this fast," Van said. "I blamed you for breaking Joe and me up. I was wrong; I broke us up. I saw you flirting with him, and I got pissed, but when I got over it, I came back and found him, well, let's just say I thought it was you in the cab of his truck."

"What?" For the first time Dana dropped her façade. "He had somebody in his truck? Why that lowdown— And you thought it was me? Ha. Who was it? Damn him, I'd been after him before you even started working at the Crab. And he never—Ugh. Who was it? Did he tell you who it was?"

"Just that it wasn't you. So I'm apologizing."

"Hell, is that what you've been talking about? You think I boinked your boyfriend? I would have. But he wasn't interested in me. Never was."

"I'm sorry I jumped to the wrong conclusion, though you weren't even aware of it. I'm still mad because you were flirting with him."

Dana grinned. "A girl can try. And what about today?"

"That is still open to debate," Suze said.

Dana started to go up the steps. Suze grabbed her by her shirt and pulled her back to the sand. "I said debate."

"You really didn't take Suze's letter?"

"No. First of all, when was I up in time to get the mail?"

Van thought back, and she couldn't think of a time when they hadn't all been together.

"And second, what would be the point? Why do I give a shit if Suze gets whatever it is she's trying to get. No skin off my nose." Dana looked from Van to Suze. "How do I know that one of you didn't do it?"

"That's absurd." Suze said. "I wouldn't steal my own mail."

"And I didn't steal it either," Van said.

Then a look of understanding crossed Dana's face. "No, Gigi was getting it on with Joe in his truck? I don't believe it."

"How did you jump from grant applications to Joe's truck?" Van asked, trying to slow down the pace of the conversation. She wasn't sure how much she should tell, or if she should even speculate around Dana. Could she be trusted?

To do what? Tell Gigi what they were thinking?

"That's it, isn't it? And Gigi took the letter and put it in my drawer."

"Another big leap," Suze said.

"No, it isn't. What the hell was she doing in my room going through my dresser?"

"Putting laundry away," Van said.

"And when did Gigi ever help out with anything? She never did shit. Gigi, can you help bring that crate of lettuce over? She'd bat her eyes and whine 'it's too heavy for me' and would get one of the guys to do it. Someone called the cops because we were too loud, and everybody would rush around so Gigi wouldn't get caught because she was the one doing the screaming.

"Good ole Gigi, never had a bad word to say about anyone. And news flash. It wasn't because she was so nice. It's because she was a spineless wonder. So yeah. I bet she took Suze's letter. I don't know why, maybe to punish Suze for being friends with you and being a professor while she married a deadbeat and now has to live with her parents."

"Pretty astute observation," Suze said.

"I'm no genius, Professor. But I know bitches."

"Gigi?"

"Yeah, precious little Gigi. That sweet-girl routine didn't fly in high school, and it certainly doesn't fly at thirty." She stopped. "Shit."

"What?"

"Oh shit."

"What?"

"Nothing. Just something Joe said." She smoothed her spiky hair back with both hands. "Just shit."

The three of them stood looking at one another for a second, then Dana visibly shook herself. "Remember when Gigi came the first day I was there? The look on her face, and the 'Why is she here?' Gigi took one look at me and decided to get me out of the house in case we started talking and you finally came to your senses about me and Joe. Well, she got me out of the house. And got you all to herself. The prize goes to Gigi."

Van and Suze both stared at her.

Then finally Suze said, "Amazing."

Dana shrugged. "Just a theory, Prof. I have to get back to work." She climbed the stairs.

Van ran after her. "So come back to Dorie's tonight."

"What? Afraid I'll try to shack up with Joe?"

"No. 'Cause we'd like to have you there."

Dana narrowed her eyes. "I'll think about." And she walked away.

As soon as Van and Suze returned to the house, Van called her uncle Nate. She told him she had some concerns and also needed advice about the house she owned. He agreed to meet her when Amelia and Gigi and the kids were at church the next morning.

Then she called Gigi at home and told her that she'd made plans to visit the Enthorpes the following day, but they would be working at renovating the Crab on Monday if she was free.

Gigi sounded disappointed but said she'd try to get over on Monday.

"Okay, done," Van said when she'd hung up. "Though I'm not sure what I should say to Uncle Nate. I'll ask him whether he thinks I should let Gigi and the kids live in the house, but what do I say about Gigi? He's bound to ask me about how she's doing."

Suze looked up from where she was stretched out on the couch. "Are you sure Dana isn't playing us?" she asked. "It wouldn't be the first time."

"I know, but I don't think so. I've become pretty good at reading people. I guess you do in my business. You learn why some cling to possessions that they don't need and that don't have any real or even sentimental value. Why they wait until they're overwhelmed to get help. What drives them to succeed. How they cope with failure, or fear, or anger. You'd be amazed at what you learn about folks just from cleaning up their messes and organizing their lives."

She looked over the plate of cheese and meat and olives. Chose an olive. "But I've been slow on the uptake here. I thought Gigi was just grieving. But now I think it's more."

"Yeah. Dana read that situation pretty accurately. I always thought Gigi was a wuss, but she was so sweet you sort of forgave her for it. And we did try to protect her."

"We did. She was my cousin and best friend growing up. Or at least I thought she was. But the truth of that somehow changes in light of what Joe told me and the theft of your grant application. I mean, what happened with Joe is really inconsequential . . ."

"I'll say." Suze laughed, then started coughing and pounding her chest. "Swallowed the wrong way." She gasped for air.

"Well, besides the lack of success, it isn't funny."

Suze shook her head energetically. "No." She burst out laughing again.

Van tried not to follow suit and gave it up. She was the first to stop. "But it's sad and pitiful. I don't think she went to Joe because she felt it was her duty to help him feel better."

"God, no. I think Dana was right on that, too. She was jealous of you. We just didn't see it."

"I know," Van said. She was serious again. "And what does that say about us? About me?"

"That we were young and clueless just like all the other young and clueless."

"But," Van said, "we're not young and clueless now."

"No. And she came close to screwing me big time."

"I know. But she did 'expose' the theft in time for you to still get your application in."

"I don't think it was because she saw the error of her ways, Van. I think it was because she saw you and Dana getting chummy and she panicked." Suze shrugged. "Or she got cold feet and couldn't take the pressure and guilt any longer."

Suze sat up. "Look, I know you're having a hard time believing that Gigi would do something like this. But it makes sense. She even announced the mail at least twice. I thought she was trying to be helpful. I don't even remember Dana being downstairs when the mail came, and most of the time I was practically sitting at the door waiting for the mail carrier."

"I know. It does make sense. It was just so much easier to blame Dana."

"I think maybe there's been too much of that already," Suze said.

"Blaming Dana?"

"Blaming in general."

Van frowned. "I suppose, but don't quote anything about it."

"I wasn't going to. I think it's time to act instead."

"I was just thinking the same thing. And I know where I have to start."

Chapter 24

Van met Nate Moran at ten the next morning at the pavilion of a nearby lake. He was sitting inside, drinking coffee from a cardboard cup. He stood when he saw Van walking across the park toward him.

When she stepped onto the platform, he handed her another cup. "I wasn't sure how you like it so I brought everything on the side."

"Black is fine, thanks." She sat down. He sat down. He seemed nervous.

"You said you needed some advice."

"I do. But it's kind of wrapped up in a lot of different things, so I was hoping you could help me. It's about my house."

"I've been having one of the boys go over and mow the grass," he said. "But I don't think anyone's been inside, since Robbie . . . your dad . . . moved out."

"When did he move out?"

"When he finally realized you weren't coming back. He took the key over to the lawyer's office and turned it in."

"He thought I was coming back?"

"Hoped you were coming back."

Van didn't want to talk about this. She knew they would have to go there, but not yet.

"It looks great, thank you."

"You been over?"

"Yeah. I've been trying to decide whether to sell it. I'd have to have a carting company come over and clear it out, then hire someone to paint it. It would take awhile."

"I see. Well, I can take care of that if you want."

Impulsively, Van placed her hand on top of his big calloused one. "You're so good to me, Uncle Nate. But you don't have to worry about it. That's not what I came to ask."

He looked tired. Burdened, maybe.

"I was thinking that maybe Gigi and the kids would like to live in it until she gets back on her feet."

Nate had been contemplating his coffee cup, but at this he looked up at her. His eyes were bloodshot but not from the usual Moran excuse. Uncle Nate was losing sleep.

"What's wrong, Uncle Nate?"

"Gigi's never been on her feet. Don't know why she just never—hell, I don't know what to do with her. She just mopes around the house all day except when she's over with you gals. Then when she gets home, Amelia lights into her for shirking her responsibilities and ignoring her children.

"The children yo-yo from being scared and quiet to acting like little heathens. And Gigi just ignores them."

"Maybe Clay's death has really . . . challenged her."

"Clay's been dead a week. Gigi's been like this ever since she moved back with us. I offered to lend them some money so they could rent a place until they rebuilt their house. But Clay didn't want to take charity, and Lord help me, I think Gigi just wanted to come home.

"And she did. And I don't think she plans on leaving."

"She can live in my house."

Nate sighed so deeply that his shoulders seemed to implode. "I appreciate it, but I'm not sure that it will fix what's wrong with Gigi."

"Depression?"

He shrugged.

"Have you thought she might need professional help?"

"You mean like a psychiatrist?"

"Maybe just a therapist; they have therapists who will see the whole family. I hear it can help in times like these."

"All fine and good, but she hasn't got insurance."

Van didn't want to touch that one. And she didn't want to offend Nate by suggesting aid.

"Maybe you can get her into the clinic and see what they can advise."

Nate nodded. "Maybe she just needs time."

Now was the time to tell Nate about the theft. She scooted closer to her uncle. She didn't know why, it just seemed the only thing she could do to let him know she wanted to help. Especially since she was about to drop something that could only hurt and embarrass him.

"Uncle Nate, I don't know quite how to say this, and it may be part of Gigi's general malaise, but I have reason to believe, I think, that— Well, Suze has been waiting for a very important letter. It was supposed to come in the mail this week. But it didn't."

"What does this have to do with Gigi?"

"Gigi found the letter in Dana's dresser yesterday. You remember Dana; she's been staying at Dorie's."

"Good for her. That Bud Albright is mean as a snake. But how did Gigi find the letter?"

"She was helping put laundry away and saw it in one of the drawers in Dana's room. She came down and showed us. We immediately turned on Dana, who of course, denied it.

"And I'm sorry to say that I'm afraid that Gigi may have taken it in order to get back at Dana for something."

"No, Gigi wouldn't do something like that. Did you ask her? What did she say?"

"I didn't ask her. Uncle Nate, she seems fragile. More fragile than grief would normally make her. I didn't want to even suggest it to her until I talked to you."

"Well, I'll talk to her." Nate suddenly went from concerned parent to someone who reminded her of her own father.

"No!" She grabbed his wrist. "It's not that big of a deal. I was just concerned for her welfare. It's not like her to do something like this."

Nate's eyes glistened, and Van prayed that he wouldn't start crying.

"Van, I would never hurt her or any of my children, if that's what you're thinking."

She shook her head. "But one thing did seem odd, and maybe she didn't really mean it, but she begged me to take her to Manhattan with me."

"For a vacation?"

"No. I think she was talking about living there. She said Amelia would keep the kids."

"Oh God." Nate dropped his head to his hands. "I don't know what to do with her."

"Just take her to someone who can tell you how to help her. I'm worried about her."

Nate nodded, suddenly resolute. "I'll deal with Gigi, and I may even take you up on your house offer, but I'll pay you rent."

"No—"

"Don't argue with me. We'll deal with this Gigi business, I promise you." He took a deep breath. Chewed on his lip. "I've listened to you, and now it's time for you to listen to me."

Van moved back ever so slightly. Was he mad that she'd meddled in their family affairs?

"Your father was a disappointed man."

She jumped to her feet.

"Sit down. I never said anything as long as your mother was alive and you were a girl. But I'm going to say it now, and you're going to listen, then we'll forget all about it if you want."

Van reluctantly sat down. She steeled herself to listen to excuses or incriminations about her father.

"Like I said, he was a disappointed man."

"That didn't give him the right—"

"No, it didn't. But I want you to know both sides of that story, before you leave again. Maybe I shoulda said something sooner, but I didn't. Now I'm going to. And you're going to sit and listen till I'm done, then you'll have your turn.

"Robbie was a smart, talented boy. More than all the rest of us put together. He always wanted to be an artist. A painter. And he was. Got himself a scholarship to art school. Oh, he had a bright future—being poor and living from whatever he could earn from painting."

It was hard for Van to imagine her father as an artistic young man. And yet she'd just seen his paintings.

"Our father wasn't so happy about his choice, but he went along with it. Mama . . . you didn't know her. She died when we were just kids and she would have been a godsend to your daddy and mamma." He drifted off, a slight smile on his face.

"At that time Robbie was going out with someone else, planned to marry her. But they had a fight or something, and he hooked up with your mother. It was spring break. All the kids were drinking and acting wild, like they do. Your mother got him at a vulnerable time. She wanted him and damn the consequences.

"And she got him. One night. One night of stupid, drunken college student madness and that was that. She got pregnant or so she said. And that it was his. That was all it took; both families demanded he do the right thing by her. There were tears shed. Some real fights. They both had tempers. She wanted him to stay and marry her. He just wanted it to all go away.

"But your mamma wasn't even out of high school, and she refused to put the baby up for adoption. He felt trapped, but he took it like a man . . . at first."

"You make it sound like the Dark Ages."

"It was around here. Still is in a lot of respects.

"Their families insisted. Robbie balked, because he loved someone else, but in the end he gave in. And there went his dreams. Lost his love. He was—and I'm sorry to say this—shackled to someone he didn't even like and someone who hated him for not loving her."

Van tried to swallow, but her mouth was dry. She wanted to deny what he was saying, to say that her mother loved her father, and that he was the monster. But since she'd been in Whisper Beach, she was remembering things, scenes were flashing in her head, scenes that she'd spent her whole life interpreting in one way and which now didn't seem like the complete truth. Still she tried to deny what Nate was saying.

"He loved you, though. I know he didn't show it. He just got caught in a downward spiral. The families got together and got him a job at the post office. Of all things, the most boring, mindless job for a man like him I can imagine. He said he'd open up a store, or work in construction, but they'd gotten it into their heads that he'd have better benefits at the post office, insurance and a pension."

Nate shook his head. "You can have no idea what that did to my brother. My baby brother."

"No. My mother was always loving toward him; he ignored her." But there had been times that her mother had instigated it. The looks, the innuendos that Van had brushed aside and buried because she didn't want to question her hatred. That hate had kept her warm at night, had made her strong, a survivor.

"Why didn't he divorce her? Or she could have divorced him."

"Not here in the Dark Ages. Though I suspect Robbie tried. In the early days he still had hope of marrying Ruth."

Van started. "Ruth?"

"That was the girl's name. I forget her last name, but she was a nice girl, and good for Robbie." He sighed.

So one night of stupidity. Van could almost laugh out loud, but it would be her undoing. He'd probably done the same thing she'd done with pretty boy, and what she thought Joe had done to her.

Like father like daughter. She wanted to throw up. No wonder he'd called her a whore.

Nate lowered his head, looked up again. "I'll never forget the night he showed up at my door. It was a few weeks after he'd returned to school. He didn't have a break, so I knew something must be wrong. It was raining hard, which looking back was pretty damn appropriate.

"He told me he'd gotten her pregnant and she wanted him to marry her."

"I thought he was nuts. We weren't even sure it was really his. Your mamma had a bit of a reputation. He didn't know, but once you were born it was pretty clear. You were a Moran through and through.

"Anyway the families swooped in and made him do the right thing. Me and my other brothers were pretty pissed. One mistake and the rest of your life is shot."

He shifted uncomfortably. "Not that he held it against you. Never."

"He hated my mother for tricking him into marrying her."

"Pretty much. His dream was ruined. Nobody even thought of that. We were all just normal folks with normal jobs, ordinary houses. But Robbie was a dreamer. And that ended for him pretty quick."

"He hated me, too."

"No never, not in his most horrible drunken state. Don't you remember anything good about him?"

Van shook her head, but there was a time at the Ocean City boardwalk, he won her a pink bear. It had been on her bed when she visited the house the other day. "No," she said, trying to push the memory away. "He destroyed my glass paintings and kicked me out of the house."

"Yeah, he'd stooped pretty low by the end. I think he was sorry."

"He was happy when she died. He cried over her casket; I thought maybe he was sorry for what he'd done. But they were tears of joy. I wanted to kill him that day."

"He wasn't happy," Nate said shortly. "If he cried, it was because he'd done his duty and she'd left his life in tatters."

"No, no." Van didn't want to hear more. She didn't want to have anything else about her life turned upside down. She tried to stand up, but Nate pulled her back down.

"He wasn't a kind man, but he was a sweet and creative boy."

"So who is this Ruth person that he lives with?"

"What are you talking about?"

"I saw him. He's painting again. He has a show over at the gallery in Whisper Beach. I saw him."

"How was he? How did he look?"

"Just fine. He looked just fine. How come I never knew he wanted to be a painter? Is that why he was so awful when I tried to do anything like that?"

"I had no idea. What did he say? He hasn't talked to the family in years."

"Nothing. Not that he would have, but I didn't give him a chance. But she came running after me. 'Your father wants to see you. Here's our address. *Our* address.' Who the hell does she think she is? Why should he get to have an 'our' when my mother didn't, when I don't?"

Nate just looked at her. Looked like he wanted to say something and then just gave up. "Her name was Ruth? Ruth . . . Singleton, I think that was her name."

Van shrugged. "We didn't get to be that good of friends."

"Vanessa Moran. Spite doesn't become you."

"Not like it became my father."

"Stop it. You don't know what you're talking about. I'll grant that you had a nasty childhood, but it took two people to make it that way. Believe me. Your mother was no saint. In fact, she wasn't even a nice person." He stood up. "Thank you for telling me about Gigi. She won't be needing your house. We take care of our own." He strode away, tossing his coffee cup in a trash receptacle without slowing his pace.

Van jumped up. "Uncle Nate, wait." He kept walking. "I'm sorry. Please wait."

He slowed. Finally stopped but didn't turn around. And Van ran to him. "I'm sorry, I'm sorry," she said as his big arms surrounded her in a hug. "It just hurts too much."

They stood silently. Then Nate gave her a final squeeze. "Ruth Singleton and Robbie were engaged when he went off to school. That was real love. I hope it's her. They were good for each other. Go see your father. Then you can decide what you want to think about him, if you never want to see him again or even acknowledge him. I'll accept that. And so will he."

They started walking back toward the street.

"And what about the house?"

"Let me talk to Amelia. She'll know what's best to do."

It was almost noon when Van ran upstairs to her room at Dorie's. It had been a long heartrending two hours. And she still hadn't decided what to do. Already her world was listing perilously to the side; another belief thrown overboard might tilt it over completely. And if it did, how would she ever right herself again?

Suze's door opened, and she followed Van across the hall. "What happened?"

"Where do I start? Come in, I've got to change. Joe is picking me up at twelve."

"Ach. That's right; okay, give me the condensed version."

"I told Nate about Gigi and the letter, not about Gigi and Joe in his truck. Old news and nobody's business. I offered the house, then we had a bit of an altercation and he said they didn't want it, but I think he'll come around."

"An altercation?"

Van nodded, stopped pulling clothes out of the closet and sat on the bed. "He told me about the circumstances of my father and mother's marriage. It wasn't pretty. I guess they were both at fault, though I'm not ready to forgive him. I don't think I ever will be. He made my life a living hell, and I was just an innocent kid. But he was in love with someone else, maybe that Ruth woman that ran after us. But the families made him marry my mother because in one stupid night he got her pregnant."

"Shite," Suze said and sat down on the bed beside her.

"Is that Chaucerian? But basically, yes, history repeats itself, only I had the good sense to run." Van pulled her knees up and hugged them. "No wonder he called me a whore. He was probably reliving his own past. Ugh. I'm just like my mother." Her voice cracked.

Suze yanked her hair hard.

"Ouch."

"No time for tears if Joe's picking you up. You're not like your mother or your father. You're you. And we all like you that way. You can wait up for me tonight and we can have a sob fest over the inequities of being women in the twenty-first century. We'll invite Dorie and Dana to join us."

Van blew out a breath and stood up. "Thanks. I needed that. What do you think I should wear?"

Suze followed Van to the closet where she'd finally hung up clothes from her suitcase. "Wow, you have such great clothes, and you haven't worn any of these since you've been here."

"I haven't exactly been anyplace that called for them. What about this?" She lifted out a swirling gauze sundress in the colors of the ocean.

"That's beautiful."

"But it calls for heels, and I don't intend to ruin my good shoes traipsing over fields. Besides, Joe said not to dress up. Which I think means really don't dress up." She took out a pair of beige cropped pants and a silk tee. "I'll throw a lightweight jacket over it in case it's too informal. I seem to remember flowered shirtwaists, and jeans with creased pleats. But that was a long time ago."

"I guess you won't be here to help me dress for La Party."

"Didn't Dana offer to do your nails?" Van pulled off her shirt and slipped the tee over her head.

"Not a chance. I'm willing to give her the benefit of the doubt, but I'm not taking a chance with my fingers. I need them to type."

"What time does the party start?"

"Fiveish, but I can push it until six and call it fashionably late. My mother won't like it, but in the words of a great English professor, 'Tough.'"

"Okay, I'll ask Joe if we can get back by fiveish. It's only lunch and a look at the vineyards. Three and a half hours should do it."

"What if it leads to something else? I can manage."

"I'm sure you can. You just have to pay attention. And it won't lead anywhere else. We both have avocations."

"You mean you're not interested?"

"I don't know. I'm not jumping into anything. I think we've all learned that doesn't pay. And I get the feeling he's not ready to take the plunge either. We'll just take it as it comes."

Van was dressed and just putting on a touch of makeup when the downstairs bell rang.

"Gawd, it's just like going on a date," Suze said in a falsetto.

"I bet that's a quote from somewhere."

"Probably," said Suze. "You don't have to hurry back. I'll survive."

"I'll be back," Van called as she jogged down the stairs.

"Now, that *is* a quote. Have fun."

Chapter 25

Joe was standing on the porch when Van opened the front door.

"You could have just called my cell. You didn't have to get out of the truck."

"Yeah, I know."

"So gallant," she said and headed down the steps. She was trying to act more relaxed than she felt. She'd managed to push the idea of seeing the Enthorpes again to the back of her mind while everything else was happening, but now it seemed like one more thing that was threatening to derail her . . . could she possibly call this a vacation?

She realized Joe had gone ahead of her and was holding the truck door open.

"Are you sure?"

"Get in. They're expecting you. Granddad even said he'd put on a tie."

"He didn't."

"He did, but I told him it was going to be casual since I had ulterior motives."

She looked at him suspiciously.

He leaned in through the door opening until his face loomed awfully close to hers. "I'm planning to hit you up for some free advice about the still room."

She breathed out. "After plying me with good home-cooked food?"

"That's the plan." He raised his eyebrows and closed the door.

She waited until they were pulling away from the curb before she said, "I don't know anything about wineries. You should have given me a heads-up, and I would have done a little research."

"Well, there's plenty of time. I installed all the vats and things last winter on the outside chance the vines produce enough grapes for a trial run."

"You didn't consider selling to another winery until your own vines get established?"

"Sure I considered it. But the whole point is to have something that is wholly Enthorpe."

She looked at his profile. "Like the dairy was. That's neat."

"Yep, if I don't lose my shirt, along with Drew's and Brett's."

"You'll be successful."

He glanced quickly over at her then back to the street. "Thanks. So what have you been up to besides revamping the Crab?"

She laughed. "Since yesterday?"

"No. Since we've hardly had time just to talk. So much weird stuff going on, and stuff being dredged up. And you letting me rattle on about the vineyard. You haven't really had a chance to talk about what you've been doing all this time . . . since you left."

"You said you've seen my website. That's what I've been doing."

"Just working?"

"Yeah. I spent some lean years while I worked my way through business school. Started the business and luckily it's really grown."

"Wait. Start at the beginning. How did you get to business school?"

"I just . . . well, after I . . . after I was better, I got a job cleaning houses. I lucked out. It was an established firm, and I had a pretty regular schedule so when I'd saved up enough money, I registered for night classes."

"But where were you living?"

"With some other girls who worked for the same service. They were from all over and some barely spoke English, but . . ." She smiled. "They were all very clean."

As Joe returned her smile, his eyes softened and Van hurried on before he asked more. There had been eight of them living in a one-bedroom fourth-floor walk-up. The stairs to the apartment might as well have been Mount Everest after a full day of cleaning.

"Occasionally clients would ask me to do something extra like reorganize a closet, help them move some furniture. All after hours, so I made a little extra money. By the time I graduated, I had a nice little side business going and had managed to save some money. I was able to quit the cleaning job and do my own business full-time. I've been lucky."

"You've been smart."

"I guess. I really didn't have a choice—" She stopped. She'd had a choice once. And she'd blown it. She wouldn't have a choice like that again. "Anyway, the business has really taken off."

"So much so that you're thinking about expanding."

"Yeah. It seems like the natural thing to do."

"What do you do for relaxation?"

"I don't."

"Don't you ever take time off?"

"You're looking at it."

Joe laughed. "I guess you haven't had any time to relax since you got back."

"Nope. It's like I showed up and the kid pulled his finger out of the dike."

"I was thinking it must be like one of those reality shows where they put a bunch of people in a house and wait for them to go berserk."

"Just like it. And my staff are going to be so disappointed that I haven't gotten a tan."

"You have another week."

"I'll probably go back on Saturday once I see that the restaurant is up and running."

Joe was silent. "Well, that's a few days."

"Except that I have a lot of stuff to get through. Like the house and deciding whether to see my father. I feel sort of bad. I met with my uncle Nate this morning to discuss Gigi. He insisted on telling me the story of my parents."

"And?"

"I won't forgive my father."

"Surely Nate didn't expect you to."

"No, but Joe, he told me things that, well, it doesn't make what he did right, but it helps me to understand."

"So will you see him?"

"I don't know. Maybe it's better to leave things alone. What if all the old anger and bitterness boils over for either one of us? Maybe seeing him will just be awful. What if he . . . I don't know. It just seems like asking for trouble.

"And it's not something I can just run out and do between working on Dorie's kitchen and trying to get help for Gigi.

"A lot of stuff has happened that needed to happen. I get that.

Still a lot to take care of. Which reminds me, Suze is taking Jerry Corso to her mother's cocktail party tonight. I told her I'd try to be back around five to help her dress."

"I heard. We can do that. I can blame her if I ask you to go out to the farm again and take a second look."

Another glance toward her and back to the road.

The warning flutter in her chest told her not to make any promises. "Sure, that works." And if lunch was a disaster, she could come up with some excuse. Or he could.

"So Suze is going out with Jerry. It's the biggest news of the year down at Mike's. Every one is giving him sartorial advice."

Van laughed. "Yikes."

"I wouldn't worry. He's a hometown boy, but he cleans up pretty good."

Jerry wasn't the only one. Joe looked at ease and comfortable with himself. He was wearing clean jeans and a polo shirt that was wrinkle free. Van thought he'd probably dressed with extra care, not for Van but for his mother.

"Why are you smiling?"

"I'm looking forward to seeing everybody again. But, Joe, are you sure—"

"Don't even finish that thought. My mother is probably ironing the tablecloth. Matt has gone back to school, but Brett's coming with his wife. Did I tell you he got married?"

"No."

"Nice girl. Wendy. You'll like her. And Dad will probably smother you with attention. So don't worry about what's going to happen today. It's all good."

"But they're not expecting us to . . . you know, be back together."

"I don't know. You're coming to lunch. Relax. Enjoy it; there are no strings. You don't even have to look at the vines if you don't want to."

"I want to."

"Good. So it's all good."

It was a relaxed drive out into the countryside. Joe talked more about the grapevines and how he came to be running Grandy's Marina. Van told him about Gigi and Suze's letter. "Suze and I apologized to Dana and asked her to come back. But I haven't confronted Gigi yet. I don't know how strong she is right now. I did tell Uncle Nate."

"I never got why everyone always tried to take care of Gigi."

"Funny, Dana and Suze said the same thing."

"Because Gigi took advantage of you. All of you but particularly you. Everybody was aware of it."

"I wasn't. Being back, though, I see that we didn't do her any favors by always shielding her."

"Gigi is . . . Gigi. And not your responsibility. She never was. And she tried to step into your place when you left. I didn't like her. She took advantage of Clay Daly, the poor jerk. That was his fault with all that stubborn macho stuff. No wife of his was going to work. She was going to stay at home to raise the kids. And it's just what Gigi wanted. He stopped coming to Mike's. He just dropped us. Probably because he was working two jobs to keep Miss Princess at home.

"Then with the hurricane, Gigi just packed up the kids and went home where it was safe and comfy and there was someone who could pay attention to her while Clay—well, it was too much for him. He lasted a couple of months, then I guess when it became apparent that Gigi wasn't interested in finding temporary lodgings, he moved out and went back to his property."

"Jeez. Is that the way everyone feels?"

"Mainly that Clay screwed up and didn't take advice or ask for help. And he paid the ultimate price."

"Nate and Amelia are worried about her, but they seem unwilling to do anything serious about it. Like send her to a therapist."

"They'd rather let her sponge off them? For how long? Some things you just can't fix, Van."

"I know. I really do . . . And Nate wants me to go see my father."

"Yeah, you're batting two for two for awkward meetings." He reached over and cupped the back of her head. "But we forgive you."

"But will I forgive him? I won't. I can't. I wasn't thinking straight when I ran to you yesterday. I just needed to be someplace . . ."

"Safe where someone understood?"

"Yes. Thank you. But I've been thinking since then. Nate said my father had gotten a scholarship to art school and wanted to marry this girl, and then he got my mother pregnant during a one-night stand." She sighed.

"He's not the first guy who had to marry a girl he knocked up. Men aren't the brightest in that situation. And in his particular case, I can't complain." He gave her a quick smile.

"Sounds like a familiar situation in our household."

"Van, don't. It was just a screwup people make all the time."

"That's why he threw me out, because it was happening to him all over again. Maybe he even thought I was expecting him to take care of me. But I wasn't. I didn't expect anyone to take care of me."

"You never did, Van."

And she still didn't.

"He was and is an artist, Joe. His paintings are good, filled with emotion—not the kind of emotion that he meted out at home. But beauty and softness. And he's living with some woman named Ruth," she added on a harsher note.

"So, are you going to see him, or not?"

"I don't know. I just remember the horrible things, but when you look at his paintings, you can't imagine the artist as anything but sensitive and caring. It's a little too much to handle. An artist. That's what I just can't wrap my mind around."

As they left the traffic behind and turned onto a two-lane county road, Van opened the window. The air was hot and dusty but it smelled so familiar, and she gratefully breathed it in, dust and all.

They came to the gate that used to mark the Enthorpe dairy but was now just an empty gaping clearing. Farther in the distance, Van could see the roofs of townhouses where once Enthorpe cows had grazed.

"Oh, Joe."

"Yep, you get used to it after a while. Sort of."

They drove on in silence. A few minutes later they turned onto a narrower road. Joe reached over and squeezed her hand then let go.

She smiled over at him. And she thanked the fates that the boy she had once loved had grown into the sensitive yet strong man sitting beside her.

Everyone was standing on the porch when the truck pulled to a stop in the drive of the sprawling farmhouse.

"The welcoming committee," Van breathed.

"They're harmless, and they love you."

Joe started to get out of the truck, but Van grabbed his arm. How could they still love her after she deserted Joe? What were they expecting from her now? Suddenly she had way too many questions that she should have been asking on the drive out instead of talking about Gigi and her father and other things that didn't require immediate attention.

"Van!" Mrs. Enthorpe was already hurrying toward them.

"What do I call her?" Van whispered urgently to Joe.

"Just call her Mom, like you always did."

"But—"

"Stop worrying."

Van didn't have time to worry further. As she got out of the truck, Mrs. Enthorpe wrapped both arms around her and hugged. "You look wonderful. Big-city life must agree with you."

"Oh, move over, honey, and give the girl some breathing room." Mr. Enthorpe, big and tall and lanky, bent over to kiss Van's cheek. "Come on inside. We got the air conditioner on."

They turned toward the house. Granddad Enthorpe was waiting on the porch. "Well, it's about time you came to visit an old man. Come on, girl, it's hot as blazes out here." Behind him Joe's brother Brett nodded and introduced Van to his wife, Wendy, as Granddad swept Van past them.

Inside was exactly as it had been, except for a new set of living room furniture, which was all color coordinated except for Granddad's recliner, even though it was worn and old and clashed with the rest. It was an act of family. Maybe stubbornness, maybe love, but familial. Van always felt that coming here.

She'd basked in that feeling, felt safe and nurtured, like she belonged. Today she only felt unbelievably sad. She was no longer a part of this wacky, boisterous, arguing, scrapping, kidding, laughing family.

"Come on, Van and Wendy. Help me out in the kitchen." Mom Enthorpe hustled the two younger women away.

"Whew," she said as soon as the kitchen door closed behind

them. "I didn't really need any help so just have a sit while I finish up here. I was just trying to give Van a chance to catch her breath from the onslaught of men."

She began spooning beans into a colander and transferring them to a serving bowl and then into a warming oven. It just seemed natural that Van and Wendy found themselves joining in the preparations.

"I feel so privileged to have two female companions at once. Since Maddy moved off to Ohio, it's been testosterone city around here."

She chatted on, answering Van's questions about Maddy, and encouraging Wendy to tell how she and Brett had met. Soon all the dishes were ready to be served. Mom Enthorpe called her husband in to carry the roast to the table. Van and Wendy helped her transport bowls and platters loaded with enough food to feed a lot more people than were actually eating. Years of hearty meals for a working family.

They all sat down, and Granddad said grace. While the food was passed, wineglasses were filled halfway at each place. Granddad pulled himself up from his chair. Took his glass.

"Well, we don't expect this wine to taste as good as the Enthorpe wine when it finally gets here. But until then, here's to family and returning friends. Van, honey, we're proud of you and that fancy business of yours."

Van blinked in surprise.

"He follows you on the Internet," Joe's father said.

"And you've done real good." Granddad winked, and they all drank.

There was general hubbub while dishes were passed, while Van struggled with a sudden urge to burst into tears. She pulled herself together and smiled across the table at the older man.

He smiled back. Nodded a couple of times and took a big helping of mashed potatoes.

Conversation slowed as they ate. It was all delicious and homemade including the seven-layer cake that Wendy and Brett had brought.

"You made this?" Van asked in disbelief. "I can't imagine."

"Oh, it's just a little time consuming. But it was one of my grandma's favorites so I learned to make it as sort of a rite of passage I guess you'd say."

"You gonna stick around for a while, Van?" Granddad asked over coffee.

"I'm staying at Dorie Lister's for a few days in Whisper Beach. I'm helping her do some streamlining at the Blue Crab."

"Haven't been there in years," he said. "That no-account Harold still gumming up the works?"

"He's off on some adventures at the moment. Suze Turner is there. I think she'll stay for the fall at least. She's working on a paper for the university she works for."

"Well, if it gets too crowded, you should come stay out here with us."

"Here, here," said Joe's dad. "There's plenty of room. When are you finishing up at the marina, son?"

"Tomorrow or the next day." Joe pushed his chair back. "Now I want to take Van out to see the vines; she has to be back in town by five."

"You go ahead," his mother said. "Maybe you can stay longer on your next visit."

Van smiled. "Lunch was delicious. Thank you."

"Don't be a stranger." Granddad winked. "I'm sure Joe won't mind. And the rest of us wouldn't mind another sprout on the family tree. Lord knows we waited long enough."

Van froze. She saw Joe and his mother exchange hurried looks. *He's told her.*

"Get on with you, old man. We'll be happy to see you anytime, Van. And don't listen to his crazy talk."

Joe guided her out of the house. "Sorry about that."

"You told your mom about me and kids."

"She wanted to know."

"You told her there is nothing between us, right? They're not really thinking—"

"I told her there was nothing between us, and that we were just friends. And she asked what I had done wrong. I spared her the details but told her that you couldn't have kids and you thought that we wouldn't want you because of that."

"You didn't."

"Well, I was more coherent in the original telling. But, Van, that wouldn't be a deal breaker if a deal ever came up."

"Goofball," she punched him lightly. She was moved, but she didn't buy it for a minute. She knew how important family was to him. "Now, show me these vines of yours."

They spent the next two hours wandering down the rows of vines, while Joe explained the growing pattern and the potential yield. Then he took her into one of the brick buildings that had been part of the milking operation.

It was a long plain rectangle with high ceilings where once hundreds of cows lined up to be milked. All that equipment and structure was gone and the room had been refitted with vats and giant barrels and equipment whose function she could only guess at.

"I have one fermentation room ready. And another space in case we expand. Two cask rooms and . . ."

"What's that machine in there?" Van pointed to a room off from the main building. "It looks like something prehistoric."

"That's the winepress. Come this way." He walked her through a doorway into a brick room that was empty. "This used to be the equipment and storage room for the dairy. I thought it might make a good wine-tasting room. Eventually."

Van stood in the center and looked around the room, taking it all in.

"I want to do a cluster of structures, be able to offer tastings and tours, and maybe even have a restaurant. Someday. But this is what I've got so far."

As Joe talked animatedly about his plans for the vineyard building, Van began to see it in her mind. Made mental notes about what he was saying he wanted and what was feasible to have. She knew nothing about vineyards, or keg rooms or tapping, but she could see the pattern.

"Seems like a lot of work."

"It is. But I'll do it by steps. It will take a few years before we have enough stock to be able to run full throttle. I've already hired a foreman who knows grape growing.

"I thought maybe we could add a store and tasting bar, maybe an event room, you know, for weddings and family reunions, stuff like that." He sighed and stuffed his hands into his jeans pockets. "First I have to get a decent crop."

The time sped; somewhere during the tour, Joe had taken Van's arm. Now he was holding her hand, though she didn't remember him taking it. And here they were back in view of the house, holding hands like a first date.

She slid her hand out of his on the pretext of brushing off her slacks, which were picking up a coating of dust. He didn't take her hand again, and she had to admit she missed his touch.

They came back to the house to say their good-byes, and the whole family came out to the porch to watch them drive away.

"So good to see you. Come back anytime." Mom Enthorpe hugged her for a long time, then stood back while her husband leaned over to kiss Van's cheek and give her a quick hug.

Van grinned back, though her throat burned. How could they still like her?

Granddad Enthorpe stood on the porch and nodded and saluted, finally saying, "Don't be a stranger."

Van smiled, nodded, waved, and couldn't manage to get a word out.

Mom Enthorpe walked them to the car. Stopped Van from getting in when Joe opened the passenger door. Gave her son a look that sent him around to the driver's side.

"I wanted to say one thing, Van."

"Okay."

"Honey, the road to love isn't always easy. And whether yours leads you back here or somewhere else, you will always be a part of our family. No matter what. And no matter how."

Van nodded, feeling her eyes filling up and trying desperately not to let her tears fall.

"Mom," Joe called from the driver's seat.

She kissed Van's cheek. "Now get back to Whisper Beach. But remember what I say."

She stood watching them until they drove out of sight of the farmhouse.

"Was she giving you a hard time?" Joe asked.

"No, she— I think she was doing what moms do. But I'm not sure what she meant."

"Hmm," he said.

"Joe . . ."

"Van, it's all good. Now let's enjoy the ride back into town."

Chapter 26

"Told you I'd be back in time," Van said, bursting into Suze's room.

"Thank God," said Dana. "I'm going to be late for my shift."

Van stuttered to a halt. "Wow, you look wow."

"Dana did my hair." Suze turned around uneasily. "Too much?"

"No!" Dana yelled.

"No, not at all," Van said. "It looks very chic."

"See, I told you. Yeesh. I don't get no respect around here. I'm gone. Have a good time."

"Like that could ever happen," Suze mumbled.

"What, having second thoughts about Jerry?"

"Hell, no. I'm having second thoughts about my mother."

"And speaking of Jerry, I hope you don't mind, but Joe is downstairs. His mother stuffed me for lunch, and he's taking me to dinner."

"Lord, it's turning into dorm central around here."

"We plan to be gone before Jerry shows up. That would be too weird. Anyway, he's really just buttering me up so I'll help him with the configurations of his planned tasting room."

"Right. I'm sure that's his only motive."

"We'll see. It's strange; it's like we're still good friends. His parents still like me as if nothing even happened. But it did. I probably should just tell him I'll send him some ideas."

"Why don't you just let it play out, instead of organizing the way it's going to go?"

"Can't help myself. So let's focus on you." Van glanced at Suze's bedside clock. It was big and round and had Minnie Mouse ears. "It's still a half hour before Jerry gets here. Maybe you should wait and put on your dress at the last minute."

Suze sank onto the bed. "This is going to be a disaster. I know I'm absentminded, and a klutz and kind of a slob, but it just gets worse when I'm around my mother and her friends. They smile, but I know they're thinking poor Karen. How did she get such a lunk of a daughter? They say hello, and then there's that awkward silence when they can't think of anything to say."

"They smile and think how brilliant you are and wonder how they will ever come up with conversation that won't sound stupid."

Suze snorted. "Have I told you lately what a good friend you are."

"BFF, that's me."

"There's no reason for you and Joe to have to hang around here. Help me into this dress. I promise not to sit, eat, or drink in it until Jerry gets here."

Suze pulled the dress up from her feet, wriggled it past her hips, and turned around for Van to zip her up.

The front doorbell echoed from below.

"He's early."

"You put on fresh lipstick. I'll let him in."

"Ugh-h-h."

"Put a smile on; you're going to have a great time." Van ran down the stairs. Joe was standing by the door. He shrugged.

Van shooed him out of the way. He disappeared into the parlor.

Van waited a beat, then opened the door. "Hi—"

"How could you?" Gigi pushed her way inside. "You're all ganging up on me just like you always did."

"Gigi, calm down. What are you talking about?"

"You told Dad I stole Suze's stupid letter. It was Dana. Dana stole it. I hate you."

Joe came out of the parlor. "Gigi, cut it out. Now."

Gigi froze, then jumped back as if she'd touched a live wire. For several seconds she stared at him, and the look was so filled with hurt, anger, and just plain craziness that Van was frightened for her.

Then Gigi switched that awful stare to Van, and back to Joe. "You told her. You told her, didn't you? Why did you have to tell?"

"Gigi, pull yourself together. And yeah, I told Van. She saw us and thought it was Dana. All these years we've both blamed Dana, when it was you. And me. I was just too stupid to realize it. Because nothing happened."

" 'Cause of you."

"Yes, because of me. Because you know something. I couldn't have lived with myself afterward."

"I hate you."

"Good, because I don't like you very much either."

"Joe," Van pleaded.

"What's happening?" Suze stood at the top of the stairs. "Jeez Louise, Gigi."

Momentarily distracted, Gigi stopped, suspended midcry.

Suze pulled off her shoes, scooped them into one hand, and ran down the stairs.

"Why did you have to tell?" Gigi sobbed.

"It was all so long ago, Gigi," Van said soothingly. "It's all right. It doesn't matter anymore."

"Doesn't it?" Joe asked, and his voice was harsh.

"Joe, please."

He turned on Gigi. "You wrecked what Van and I had between us, let us all think it was Dana's fault, which we all believed, even Dana, who's been living up to her bad-girl role ever since. That was partially her responsibility. But it was also yours. You've never taken responsibility for anything, not even your marriage or your children. It's about time you started."

"Go, Joe," Suze said under her breath.

"You never liked me. None of you ever liked me."

"Gigi, that's crazy," Van said. "We were best friends, remember?"

"Until Suze and Dana and Joe came along."

"How can you say that? We included you in everything. We even made sure that you didn't get into trouble."

"Because I was sweet Gigi, the good girl. I didn't want to be the good girl." Tears were falling fast, drenching her face. Her nose began to run.

"Well, then you should have said so." Suze dropped her shoes, opened her clutch purse, and handed Gigi a tissue.

Gigi snatched it from her without a thank-you and wiped her nose.

"Let's just forget the past, okay?" Van said.

"Fine for you. You're successful and live in New York City. Why would you want to remember the past? You came from nothing. We were embarrassed that you were part of our family."

Van flinched.

"That's enough, Gigi," Joe said.

"You wouldn't have gotten out if I hadn't given you all my money."

"Dammit, Gigi. I paid it back and more. And before you rewrite that part of history, you insisted that I take it. Now I understand why. It wasn't that you cared about me. It was guilt money."

"And I don't want your stupid house."

"Fine," Van said, suddenly weary of the whole mess. "I'm sorry that you are unhappy. I'm sorry that you're a widow. But I'm not sorry about what I made out of my life. Which I will be going back to in a few days. Go home, Gigi. Do something about your life."

"Wait a minute." Suze stepped in front of the door. "I want to know why you took that letter. What did I ever do to you?"

"Nothing. I didn't."

Van had never seen this surly side of Gigi, but she suddenly understood. "Most favored nation," she said to Suze.

Suze nodded, opened the door, and stepped aside.

Gigi looked at the open door, then at Suze. She took a step forward, then flung herself at Suze, screaming and slashing and kicking.

Joe and Van grabbed for her and pulled her away. Joe held on to her as she flailed. "I think you better call her father."

Footsteps sounded on the porch. Nate and Jerry Corso both came to the door.

"I got here as soon as I realized she'd left home," Nate said. "I shouldn't have said anything to her. Gigi, you're making a spectacle of yourself. It's time to come home."

"Uncle Nate—"

He held up his hand. "You don't have to explain. You were right, Van. We've ignored this too long. We'll take care of her. I'll send the boys over to get her car."

He led Gigi, suddenly docile, out of the house.

Van watched them go. She could hear Gigi already telling Nate that it wasn't her fault. She closed the door.

"Whew," Joe said and pulled Van close. "Hi, Jer."

"Uh, am I too early?" Jerry looked from Joe to Suze.

Suze stood stock-still against the wall. Her hair had been pulled out of its pins. Her dress was crumpled. Her lipstick was smeared, and there was a scratch on her cheek.

She looked in horror at Jerry, clean and well put together in his summer suit.

Van caught her eye. Then Van fought with a smile. And a bubble of laughter welled up inside her. Suze's expression broke; for a few interminable seconds, Van didn't know if she teetered between laughter or tears. Then they both caved in to the ridiculous.

"We'll be back in a minute . . . or two," Van said. "Make yourselves at home."

She led Suze up the stairs to her room.

They sat on the bed side by side, speechless now that their adrenaline was beginning to subside.

"Did that just happen?" Suze said.

"I'm afraid so."

"Do you think we were really like that?"

"You mean, did we enable her? I guess maybe we did." Van sighed. "I know I did. She just always seemed like she needed taking care of. She's right, though. We were best friends, when we were younger. We grew up together. Then we got to high school, and we weren't so close. She had a comfy home and I had hell. I didn't have the energy to put into her.

"Then you and Dana came to work at the restaurant. Dana was my least favorite of the group. She was the crazy one, the troublemaker. I didn't always like her even then. But it was really Gigi who didn't quite fit in. I didn't see it. I wish I had."

Suze stood up. "Stop it. Don't you even think about taking responsibility for what just happened downstairs."

"I'm not. I was just thinking that no matter how hard you try to forget and ignore your past, pretend it wasn't what it was, it's still always there."

"That's very profound for a professional apartment organizer," Suze quipped, but there was understanding in her eyes.

"It just took a hammer for me to grow up. Which I think I just did."

"Cool. Now I hate to sound selfish, but if we can stop obsessing about Gigi, what am I going to do?"

Van took in Suze's hair, her face, her dress. "Call in sick?"

Suze groaned.

"Let me rephrase that. What do you want to do?"

"OMG, IT'S LIKE I stepped into a time machine." Dana, order pad poised in front of her, looked over the group. "And what the hell happened to your hair? And why aren't you at that cocktail party?"

"Long story," Suze said. "When do you get off?"

"Late, but I have a break in an hour."

"Great. We'll eat, and then we'll fill you in on your break."

They ordered, though Van didn't feel much like eating; she looked out at the beach wondering how it had all come to this. Suze had called her mother and canceled due to "an unfortunate accident." Her mother wasn't happy until Suze said she'd be wearing a Band-Aid over her check and had a fat lip. "I fell."

Van could hear Karen Turner at the other end commiserating and clucking and pretty much telling her daughter that she was such a klutz. And Van realized that no family was without its bit of dysfunction.

Suze hung up. "I think she was actually relieved to not have to deal with me tonight."

"Does that hurt your feelings?"

"Nah. My father is kind of a klutz, too. Runs in his side of the family. A cross she must bear."

When they returned downstairs, Suze was wearing a pair of black capris and a knit tee that she'd bought the other day. Van had tried to repair her hairstyle, but admitted defeat, and now it was swirling curly about Suze's head. She looked much younger than she was.

Jerry had divested himself of jacket and tie and had unbuttoned the top button of his dress shirt and rolled up the sleeves. He seemed a lot happier. And actually so did Suze.

They'd walked double-date style to the Blue Crab. Van and Joe led and Suze and Jerry lagged behind, laughing and talking like they'd been seeing each other forever.

That had felt weird enough to Van, who was still upset over the scene with Gigi and her subsequent call to the Moran house. Amelia had answered and had practically accused Van of upsetting her daughter. Twelve years ago, Van would have rushed right over and apologized, done something special with her cousin until she was forgiven.

But not this time. This time the stakes were higher for everyone but especially for Gigi. She needed some serious therapy, and Van wanted to make sure she got it, instead of having excuses made for her. She'd find a way to talk directly to Nate the next time she called.

Joe wrapped an arm around her waist and pulled her close. "Stop thinking."

"Can't help it. I've got a lot to sort out."

He kissed the top of her head. She wanted to tell him to stop, but it would take too much energy. She felt dragged out. And she was glad of the warmth and strength of his arm. Even though she knew this happy couples scenario would have to end soon before they all started believing it. Especially her.

Because as she'd looked over the rows of young vines earlier that afternoon, she'd felt an echo of that thrill when she'd looked over the dairy herd years before. Something to grow, a life to live. Yeesh, she was on sensory and emotional overload.

"Van? Yoo hoo, Van."

"Huh?"

"Do you want a beer or something?" Dana's face loomed over her, and Van realized she'd been in the nether. Joe was right. No more thinking.

"Would it be weird to have a cup of hot tea?"

"Definitely," Dana said. "Milk or lemon."

"So do you think Gigi had some kind of breakdown?" Jerry asked when Dana had finished taking her order.

"Sure feels like it," Suze said.

It felt like it to Van, too. Actually it felt like they had all broken down. Or something had. Maybe it was a good thing. Maybe not.

Dana brought their drinks. The tea was hot and calming. Van could feel Joe glancing at her. She wanted to tell him she was fine. But she wasn't sure she was. Though of course she was. She'd made it this far; she wouldn't give up without a fight. But she felt sorry for Gigi, and slightly responsible.

And she knew that was probably not a good thing. Funny how one little insignificant event in the past, like Dana and Joe flirting or him not having sex in the truck with Gigi, could bear such unexpected fruit down the road. Or in her case no fruit at all.

"What?" Suze asked.

"I was thinking about you and mixed metaphors."

"Hate 'em."

Van smiled. "I knew you would."

After dinner they all walked out to Whisper Beach, though Jerry groused about his shoes until Suze made him sit down and take them off.

Van suspected he was more worried about what he was going to say to Dana than he was about getting his shoes wet. He'd told them during dinner that Bud had left town.

"Gone to Florida—his sister and brother-in-law live down there—and checked himself into a rehab center."

"That's good," Van said.

"I'm not sure if he told Dana or not."

"She'll be better off without him," Joe said.

"I know that. We all do, except maybe Dana. But somebody's got to tell her."

"Maybe she can move in with Suze and Dorie," Van suggested. "Support group and all that."

Suze frowned over that. "As long as she doesn't expect one big party. I have work to do."

"You seem pretty confident about getting that grant."

"Actually, it has nothing to do with the grant. I'm writing this paper even if I have to work for Dorie . . . as soon as Dana and I talk her into opening for the winter."

"When did this all happen?"

"Me and the terror bonded over my hair this afternoon." Suze turned to Jerry. "I'm sorry you missed it. I looked really nice."

"I think you look great the way you are," Jerry said.

Joe looked at Van and batted his eyelashes.

Van bit her lip to keep from laughing.

"Here she comes."

Dana was standing on the pier looking down at them. "You expect me to get my feet all sandy and then have to go back to work?"

"Yeah, we do," Joe called up to her. "Come on down; Jerry has something he wants to say."

"Jeez, Joe," Jerry said under his breath.

Dana slid off the pier and jumped to the ground. They could hear her grousing all the way to where they waited for her.

"So what's the big powwow about? I thought we decided I didn't take the damn application letter."

"What?" Jerry asked.

"Long story," Joe said. "Go on."

Jerry stepped forward. "Dana?"

"Jerry?"

"I just thought you should know, Bud's left town."

Dana screwed up her face.

"I know you're upset but—"

"You hauled my butt down here just to tell me that? I know. He texted me. Gone off to rehabilitate himself. Good luck with that one."

"You're okay?"

"Me? Hell, yeah. I feel, I don't know, a big weight lifted off me. I hope he doesn't come back. Sounds awful, doesn't it? I thought I loved him, but I don't. And I don't think he can love anybody no matter how much he gets rehabilitated. I think he has a sickness, ya know? I'm better now.

"Dorie says I have to go to some group grope session. Say stuff like I'm Dana Mulvanney and I'm a dumb shit 'cause I let a guy beat me up. Yeah, I got it. I'll do it. I'm cool. Is that it?"

"Dana." Van stepped toward her.

Dana stepped back. "No group hugs or anything; I gotta reputation to maintain."

"Dana, you've got a reputation you need to lose."

"Aw, Joe, that's the sexiest thing you ever said to me."

"You're hopeless."

"No, she's not," Suze said. "When I'm not researching misanthropic literature of the Chaucerian period, Dana and I are going to get us some self-esteem."

Dana snorted. "I gotta get back." She turned and walked back up the beach.

"Are you really going to do that?" Van asked.

"Why not? You know what they say?"

"No, what?"

"'Tain't what you do, it's the way that cha do it."

"That's not Chaucer." Jerry said.

"No. Ella Fitzgerald."

Suze and Jerry decided to walk into town for ice cream, but Van and Joe stayed on the beach. The last of the Sunday crowd had gone, and they were alone except for the sounds coming from the restaurant.

"Do you think Bud will come back?" Van asked as the dusk turned into dark.

"Who knows. We'll all be better off with him gone. I hope that he can change, but I don't have much hope. At least the clam diggers will be someone else's problem now."

"The clam diggers?"

"Poachers. Bud had a real thing about them. Grandy's coming back and he can deal with them—or not."

"Then you'll move back to the farm?"

"Yeah, I'll have to bunk in the main house since I loaned my house to my foreman and his family."

Van shuddered.

"What?"

"Just thinking about Gigi living back at home."

Joe laughed. "Don't worry; my mother would never put up with that kind of stuff."

"I know. She's really great. Your whole family is."

"Well."

"Don't say it."

"What? I was just going to repeat what she told you, that you're welcome anytime."

"Thanks."

"Think you'll get out to see us before you go back to the city?"

Van shrugged. "Tomorrow I start overhauling the Crab. Everyone's coming in at noon."

"That should be interesting. The Crab has been hobbling along the same way for as long as I can remember. You might want to stick around an extra week or so, to make sure they can find everything once you fix it."

"I can't. I've already been away from work too long."

"They can't manage without you?"

"I'm afraid they manage just fine. One of the reasons I need to get back."

"You said you were going to expand. Have you decided where?"

"No. I've looked at Boston and Philadelphia; those are the most obvious choices. But the overhead is high and I'm not sure it will be cost-effective. I doubt if they'll pay in Philly like they do in Manhattan."

"Hmmm. Have you ever thought about doing something here?"

"Here? The Crab is an act of love and payback to Dorie. And I'll look into some ideas for the winery. But after that . . . look around."

"I don't mean right here. But what about Suze's town? Some of those families have started living here year-round. And the ones who do come down are entertaining all the time."

"I'm sure they have a staff for that."

"Maybe. But the overhead would be lower and you'd have this." He looked out to the ocean, rolling dark against the sand, the shush-shush a slow lazy counterpoint to the surf.

"It's tempting. But I don't think so. I'm not sure I could ever be comfortable here again."

"Van, I'm sorry for all that nonsense I put you through. I was just dumb. I wished you had just said something. We always told each other everything, didn't we?"

"It wasn't your fault. I kind of lost my head. Life at home was unbearable, and I jumped to conclusions. I was wrong. I was wrong about so many things. Maybe I was wrong about everything."

"Not about how we felt about each other."

"No, I don't think so."

The lights in the restaurant went off. Joe put his arm around her, and she relaxed into his shoulder. It was comfortable. Undemanding. Safe. But the feeling belonged in the past.

"We'd better get back. Dorie will want to go over a schedule for tomorrow."

He jumped up and pulled Van to her feet. Then he pulled her against him. He kissed her, gently. And for a moment they were young and looking forward instead of two people who had gone their separate ways.

Chapter 27

Dorie's house was empty when Joe and Van walked up the front steps. "Suze and Jerry must still be out," Van said.

"Looks that way. Dorie and Dana, too."

"Well, thanks for lunch . . . and dinner."

"I'll see you before you leave?"

"Sure. I'll be working at the restaurant for the next couple of days. I'll probably go back on Saturday to give myself a day to get back up to speed. Send me some ideas you like, or photos, and a list of what you need where, and I'll see what I can come up with."

Joe nodded.

"Well, I'd invite you in but . . ." She breathed out a laugh. "I wouldn't know what to do with you."

"I have a few ideas, but I don't think we're there yet."

She shook her head.

"Maybe never."

She shrugged.

"Or maybe later." He smiled. Raised his eyebrows in a way that had always made her laugh, and she fell into a place she knew so well and felt so comfortable in.

"I'm staying out at the farm. Call me if you need anything. Or if you want to come out."

"Thanks, I will."

"Save Friday for me."

She hesitated. "Okay. But Joe—"

He kissed her, fast, unexpectedly, cutting off the rest of her sentence.

"See you on Friday. Good night."

"Good night."

He walked out to his truck, waved over the hood, and drove off into the night.

Van watched him go. She couldn't decide whether what she was feeling was surprise, disappointment, or confusion; whether things were closing or opening. And whether she should accept the former or hope for the latter.

Okay, he probably should have maneuvered her into prolonging the night. It wasn't that he didn't want to. It's just that he didn't want to make any rash moves with Van.

He wasn't even sure if he wanted to risk getting involved with her again. He drove to the farm. Maybe someone would still be up.

The porch light was on, and a light in the kitchen glowed through the café curtains. Joe pulled into the drive and stopped at the house. The kitchen door opened and his mother stepped out.

"Joe? I thought you were coming tomorrow."

"I was but— Hell, I don't know."

"You'd better come in. Your father and I were just having some decaf."

Joe stepped into the kitchen. His dad looked up in surprise. "What brings you here again so soon?"

"Indecision."

"Would this have anything to do with Van?"

"Yeah." Joe pulled out a chair and sat down.

His mother poured him a cup of coffee and sat down. "You both seemed very relaxed today. Actually I was surprised at how easily she fit back into the family. I expected her to be a bit skittish. She always had this edge that made me think she was on the verge of running. But not today."

"Probably because she knows she's leaving." Joe took a sip of hot coffee.

"So what's the problem?" his dad asked.

"I don't know that there is a problem. She's willing to do some work on the winery, just some organizational stuff."

"Good. And?"

"Well, she's changed."

"Oh my goodness," his mother said. "Of course she has. Are you hungry? Can I make you a plate?"

Joe laughed. "Thanks, but we went to the Crab with Suze Turner and Jerry."

"Jerry Corso? And Suze is the college professor, right?"

"Yes."

"Well, I never," said his father. "Bet that was an interesting night."

"You can say that again. Suze had to go to this cocktail party and needed a date." He told them about Gigi freaking out and attacking Suze.

"And she always seemed like such a nice girl," his mother said.

"Those nice girls'll fool you every time." Joe Junior winked at his wife.

Joe looked away. A combination of TMI and envy.

He wanted what his parents had. He hadn't found anyone he thought he could spend his life with, except Van, and that had been a lifetime ago. Especially for Van. And there wouldn't be any children.

"So do you think maybe there could be a future for the two of you?"

Joe shrugged. He didn't know why he was feeling so ambivalent.

"'Cause there haven't been that many women visiting the old farmstead."

"I know."

"Did you ask how she felt?"

"No. I don't even know how I feel."

"Well, then, don't rush into anything."

"I know, Dad, look before I leap."

His mother laughed. "Unlike your father. And look what he got."

"I was lucky. And I know it. But Van is carrying a lot of baggage. Make sure she's the one for the right reasons."

"I feel a little pressed for time. She agreed to see me on Friday, but she's leaving on Saturday."

"New York is only a train ride away. What? Two hours max."

"Besides," his mother added. "Neither of you should make any decisions until you get to know each other better."

"For crying out loud," called a voice from the living room. "Marry the girl already; you've waited long enough."

Joe's father called out. "Thanks for your input, Pop. Your grandson has his own ideas."

"If you don't want her, I'll marry her."

"Good night, Pop."

"He means well," his mother said.

"That's what's got me . . . I don't know if I want to invest the time and emotional wringing out that finding out might entail."

"Well, that's something only you can decide."

"I know, but why didn't I try before now? I knew where she was. We all did, watched her career. I never once called her, went into the city to see her. I figured it was over. I knew she would never come back here, and my life was here on the farm."

"Well, she did come back," his father said. "If only for a couple of weeks. Is it any different now?"

"Not really, but I'm beginning to think the commute might not be that bad. I mean, just to see what might happen."

"I think that's an excellent plan." His mother patted his hand. "And there's no reason you have to wait until Friday to see her. Go make yourself a fixture. See how things play out."

"Listen to your mother, son. She's been playing me for years."

"Joseph Enthorpe."

Joe covered his eyes with his hand.

"Look, you've gone and embarrassed the boy."

"Me?" Joe's father said innocently.

She threw her napkin at him. "Go to bed, both of you. And in the morning, Joe, you're going back into town and see what happens."

"Yes, ma'am. I guess that's what I'll do, but I wanted to take a look over the fields."

His father waved the idea away. "The fields will be here when you get back. Van might not be. And, son, this is going to sound old-fashioned, but—"

"Enough, enough," said Joe, standing. "I'm not going to do anything that I would normally be inclined to do. Not with Van, not with her history."

"All or nothing isn't a bad thing," his father said.

Joe nodded. He definitely felt that way about Van. That was one thing he was sure of.

"Joe, come let me get you a fresh towel. Honey, you can put our cups in the dishwasher."

"Yes, ma'am."

Joe followed his mother to the linen closet. She handed him a towel and face cloth, but held on to them. "I didn't tell your father about Van not being able to conceive. I didn't think it was something that is any of his or Pop's business. But if that's what's holding you back, then think long and hard before you make any commitments.

"But don't feel like you're obligated to carry on the family line. We won't lack for grandchildren, and there are plenty of poor children in the world who need loving families. They're just as important as every other child on this earth. Remember that."

"I will, thanks."

She let go of the towels, and Joe went down the hall to bed.

On Monday morning, Van was drinking coffee and listing priorities when Dorie and Dana left for the Crab.

"Suze and I will meet you there at noon," she said distractedly. That would give the staff four hours to complete their usual

Monday morning cleanup. Then while they were taking a break, Van, Dorie, and Cubby could organize the afternoon.

"Make sure Suze gets to the post office first," Dorie said. "I'm getting used to having her around."

"Will do." Van went back to her notes. She'd have Cubby divide them into teams; hopefully, there would be enough volunteers to have several teams. Two for the dining room and the rest in the kitchen.

Whenever a nonrestaurant thought intruded, like what to do about Gigi or whether she should pursue any kind of relationship with Joe, Van flipped to the back and wrote it down. Not that those things on a back page were of less importance, just of less immediacy.

Today was restaurant day.

She was ready if a little tired; she and Suze had stayed up telling Dorie about the events that led up to Gigi's breakdown. Van thought that Suze had earned a little credit with Dana now that she had the scars of what Dana called a catfight. It was much more serious than that. But Nate and Amelia would have to take care of it. That was one mess that Van couldn't fix.

She yawned again, considered a fresh cup of coffee, and decided against it. She knew from experience that adrenaline would kick in as soon as she got on the job.

She had just closed her notebook when she heard Suze clomping down the stairs. She smiled, in sheer enjoyment.

Suze burst through the kitchen door.

"Can you drive me to the post office?"

"You betcha. Give me two seconds." Van poured the dregs of her coffee down the sink and put her cup in the dishwasher and went out into the hall.

Suze followed her.

Van stopped at the hall mirror to check her makeup and clothing.

"Really," Suze said. "You put on makeup to clean a greasy dirty kitchen?"

"Always. Never face the world when you are not at your best." *Even if the world you're facing is unknown territory,* Van added to herself.

"I'll be right back."

When Suze came down the stairs again, she'd changed clothes, pulled her hair back, and actually was wearing mascara. "This might not be my best, but it's the best I can do."

They laughed all the way to the post office.

When they walked into the Blue Crab's kitchen twenty minutes later, the whole staff was already at work moving appliances and workstations away from the wall. The room was steamy with hot water and detergent.

Van looked at her watch. Dorie, soap suds up to her elbows, waved her over.

"I know, we're supposed to have finished cleaning and be on break. But we got a little carried away and decided to scrub the whole place first. I hope that's okay."

"Sure. I'll make adjustments if need be. How long do you think you'll be?"

"Almost done. Go check out the dining room."

Van and Suze went out to see what was going on.

"Wow," Suze said.

"I'll say." The tables had been pushed to the street end of the long room and were stacked two high. Chairs filled in the empty spaces or were upturned on the tabletops. The cashier's desk and the condiment counter were piled high with everything else.

At the opposite end a half-dozen people were busy with mops

and rags and squeegees. Dana strode back and forth pointing out things and giving instructions.

"A prodigious effort," Suze said under her breath.

It *was* a bit daunting, but nothing Van couldn't handle. In fact, this should be easy. Tables would more or less stay put when they were reconfigured; reconfiguring the staff habits would be the challenge. That's why she had Dorie.

"And get a load of Dana," Suze asked. "Who knew she had drill-sergeant skills?"

"Just one surprise after another."

"Huh," Suze agreed. "Now what? You've got this look on your face."

"I do? It must be my oh-yeah-this-is-going-to-work face."

"You had doubts?" Suze eyes opened in mock astonishment.

"No."

Cubby saw Van and hurried over. "Dorie said you were going to change the tables around anyway, so I figured we might as well give the place a major cleaning."

"The mark of a good manager," Van said.

"We put all the condiments and stuff over on the counter. Dorie said you wanted them out of sight."

"Yes, and I found several ideas on the Internet last night. Take a look at these." She pushed the stack of menus over and put her bags on the only uncluttered square foot of counter space on the hostess station. Pulled out her iPad. "We can do this several ways." She showed him several screen shots. "But until Dorie gives the go-ahead for ordering, I say—"

"While you're doing that, what do you want me to do?" Suze asked.

"For starters, I wish you'd go out and burn those menus. Or

at least round them up and come up with an idea for menus that doesn't involve specials in little plastic compartments. Then see if we can get them printed by the weekend. If not, make sure they get cleaned up, no more stickiness, and we'll do the redesigning during happy hour."

Van gathered up the pile of plastic menus and thrust them at Suze. "Then I'll come up with a few good men with some boxes and have them get the rest of this stuff out of here."

"That would be us," said a familiar voice behind her.

Joe and Jerry stood shoulder to shoulder, loaded up with broken-down boxes, tape, buckets, and a few other things that weren't recognizable.

"What are you two doing here?" Van asked.

Suze just stood there with her mouth open.

"Earning brownie points," Jerry said, looking at Suze. "I hope. Where do you want these?"

Suze closed her mouth and said, "I'll show you." He shrugged and followed Suze over to the counter.

"And what about you?" Van asked Joe.

"My mother made me come."

Van laughed. "No, really."

"Really. She said it was about time I stopped sitting around waiting for something to happen and come see if you needed help. You don't want to know what Granddad said."

"I'm sure I don't."

"So what are the chances of me earning some brownie points, too?"

"Pretty good," Van said. "Pretty good."

It was a long day, but they didn't stop until the dining room had a new configuration, the kitchen had been cleaned until it sparkled, well, almost, and the workstations were organized so that people weren't constantly running into one another as they moved from one job to the next.

Van had set up a new traffic pattern and spent half an hour practicing with the waitstaff and busers.

"A couple more days of practice and they should be ready for the restaurant to open on Friday evening," she told Dorie.

"And hopefully, they'll be able to keep the part-timers on track. Lord, I'm tired. I don't suppose you girls will be around tonight to order takeout?" She shot a look over to where Suze was talking to Joe and Jerry.

"Oh, I think we might convince two guys to join us."

Chapter 28

Owen was scrubbing an old fishing boat when Joe walked bleary-eyed to the door the next morning.

He'd stayed up late talking to Van, and if he hadn't been living at the marina, he would have taken her home. Or would have tried anyway. Except he didn't exactly have a home to take her to even if she wanted to go. He couldn't very well take her to the farm, not for the reasons he wanted.

And he'd given his own house away. For a crazy moment he thought of her old house but immediately nixed that idea. Was he crazy? Maybe a little bit.

"Hey, Joe, you gonna stand there all day?" Owen was already drenched and wearing a few suds.

He seemed so happy, Joe hated to break it to him that his job was coming to an end.

"Turn off that hose and come over here for a sec."

Owen's face fell. And he slowly went over to turn off the water, even more slowly walked toward Joe.

"Did I do something wrong?"

"No. You've done great." Joe felt for the kid, wondering how often he got into trouble.

"Just wanted to know if you've had breakfast."

Owen broke into a smile. "Yeah, we had scrambled eggs and toast and orange juice."

And Joe bet Owen paid for it with the twenty bucks a day Joe had been giving him.

"Listen. I'm moving back to the farm today."

Owen just looked at him.

"I've just been staying here helping out the owner. He's been sick."

Owen still just stood there.

"He's been in the hospital."

"Then who's gonna take care of the marina?"

"Well, most of the boats will go into dry dock when the weather changes."

"What about the others?"

Disbelief had turned to a kind of belligerence, or maybe just panic. Joe began to feel a little guilty about setting Owen up with cash, then snatching it away. He should have explained up front that it was a temporary job. He would have done that with any worker he hired at the vineyard. But he hadn't really expected Owen to keep coming back. And now he realized he'd inadvertently set the kid up for a fall.

"How old are you, Owen?"

"Twelve . . . almost."

"You'll be going to school next week."

"I'd rather go to work."

Joe smiled. "Yeah, twenty bucks feels like a lot of money right now. But if you stay in school, you'll make a lot more than that when you graduate."

"Don't like school so much."

"I know. I didn't like it so much either. But I went and finished and went to college."

"And now you own a farm?"

Yeah, he did.

"You got cows and chickens and things?"

"Used to. Now I grow grapes."

"Huh. That's a weird thing to grow."

"It used to be a dairy farm."

"You had cows that made milk and stuff?"

Joe nodded.

"Bet you could have milk anytime you wanted."

"Pretty much."

"Then why did you stop having cows?"

"Long story."

"Now you make grape juice?"

"Sort of."

"You need help on that farm?"

"It's kind of far from here."

"I got a bike."

This was a lot harder than Joe thought it would be. How did you tell a kid no without disappointing him? It wasn't something that he'd ever thought about. No, that wasn't entirely true. He'd seen Brett say no to his kids. It looked easy. But this wasn't easy.

"It's a little too far to ride a bike to."

"Nuh-uh."

"But I was thinking that maybe Grandy could use you a couple of days a week after school. If you're into that. I'd have to ask him."

Grandy probably could use the help and if he couldn't pay the kid much, well, Joe could subsidize the salary for a little longer.

"Is Grandy nice?"

"Yep."

"Then I guess it would be all right, but—"

"But what?"

"I don't want you to go."

Joe had meant to go over to the Crab and help out again today. Mainly because he wanted to see more of Van, but he also felt a responsibility to Owen. He should have explained right up front that it would only be for a few days.

If he was surprised to see Owen the first day, Joe had been doubly surprised when the boy had come two days in a row. But it was more than that. He actually enjoyed the kid's company.

He'd always thought he'd have a bunch of kids, several sons, like his dad and granddad did. To work side by side to build something together. But maybe his mother was right. There were a lot of kids who needed homes.

Would he feel more deeply about a kid who was his blood than he would about a chosen kid? God, he didn't know. And was it really that important? Why was he thirty-three and unmarried if he wanted kids so much? Why hadn't he just settled on a good woman who would be a good mother?

Joe was beginning to think he knew. Had known all along. His granddad had told him in no uncertain terms when Van had left all those years ago. "You're lucky if you find the right woman to spend this life with. Don't expect to find another one."

Granddad had been pretty mad that Joe had screwed up with Van. His whole family loved her.

"Joe, you mad?"

"What? No? Just thinking."

"About your vineyard?"

"No, about my girlfriend."

"Did that other one mess up things for you?"

"No. She tried." But only halfheartedly, Joe realized. "But it didn't work."

"Are you going to marry her?"

"Well, that's what I was thinking about." He could slip back into the life he'd been living until a week ago. He was happy with it. It was a good life. Or he could take the chance of getting to know Van better.

And still he couldn't make the leap. He was afraid he might not bounce back if things fell apart again.

He needed to see her, talk to her, just to make sure it was real. But here was Owen, long-faced, disappointed, and maybe just a little scared. He'd said he lived with his mother and sisters. No talk of a father. And Joe knew he couldn't just walk away. Not at this moment.

"So, Owen, do you know how to swim?"

VAN SAT STARING at her phone as her coffee grew cold. She wanted to see how Gigi was, but she didn't want to take the chance of Amelia answering. Amelia would blame Van for Gigi's sudden breakdown.

And for once Van wasn't willing to take responsibility. It had not been her fault. All this time Gigi had let Van think that Dana had seduced Joe away. When it had been Gigi doing the seducing.

And after all this time, Van might have been able to dismiss her betrayal and get on with things if Gigi hadn't sabotaged Suze and Dana. It made Van angry all over again.

Gigi had manipulated them all to keep her secret nonliaison with Joe secret—and for what?

Still, she was Van's cousin. And Van did share in her unhappiness; even after all the nonsense, she still cared about her cousin.

She picked up her phone, and hoping Amelia wasn't home, she made the call.

Nate answered. "I'm glad you called. I wanted to tell you that we took Gigi to the clinic last night. She's seeing a doctor. She knows she caused a lot of trouble and she's sorry, but she doesn't want to see you, Van. Not yet."

Van was ashamed of how relieved she felt. She wouldn't know what to say. Gigi would apologize and start crying—Van knew the drill.

"I understand. It's better if she just concentrates on getting better, and I think that will be easier without me in the equation."

"But I want to apologize to you. I had no idea."

"Nate, don't apologize. It isn't your fault." It wasn't anyone's fault, or maybe it was all their faults that Gigi had come to this. But it was time for Gigi to take responsibility for her life. And she could only do that herself.

"Are you planning to stay for a while?"

"I leave on Saturday, so I might not see you before I go." Van took a breath, made a decision. "But I'll stay in touch."

"Good. Good. I'd like that."

Van hung up, waiting to feel relief or a sense of loss. Relief won out.

Van thought she had taken responsibility for her choices in life a long time ago. And to a certain extent she had. But coming back had unraveled the mesh that held that belief together.

She'd been wrong or only partially right about more than she cared to admit. Over the years she had built a rational system that worked. And it might have stayed in place if she'd just stayed away.

But she hadn't. And she couldn't even credit Clay Daly's funeral or her drive down the Garden State Parkway. She'd known for quite a while that she'd reached as far as she could go without cutting the invisible bands that held her.

Only she'd been wrong about that, too. Those bands once cut didn't set her free at all. Not in the sense of floating away to a happy future.

They had allowed her to float back down to earth and be comfortable there. To accept her place there.

All but one. One tie still threatened to drag her down, hold her back. And she was going to face that final Gordian knot this morning. At least she would try.

Joe maneuvered the marina hire cruiser, *Shore Baby,* out of the river and onto open water. He hadn't had a hire in a week, and the *Baby* would be going into dry dock since Grandy wouldn't be able to take it out by himself for a while.

So Joe was taking a final spin. And he was taking Owen for an inaugural boat ride. The kid lived on the river, within walking distance of the shore, and he'd never been in a boat.

He said he could swim, but Joe wasn't taking any chances. He handed him an orange life vest.

Owen looked skeptical, but Joe tightened it around him.

"How come you don't have to wear one?"

Instead of explaining marine laws, Joe put on one, too, which earned him a big grin. And made him feel a little sad.

"Ready?" he asked.

Owen nodded, grinned back at him, but the grin turned to surprise when Joe fired up the motor and eased the boat away from the moorings. And when Joe pushed the shift lever forward and the boat reared up as it took off, Owen clutched the straps of Joe's preserver and held on for dear life.

Joe smiled, put his arm around the boy and pulled him in front of him while he steered.

"Look straight ahead; there's the ocean." Joe leaned over and pointed to the opening between the two retaining seawalls.

Owen leaned back against him. "Are we going out there?"

"Want to?"

Owen looked back at him, frowning. Then nodded.

"Okay, here we go." Joe opened the throttle, and they shot past the Blue Crab, past Whisper Beach, and into the open sea.

When they were clear of the shore, Joe swung the boat toward the south. The water was pretty calm, so he had time to think about what was going on in his life.

He looked down at Owen, whose long hair was snapping around in the wind as he tried to see everything on the shore and out to sea.

Joe slowed down. "You want to steer?"

A big nod. Owen smiled up at him. And Joe was hit by such a strong longing that it staggered him. His mother asked him how important having kids was. It meant a lot. If Joe had any questions before, Owen's smile had clinched it.

He wanted kids. There it was. He wanted a large family. Like the one he grew up in. He wanted his own kids, but could he be content with someone else's?

Chapter 29

Van drove to the address on the card Ruth had given her. Parked across the street from a Craftsman-type bungalow on a modest street in one of the older blue-collar neighborhoods.

It was freshly painted white with magenta shutters—which seemed totally incongruous to Van—and a gray front porch. Pots of geraniums hung from the porch eaves.

Van looked at the address on the card. Looked at the black numbers on the curb. This was the place. Still she sat there.

Maybe they wouldn't be home, or maybe he wouldn't let her in. The front door opened, and Ruth came onto the porch. She was wearing bright blue clam diggers and an oversized purple shirt. The woman sure liked color.

She carried a watering can to the pots, watered the first, moved to the next, watered it, and the next. Then she stepped into the opening above the porch steps and looked directly at Van.

How did she know she was out here?

Or was she just wondering who was parked across the street and not getting out of the car?

She smiled. Waved Van to come. Then she stood motionless while Van deliberated on whether to accept her invitation—challenge?—or to drive away.

Van opened the car door and got out. Took the long walk across the narrow street and walked to the bottom of the steps. Looked up.

"I'm so glad you came." Ruth stepped aside, and Van climbed the stairs. She wished she'd brought Suze with her. Suze would have some apt literary quote to put the situation in perspective.

But Van couldn't think of a thing to think or say.

Inside, the house was cool and bright. Was it possible that her father lived here? With all this color and sunshine? And strangely enough, she didn't resent the idea.

"Have a seat," Ruth said. "Robbie is working out back. He has a studio in the garage. He'll be taking a break soon."

Van flinched. She couldn't help herself. The idea of him coming inside and discovering her propelled a full-scale panic in her.

"He doesn't expect anything from you. Except maybe anger and recriminations. He knows he was wrong, the way he treated you and your mother."

Van didn't want to hear excuses for him by this honey-voiced woman. She turned to say so, but what she asked was, "Were you the girl he wanted to marry? Were you the one he cheated on with my mother?"

Van thought she must have blurted those words to upset the calm that emanated from this woman.

Ruth merely said, "Yes."

"And you forgave him?"

Ruth smiled and stepped fully into the room. "Eventually. It ruined my life, too, for a while."

Van wanted to say *Not for as long as it ruined ours*. But she didn't know that. She didn't know what Ruth had suffered. And this was a new side of herself that she wasn't totally comfortable with.

She'd carried her perception, her hurt, for so long, nurtured it like she would have all the children she wouldn't have. It was hard to let go just because he now lived in a nice house, with a woman who seemed at peace with herself, and painted pictures of things he never even noticed when he'd been her father.

Been her father. God help her, he was still her father and always would be. She could walk away and pretend that none of this was happening. Could let life go on with the seed of anger and pain that she could bring out and polish when she began to forget. Or she could face the reality of now.

She turned to leave.

And a reflection of light caught her eye. A glass case sitting on a table, and inside, ragged pieces of sea glass. She could see the tiny pictures painted on them, and she knew if she moved closer, she would recognize them as her own work. And she knew there would be twenty of them. Just as there had been the day she'd climbed out the window to escape his anger.

He hadn't thrown them away, but why? Why had he kept them? To remind him of what a horrible man he'd been? To remember her? To punish himself for all the harm he'd done?

Emotions were tumbling inside her so violently that Van had to fight not to be sick.

Ruth came to stand beside her. "Didn't you ever wonder what inspired you to paint?"

"I just needed money."

"You could have gotten another part-time job. Babysat. Licked envelopes."

"He never— never—" Van couldn't go on.

"I know."

"I won't forgive him."

"I don't expect you to."

Van whirled around. He was standing there in an old white shirt with the collar torn off and covered in paint smears, paint-covered jeans, and socks.

He looked old, but handsome. And a betraying memory bubbled up from deep inside her. They were on the beach. She was only four or five, and he was in swim trunks. They sat across from each other, a big lopsided sand castle between them, and she'd said, *This is your castle, Daddy.* Because he had been like a fairy prince to her, and he'd looked sad.

Van bit her lip. Of course that was before the days she'd understood what was happening between her parents. She was not going to be beguiled by memories like that. They were probably fabricated out of her longing to be loved.

He didn't come farther into the room, but stood in the opening, half silhouetted by the shadows missed by the sun.

"I was a bad man. I mistreated you and your mother."

"Uncle Nate told me what happened."

He nodded once, a slight jerky movement. His hair was thick and white, though he couldn't be much over fifty. She didn't even know how old her father was.

She glanced over to Ruth, who stood there silent, but not alarmed or pained that they were talking about something that had also impacted her life. And the way she was watching Robbie Moran, Van thought she must be comfortable to live with.

Van wondered how Ruth could forgive him for all he'd done to her, but it was obvious that she had and that they were happy together.

"I can't make it up to you. I can only say I'm sorry. And I know that isn't enough."

Van just looked at him. His face was tanned, wrinkled beyond his years, but there was a calmness there she couldn't remember ever seeing. He must never have felt that way when they'd lived together.

And suddenly she had a million questions that she knew would be better unasked. *Why couldn't you make the best of it? Why did you let yourself become eaten by rage? Why did you transfer that hatred to us? To me?*

Maybe he'd been trapped into marrying her mother, but—

"A better man would have risen above what happened. I was not a better man. I am now. Though I know it's too late for us. I'm glad you're successful. I hope you're happy."

"I am." But was she? Really? Van felt Ruth's hand lightly touch her back. A gesture of comfort? Or a connection to her father that Ruth and Van both knew she couldn't manage on her own?

Her father smiled; his eye were shiny and bright, but Van knew he wouldn't cry, not while she was here.

"I'm glad you're painting again," she said.

He nodded. Again quick and sharp.

"I— I never knew."

"No," he said.

And she could hear the regret in his voice. She couldn't forgive him. But she knew now that it wasn't all his fault.

"I always loved you, Van. Even when I didn't act like it. Even in those dark days when I forgot that I did. But I always did."

A jagged breath escaped Van, and she looked away. This was

so not what she'd wanted to do. Ruth's hand stroked her back, calming her.

"Maybe, Van, you'd like to sit down."

"No, thank you." Van latched on to something real. "I'm meeting Dorie at the Blue Crab." She glanced at her father. "I'm helping her to reorganize the kitchen."

He nodded. This time the awkwardness was gone, like a clean wind had just blown through and left the calm again.

"Are you staying long?" Ruth asked.

"Until Saturday. But I'll probably be back—off and on—to keep the restaurant operating efficiently." What was she saying? She couldn't really think she would be back. The whole point was closure, not reopening. She was almost there.

"I really have to go. I can't be late." Van started toward the door. She couldn't run away. She'd done that once. Besides, her father was standing in the doorway.

"I'll walk you to the door," Ruth said.

They walked past her father. Van stopped. Reached up and kissed him quickly on the cheek, shocking herself with a burst of love as horrifying as it was longed for.

Once on the porch, she let out her breath.

"It's fine," Ruth said. "Small doses. Will we see you again before you leave?"

Van thought. Would the woman really wish to put them all through that again? She studied Ruth's face and realized that not only would she welcome Van, but she was looking forward to it.

"I— Maybe."

"How about Thursday for an early dinner? We have a lovely screened porch out back."

"I—"

Ruth smiled at her; she already knew the answer.

"Okay."

They walked together across the street. Decided on an hour, and Van got into the car.

"Thank you," Ruth said and stood in the street as Van drove away.

As soon as Van had driven a few blocks, she pulled to the curb to pull herself together. She wasn't sure what had just happened, she just knew she'd agreed to come to dinner. She must be going stark raving mad.

She fumbled in her bag for her phone, pressed speed dial.

"Suze?"

"That's me."

"Can you take a break?"

"Sure. I was going over to the Crab in a bit."

"Well, come with me now."

"Where are we going?

"To get ice cream and then we're going to the beach."

"HE LOOKED LIKE an old man, a nice old man," Van said as she and Suze sat in her car eating triple scoops of their favorite flavors.

"He isn't really old," Suze reminded her. "Though life has probably dealt him some premature aging blows. But nice-looking now doesn't make up for the eighteen years of misery he put you and your mother through."

"I know it doesn't. And I told him that. Except I've started remembering the early years and times that weren't so awful. I don't know how he felt about my mother then—from all accounts he already hated her for wrecking his life—but he did stuff with me. I think he did love me. At least at first."

"Are you sure you're remembering correctly and not just wish-fulfilling?"

"Not entirely. And like you said, it doesn't make up for all the other times. But it's good to know there were some good times, at least between him and me."

"And Ruth?"

"I don't know. If I met them now, I would think, what a nice couple. She's totally calm and loving, almost too calm and loving. Usually people like that you expect to cross over to the lunatic fringe and go on a rampage. But I don't know. Maybe they're just happy at last." Van paused to eat some ice cream. "He asked me if I was happy."

"And you said . . ."

"I said yes. Because I am."

"You don't sound so sure of that."

Van watched a drip of ice cream drop off Suze's plastic spoon and land . . . back in her cup. Amazing.

"I am, but being back even for a couple of weeks, even with all the angsting and hair tearing, has made we wonder how important it is to cut yourself off from your past. Even if you don't like your past very much."

"Like the baby and the bathwater."

"Which is exactly what I did. In my case, literally."

"Sorry. That was a grossly inappropriate analogy."

"True but true." Van scraped the last of her ice cream from the cardboard dish.

"Give me that; I'll toss them in the trash." Suze got out, deposited their ice cream dishes, and climbed back into the car.

Van gave her the once-over. "You know you managed to eat that entire dish without dropping anything down your front."

Suze looked down at her striped tee. "Ah, but the day is still young. So are you going to dinner on Thursday?"

"I think I am. I'm feeling like I can pretty much handle anything Whisper Beach shovels up."

"What about Joe?"

"I said 'almost.' There's still some spark between us. Actually, it feels a little like coming home in a get-to-know-you way."

"That is a really convoluted explanation."

"I know, but that's what it is. We have history, mostly good history but it's ancient history. Maybe we've changed too much. Neither one of us is ready to look too deep. We're taking a wait-and-see approach."

"That gives you three more days, if you're really leaving Saturday."

"And I'll take them as they come. There's still the children thing to be considered. That's what's really holding me back."

"You should talk to him. Openly. All out. What you feel, what he wants, the whole nine yards."

Van smiled at her friend. "Like you say, we only have a few more days. But enough about me. What about you and Jerry? I didn't even hear you come in last night."

"Not to worry. I came in. I've never laughed so much since the last faculty meeting. The faculty meeting was absurd; Jerry was just really funny. Who knew?"

"Are you going to see him again?"

Suze shrugged. "If I'm not too busy."

Van smacked her on the arm. "You seem pretty confident for someone who just got her grant application off hours before the deadline."

"I know, but I just have a feeling that something, if not the grant, will turn up. For both of us."

The Crab opened as always on Friday night. They'd spent two more days spiffing up the restaurant. New menus had been printed, a rush order that Van had paid for as a reopening-night present. She had managed to get a tan, and although Suze was still waiting to hear from the grant committee, she had decided to stay on with Dorie regardless.

Occasionally Van caught Dana looking out at Whisper Beach, and she wondered if she was missing Bud. Van hoped not. Dana was not so bad, if given the right environment. And she deserved that. They all did.

Van had seen Joe three times that week and they'd begun to talk, but not about the subject that concerned each of them the most.

Dinner with her father and Ruth had gone as well as could be expected. It helped Van to see that someone could love her father—someone who wasn't needy or demanding, but who seemed to enjoy being with him. It was a different experience and sometimes a little hard to watch, but she was learning to listen to the present rather than to keep rerunning the past. Would she and her father ever be close? She couldn't see it now, but down the road, in *that* present, who knew?

She was willing to find out.

Van, Suze, Joe, and Jerry dressed up for the opening. Dana had redone Suze's hair and nails though she groused that they were hardly long enough to get color on. Suze donned her new black dress, and Van wore one of the dresses she'd brought on vacation but had never worn.

The place was packed, and Van felt proud. Dorie was in her element. And there wasn't one near miss that Van could see.

"It's just like that television show," Suze said. "The one where people come in and say 'oh this looks so much better.' You know the one?"

None of them knew it.

"In my defense," Van said. "I don't have too much time for television." Or anything much more than work, she realized.

"I don't watch the Cooking Channel," Jerry said. "I'm a cop."

"Big tuffy," Suze said, then gave him a Suze grin.

Joe shrugged. "I actually do watch the Food Channel, which reminds me, I've been meaning to ask you what you think about putting a . . ."

He had to draw his ideas for a dining terrace with a fork, since for the evening at least, the paper placemats had been replaced by tablecloths rented for the occasion. Joe's plans were good, but it would be a long time before they were ready to implement them.

They? Had she really just thought that?

Maybe there would be a "they"; it didn't have to be settled this week.

AFTER THE RESTAURANT closed, everyone gathered in the kitchen.

"You did a fabulous job," Dorie told Van. "Thank you. I think there's some life in the old dog yet. And I'm not talking about me."

"You're not an old dog," Cubby said. "You're one hot mama."

Dorie laughed. "Well, maybe lukewarm. Seriously though, thank you, Van, for taking time out of your vacation to revitalize the Crab."

"Hardly a vacation," Suze said.

"Yeah, but better than the movies," Dana added.

"And," Dorie continued, "thanks to all of you and the extra hours you put in. And to Dana, our new assistant front-of-house manager. And— Aw, heck, I'm getting all choked up. Hold that thought. I'll be right back. Nobody go anywhere." She hurried out of the room.

Van looked at Suze. "Please tell me she's not going to drag Harold out from the deep freeze."

"I think something better."

Dorie came back a minute later, a bottle of champagne in each hand. "And thank you to Suze for furnishing us with a little bubbly for the occasion."

Cubby took a bottle, popped the cork, and filled the glasses that had magically appeared.

Everyone took a glass and raised it to Dorie.

"Told you we'd find something to celebrate," Suze said.

"And you were right," Van said and clinked her glass with Suze's.

"So, Van," Jerry said, "Suze said you're thinking about expanding."

"Yes, I've been thinking about it for a while."

"Really?" Jerry glanced at Joe. "Where to?"

"I was considering Boston or Philly."

"Oh yeah?"

"Yeah. But lately I've been thinking about something a little closer to Manhattan."

"Would that some place be as close as Whisper Beach?"

"Maybe. It's not a bad commute."

"Commute? Really?" asked Joe.

Van shrugged. "I'm thinking about it. I have friends and family here, and a room at Dorie's."

"That would be great," Joe said.

"I think it's worth looking into, don't you?"

"Me? Absolutely."

"And so do I," called Dorie from across the room. "So do I."

There was a lot still to consider, to think through, to talk through, and plan, but this time Van wouldn't let her fears drive her away. If things didn't work out, well, at least she would have tried. And if they did, well, that would be even better.

Book Club Questions

1. Van left Whisper Beach twelve years ago and hasn't been back or communicated with anyone. Why do you think she chose a funeral for her return?

2. What is it about coming "home" to Whisper Beach that Van is most afraid of? Is it one major reason or many reasons that add up to overwhelm her? Is her fear valid or has she built the fear out of proportion?

3. Van isn't very sympathetic to Dana at first, if ever. Do you think in her heart Van thinks Dana deserves unhappiness because of what she did years before? What, if anything, changes her mind?

4. Can Van and Dana ever really be friends?

5. Why is Suze so adamant about not taking her family's money? What kinds of "strings" are attached if she does accept help? How important is it to make it on your own?

6. Gigi says that she always did what was right, and look where it got her; widowed, unemployed with two small children to support. Do you feel sympathetic towards her? Or do you think she allowed people to take care of her and expects them to continue to do so? Why do you think Gigi always tried to do what was right? Or did she?

7. Van and Joe get off to a rocky start because of Van's preconceptions. Do you think seeing Joe surrounded by wine bottles triggered her memory of childhood and colored her expectations of how Joe had turned out? What does her reaction say about Van?

8. Suze spends most of the book waiting for her grant application. What was the motivation for the theft of the application? Was it to hurt Suze or Van or something else entirely, like jealousy?

9. Van has been thinking about expanding her business. When Joe suggests the possibility of opening a branch in Whisper Beach, she is skeptical. What factors changed her mind? Do you think it is a viable choice? Will it be possible for her to run a successful, fulfilling business in her childhood home?

10. What do you think about Dorie and the way she has chosen to live her life? Why does she stay married to Harold? Is she destined to failure or can she make a success of the restaurant?

11. There are successes and failures among this once close-knit group. Were there victims in this story? Gigi? Van's father? Van? Joe? Dana? Suze? Dorie? Bud? How did each of them cope with their situations? Who were the sympathetic characters?

12. Do Van and her father have a chance of developing a positive relationship? What are some of the challenges that they face?

13. Van has buried her desire for children by nurturing her career. Knowing how much Joe wants to have a family, will this be a deterrent for any future together? Do you think either of them will be happy with adoption, or will there always be hidden accusations and insecurities?

14. Much is made about one little episode when they were all teenagers. All their lives seemed to be affected by it in one way or another. Do people get over the humiliation or hurt they experienced as children or teenagers? Or will it always be a part of them that they can't overcome?

15. It is hard enough to get over something inside yourself, how hard is it to change other peoples' perceptions of you as a person? Will people always look at Van and remember her as the girl who ran away, or will they see the successful businesswoman that she has become?

16. Do you think the lingering and erupting emotions in Whisper Beach were more than the teenage episode should have provoked? Or was that incident merely a catalyst for some underlying reasons that existed then and now?